THE HARBOR-MASTER

The Hippocampus Press Classics of Gothic Horror Series

Edited by S. T. Joshi

Johnson Looked Back: The Collected Weird Stories of Thomas Burke
The Harbor-Master: Best Weird Stories of Robert W. Chambers
Lost Ghosts: The Complete Weird Stories of Mary E. Wilkins Freeman
Back There in the Grass: The Horror Tales of
Irvin S. Cobb and Gouverneur Morris
The Mummy's Foot and Other Fantastic Tales, Théophile Gautier
Twin Spirits: The Complete Weird Stories of W. W. Jacobs
From the Dead: The Complete Weird Stories of E. Nesbit
Frankenstein and Others: The Complete Weird Fiction of Mary Shelley

THE HARBOR-MASTER

BEST WEIRD STORIES OF ROBERT W. CHAMBERS

Edited, with an Introduction, by S. T. Joshi

Hippocampus Press

New York

Published by Hippocampus Press
P.O. Box 641, New York, NY 10156.
www.hippocampuspress.com

Cover art © 2021 by Aeron Alfrey
Cover design and "Classics of Gothic Horror" logo by Dan Sauer,
dansauerdesign.com
Hippocampus Press logo designed by Anastasia Damianakos.
Photo on page 301 by Emily Marija Kurmis.

First Edition
1 3 5 7 9 8 6 4 2

ISBN13: 978-1-61498-327-9

Contents

INTRODUCTION

Robert W. Chambers (1865-1933) is the very embodiment of the cult writer. Although in his day he was an immensely popular author of historical and romance novels, he is today remembered for a handful of books he wrote early in his career—books that powerfully fuse mystery, supernatural horror, and psychological aberration into a uniquely unnerving amalgam. The pinnacle of his achievement in this realm is *The King in Yellow* (1895), a title that has covertly inspired generations of horror writers, beginning with H. P. Lovecraft. The revelation that Nic Pizzolatto, creator of the television show *True Detective,* has been inspired by Chambers, Lovecraft, Ligotti, and other weird writers has given Chambers a mini-boom—just about the last thing its author would have expected for work that he appeared to repudiate after he had capitulated to the Sirens' song of bestsellerdom.

Of the life of Robert William Chambers we know surprisingly little. Born in Brooklyn on May 26, 1865, he entered the Art Students' League around the age of twenty, where the artist Charles Dana Gibson was his fellow-student. From 1886 to 1893 he studied art in Paris, at the Ecole des Beaux Arts and at the Académie Julian, and his work was displayed at the Salon as early as 1889. Returning to New York, he succeeded in selling his illustrations to *Life, Truth,* and *Vogue* ("the three most frivolous and ephemeral publications of any commercial standing that New York has ever known," as John Curtis Underwood termed them[1]); but for reasons still not entirely clear he turned to writing and produced his first "novel," *In the Quarter* (1894), really a series of loosely connected character sketches of artist life in Paris. C. C. Baldwin

---

1. John Curtis Underwood, "Robert W. Chambers and Commercialism," in *Literature and Insurgency: Ten Studies in Racial Evolution* (New York: Mitchell Kennerley, 1914), 452.

suggested that Chambers was inspired "to make use of his Latin Quarter experiences"[2] by Henri Murger's *Scènes de la vie de Bohème* (1851; the novel upon which Puccini's opera *La Bohème* is based), and this may be right; although there is no way to ascertain whether it was so specific a literary influence as this. That Chambers was not, in any case, sincerely interested in capturing his own experiences is testified by the fact that he completely dropped the "Gallic studio atmosphere" after *The Mystery of Choice* (1897), presumably because it no longer proved popular. With *The King in Yellow,* Chambers's career as a writer was established—not because he had felt himself a born writer but because that collection of short stories was (probably in spite rather than because of the weird tales contained in it) successful. Chambers had somehow caught the public eye; he knew what the public wanted and gave it to them.

Although from time to time he returned to weird fiction, Chambers never did so with the gripping and almost nightmarish intensity of *The King in Yellow.* Instead, he wrote an endless succession of novels and tales that, while superficially dealing with a wide range of topics—the Franco-Prussian War; the American Revolution; modern New York society; World War I; the Civil War—all contained an unending procession of pretentious and dim-witted fellows (usually of independent means and attemptedly cynical temperament) falling in love at the least provocation with an equally endless parade of simpering and virtuous women who, although capable of blushing instantly at the slightest suggestion of impropriety, nevertheless give themselves body and soul to their male pursuers after what proves to be a merely token resistance. Some passages in Chambers's works would probably have been considered salacious at the time of their writing, and the only fitting modern parallels are Harlequin romances. It is doubtful whether any of Chambers's work would serve even as raw material for historical or sociological analysis of the period, since even in his own day he was castigated for producing wooden and unrealistic characters; of his females in particular Frederic Taber Cooper remarked: "They are all of them what men

---

2. C. C. Baldwin, "Robert W. Chambers," in *The Men Who Make Our Novels,* rev. ed. (New York: Dodd, Mead, 1924), 92.

like to think women to be, rather than the actual women themselves."[3] It is not, then, surprising that nearly the whole of Chambers's output—of which I have counted eighty-seven different volumes, including novels, short story collections, one volume of poems, one drama, juvenile books on nature, and even an opera libretto—has lapsed into obscurity.

There is not much to tell of Chambers's later life. At least two of his novels reached official best-seller status—*The Fighting Chance* (1906) and *The Younger Set* (1907), both selling some 200,000 copies—and Chambers settled into a luxurious and elegantly furnished mansion in Broadalbin, in upstate New York. Like Lord Dunsany, Chambers liked the "great outdoors" and was an ardent hunter and fisherman. He collected butterflies, Oriental rugs and vases, and—if the photograph of his study printed in Rupert Hughes's laudatory sketch of Chambers in *Cosmopolitan* is any guide—he was in no small way a bibliophile. He died, presumably in comfort and peace, on December 16, 1933.

Of the pleasantness of Chambers's character there seems no doubt: Hughes unhesitatingly said that "Bob Chambers is the salt of the earth,"[4] and Joyce Kilmer's interview with him in 1917 reveals him to be genial, completely lacking in the arrogance of success, and even fairly perceptive about writing and writers; his concluding advice to the would-be author ("Let him not take himself too seriously!") is surely a reference to himself.[5] It is, however, ironic that Chambers's very popularity drove each of his works into obscurity as its successor emerged; and so early as 1927 August Derleth complained in a letter to H. P. Lovecraft that even *The King in Yellow*—the most widely reprinted of his works both during and after his lifetime—was becoming difficult of access.[6]

---

3. Frederic Taber Cooper, "Robert W. Chambers," in *Some American Story Tellers* (New York: Henry Holt, 1911), 86.

4. Rupert Hughes, "The Art of Robert W. Chambers," *Cosmopolitan* 65 (June 1918): 116.

5. Joyce Kilmer, "What Is Genius? Robert W. Chambers," In *Literature in the Making* (New York & London: Harper, 1917), 85.

6. See H. P. Lovecraft to August Derleth, May 6, 1927 and May 16, 1927; in *Essential Solitude: The Letters of H. P. Lovecraft and August Derleth,* ed. David E. Schultz and S. T. Joshi (New York: Hippocampus Press, 2008), 1.87, 88.

Chambers's fantastic writing is limited principally to five volumes—*The King in Yellow* (1895), *The Mystery of Choice* (1897), *In Search of the Unknown* (1904), *Police!!!* (1915), and the novel *The Slayer of Souls* (1920)—while several ancillary volumes contain weird matter in lesser degrees—*The Maker of Moons* (1896), *The Tracer of Lost Persons* (1906), and *The Tree of Heaven* (1907). This wide scattering of his fantastic writing shows that Chambers never considered himself a writer of weird fiction in the tradition of Poe and Bierce (although he was influenced by both), but seems to have written such work whenever the mood struck him. It is, of course, to be noted that three of the eight works listed date to Chambers's very early period; and future generations of readers have confirmed C. C. Baldwin's remark on Chambers's output: "Had I my choice I'd take the first three or four [of his books] and let the rest go hang."[7]

One phase of the inspiration for *The King in Yellow*—a collection of short stories of which only the first six are fantastic, and of these the first four are loosely interrelated—is sufficiently obvious. Chambers must have read Ambrose Bierce's collection *Tales of Soldiers and Civilians* (1891)—or the English edition of 1892, *In the Midst of Life*—shortly after his return to America from France, for he adopts certain cryptic allusions and names coined in some of Bierce's tales and appropriates them for his own.[8] The focus of these first four tales in *The King in Yellow* is a mysterious drama (apparently in two acts) called *The King in Yellow,* which incites a peculiar fear and desperation upon reading. Chambers has, however, willfully altered the components he derived from Bierce, and it is in any case not clear whether the Bierce influence really extends beyond these borrowed names. Bierce indeed created Carcosa,

---

7. Baldwin, 90.

8. The stories by Bierce that principally influenced Chambers—"Haïta the Shepherd" and "An Inhabitant of Carcosa"—were originally collected in *Tales of Soldiers and Civilians,* but in later editions were transferred to the revised edition of *Can Such Things Be?,* whose original edition (1893) did not contain them, hence could not have been the volume that influenced Chambers. Since, however, it is these later editions that have subsequently been reprinted, the two tales can now be found in modern editions of *Can Such Things Be?*

which he describes in "An Inhabitant of Carcosa" as some great city of the distant past. Chambers maintains this notion, but in Bierce Hali was simply a prophet who is "quoted" as the epigraphs for the tales "An Inhabitant of Carcosa" and "The Death of Halpin Frayser" (1891). Finally, Chambers borrows the term "Hastur" from Bierce; but whereas Bierce envisioned Hastur as a god of the shepherds (see "Haïta the Shepherd"), Chambers regards Hastur alternately as a place or as a person. (It is to be noted that Lovecraft, when mentioning such things as Carcosa, the Lake of Hali, and the like in his own tales, was consciously following Chambers, although he knew full well the Biercian origin of these terms. His one mention of Hastur in "The Whisperer in Darkness" is entirely inconclusive, and it cannot be determined what he meant by this term.)

From the first four stories in *The King in Yellow* we learn a few more details about the contents of Chambers's mythical play: there are at least three characters, Cassilda, Camilla, and the King in Yellow himself; aside from places such as Hastur and the Lake of Hali, we learn of regions called Demhe, Yhtill, and Alar; finally, there are other details such as the Pallid Mask and the Yellow Sign. It is obvious that Chambers intended to leave these citations vague and unexplained; he wished merely to provide dark hints as to the possible worlds of horror and awe to which his mythical book was a guide. Although in "The Silent Land" (in *The Maker of Moons*) Chambers twice makes mention of a "King in Carcosa," he never develops this "King in Yellow mythology" elsewhere.

The tales in *The King in Yellow* differ widely in tone, flavor, and quality. The first, "The Repairer of Reputations," is a bizarre tale of the future (its setting is New York in 1920) in which Chambers, aside from oddly predicting a general European war, imagines a quasi-utopia with euthanasia chambers for those who wish to slough off the burden of existence, while Chicago and New York rise "white and imperial" in a new age of architecture wherein the "horrors" of Victorian design are repudiated. Nevertheless, the tale cannot be called science fiction (on which see further below), since the futuristic setting does not in the end have any role in the story line, which concerns a demented young man who imagines that he is the King in Yellow and that his cousin is vying for the throne. Such a bald description cannot begin to convey the otherworldly, nightmarish quality of the tale, where the unexplained elements of Chambers's "King in Yellow mythology," along with a prose style bordering upon the extravagant and an intentionally chaotic exposition, create an atmosphere of chilling horror. "The Mask," in contrast, is an exquisitely beautiful tale set in France concerning a sculptor who has discovered a fluid capable of petrifying any plant or animal such that it resembles the finest marble. Several portions of the narration, especially toward the end, are pure poetry.

"The Yellow Sign" is generally considered to be the best tale in *The King in Yellow,* and deals horrifyingly with the nameless fate of an artist who has found the Yellow Sign. The story presents an unforgettable image of the loathsome hearse-driver who is a harbinger for the narrator's death—a soft, pudgy, wormlike creature who has one of his fingers torn off in a tussle and who, when found in the artist's studio at the end, is pronounced to have been dead for months. "The Demoiselle d'Ys," in spite of its inclusion of Hastur as a minor character, is not part of the "King in Yellow mythology," but is another hauntingly beautiful tale about a man who is supernaturally transplanted into the medieval age while hunting in the Breton countryside and falls in love with a lovely huntress three centuries dead. The rest of *The King in Yellow* contains a series of fine prose-poems ("The Prophet's Paradise") followed by two gripping tales dealing with the Franco-Prussian War (1870–71), in which France suffered a humiliating military defeat at the hands of Prussia.

The Maker of Moons (1896) features an extraordinary novella as its title story, a tale of the mysterious East that introduces us to more unexplained and allusive names and places, notably Yian (probably the source of the "Yian-Ho" cited in some of Lovecraft's tales). Another fine contribution to the volume is "A Pleasant Evening," an effective ghost story.

The Mystery of Choice (1897) is an undeservedly forgotten collection, and—in its more refined and controlled prose style, greater unity of theme, and exquisite pathos—ranks close to *The King in Yellow* in quality. The first five stories are linked by a common setting—Brittany—and some recurring characters; and although the first ("The Purple Emperor") is an amusing parody on the detective story, the rest of the collection contains fine tales of fantasy and even science fiction. "Pompe Funèbre" is a resonant prose-poem on the omnipresence of death in the natural world, including the human realm. "The Messenger" is a complex and richly textured tale with a subtle supernatural element and a magnificent atmosphere of cumulative horror, focusing on a "Black Priest" who betrayed the French and allowed the British to capture a fort in Brittany in 1760. He was executed, but vowed to return from the dead if his remains were disturbed. He has in fact done so? And what relation does he hold to an earlier Black Priest from the Middle Ages?

With *In Search of the Unknown* (1904) Chambers begins to take another tack—the mingling of weirdness, humor, and romance—and readers must judge for themselves how felicitous this union is. His conceptions are as fertile as ever (we are here concerned with a series of tales depicting successive searches for lost species of animals, including a loathsome half-man and half-amphibian called "the harbor-master," a group of invisible creatures apparently in the shape of beautiful women, and the like), but in every tale the narrator attempts to flirt with a pretty girl, only to lose her at the last moment to some rival. The volume, although purporting to be a novel, is in fact a series of short stories stitched together from disparate sources. The first five chapters were in fact published separately in 1899 as "The Harbor-Master"; and Chambers has borrowed stories from *The Maker of Moons* ("The Man at the Next Table") and *The Mystery of Choice* ("A Matter of Interest") and fused them into the narrative.

The Tree of Heaven (1907) is not exclusively fantastic, but contains some very fine moments. The construction of the "novel" is ingenious: at the outset an odd mystic utters prophecies to a group of his friends, and the subsequent episodes are concerned with their fulfillment. For once the love element is not extrinsic to the plot, and in several of these tales love is simply given a supernatural dimension that creates a profundity and poignancy not often found in Chambers. The superb atmosphere of delicate pathos and dream-fantasy maintained some of these tales—notably "The Carpet of Belshazzar," the frame story, and "The Sign of Venus," a wistful story of an astral body—may place this volume only behind *The King in Yellow* and *The Mystery of Choice* as Chambers's finest.

Police!!! (1915) is a sequel to *In Search of the Unknown,* and is another collection of tales where searches are made into lost species—

including mammoths in the glaciers of Canada, a group of "cave-ladies" in the Everglades, and the like. This book places still greater emphasis on humor than its predecessor, and several of the tales are quite amusing; but there also seems to be a slight decline in Chambers's fertility of invention: the amphibian man in "The Third Eye" too closely resembles the harbor-master, while in "Un Peu d'Amour" we encounter an irascible character obviously reminiscent of a similar character in the first segment of *In Search of the Unknown*. But even here there are some gripping moments: "Un Peu d'Amour" presents some horrifying glimpses of a gigantic worm burrowing beneath the fields of upstate New York, while another tale ("The Ladies of the Lake") discloses a school of huge minnows the size of Pullman cars.

With *The Slayer of Souls* (1920), however, Chambers reaches the nadir of his career. Even if we could swallow the appallingly tasteless premise—that "Anarchists, terrorists, Bolshevists, Reds of all shades and degrees, are now believed to represent in modern times"[9] the descendants of the devil-worshipping Yezidi sect of inner Asia, which is poisoning the minds of misguided leftists and labor unionists for the overthrow of good and the establishment of evil, whatever that means—there is no escaping the tedium of the whole work, which is concerned with the efforts of the U.S. Secret Service, along with a young woman who, although having lived for years with these evil Chinese, has now defected and converted to Christianity, to hunt down the eight leading figures of the sect and exterminate them. This happens with mechanical regularity, and it is no surprise that civilisation is saved in the end for God-fearing Americans. The novel—an elaboration of the title story of *The Maker of Moons* (1896), although that tale is handled far better and contains some delicate moments of shimmering fantasy—is further crippled by a ponderous and entirely humourless style, and with characters so moronic that they cannot reconcile themselves to the supernatural even after repeated exposure to it. And the crowning absurdity is that the origin of all these evils is a "black planet . . . not a hundred miles"[10] from the earth! There is not a single redeeming element in this novel.

---

9. Robert W. Chambers, *The Slayer of Souls* (New York: George H. Doran, 1920), 39.

10. Ibid., 290.

Some general remarks can now be made on Chambers' fantastic work. One of its most interesting features is a proto-science-fictional element that emerges in some works cheek by jowl with the overt supernaturalism of other tales. We have seen that "The Repairer of Reputations" is set in the future; but "The Mask" actually makes greater use of a science-fictional principle of great importance: the scientific justification for a fantastic event. Chambers never precisely explains the nature of the petrifying fluid used in the story, but we are led to believe that it would not be beyond the bounds of chemistry to encompass it. Similarly, in "A Matter of Interest" elaborate attempts are made at the outset to establish the veracity and accuracy of the narrative, which concerns the discovery of the last living dinosaur (the "thermosaurus"). Other segments of *In Search of the Unknown* are even more emphatic on the point, and one of the characters vigorously denies the supernatural character of the harbor-master: "'I don't think that the harbor-master is a spirit or a sprite or a hobgoblin, or any sort of damned rot. Neither do I believe it to be an optical illusion.'" Less scientific justification is presented for the creatures in *Police!!!*, but even here few strain credulity beyond the breaking-point. Even *The Slayer of Souls* enunciates the principle: "'We're up against something absolutely new. Of course, it isn't magic. It can, of course, be explained by natural laws about which we happen to know nothing at present.'"[11] Unfortunately, in this case little effort is made to coordinate the bizarre events into a plausibly scientific framework.

Chambers's influence on subsequent weird writing is significant. Several leading weird writers of the next generation—Lovecraft, Clark Ashton Smith, A. Merritt—professed to have been impressed with his work (especially—and almost exclusively—*The King in Yellow*), but in Lovecraft's case at any rate the influence does not seem to extend much beyond the borrowing of names from Chambers's "King in Yellow mythology"; the general "cosmic" attitude of both Lovecraft and Smith was clearly established before they ever encountered its dim adumbration in Chambers. Indeed, there are some anomalies in Chambers's influence on Lovecraft. In the latter's short novel *The Dream-Quest of Unknown*

---

11. Ibid., 173–74.

Kadath there are cryptic references to a "high-priest not to be described, which wears a yellow silken mask over his face."[12] This would seem to be an unmistakable allusion to the Pallid Mask; but we know that Lovecraft completed his novel on January 22, 1927, but did not read *The King in Yellow* until March 1927. It is a remarkable case of literary parallelism. Lovecraft went on to state whimsically that Chambers was inspired to create *The King in Yellow* by the *Necronomicon* of the mad Arab Abdul Alhazred—a volume of occult lore that Lovecraft himself had invented.[13]

Lovecraft was, indeed, central to the revival of Chambers's reputation as a weird writer. Lovecraft devoted several pages to *The King in Yellow* in his essay "Supernatural Horror in Literature" (1927), and the wide dissemination of that essay led many readers to seek out Chambers's phantom volume. It was reprinted in paperback in the 1960s, and many subsequent editions have followed. Chambers's work also inspired a host of writers, from James Blish to Karl Edward Wagner, who sought to duplicate the cryptic allusiveness of *The King in Yellow*. The contemporary writer Joseph S. Pulver, Sr., developed a veritable obsession with this book, writing poignant short stories based on it, such as "Carl Lee & Cassilda," which transfers the characters of Chambers's imaginary play into a gritty, hard-boiled realm of crime and perversion. Pulver also compiled an anthology of original stories based on Chambers's work, *A Season in Carcosa* (2012), with scintillating contributions by such contemporary writers as Joel Lane, Simon Strantzas, Ann K. Schwader, Richard Gavin, Gemma Files, Laird Barron, and John Langan.

How long the recent "Chambers boom" will last is anyone's guess; but the fact remains that Chambers has attained permanent status as a minor but distinctive writer of weird fiction whose work resonates through the decades chiefly because he exercised artistic restraint in his conceptions and in particular to his allusions to the "King in Yellow mythology." It is precisely because Chambers deliberately failed to define what he meant by such terms as Carcosa, Hastur, and Cassilda that

---

12. H. P. Lovecraft, *Collected Fiction: A Variorum Edition,* ed. S. T. Joshi (New York: Hippocampus Press, 2015), 2.110.

13. See "History of the 'Necronomicon,'" in *Collected Fiction,* 2.408.

these terms have developed an almost talismanic power to inspire fear, wonder, and terror in today's readers, who can imagine scenarios far more chilling than any author could ever put on paper. The wide range of Chambers's weird work—from clutching horror to ethereal beauty—indicates that he was a master of tone, atmosphere, and prose rhythm; and it is these qualities that will allow his work to last well into the new millennium.

THE HARBOR-MASTER

The Repairer of Reputations

"Ne raillons pas les fous; leur folie dur plus longtemps que la notre
. . . Voilà toute la difference."

I

Toward the end of the year 1920 the Government of the United
States had practically completed the programme, adopted during
the last months of President Winthrop's administration. The country
was apparently tranquil. Everybody knows how the Tariff and Labor
questions were settled. The war with Germany, incident on that country's seizure of the Samoan Islands, had left no visible scars upon the
republic, and the temporary occupation of Norfolk by the invading army had been forgotten in the joy over repeated naval victories and the
subsequent ridiculous plight of General Von Gartenlaube's forces in the
State of New Jersey. The Cuban and Hawaiian investments had paid
one hundred per cent. and the territory of Samoa was well worth its cost
as a coaling station. The country was in a superb state of defence. Every
coast city had been well supplied with land fortifications; the army under
the parental eye of the General Staff, organized according to the Prus-
sian system, had been increased to 300,000 men with a territorial reserve of a million; and six magnificent squadrons of cruisers and
battleships patrolled the six stations of the navigable seas, leaving a
steam reserve amply fitted to control home waters. The gentlemen from
the West had at last been constrained to acknowledge that a college for
the training of diplomats was as necessary as law schools are for the
training of barristers; consequently we were no longer represented
abroad by incompetent patriots. The nation was prosperous. Chicago,
for a moment paralyzed after a second great fire, had risen from its ruins, white and imperial, and more beautiful than the white city which

had been built for its plaything in 1893. Everywhere good architecture was replacing bad, and even in New York, a sudden craving for decency had swept away a great portion of the existing horrors. Streets had been widened, properly paved and lighted, trees had been planted, squares laid out, elevated structures demolished and underground roads built to replace them. The new government buildings and barracks were fine bits of architecture, and the long system of stone quays which completely surrounded the island had been turned into parks which proved a godsend to the population. The subsidizing of the state theatre and state opera brought its own reward. The United States National Academy of Design was much like European institutions of the same kind. Nobody envied the Secretary of Fine Arts, either his cabinet position or his portfolio. The Secretary of Forestry and Game Preservation had a much easier time, thanks to the new system of National Mounted Police. We had profited well by the latest treaties with France and England; the exclusion of foreign-born Jews as a measure of national self-preservation, the settlement of the new independent Negro state of Suanee, the checking of immigration, the new laws concerning naturalization, and the gradual centralization of power in the executive all contributed to national calm and prosperity. When the Government solved the Indian problem and squadrons of Indian cavalry scouts in native costume were substituted for the pitiable organizations tacked on to the tail of skeletonized regiments by a former Secretary of War, the nation drew a long sigh of relief. When, after the colossal Congress of Religions, bigotry and intolerance were laid in their graves and kindness and charity began to draw warring sects together, many thought the millennium had arrived, at least in the new world, which after all is a world by itself.

But self-preservation is the first law, and the United States had to look on in helpless sorrow as Germany, Italy, Spain and Belgium writhed in the throes of Anarchy, while Russia, watching from the Caucasus, stooped and bound them one by one.

In the city of New York the summer of 1899 was signalized by the dismantling of the Elevated Railroads. The summer of 1900 will live in the memories of New York people for many a cycle; the Dodge Statue was removed in that year. In the following winter began that agitation for the repeal of the laws prohibiting suicide which bore its final fruit in the month of April, 1920, when the first Government Lethal Chamber was opened on Washington Square.

I had walked down that day from Dr. Archer's house on Madison Avenue, where I had been as a mere formality. Ever since that fall from my horse, four years before, I had been troubled at times with pains in the back of my head and neck, but now for months they had been absent, and the doctor sent me away that day saying there was nothing more to be cured in me. It was hardly worth his fee to be told that; I knew it myself. Still I did not begrudge him the money. What I minded was the mistake which he made at first. When they picked me up from the pavement where I lay unconscious, and somebody had mercifully sent a bullet through my horse's head, I was carried to Doctor Archer, and he, pronouncing my brain affected, placed me in his private asylum where I was obliged to endure treatment for insanity. At last he decided that I was well, and I, knowing that my mind had always been as sound as his, if not sounder, "paid my tuition" as he jokingly called it, and left. I told him, smiling, that I would get even with him for his mistake, and he laughed heartily, and asked me to call once in a while. I did so, hoping for a chance to even up accounts, but he gave me none, and I told him I would wait.

The fall from my horse had fortunately left no evil results; on the contrary it had changed my whole character for the better. From a lazy young man about town, I had become active, energetic, temperate, and above all—oh, above all else—ambitious. There was only one thing which troubled me. I laughed at my own uneasiness, and yet it troubled me.

During my convalescence I had bought and read for the first time, "The King in Yellow." I remembered after finishing the first act that it occurred to me that I had better stop. I started up and flung the book into the fireplace; the volume struck the barred grate and fell open on the hearth in the fire-light. If I had not caught a glimpse of the opening words in the second act I should never have finished it, but as I stooped to pick it up, my eyes became riveted to the open page, and with a cry of terror, or perhaps it was of joy so poignant that I suffered in every nerve, I snatched the thing out of the coals and crept to my bedroom, where I read it and reread it, and wept and laughed and trembled with a horror which at times assails me yet. This is the thing that troubles me, for I cannot forget Carcosa where black stars hang in the heavens; where the shadows of men's thoughts lengthen in the afternoon, when the twin suns sink into the Lake of Hali; and my mind will bear forever the memory of the Pallid Mask. I pray God will curse the writer, as the writer has cursed the world with this beautiful, stupendous creation, terrible in its simplicity, irresistible in its truth—a world which now trembles before the King in Yellow. When the French Government seized the translated copies which had just arrived in Paris, London, of course, became eager to read it. It is well known how the book spread like an infectious disease, from city to city, from continent to continent, barred out here, confiscated there, denounced by press and pulpit, censured even by the most advanced of literary anarchists. No definite principles had been violated in those wicked pages, no doctrine promulgated, no convictions outraged. It could not be judged by any known standard, yet, although it was acknowledged that the supreme note of art had been struck in "The King in Yellow," all felt that human nature could not bear the strain, nor thrive on words in which the essence of purest poison lurked. The very banality and innocence of the first act only allowed the blow to fall afterward with more awful effect.

It was, I remember, the 13th day of April, 1920, that the first Government Lethal Chamber was established on the south side of Washington Square, between Wooster Street and South Fifth Avenue. The block which had formerly consisted of a lot of shabby old buildings, used as cafés and restaurants for foreigners, had been acquired by the Government in the winter of 1898. The French and Italian cafés were torn down; the whole block was enclosed by a gilded iron railing, and converted into a lovely garden with lawns, flowers and fountains. In the centre of the garden stood a small, white building, severely classical in architecture, and surrounded by thickets of flowers. Six Ionic columns supported the roof, and the single door was of bronze. A splendid marble group of "The Fates" stood before the door, the work of a young American sculptor, Boris Yvain, who had died in Paris when only twenty-three years old.

The inauguration ceremonies were in progress as I crossed University Place and entered the square. I threaded my way through the silent throng of spectators, but was stopped at Fourth Street by a cordon of police. A regiment of United States lancers were drawn up in a hollow square around the Lethal Chamber. On a raised tribune facing Washington Park stood the Governor of New York, and behind him were grouped the Mayor of New York and Brooklyn, the Inspector-General of Police, the Commandant of the state troops, Colonel Livingston, military aide to the President of the United States, General Blount, commanding at Governor's Island, Major-General Hamilton, commanding the garrison of New York and Brooklyn, Admiral Buffby of the fleet in the North River, Surgeon-General Lanceford, the staff of the National Free Hospital, Senators Wyse and Franklin of New York, and the Commissioner of Public Works. The tribune was surrounded by a squadron of hussars of the National Guard.

The Governor was finishing his reply to the short speech of the Surgeon-General. I heard him say: "The laws prohibiting suicide and providing punishment for any attempt at self-destruction have been repealed. The Government has seen fit to acknowledge the right of man to end an existence which may have become intolerable to him, through physical suffering or mental despair. It is believed that the community will be benefited by the removal of such people from their midst. Since the passage of this law, the number of suicides in the United States has not increased. Now that the Government has determined to establish a Lethal Chamber in every city, town and village in the country, it remains to be seen whether or not that class of human creatures from whose desponding ranks new victims of self-destruction fall daily will accept the relief thus provided." He paused, and turned to the white Lethal Chamber. The silence in the street was absolute. "There a painless death awaits him who can no longer bear the sorrows of this life. If death is welcome let him seek it there." Then quickly turning to the military aide of the President's household, he said, "I declare the Lethal Chamber open," and again facing the vast crowd he cried in a clear voice: "Citizens of New York and of the United States of America, through me the Government declares the Lethal Chamber to be open."

The solemn hush was broken by a sharp cry of command, the squadron of hussars filed after the Governor's carriage, the lancers wheeled and formed along Fifth Avenue to wait for the commandant of the garrison, and the mounted police followed them. I left the crowd to gape and stare at the white marble Death Chamber, and, crossing South Fifth Avenue, walked along the western side of that thoroughfare to Bleecker Street. Then I turned to the right and stopped before a dingy shop which bore the sign,

Hawberk, Armorer.

I glanced in at the doorway and Hawberk busy in his little shop at the end of the hall. He looked up, and catching sight of me cried in his deep, hearty voice, "Come in, Mr. Castaigne!" Constance, his daughter, rose to meet me as I crossed the threshold, and held out her pretty hand, but I saw the blush of disappointment on her cheeks, knew that it was another Castaigne she had expected, my cousin Louis. I smiled at her confusion and complimented her on the banner which she was embroidering from a colored plate. Old Hawberk sat riveting the worn greaves of some ancient suit of armor, and the ring! ting! ting! of his little hammer sounded pleasantly in the quaint shop. Presently he dropped his hammer, and fussed about for a moment with a tiny wrench. The soft clash of the mail sent a thrill of pleasure through me. I loved to hear the music of steel brushing against steel, the mellow shock of the mallet on thigh pieces, and the jingle of chain armor. That was the only reason I went to see Hawberk. He had never interested me personally, nor did Constance, except for the fact of her being in love with Louis. This did occupy my attention, and sometimes even kept me awake at night. But I knew in my heart that all would come right, and that I should arrange their future as I expected to arrange that of my kind doctor, John Archer. However, I should never have troubled myself about visiting them just then, had it not been, as I say, that the music of the tinkling hammer had for me this strong fascination. I would sit for hours, listening and listening, and when a stray sunbeam struck the inlaid steel, the sensation it gave me was almost too keen to endure. My eyes would become fixed, dilating with a pleasure that stretched every nerve almost to breaking, until some movement of the old armorer cut off the ray of sunlight, then, still thrilling secretly, I leaned back and listened again to the sound of the polishing rag, swish! swish! rubbing rust from the rivets.

Constance worked with the embroidery over her knees, now and then pausing to examine more closely the pattern in the colored plate from the Metropolitan Museum.

"Who is this for?" I asked.

Hawberk explained, that in addition to the treasures of armor in the Metropolitan Museum of which he had been appointed armorer, he also had charge of several collections belonging to rich amateurs. This was the missing greave of a famous suit which a client of his had traced to a little shop in Paris on the Quai d'Orsay. He, Hawberk, had negotiated for and secured the greave, and now the suit was complete. He laid down his hammer and read me the history of the suit, traced since 1450 from owner to owner until it was acquired by Thomas Stainbridge. When his superb collection was sold, this client of Hawberk's bought the suit, and since then the search for the missing greave had been pushed until it was, almost by accident, located in Paris.

"Did you continue the search so persistently without any certainty of the greave being still in existence?" I demanded.

"Of course," he replied coolly.

Then for the first time I took a personal interest in Hawberk.

"It was worth something to you," I ventured.

"No," he replied, laughing, "my pleasure in finding it was my reward."

"Have you no ambition to be rich?" I asked smiling.

"My one ambition is to be the best armorer in the world," he answered gravely.

Constance asked me if I had seen the ceremonies at the Lethal Chamber. She herself had noticed cavalry passing up Broadway that morning, and had wished to see the inauguration, but her father wanted the banner finished, and she had stayed at his request.

"Did you see your cousin, Mr. Castaigne, there?" she asked with the slightest tremor of her soft eyelashes.

"No," I replied carelessly. "Louis' regiment is manoeuvreing out in Westchester County." I rose and picked up my hat and cane.

"Are you going upstairs to see the lunatic again?" laughed old Hawberk. If Hawberk knew how I loathe that word "lunatic," he would never use it in my presence. It rouses certain feelings within me which I do not care to explain. However, I answered him quietly: "I think I shall drop in and see Mr. Wilde for a moment or two."

"Poor fellow," said Constance, with a shake of her head, "it must be hard to live alone year after year, poor, crippled and almost demented. It is very good of you, Mr. Castaigne, to visit him as often as you do."

"I think he is vicious," observed Hawberk, beginning again with his hammer. I listened to the golden tinkle on the greave plates; when he had finished I replied:

"No, he is not vicious, nor is he in the least demented. His mind is a wonder chamber, from which he can extract treasures that you and I would give years of our lives to acquire."

Hawberk laughed.

I continued a little impatiently: "He knows history as no one else could know it. Nothing, however trivial, escapes his search, and his memory is so absolute, so precise in details, that were it known in New York that such a man existed the people could not honor him enough."

"Nonsense," muttered Hawberk, searching on the floor for a fallen rivet.

"Is it nonsense," I asked, managing to suppress what I felt, "is it nonsense when he says that the tassets and cuissards of the enamelled suit of armor commonly known as the 'Prince's Emblazoned' can be found among a mass of rusty theatrical properties, broken stoves and ragpicker's refuse in a garret in Pell Street?"

Hawberk's hammer fell to the ground, but he picked it up and asked, with a great deal of calm, how I knew that the tassets and left cuissard were missing from the "Prince's Emblazoned."

"I did not know until Mr. Wilde mentioned it to me the other day. He said they were in the garret of 998 Pell Street."

"Nonsense," he cried, but I noticed his hand trembling under his leathern apron.

"Is this nonsense too?" I asked pleasantly. "Is it nonsense when Mr. Wilde continually speaks of you as the Marquis of Avonshire and of Miss Constance—"

I did not finish, for Constance had started to her feet with terror written on every feature. Hawberk looked at me and slowly smoothed his leathern apron. "That is impossible," he observed, "Mr. Wilde may know a great many things—"

"About armor, for instance, and the 'Prince's Emblazoned,'" I interposed, smiling.

"Yes," he continued, slowly, "about armor also—maybe—but he is wrong in regard to the Marquis of Avonshire, who, as you know, killed his wife's traducer years ago, and went to Australia where he did not long survive his wife."

"Mr. Wilde is wrong," murmured Constance. Her lips were blanched but her voice was sweet and calm.

"Let us agree, if you please, that in this one circumstance Mr. Wilde is wrong," I said.

II

I climbed the three dilapidated flights of stairs, which I had so often I climbed before, and knocked at a small door at the end of the corridor. Mr. Wilde opened the door and I walked in.

When he had double-locked the door and pushed a heavy chest against it, he came and sat down beside me, peering up into my face with his little light-colored eyes. Half a dozen new scratches covered his nose and cheeks, and the silver wires which supported his artificial ears had become displaced. I thought I had never seen him so hideously fascinating. He had no ears. The artificial ones, which now stood out at an angle from the fine wire, were his one weakness. They were made of wax and painted a shell pink, but the rest of his face was yellow. He might better have revelled in the luxury of some artificial fingers for his left hand, which was absolutely fingerless, but it seemed to cause him no inconvenience, and he was satisfied with his wax ears. He was very small, scarcely higher than a child of ten, but his arms were magnificently developed, and his thighs as thick as any athlete's. Still, the most remarkable thing about Mr. Wilde was that a man of his marvelous intelligence and knowledge should have such a head. It was flat and pointed, like the heads of many of those unfortunates whom people imprison in asylums for the weak-minded. Many called him insane but I knew him to be as sane as I was.

I do not deny that he was eccentric; the mania he had for keeping that cat and teasing her until she flew at his face like a demon, was certainly eccentric. I never could understand why he kept the creature, nor what pleasure he found in shutting himself up in his room with the surly, vicious beast. I remembered once, glancing up from the manuscript I was studying by the light of some tallow dips, and seeing Mr. Wilde squatting motionless on his high chair, his eyes fairly blazing with excitement, while the cat, which had risen from her place before the stove, came creeping across the floor right at him. Before I could move she flattened her belly to the ground, crouched, trembled, and sprang into his face. Howling and foaming they rolled over and over the floor, scratching and clawing, until the cat screamed and fled under the cabinet, and Mr. Wilde turned over on his back, his limbs contracting and curling up like the legs of a dying spider. He was eccentric.

Mr. Wilde had climbed into his high chair, and, after studying my face, picked up a dog's-eared ledger and opened it.

"Henry B. Matthews," he read, "bookkeeper with Whysot Whysot and Company, dealers in church ornaments. Called April 3d. Reputation damaged on the race-track. Known as a welcher. Reputation to be repaired by August 1st. Retainer Five Dollars." He turned the page and ran his fingerless knuckles down the closely-written columns.

"P Greene Dusenberry, Minister of the Gospel, Fairbeach, New Jersey. Reputation damaged in the Bowery. To be repaired as soon as possible. Retainer $100."

He coughed and added, "Called, April 6th."

"Then you are not in need of money, Mr. Wilde," I inquired.

"Listen," he coughed again.

"Mrs. C. Hamilton Chester, of Chester Park, New York City. Called April 7th. Reputation damaged at Dieppe, France. To be repaired by October 1st. Retainer $500.

"Note—C. Hamilton Chester, Captain, U.S.S. *Avalanche* ordered home from South So. Squadron October 1st."

"Well," I said, "the profession of a Repairer of Reputations is lucrative."

His colorless eyes sought mine. "I only wanted to demonstrate that I was correct. You said it was impossible to succeed as a Repairer of Reputations; that even if I did succeed in certain cases it would cost me more than I would gain by it. To-day I have five hundred men in my employ, who are poorly paid, but who pursue the work with an enthusiasm which possibly may be born of fear. These men enter every shade and grade of society; some even are pillars of the most exclusive social temples; others are the prop and pride of the financial world; still others, hold undisputed sway among the 'Fancy and the Talent.' I choose them at my leisure from those who reply to my advertisements. It is easy enough, they are all cowards. I could treble the number in twenty days if I wished. So you see, those who have in their keeping the reputations of their fellow-citizens, I have in my pay."

"They may turn on you," I suggested.

He rubbed his thumb over his cropped ears, and adjusted the wax substitutes. "I think not," he murmured thoughtfully, "I seldom have to apply the whip, and then only once. Besides, they like their wages."

"How do you apply the whip?" I demanded.

His face for a moment was awful to look upon. His eyes dwindled to a pair of green sparks.

"I invite them to come and have a little chat with me," he said in a soft voice.

A knock at the door interrupted him, and his face resumed its amiable expression.

"Who is it?" he inquired.

"Mr. Steylette," was the answer.

"Come to-morrow," replied Mr. Wilde.

"Impossible," began the other, but was silenced by a sort of bark from Mr. Wilde.

"Come to-morrow," he repeated.

We heard somebody move away from the door and turn the corner by the stairway.

"Who is that?" I asked.

"Arnold Steylette, Owner and Editor in Chief of the great New York daily."

He drummed on the ledger with his fingerless hand adding: "I pay him very badly, but he thinks it a good bargain."

"Arnold Steylette!" I repeated amazed.

"Yes," said Mr. Wilde with a self-satisfied cough.

The cat, which had entered the room as he spoke, hesitated, looked up at him and snarled. He climbed down from the chair and squatting on the floor, took the creature into his arms and caressed her. The cat ceased snarling and presently began a loud purring which seemed to increase in timbre as he stroked her.

"Where are the notes?" I asked. He pointed to the table, and for the hundredth time I picked up the bundle of manuscript entitled

"THE IMPERIAL DYNASTY OF AMERICA."

One by one I studied the well-worn pages, worn only by my own handling, and although I knew all by heart, from the beginning, "When from Carcosa, the Hyades, Hastur, and Aldebaran," to "Castaigne, Louis de Calvados, born December 19th, 1877," I read it with an eager rapt attention, pausing to repeat parts of it aloud, and dwelling especially on "Hildred de Calvados, only son of Hildred Castaigne and Edythe Landes Castaigne, first in success," etc., etc.

When I finished, Mr. Wilde nodded and coughed.

"Speaking of your legitimate ambition," he said, "how do Constance and Louis get along?"

"She loves him," I replied simply.

The cat on his knee suddenly turned and struck at his eyes, and he flung her off and climbed on to the chair opposite me.

"And Doctor Archer! But that's a matter you can settle any time you wish," he added.

"Yes," I replied, "Doctor Archer can wait, but it is time I saw my cousin Louis."

"It is time," he repeated. Then he took another ledger from the table and ran over the leaves rapidly.

"We are now in communication with ten thousand men," he muttered. "We can count on one hundred thousand within the first twenty-eight hours, and in forty-eight hours the state will rise *en masse*. The country follows the state, and the portion that will not, I mean California and the Northwest, might better never have been inhabited. I shall not send them the Yellow Sign."

The blood rushed to my head, but I only answered, "A new broom sweeps clean."

"The ambition of Caesar and of Napoleon pales before that which could not rest until it had seized the minds of men and controlled even their unborn thoughts," said Mr. Wilde.

"You are speaking of the King in Yellow," I groaned with a shudder.

"He is a king whom emperors have served."

"I am content to serve him," I replied.

Mr. Wilde sat rubbing his ears with his crippled hand. "Perhaps Constance does not love him," he suggested.

I started to reply, but a sudden burst of military music from the street below drowned my voice. The twentieth dragoon regiment, formerly in garrison at Mount St. Vincent, was returning from the manoeuvres in Westchester County, to its new barracks on East Washington Square. It was my cousin's regiment. They were a fine lot of fellows, in their pale-blue, tight-fitting jackets, jaunty busbys and white riding breeches with the double yellow stripe, into which their limbs seemed molded. Every other squadron was armed with lances, from the metal points of which fluttered yellow and white pennons. The band passed, playing the regimental march, then came the colonel and staff, the horses crowding and trampling, while their heads bobbed in unison, and the pennons fluttered from their lance points. The troopers, who rode with the beautiful English seat, looked brown as berries from their bloodless campaign among the farms of Westchester, and the music of their sabres against the stirrups, and the jingle of spurs and carbines was delightful to me. I saw Louis riding with his squadron. He was as handsome an officer as I have ever seen. Mr. Wilde, who had mounted a chair by the window, saw him too, but said nothing. Louis turned and looked straight at Hawberk's shop as he passed, and I could see the flush on his brown cheeks. I think Constance must have been at the window. When the last troopers had clattered by, and the last pennons vanished into South Fifth Avenue, Mr. Wilde clambered out of his chair and dragged the chest away from the door.

"Yes," he said, "it is time that you saw your cousin Louis."

He unlocked the door and I picked up my hat and stick and stepped into the corridor. The stairs were dark. Groping about, I set my foot on something soft, which snarled and spit, and I aimed a murderous blow at the cat, but my cane shivered to splinters against the balustrade, and the beast scurried back into Mr. Wilde's room.

Passing Hawberk's door again I saw him still at work on the armor, but I did not stop, and stepping out into Bleecker Street, I followed it to Wooster, skirted the grounds of the Lethal Chamber, and crossing Washington Park went straight to my rooms in the Benedick. Here I lunched comfortably, read the *Herald* and the *Meteor,* and finally went to the steel safe in my bedroom and set the time combination. The three and three-quarter minutes which it is necessary to wait, while the time lock is opening, are to me golden moments. From the instant I set the combination to the moment when I grasp the knobs and swing back the solid steel doors, I live in an ecstasy of expectation. Those moments must be like the moments passed in Paradise. I know what I am to find at the end of the time limit. I know what the massive safe holds secure for me, for me alone, and the exquisite pleasure of waiting is hardly enhanced when the safe opens and I lift, from its velvet crown, a diadem of purest gold, blazing with diamonds. I do this every day, and yet the joy of waiting and at last touching the diadem, only seems to increase as the days pass. It is a diadem fit for a King among kings, an Emperor among emperors. The King in Yellow might scorn it, but it shall be worn by his royal servant.

I held it in my arms until the alarm on the safe rang harshly, and then tenderly, proudly, I replaced it and shut the steel doors. I walked slowly back into my study, which faces Washington Square, and leaned on the windowsill. The afternoon sun poured into my windows, and a gentle breeze stirred the branches of the elms and maples in the park, now covered with buds and tender foliage. A flock of pigeons circled about the tower of the Memorial Church; sometimes alighting on the purple tiled roof, sometimes wheeling downward to the lotos fountain in front of the marble arch. The gardeners were busy with the flower beds around the fountain, and the freshly-turned earth smelled sweet and spicy. A lawn mower, drawn by a fat white horse, clinked across the green sward, and watering carts poured showers of spray over the asphalt drives. Around the statue of Peter Stuyvesant, which in 1897 had replaced the monstrosity supposed to represent Garibaldi, children played in the spring sunshine, and nurse girls wheeled elaborate baby-carriages with a reckless disregard for the pasty-faced occupants, which could probably be explained by the presence of half a dozen trim dragoon troopers languidly lolling on the benches. Through the trees, the Washington Memorial Arch glistened like silver in the sunshine, and beyond, on the eastern extremity of the square the gray stone barracks of the dragoons, and the white granite artillery stables were alive with color and motion.

I looked at the Lethal Chamber on the corner of the square opposite. A few curious people still lingered about the gilded iron railing, but inside the grounds the paths were deserted. I watched the fountains ripple and sparkle; the sparrows had already found this new bathing nook, and the basins were crowded with the dusty-feathered little things. Two or three white peacocks picked their way across the lawns, and a drab-colored pigeon sat so motionless on the arm of one of the Fates, that it seemed to be a part of the sculptured stone.

As I was turning carelessly away, a slight commotion in the group of curious loiterers around the gates attracted my attention. A young man had entered, and was advancing with nervous strides along the gravel path which leads to the bronze doors of the Lethal Chamber. He paused a moment before the Fates, and as he raised his head to those three mysterious faces, the pigeon rose from its sculptured perch, circled about for a moment and wheeled to the east. The young man pressed his hands to his face, and then with an undefinable gesture sprang up the marble steps, the bronze doors closed behind him, and half an hour later the loiterers slouched away, and the frightened pigeon returned to its perch in the arms of Fate.

I put on my hat and went out into the park for a little walk before dinner. As I crossed the central driveway a group of officers passed, and one of them called out, "Hello, Hildred," and came back to shake hands with me. It was my cousin Lou is, who stood smiling and tapping his spurred heels with his riding-whip.

"Just back from Westchester," he said; "been doing the bucolic; milk and curds, you know, dairy-maids in sunbonnets, who say 'haeow' and 'I don't think' when you tell them they are pretty. I'm nearly dead for a square meal at Delmonico's. What's the news?"

"There is none," I replied pleasantly. "I saw your regiment coming in this morning."

"Did you? I didn't see you. Where were you?"

"In Mr. Wilde's window."

"Oh hell!" he began impatiently, "that man is stark mad! I don't understand why you—"

He saw how annoyed I felt by this outburst, and begged my pardon.

"Really, old chap," he said, "I don't mean to run down a man you like, but for the life of me I can't see what the deuce you find in common with Mr. Wilde. He's not well-bred, to put it generously; he's hideously deformed; his head is the head of a criminally insane person. You know yourself he's been in an asylum—"

"So have I," I interrupted calmly.

Louis looked startled and confused for a moment, but recovered and slapped me heartily on the shoulder.

"You were completely cured," he began, but I stopped him again.

"I suppose you mean that I was simply acknowledged never to have been insane."

"Of course that—that's what I meant," he laughed.

I disliked his laugh because I knew it was forced, but I nodded gaily and asked him where he was going. Louis looked after his brother officers who had now almost reached Broadway.

"We had intended to sample a Brunswick cocktail, but to tell you the truth I was anxious for an excuse to go and see Hawberk instead. Come along, I'll make you my excuse."

We found old Hawberk, neatly attired in a fresh spring suit, standing at the door of his shop and sniffing the air.

"I had just decided to take Constance for a little stroll before dinner," he replied to the impetuous volley of questions from Louis. "We thought of walking on the park terrace along the North River."

At that moment Constance appeared and grew pale and rosy by turns as Louis bent over her small gloved fingers. I tried to excuse myself, alleging an engagement up-town, but Louis and Constance would not listen, and I saw I was expected to remain and engage old Hawberk's attention. After all it would be just as well if I kept my eye on Louis, I thought, and when they hailed a Spring Street horsecar, I got in after them and took my seat beside the armorer.

The beautiful line of parks and granite terraces overlooking the wharves along the North River, which were built in 1910 and finished in the autumn of 1917, had become one of the most popular promenades in the metropolis. They extended from the battery to 190th Street, overlooking the noble river and affording a fine view of the Jersey shore and the Highlands opposite. Cafés and restaurants were scattered here and there among the trees, and twice a week military bands from the garrison played in the kiosques on the parapets.

We sat down in the sunshine on the bench at the foot of the equestrian statue of General Sheridan.[6] Constance tipped her sunshade to shield her eyes, and she and Louis began a murmuring conversation which was impossible to catch. Old Hawberk, leaning on his ivory-headed cane, lighted an excellent cigar, the mate to which I politely refused, and smiled at vacancy. The sun hung low above the Staten Island woods, and the bay was dyed with golden hues reflected from the sun-warmed sails of the shipping in the harbor.

Brigs, schooners, yachts, clumsy ferry-boats, their decks swarming with people, railroad transports carrying lines of brown, blue and white freight cars, stately sound steamers, *declassé* tramp steamers, coasters, dredgers, scows, and everywhere pervading the entire bay impudent little tugs puffing and whistling officiously;—these were the crafts which churned the sunlit waters as far as the eye could reach. In calm contrast to the hurry of sailing vessel and steamer a silent fleet of white warships lay motionless in midstream.

Constance's merry laugh aroused me from my reverie.

"What *are* you staring at?" she inquired.

"Nothing—the fleet," I smiled.

Then Louis told us what the vessels were, pointing out each by its relative position to the old Red Fort on Governor's Island.

"That little cigar-shaped thing is a torpedo boat," he explained; "there are four more lying close together. They are the *Tarpon,* the *Falcon,* the *Sea Fox* and the *Octopus.* The gun-boats just above are the *Princeton,* the *Champlain,* the *Still Water* and the *Erie.* Next to them lie the cruisers *Farragut* and *Los Angeles,* and above them the battleships *California* and *Dakota,* and the *Washington* which is the flag-ship.

Those two squatty-looking chunks of metal which are anchored there off Castle William are the double-turreted monitors *Terrible* and *Magnificent;* behind them lies the ram, *Osceola.*"

Constance looked at him with deep approval in her beautiful eyes.

"What loads of things you know for a soldier," she said, and we all joined in the laugh which followed.

Presently Louis rose with a nod to us and offered his arm to Constance, and they strolled away along the river wall. Hawberk watched them for a moment and then turned to me.

"Mr. Wilde was right," he said. "I have found the missing tassets and left cuissard of the 'Prince's Emblazoned,' in a vile old junk garret in Pell Street."

"998?" I inquired, with a smile.

"Yes."

"Mr. Wilde is a very intelligent man," I observed.

"I want to give him the credit of this most important discovery," continued Hawberk. "And I intend it shall be known that he is entitled to the fame of it."

"He won't thank you for that," I answered sharply; "please say nothing about it."

"Do you know what it is worth?" said Hawberk.

"No, fifty dollars, perhaps."

"It is valued at five hundred, but the owner of the 'Prince's Emblazoned' will give two thousand dollars to the person who completes his suit; that reward also belongs to Mr. Wilde."

"He doesn't want it! He refuses it!" I answered angrily. "What do you know about Mr. Wilde? He doesn't need the money. He is rich—or will be—richer than any living man except myself. What will we care for money then—what will we care, he and I, when—when—"

"When what?" demanded Hawberk, astonished.

"You will see," I replied, on my guard again.

He looked at me narrowly, much as Doctor Archer used to, and I knew he thought I was mentally unsound. Perhaps it was fortunate for him that he did not use the word lunatic just then.

"No," I replied to his unspoken thought, "I am not mentally weak; my mind is as healthy as Mr. Wilde's. I do not care to explain just yet what I have on hand, but it is an investment which will pay more than mere gold, silver and precious stones. It will secure the happiness and prosperity of a continent—yes, a hemisphere!"

"Oh," said Hawberk.

"And eventually," I continued more quietly, "it will secure the happiness of the whole world."

"And incidentally your own happiness and prosperity as well as Mr. Wilde's?"

"Exactly," I smiled. But I could have throttled him for taking that tone.

He looked at me in silence for a while and then said very gently, "Why don't you give up your books and studies, Mr. Castaigne, and take a tramp among the mountains somewhere or other? You used to be fond of fishing. Take a cast or two at the trout in the Rangeleys."

"I don't care for fishing any more," I answered, without a shade of annoyance in my voice.

"You used to be fond of everything," he continued; "athletics, yachting, shooting, riding—"

"I have never cared to ride since my fall," I said quietly.

"Ah, yes, your fall," he repeated, looking away from me.

I thought this nonsense had gone far enough, so I turned the conversation back to Mr. Wilde; but he was scanning my face again in a manner highly offensive to me.

"Mr. Wilde," he repeated, "do you know what he did this afternoon? He came down stairs and nailed a sign over the hall door next to mine; it read:

MR. WILDE,
REPAIRER OF REPUTATIONS,
3d Bell.

Do you know what a Repairer of Reputations can be?"

"I do," I replied, suppressing the rage within.

"Oh," he said again.

Louis and Constance came strolling by and stopped to ask if we would join them. Hawberk looked at his watch. At the same moment a puff of smoke shot from the casemates of Castle William, and the boom of the sunset gun rolled across the water and was re-echoed from the Highlands opposite. The flag came running down from the flag-pole, the bugles sounded on the white decks of the warships, and the first electric light sparkled out from the Jersey shore.

As I turned into the city with Hawberk I heard Constance murmur something to Louis which I did not understand; but Louis whispered, "My darling," in reply; and again, walking ahead with Hawberk through the square I heard a murmur of "sweetheart," and "my own Constance," and I knew the time had nearly arrived when I should speak of important matters with my cousin Louis.

III

One morning early in May I stood before the steel safe in my bedroom, trying on the golden jewelled crown. The diamonds flashed fire as I turned to the mirror, and the heavy beaten gold burned like a halo about my head. I remembered Camilla's agonized scream and the awful words echoing through the streets of Carcosa. They were the last lines in the first act, and I dared not think of what followed—dared not, even in the spring sunshine, there in my own room, surrounded with familiar objects, reassured by the bustle from the street and the voices of the servants in the hallway outside. For those poisoned words had dropped slowly into my heart, as death-sweat drops upon a bed-sheet and is absorbed. Trembling, I put the diadem from my head and wiped my forehead, but I thought of Hastur and of my own rightful ambition, and I remembered Mr. Wilde as I had last left him, his face all torn and bloody from the claws of that devil's creature, and what he said—ah, what he said! The alarm bell in the safe began to whirr harshly, and I knew my time was up; but I would not heed it, and replacing the flashing circlet upon my head I turned defiantly to the mirror. I stood for a long time absorbed in the changing expression of my own eyes. The mirror reflected a face which was like my own, but whiter, and so thin that I hardly recognized it. And all the time I kept repeating between my clenched teeth, "The day has come! the day has come!" while the alarm in the safe whirred and clamored, and the diamonds sparked and flamed above my brow. I heard a door open but did not heed it. It was only when I saw two faces in the mirror;—it was only when another face rose over my shoulder, and two other eyes met mine. I wheeled like a flash and seized a long knife from the dressing-table, and my cousin sprang back very pale, crying: "Hildred! for God's sake!" then as my hand fell, he said: "It is I, Louis, don't you know me?" I stood silent. I could not have spoken for my life. He walked up to me and took the knife from my hand.

"What is all this?" he inquired, in a gentle voice. "Are you ill?"

"No," I replied. But I doubt if he heard me.

"Come, come, old fellow," he cried, "take off that brass crown and toddle into the study. Are you going to a masquerade? What's all this theatrical tinsel anyway?"

I was glad he thought the crown was made of brass and paste, yet I didn't like him any the better for thinking so. I let him take it from my hand, knowing it was best to humor him. He tossed the splendid diadem in the air, and catching it, turned to me smiling.

"It's dear at fifty cents," he said. "What's it for?"

I did not answer, but took the circlet from his hands, and placing it in the safe shut the massive steel door. The alarm ceased its infernal din at once. He watched me curiously, but did not seem to notice the sudden ceasing of the alarm. He did, however, speak of the safe as a biscuit box. Fearing lest he might examine the combination I led the way into the study. Louis threw himself on the sofa and flicked at flies with his eternal riding-whip. He wore his fatigue uniform with the braided jacket and jaunty cap, and I noticed that his riding-boots were all splashed with red mud.

"Where have you been?" I inquired.

"Jumping mud creeks in Jersey," he said. "I haven't had time to change yet; I was rather in a hurry to see you. Haven't you got a glass of something? I'm dead tired; been in the saddle twenty-four hours."

I gave him some brandy from my medicinal store, which he drank with a grimace.

"Damned bad stuff," he observed. "I'll give you an address where they sell brandy that is brandy."

"It's good enough for my needs," I said indifferently. "I used it to rub my chest with." He stared and flicked at another fly.

"See here, old fellow," he began, "I've got something to suggest to you. It's four years now that you've shut yourself up in here like an owl, never going anywhere, never taking any healthy exercise, never doing a damned thing but poring over those books up there on the mantelpiece."

He glanced along the row of shelves. "Napoleon, Napoleon, Napoleon!" he read. "For heaven sake, have you nothing but Napoleons there?"

"I wish they were bound in gold," I said. "But wait, yes, there is another book, 'The King in Yellow.'" I looked him steadily in the eye.

"Have you never read it?" I asked.

"I? No, thank God! I don't want to be driven crazy."

I saw he regretted his speech as soon as he had uttered it. There is only one word which I loathe more than I do lunatic and that word is crazy. But I controlled myself and asked him why he thought "The King in Yellow" dangerous.

"Oh, I don't know," he said, hastily. "I only remember the excitement it created and the denunciations from pulpit and press. I believe the author shot himself after bringing forth this monstrosity, didn't he?"

"I understand he is still alive," I answered.

"That's probably true," he muttered; "bullets couldn't kill a fiend like that."

"It is a book of great truths," I said.

"Yes," he replied, "Of 'truths' which send men frantic and blast their lives. I don't care if the thing is, as they say, the very supreme essence of art. It's a crime to have written it and I for one shall never open its pages."

"Is that what you have come to tell me?" I asked.

"No," he said, "I came to tell you that I am going to be married."

I believe for a moment my heart ceased to beat, but kept my eyes on his face.

"Yes," he continued, smiling happily, "married to the sweetest girl on earth."

"Constance Hawberk," I said mechanically.

"How did you know?" he cried, astonished. "I didn't know it myself until that evening last April, when we strolled down to the embankment before dinner."

"When is it to be?" I asked.

"It was to have been next September, but an hour ago a despatch came ordering our regiment to the Presidio, San Francisco. We leave at noon tomorrow. To-morrow," he repeated. "Just think, Hildred, to-morrow I shall be the happiest fellow that ever drew breath in this jolly world, for Constance will go with me."

I offered him my hand in congratulation, and he seized and shook it like the good-natured fool he was—or pretended to be.

"I am going to get my squadron as a wedding present," he rattled on. "Captain and Mrs. Louis Castaigne, eh, Hildred?"

Then he told me where it was to be and who were to be there, and made me promise to come and be best man. I set my teeth and listened to his boyish chatter without showing what I felt, but—

I was getting to the limit of my endurance, and when he jumped up, and, switching his spurs till they jingled, said he must go, I did not detain him. "There's one thing I want to ask of you," I said quietly.

"Out with it, it's promised," he laughed.

"I want you to meet me for a quarter of an hour's talk to-night."

"Of course, if you wish," he said, somewhat puzzled. "Where?"

"Anywhere, in the park there."

"What time, Hildred?"

"Midnight."

"What in the name of—" he began, but checked himself and laugh-ingly assented. I watched him go down the stairs and hurry away, his sa-bre banging at every stride. He turned into Bleecker Street, and I knew he was going to see Constance. I gave him ten minutes to disappear and then followed in his footsteps, taking with me the jewelled crown and the silken robe embroidered with the Yellow Sign. When I turned into Bleecker Street, and entered the doorway which bore the sign,

MR. WILDE,
REPAIRER OF REPUTATIONS,
3d Bell,

I saw old Hawberk moving about in his shop, and imagined I heard Constance's voice in the parlor; but I avoided them both and hurried up the trembling stairways to Mr. Wilde's apartment. I knocked, and entered without ceremony. Mr. Wilde lay groaning on the floor, his face covered with blood, his clothes torn to shreds. Drops of blood were scattered about over the carpet, which had also been ripped and frayed in the evidently recent struggle.

"It's that cursed cat," he said, ceasing his groans, and turning his colorless eyes to me; "she attacked me while I was asleep. I believe she will kill me yet."

This was too much, so I went into the kitchen and seizing a hatchet from the pantry, started to find the infernal beast and settle her then and there. My search was fruitless, and after a while I gave it up and came back to find Mr. Wilde squatting on his high chair by the table. He had washed his face and changed his clothes. The great furrows which the cat's claws had ploughed up in his face he had filled with collodion, and a rag hid the wound in his throat. I told him I should kill the cat when I came across her, but he only shook his head and turned to the open ledger before him. He read name after name of the people who had come to him in regard to their reputation, and the sums he had amassed were startling.

"I put the screws on now and then," he explained.

"One day or other some of these people will assassinate you," I insisted. "Do you think so?" he said, rubbing his mutilated ears.

It was useless to argue with him, so I took down the manuscript entitled Imperial Dynasty of America, for the last time I should ever take it down in Mr. Wilde's study. I read it through, thrilling and trembling with pleasure. When I had finished Mr. Wilde took the manuscript and, turning to the dark passage which leads from his study to his bed-chamber, called out in a loud voice, "Vance." Then for the first time, I noticed a man crouching there in the shadow. How I had overlooked him during my search for the cat, I cannot imagine.

"Vance, come in," cried Mr. Wilde.

The figure rose and crept toward us, and I shall never forget the face that he raised to mine, as the light from the window illuminated it.

"Vance, this is Mr. Castaigne," said Mr. Wilde. Before he had finished speaking, the man threw himself on the ground before the table, crying and gasping, "Oh, God! Oh, my God! Help me! Forgive me— Oh, Mr. Castaigne, keep that man away. You cannot, you cannot mean it!

You are different—save me! I am broken down—I was in a madhouse and now—when all was coming right—when I had forgotten the King— the King in Yellow and—but I shall go mad again—I shall go mad—"

His voice died into a choking rattle, for Mr. Wilde had leapt on him and his right hand encircled the man's throat. When Vance fell in a heap on the floor, Mr. Wilde clambered nimbly into his chair again, and rubbing his mangled ears with the stump of his hand, turned to me and asked me for the ledger. I reached it down from the shelf and he opened it. After a moment's searching among the beautifully written pages, he coughed complacently, and pointed to the name Vance.

"Vance," he read aloud, "Osgood Oswald Vance." At the sound of his name, the man on the floor raised his head and turned a convulsed face to Mr. Wilde. His eyes were injected with blood, his lips tumefied. "Called April 28th," continued Mr. Wilde. "Occupation, cashier in the Seaforth National Bank; has served a term of forgery at Sing Sing, from whence he was transferred to the Asylum for the Criminal Insane. Pardoned by the Governor of New York, and discharged from the Asylum, January 19, 1918. Reputation damaged at Sheepshead Bay. Rumors that he lives beyond his income. Reputation to be repaired at once. Retainer $1,500.

"Note—has embezzled sums amounting to $30,000 since March 20th, 1919, excellent family, and secured present position through uncle's influence. Father, President of Seaforth Bank."

I looked at the man on the floor.

"Get up, Vance," said Mr. Wilde in a gentle voice. Vance rose as if hypnotized. "He will do as we suggest now," observed Mr. Wilde, and opening the manuscript, he read the entire history of the Imperial Dynasty of America. Then in a kind and soothing murmur he ran over the important points with Vance, who stood like one stunned. His eyes were so blank and vacant that I imagined he had become half-witted, and remarked it to Mr. Wilde who replied that it was of no consequence anyway. Very patiently we pointed out to Vance what his share in the affair would be, and he seemed to understand after a while. Mr. Wilde explained the manuscript, using several volumes on heraldry to substantiate the result of his researches. He mentioned the establishment of the Dynasty in Carcosa, the lake which connected Hastur, Al-

debaran and the mystery of the Hyades. He spoke of Cassilda and Camilla, and sounded the cloudy depths of Demhe, and the lake of Hali.
"The scalloped tatters of the King in Yellow must hide Yhtill forever,"
he muttered, but I do not believe Vance heard him. Then by degrees he
led Vance along the ramifications of the Imperial family, to Uoht and
Thale, from Naotalba and Phantom of Truth, to Aldones, and then
tossing aside his manuscript and notes, he began the wonderful story of
the Last King. Fascinated and thrilled I watched him. He threw up his
head, his long arms were stretched out in a magnificent gesture of pride
and power, and his eyes blazed deep in their sockets like two emeralds.
Vance listened stupefied. As for me, when at last Mr. Wilde had finished, and pointing to me, cried, "The cousin of the King!" my head
swam with excitement.

Controlling myself with a superhuman effort, I explained to Vance
why I alone was worthy of the crown and why my cousin must be exiled
or die. I made him understand that my cousin must never marry, even
after renouncing all his claims, and how that least of all he should marry
the daughter of the Marquis of Avonshire and bring England into the
question. I showed him a list of thousands of names which Mr. Wilde
had drawn up; every man whose name was there had received the Yellow Sign which no living human being dared disregard. The city, the
state, the whole land, were ready to rise and tremble before the Pallid
Mask.

The time had come, the people should know the son of Hastur,
and the whole world bow to the Black Stars which hang in the sky over
Carcosa.

Vance leaned on the table, his head buried in his hands. Mr. Wilde
drew a rough sketch on the margin of yesterday's *Herald* with a bit of
lead pencil. It was a plan of Hawberk's rooms. Then he wrote out the
order and affixed the seal, and shaking like a palsied man I signed my
first writ of execution with my name Hildred-Rex.

Mr. Wilde clambered to the floor and unlocking the cabinet, took a
long square box from the first shelf. This he brought to the table and
opened. A new knife lay in the tissue paper inside and I picked it up
and handed it to Vance, along with the order and the plan of Hawberk's

apartment. Then Mr. Wilde told Vance he could go; and he went, shambling like an outcast of the slums.

I sat for a while watching the daylight fade behind the square tower of the Judson Memorial Church, and finally, gathering up the manuscript and notes, took my hat and started for the door.

Mr. Wilde watched me in silence. When I had stepped into the hall I looked back. Mr. Wilde's small eyes were still fixed on me. Behind him, the shadows gathered in the fading light. Then I closed the door behind me and went out into the darkening streets.

I had eaten nothing since breakfast, but I was not hungry. A wretched half-starved creature, who stood looking across the street at the Lethal Chamber, noticed me and came up to tell me a tale of misery. I gave him money, I don't know why, and he went away without thanking me. An hour later another outcast approached and whined his story. I had a blank bit of paper in my pocket, on which was traced the Yellow Sign and I handed it to him. He looked at it stupidly for a moment and then with an uncertain glance at me, folded it with what seemed to me exaggerated care and placed it in his bosom.

The electric lights were sparkling among the trees, and the new moon shone in the sky above the Lethal Chamber. It was tiresome waiting in the square; I wandered from the Marble Arch to the artillery stables, and back again to the lotos fountain. The flowers and grass exhaled a fragrance which troubled me. The jet of the fountain played in the moonlight, and the musical splash of falling drops reminded me of the tinkle of chained mail in Hawberk's shop. But it was not so fascinating, and the dull sparkle of the moonlight on the water brought no such sensations of exquisite pleasure, as when the sunshine played over the polished steel of a corselet on Hawberk's knee. I watched the bats darting and turning above the water plants in the fountain basin, but their rapid, jerky flight set my nerves on edge, and I went away again to walk aimlessly to and fro among the trees.

The artillery stables were dark, but in the cavalry barracks the officer's windows were brilliantly lighted, and the sallyport was constantly filled with troopers in fatigue, carrying straw and harness and baskets filled with tin dishes.

Twice the mounted sentry at the gates was changed, while I wandered up and down the asphalt walk. I looked at my watch. It was nearly time. The lights in the barracks went out one by one, the barred gate was closed, and every minute or two an officer passed in through the side wicket, leaving a rattle of accoutrements and a jingle of spurs on the night air. The square had become very silent. The last homeless loiterer had been driven away by the gray-coated park policemen, the car tracks along Wooster Street were deserted, and the only sound which broke the stillness was the stamping of the sentry's horse and the ring of his sabre against the saddle pommel. In the barracks, the officer's quarters were still lighted, and military servants passed and repassed before the bay windows. Twelve o'clock sounded from the new spire of St. Francis Xavier, and at the last stroke of the sad-toned bell a figure passed through the wicket beside the portcullis, returned the salute of the sentry, and crossing the street entered the square and advanced toward the Benedick apartment house.

"Louis," I called.

The man pivoted on his spurred heels and came straight toward me.

"Is that you, Hildred?"

"Yes, you are on time."

I took his offered hand, and we strolled toward the Lethal Chamber.

He rattled on about his wedding and the graces of Constance, and their future prospects, calling my attention to his captain's shoulder-straps, and the triple gold arabesque on his sleeve and fatigue cap. I believe I listened as much to the music of his spurs and sabre as I did to his boyish babble, and at last we stood under the elms on the Fourth Street corner of the square opposite the Lethal Chamber. Then he laughed and asked me what I wanted, with him. I motioned him to a seat on a bench under the electric light, and sat down beside him. He looked at me curiously, with that same searching glance which I hate and fear so in doctors. I felt the insult of his look, but he did not know it, and I carefully concealed my feelings.

"Well, old chap," he enquired, "what can I do for you?"

I drew from my pocket the manuscript and notes of the Imperial Dynasty of America, and looking him in the eye said:

"I will tell you. On your word as a soldier, promise me to read this manuscript from beginning to end, without asking me a question. Promise me to read these notes in the same way, and promise me to listen to what I have to tell later."

"I promise, if you wish it," he said pleasantly. "Give me the paper, Hildred."

He began to read, raising his eyebrows with a puzzled whimsical air, which made me tremble with suppressed anger. As he advanced, his eyebrows contracted, and his lips seemed to form the word, "rubbish."

Then he looked slightly bored, but apparently for my sake read, with an attempt at interest, which presently ceased to be an effort. He started when in the closely-written pages he came to his own name, and when he came to mine he lowered the paper, and looked sharply at me for a moment. But he kept his word, and resumed his reading, and I let the half-formed question die on his lips unanswered. When he came to the end and read the signature of Mr. Wilde, he folded the paper carefully and returned it to me. I handed him the notes, and he settled back, pushing his fatigue cap up to his forehead, with a boyish gesture, which I remembered so well in school. I watched his face as he read, and when he finished I took the notes with the manuscript, and placed them in my pocket. Then I unfolded a scroll marked with the Yellow Sign. He saw the sign, but he did not seem to recognize it, and I called his attention to it somewhat sharply.

"Well," he said, "I see it. What is it?"

"It is the Yellow Sign," I said, angrily.

"Oh, that's it, is it?" said Louis, in that flattering voice, which Doctor Archer used to employ with me, and would probably have employed again, had I not settled his affair for him.

I kept my rage down and answered as steadily as possible, "Listen, you have engaged your word?"

"I am listening, old chap," he replied soothingly.

I began to speak very calmly.

"Dr. Archer, having by some means become possessed of the secret of the Imperial Succession, attempted to deprive me of my right, alleging that because of a fall from my horse four years ago, I had become mentally deficient. He presumed to place me under restraint in his own house in hopes of either driving me insane or poisoning me. I have not forgotten it. I visited him last night and the interview was final."

Louis turned quite pale, but did not move. I resumed triumphantly, "There are yet three people to be interviewed in the interests of Mr. Wilde and myself. They are my cousin Louis, Mr. Hawberk, and his daughter Constance."

Louis sprang to his feet and I arose also, and flung the paper marked with the Yellow Sign to the ground.

"Oh, I don't need that to tell you what I have to say," I cried with a laugh of triumph. "You must renounce the crown to me, do you hear, to me."

Louis looked at me with a startled air, but recovering himself said kindly, "Of course I renounce the—what is it I must renounce?"

"The crown," I said angrily.

"Of course," he answered, "I renounce it. Come, old chap, I'll walk back to your rooms with you."

"Don't try any of your doctor's tricks on me," I cried, trembling with fury. "Don't act as if you think I am insane."

"What nonsense," he replied. "Come, it's getting late, Hildred."

"No," I shouted, "you must listen. You cannot marry, I forbid it. Do you hear? I forbid it. You shall renounce the crown, and in reward I grant you exile, but if you refuse you shall die."

He tried to calm me but I was roused at last, and drawing my long knife barred his way.

Then I told him how they would find Dr. Archer in the cellar with his throat open, and I laughed in his face when I thought of Vance and his knife, and the order signed by me.

"Ah, you are the King," I cried, "but I shall be King. Who are you to keep me from Empire over all the habitable earth! I was born the cousin of a king, but I shall be King!"

Louis stood white and rigid before me. Suddenly a man came running up Fourth Street, entered the gate of the Lethal Temple, traversed the path to the bronze doors at full speed, and plunged into the death chamber with the cry of one demented, and I laughed until I wept tears, for I had recognized Vance, and knew that Hawberk and his daughter were no longer in my way.

"Go," I cried to Louis, "you have ceased to be a menace. You will never marry Constance now, and if you marry anyone else in your exile, I will visit you as I did my doctor last night. Mr. Wilde takes charge of you to-morrow." Then I turned and darted into South Fifth Avenue, and with a cry of terror Louis dropped his belt and sabre and followed me like the wind. I heard him close behind me at the corner of Bleecker Street, and I dashed into the doorway under Hawberk's sign. He cried, "Halt, or I fire!" but when he saw that I flew up the stairs leaving Hawberk's shop below, he left me and I heard him hammering and shouting at their door as though it was possible to arouse the dead.

Mr. Wilde's door was open, and I entered crying, "It is done, it is done! Let the nations rise and look upon their King!" but I could not find Mr. Wilde, so I went to the cabinet and took the splendid diadem from its case. Then I drew on the white silk robe, embroidered with the Yellow Sign, and placed the crown upon my head. At last I was King, King by my right in Hastur, King because I knew the mystery of the Hyades, and my mind had sounded the depths of the Lake of Hali. I was King! The first gray pencillings of dawn would raise a tempest which would shake two hemispheres. Then as I stood, my every nerve pitched to the highest tension, faint with the joy and splendor of my thought, without, in the dark passage, a man groaned.

I seized the tallow dip and sprang to the door. The cat passed me like a demon, and the tallow dip went out, but my long knife flew swifter than she, and I heard her screech, and I knew that my knife had found her. For a moment I listened to her tumbling and thumping about in the darkness, and then when her frenzy ceased, I lighted a lamp and raised it over my head. Mr. Wilde lay on the floor with his throat torn open. At first I thought he was dead, but as I looked, a green sparkle came into his sunken eyes, his mutilated hand trembled, and then a spasm stretched his mouth from ear to ear. For a moment my terror and despair gave place to hope, but as I bent over him his eyeballs rolled clean around in his head, and he died. Then while I stood, transfixed with rage and despair, seeing my crown, my empire, every hope and every ambition, my very life, lying prostrate there with the dead master, they came, seized me from behind, and bound me until my veins stood out like cords, and my voice failed with paroxysms of my frenzied screams. But I still raged, bleeding and infuriated among them, and more than one policeman felt my sharp teeth. Then when I could no longer move they came nearer; I saw old Hawberk, and behind him my cousin Louis' ghastly face, and farther away, in the corner, a woman, Constance, weeping softly.

"Ah! I see it now!" I shrieked. "You have seized the throne and the empire. Woe! woe to you who are crowned with the crown of the King in Yellow!"

[EDITOR'S NOTE: Mr. Castaigne died yesterday in the Asylum for the Criminal Insane.]

The Mask

CAMILLA: You, sir, should unmask.

STRANGER: Indeed?

CASSILDA: Indeed it's time. We all have laid aside disguise but you.

STRANGER: I wear no mask.

CAMILLA: (Terrified, aside to Cassilda.) No mask? No mask!

—THE KING IN YELLOW: Act 1—Scene 2d.

I

Although I knew nothing of chemistry, I listened fascinated. He picked up an Easter lily which Geneviève had brought that morning from Notre Dame and dropped it into the basin. Instantly the liquid lost its crystalline clearness. For a second the lily was enveloped in a milk-white foam, which disappeared, leaving the fluid opalescent. Changing tints of orange and crimson played over the surface, and then what seemed to be a ray of pure sunlight struck through from the bottom where the lily was resting. At the same instant he plunged his hand into the basin and drew out the flower. "There is no danger," he explained, "if you choose the right moment. That golden ray is the signal."

He held the lily toward me and I took it in my hand. It had turned to stone, to the purest marble.

"You see," he said, "it is without a flaw. What sculptor could reproduce it?"

The marble was white as snow, but in its depths the veins of the lily were tinged with palest azure, and a faint flush lingered deep in its heart.

"Don't ask me the reason of that," he smiled, noticing my wonder. "I have no idea why the veins and heart are tinted, but they always are. Yesterday I tried one of Geneviève's gold fish,—there it is."

53

The fish looked as if sculptured in marble. But if you held it to the light the stone was beautifully veined with a faint blue, and from somewhere within came a rosy light like the tint which slumbers in an opal. I looked into the basin. Once more it seemed filled with clearest crystal.

"If I should touch it now?" I demanded.

"I don't know," he replied, "but you had better not try."

"There is one thing I'm curious about," I said, "and that is where the ray of sunlight came from."

"It looked like a sunbeam true enough," he said. "I don't know, it always comes when I immerse any living thing. Perhaps," he continued smiling, "perhaps it is the vital spark of the creature escaping to the source from whence it came."

I saw he was mocking and threatened him with a mahl-stick, but he only laughed and changed the subject.

"Stay to lunch. Geneviève will be here directly."

"I saw her going to early mass," I said, "and she looked as fresh and sweet as that lily—before you destroyed it."

"Do you think I destroyed it?" said Boris gravely.

"Destroyed, preserved, how can we tell?"

We sat in the corner of a studio near his unfinished group of "The Fates." He leaned back on the sofa, twirling a sculptor's chisel and squinting at his work.

"By the way," he said, "I have finished pointing up that old academic Ariadne and I suppose it will have to go to the Salon. It's all I have ready this year, but after the success the 'Madonna' brought me I feel ashamed to send a thing like that."

The "Madonna," an exquisite marble for which Genèvieve had sat, had been the sensation of last year's Salon. I looked at the Ariadne. It was a magnificent piece of technical work, but I agreed with Boris that the world would expect something better of him than that. Still it was impossible now to think of finishing in time for the Salon, that splendid terrible group half shrouded in the marble behind me. "The Fates" would have to wait.

We were proud of Boris Yvain. We claimed him and he claimed us on the strength of his having been born in America, although his father was French and his mother was a Russian. Every one in the Beaux Arts called him Boris. And yet there were only two of us whom he addressed in the same familiar way; Jack Scott and myself.

Perhaps my being in love with Geneviève had something to do with his affection for me. Not that it had ever been acknowledged between us. But after all was settled, and she had told me with tears in her eyes that it was Boris whom she loved, I went over to his house and congratulated him. The perfect cordiality of that interview did not deceive either of us, I always believed, although to one at least it was a great comfort. I do not think he and Geneviève ever spoke of the matter together, but Boris knew.

Geneviève was lovely. The Madonna-like purity of her face might have been inspired by the Sanctus in Gounod's Mass. But I was always glad when she changed that mood for what we called her "April Manoeuvres." She was often as variable as an April day. In the morning grave, dignified and sweet, at noon laughing, capricious, at evening whatever one least expected. I preferred her so rather than in that Madonna-like tranquillity which stirred the depths of my heart. I was dreaming of Geneviève when he spoke again.

"What do you think of my discovery, Alec?"

"I think it wonderful."

"I shall make no use of it, you know, beyond satisfying my own curiosity so far as may be and the secret will die with me."

"It would be rather a blow to sculpture, would it not? We painters lose more than we ever gain by photography."

Boris nodded, playing with the edge of the chisel.

"This new vicious discovery would corrupt the world of art. No, I shall never confide the secret to anyone," he said slowly.

It would be hard to find any one less informed about such phenomena than myself; but of course I had heard of mineral springs so saturated with silica that the leaves and twigs which fell into them were turned to stone after a time. I dimly comprehended the process, how the silica replaced the vegetable matter, atom by atom, and the result was a duplicate of the object in stone. This I confess had never interested me greatly, and as for the ancient fossils thus produced, they disgusted me. Boris, it appeared, feeling curiosity instead of repugnance, had investigated the subject, and had accidentally stumbled on a solution which, attacking the immersed object with a ferocity unheard of, in a second did the work of years. This was all I could make out of the strange story he had just been telling me. He spoke again after a long silence.

"I am almost frightened when I think what I have found. Scientists would go mad over the discovery. It was so simple too; it discovered itself. When I think of that formula, and that new element precipitated in metallic scales—"

"What new element?"

"Oh, I haven't thought of naming it, and I don't believe I ever shall. There are enough precious metals now in the world to cut throats over."

I pricked up my ears. "Have you struck gold, Boris?"

"No, better;—but see here, Alec!" he laughed, starting up. "You and I have all we need in this world. Ah! how sinister and covetous you look already!" I laughed too, and told him I was devoured by the desire for gold, and we had better talk of something else; so when Genevieve came in shortly after, we had turned our backs on alchemy.

Geneviève was dressed in silvery gray from head to foot. The light glinted along the soft curves of her fair hair as she turned her cheek to Boris; then she saw me and returned my greeting. She had never before failed to blow me a kiss from the tips of her white fingers, and I promptly complained of the omission. She smiled and held out her hand which dropped almost before it had touched mine; then she said, looking at Boris,

"You must ask Alec to stay for luncheon." This also was something new. She had always asked me herself until to-day.

"I did," said Boris shortly.

"And you said yes, I hope," she turned to me with a charming conventional smile. I might have been an acquaintance of the day before yesterday. I made her a low bow. "J'avais bien l'honneur, madame," but refusing to take up our usual bantering tone she murmured a hospitable commonplace and disappeared. Boris and I looked at one another.

"I had better go home, don't you think?" I asked.

"Hanged if I know!" he replied frankly.

While we were discussing the advisability of my departure Geneviève reappeared in the doorway without her bonnet. She was wonderfully beautiful, but her color was too deep and her lovely eyes were too bright. She came straight up to me and took my arm.

"Luncheon is ready. Was I cross, Alec? I thought I had a headache but I haven't. Come here, Boris;" and she slipped her other arm through his. "Alec knows that after you there is no one in the world whom I like as well as I like him, so if he sometimes feels snubbed it won't hurt him."

"A la bonheur!" I cried, "who says there are no thunderstorms in April?"

"Are you ready?" chanted Boris. "Aye ready;" and arm in arm we raced into the dining-room scandalizing the servants. After all we were not so much to blame; Geneviève was eighteen, Boris was twenty-three and I not quite twenty-one.

II

Some work that I was doing about this time on the decoration for Geneviève's boudoir kept me constantly at the quaint little hotel in the rue Sainte-Cecile. Boris and I in those days labored hard but as we pleased, which was fitfully, and we all three, with Jack Scott, idled a great deal together.

One quiet afternoon I had been wandering alone over the house examining curios, prying into odd corners, bringing out sweetmeats and cigars from strange hiding-places, and at last I stopped in the bathing-room. Boris all over clay stood there washing his hands.

The room was built of rose-colored marble excepting the floor which was tesselated in rose and gray. In the centre was a square pool sunken below the surface of the floor; steps led down into it, sculptured pillars supported a frescoed ceiling. A delicious marble Cupid appeared to have just alighted on his pedestal at the upper end of the room. The whole interior was Boris' work and mine. Boris, in his working clothes of white canvas, scraped the traces of clay and red modelling wax from his handsome hands, and coquetted over his shoulder with the Cupid.

"I see you," he insisted, "don't try to look the other way and pretend not to see me. You know who made you, little humbug!"

It was always my role to interpret Cupid's sentiments in these conversations, and when my turn came I responded in such a manner, that Boris seized my arm and dragged me toward the pool, declaring he would duck me. Next instant he dropped my arm and turned pale. "Good God!" he said, "I forgot the pool is full of the solution!"

I shivered a little, and drily advised him to remember better where he had stored the precious liquid.

"In Heaven's name why do you keep a small lake of that grewsome stuff here of all places!" I asked.

"I want to experiment on something large," he replied.

"On me, for instance!"

"Ah! that came too close for jesting; but I do want to watch the action of that solution on a more highly organized living body; there is that big white rabbit," he said, following me into the studio.

Jack Scott, wearing a paint-stained jacket, came wandering in, appropriated all the Oriental sweetmeats he could lay his hands on, looted the cigarette case, and finally he and Boris disappeared together to visit the Luxembourg gallery, where a new silver bronze by Rodin and a landscape of Monet's were claiming the exclusive attention of artistic France. I went back to the studio, and resumed my work. It was a Renaissance screen, which Boris wanted me to paint for Geneviève's boudoir. But the small boy who was unwillingly dawdling through a series of poses for it, to-day refused all bribes to be good. He never rested an instant in the same position, and inside of five minutes, I had as many different outlines of the little beggar.

"Are you posing, or are you executing a song and dance, my friend?" I inquired.

"Whichever monsieur pleases," he replied with an angelic smile.

Of course I dismissed him for the day, and of course I paid him for the full time, that being the way we spoil our models.

After the young imp had gone, I made a few perfunctory daubs at my work, but was so thoroughly out of humor, that it took me the rest of the afternoon to undo the damage I had done, so at last I scraped my palette, stuck my brushes in a bowl of black soap, and strolled into the smoking-room. I really believe that, excepting Genevieve's apartments, no room in the house was so free from the perfume of tobacco as this one. It was a queer chaos of odds and ends hung with threadbare tapestry. A sweet-toned old spinet in good repair stood by the window. There were stands of weapons, some old and dull, others bright and modern, festoons of Indian and Turkish armor over the mantel, two or three good pictures, and a pipe-rack. It was here that we used to come for new sensations in smoking. I doubt if any type of pipe ever existed which was not represented in that rack. When we had selected one, we immediately carried it somewhere else and smoked it; for the place was, on the whole, more gloomy and less inviting than any in the house. But this afternoon, the twilight was very soothing, the rugs and skins on the floor looked brown and soft and drowsy; the big couch was piled with cushions, I found my pipe and curled up there for an unaccustomed smoke in the smoking-room. I had chosen one with a long flexible stem, and lighting it fell to dreaming. After a while it went out, but I did not stir. I dreamed on and presently fell asleep.

I awoke to the saddest music I had ever heard. The room was quite dark, I had no idea what time it was. A ray of moonlight silvered one edge of the old spinet, and the polished wood seemed to exhale the sounds as perfume floats above a box of sandal wood. Some one rose in the darkness, and came away weeping quietly, and I was fool enough to cry out "Geneviève!"

She dropped at my voice, and I had time to curse myself while I made a light and tried to raise her from the floor. She shrank away with a murmur of pain. She was very quiet, and asked for Boris. I carried her to the divan, and went to look for him, but he was not in the house, and the servants were gone to bed. Perplexed and anxious, I hurried back to Geneviève. She lay where I had left her, looking very white.

"I can't find Boris nor any of the servants," I said.

"I know," she answered faintly, "Boris has gone to Ept with Mr. Scott. I did not remember when I sent you for him just now."

"But he can't get back in that case before to-morrow afternoon, and—are you hurt? Did I frighten you into falling? What an awful fool I am, but I was only half awake."

"Boris thought you had gone home before dinner. Do please excuse us for letting you stay here all this time."

"I have had a long nap," I laughed, "so sound that I did not know whether I was still asleep or not when I found myself staring at a figure that was moving toward me, and called out your name. Have you been trying the old spinet? You must have played very softly."

I would tell a thousand more lies worse than that one to see the look of relief that came into her face. She smiled adorably and said in her natural voice: "Alec, I tripped on that wolf's head, and I think my ankle is sprained. Please call Marie and then go home."

I did as she bade me and left her there when the maid came in.

III

At noon next day when I called, I found Boris walking restlessly about his studio.

"Geneviève is asleep just now," he told me, "the sprain is nothing, but why should she have such a high fever? The doctor can't account for it; or else he will not," he muttered.

"Geneviève has a fever?" I asked.

"I should say so, and has actually been a little light-headed at intervals all night. The idea! gay little Geneviève, without a care in the world,—and she keeps saying her heart's broken, and she wants to die!"

My own heart stood still.

Boris leaned against the door of his studio, looking down, his hands in his pockets, his kind, keen eyes clouded, a new line of trouble drawn "over the mouth's good mark, that made the smile." The maid had orders to summon him the instant Geneviève opened her eyes. We waited and waited, and Boris growing restless wandered about, fussing with modelling wax and red clay. Suddenly he started for the next room. "Come and see my rose-colored bath full of death," he cried.

"Is it death?" I asked to humor his mood.

"You are not prepared to call it life, I suppose," he answered. As he spoke he plucked a solitary gold fish squirming and twisting out of its globe. "We'll send this one after the other—wherever that is," he said. There was feverish excitement in his voice. A dull weight of fever lay on my limbs and on my brain as I followed him to the fair crystal pool with its pink-tinted sides; and he dropped the creature in. Falling, its scales flashed with a hot orange gleam in its angry twistings and contortions; the moment it struck the liquid it became rigid and sank heavily to the bottom. Then came the milky foam, the splendid hues radiating on the surface and then the shaft of pure serene light broke through from seemingly infinite depth. Boris plunged in his hand and drew out an exquisite marble thing, blue-veined, rose-tinted and glistening with opalescent drops.

"Child's play," he muttered, and looked wearily, longingly at me,—as if I could answer such questions! But Jack Scott came in and entered into the "game" as he called it with ardor. Nothing would do but to try the experiment on the white rabbit then and there. I was willing that Boris should find distraction from his cares, but I hated to see the life go out of a warm, living creature and I declined to be present. Picking up a book at random I sat down in the studio to read. Alas, I had found "The King in Yellow." After a few moments which seemed ages, I was putting it away with a nervous shudder, when Boris and Jack came in bringing their marble rabbit. At the same time the bell rang above and a cry came from the sick room. Boris was gone like a flash, and the next moment he called, "Jack, run for the doctor; bring him back with you. Alec, come here."

I went and stood at her door. A frightened maid came out in haste and ran away to fetch some remedy. Geneviève, sitting bolt upright, with crimson cheeks and glittering eyes, babbled incessantly and resisted Boris' gentle restraint. He called me to help. At my first touch she sighed and sank back, closing her eyes, and then—then—as we still bent above her, she opened them again, looked straight into Boris' face, poor fever-crazed girl, and told her secret. At the same instant, our three lives turned into new channels; the bond that had held us so long together snapped forever and a new bond was forged in its place, for she had spoken my name, and as the fever tortured her, her heart poured out its load of hidden sorrow. Amazed and dumb I bowed my head, while my face burned like a live coal, and the blood surged in my ears, stupefying me with its clamor. Incapable of movement, incapable of speech, I listened to her feverish words in an agony of shame and sorrow. I could not silence her, I could not look at Boris. Then I felt an arm upon my shoulder, and Boris turned a bloodless face to mine.

"It is not your fault, Alec, don't grieve so if she loves you—" but he could not finish; and as the doctor stepped swiftly into the room saying— "Ah, the fever!" I seized Jack Scott and hurried him to the street saying, "Boris would rather be alone." We crossed the street to our own apartments and that night, seeing I was going to be ill too, he went for the doctor again. The last thing I recollect with any distinctness was hearing Jack say, "For Heaven's sake, doctor, what ails him, to wear a face like that?" and I thought of "The King in Yellow" and the Pallid Mask.

I was very ill, for the strain of two years which I had endured since that fatal May morning when Geneviève murmured, "I love you, but I think I love Boris best" told on me at last. I never imagined that it could become more than I could endure. Outwardly tranquil, I had deceived myself. Although the inward battle raged night after night, and I, lying alone in my room, cursed myself for rebellious thoughts unloyal to Boris and unworthy of Geneviève, the morning always brought relief, and I returned to Geneviève and to my dear Boris with a heart washed clean by the tempests of the night.

Never in word or deed or thought while with them, had I betrayed my sorrow even to myself.

The mask of self-deception was no longer a mask for me, it was a part of me. Night lifted it, laying bare the stifled truth below; but there was no one to see except myself, and when day broke the mask fell back again of its own accord. These thoughts passed through my troubled mind as I lay sick, but they were hopelessly entangled with visions of white creatures, heavy as stone, crawling about in Boris' basin,—of the wolf's head on the rug, foaming and snapping at Geneviève, who lay smiling beside it. I thought, too, of The King in Yellow wrapt in the fantastic colors of his tattered mantle, and that bitter cry of Cassilda, "Not upon us, oh King, not upon us!" Feverishly I struggled to put it from me, but I saw the lake of Hali, thin and blank, without a ripple or wind to stir it, and I saw the towers of Carcosa behind the moon. Aldebaran, The Hyades, Alar, Hastur, glided through the cloud rifts which fluttered and flapped as they passed like the scolloped tatters of The King in Yellow. Among all these, one sane thought persisted. It never wavered, no matter what else was going on in my disordered mind, that my chief reason for existing, was to meet some requirement of Boris and Geneviève.

What this obligation was, its nature, was never clear; sometimes it seemed to be protection, sometimes support, through a great crisis. Whatever it seemed to be for the time, its weight rested only on me, and I was never so ill or so weak that I did not respond with my whole soul. There were always crowds of faces about me, mostly strange, but a few I recognized, Boris among them. Afterward they told me that this could not have been, but I know that once at least he bent over me. It was only a touch, a faint echo of his voice, then the clouds settled back on my senses, and I lost him, but he *did* stand there and bend over me once at least.

At last, one morning I awoke to find the sunlight falling across my bed, and Jack Scott reading beside me. I had not strength enough to speak aloud, neither could I think, much less remember, but I could smile feebly, as Jack's eye met mine, and when he jumped up and asked eagerly if I wanted anything, I could whisper, "Yes, Boris." Jack moved to the head of my bed, and leaned down to arrange my pillow: I did not see his face, but he answered heartily, "You must wait, Alec, you are too weak to see even Boris."

I waited and I grew strong; in a few days I was able to see whom I would, but meanwhile I had thought and remembered. From the moment when all the past grew clear again in my mind, I never doubted what I should do when the time came, and I felt sure that Boris would have resolved upon the same course so far as he was concerned; as for what pertained to me alone, I knew he would see that also as I did. I no longer asked for anyone. I never inquired why no message came from them; why during the week I lay there, waiting and growing stronger, I never heard their names spoken. Preoccupied with my own searchings for the right way, and with my feeble but determined fight against despair, I simply acquiesced in Jack's reticence, taking for granted that he was afraid to speak of them, lest I should turn unruly and insist on seeing them. Meanwhile I said over and over to myself, how it would be when life began again for us all. We would take up our relations exactly as they were before Geneviève fell ill. Boris and I would look into each other's eyes and there would be neither rancor nor cowardice nor mistrust in that glance. I would be with them again for a little while in the dear intimacy of their home, and then, without pretext or explanation, I would disappear from their lives forever. Boris would know, Geneviève—the only comfort was that she would never know. It seemed, as I thought it over, that I had found the meaning of that sense of obligation which had persisted all through my delirium, and the only possible answer to it. So, when I was quite ready, I beckoned Jack to me one day, and said,

"Jack, I want Boris at once; and take my dearest greeting to Geneviève. . . ."

When at last he made me understand that they were both dead, I fell into a wild rage that tore all my little convalescent strength to atoms. I raved and cursed myself into a relapse, from which I crawled forth some weeks afterward a boy of twenty-one who believed that his youth was gone forever. I seemed to be past the capability of further suffering, and one day when Jack handed me a letter and the keys to Boris' house, I took them without a tremor and asked him to tell me all. It was cruel of me to ask him, but there was no help for it, and he leaned wearily on his thin hands, to reopen the wound which could never entirely heal. He began very quietly.

"Alec, unless you have a clue that I know nothing about, you will not be able to explain any more than I, what has happened. I suspect that you would rather not hear these details, but you must learn them, else I would spare you the relation. God knows I wish I could be spared the telling. I shall use few words.

"That day when I left you in the doctor's care and came back to Boris, I found him working on the 'Fates.' Geneviève, he said, was sleeping under the influence of drugs. She had been quite out of her mind, he said. He kept on working, not talking any more, and I watched him. Before long, I saw that the third figure of the group—the one looking straight ahead, out over the world—bore his face; not as you ever saw it, but as it looked then and to the end. This is one thing for which I should like to find an explanation, but I never shall.

"Well, he worked and I watched him in silence, and we went on that way until nearly midnight. Then we heard a door open and shut sharply, and a swift rush in the next room. Boris sprang through the doorway and I followed; but we were too late. She lay at the bottom of the pool, her hands across her breast. Then Boris shot himself through the heart." Jack stopped speaking, drops of sweat stood under his eyes, and his thin cheeks twitched. "I carried Boris to his room. Then I went back and let that hellish fluid out of the pool, and turning on all the water, washed the marble clean of every drop. When at length I dared descend the steps, I found her lying there as white as snow. At last, when I had decided what was best to do, I went into the laboratory, and first emptied the solution in the basin into the waste-pipe; then I poured the contents of every jar and bottle after it. There was wood in the fireplace, so I built a fire, and breaking the locks of Boris' cabinet I burnt every paper, notebook and letter that I found there. With a mallet from the studio I smashed to pieces all the empty bottles, then loading them into a coal scuttle, I carried them to the cellar and threw them over the red-hot bed of the furnace. Six times I made the journey, and at last, not a vestige remained of anything which might again aid in seeking for the formula which Boris had found. Then at last I dared call the doctor. He is a good man, and together we struggled to keep it from the public. Without him I never could have succeeded. At last we got the servants paid and sent away into the country, where old Rosier keeps them quiet with stories of Boris' and Geneviève's travels in distant lands, from whence they will not return for years. We buried Boris in the little cemetery of Sèvres. The doctor is a good creature and knows when to pity a man who can bear no more. He gave his certificate of heart disease and asked no questions of me."

Then lifting his head from his hands, he said, "Open the letter, Alec; it is for us both."

I tore it open. It was Boris' will dated a year before. He left everything to Geneviève, and in case of her dying childless, I was to take control of the house in the Rue Sainte-Cécile, and Jack Scott, the management at Ept. On our deaths the property reverted to his mother's family in Russia, with the exception of the sculptured marbles executed by himself. These he left to me.

The page blurred under our eyes, and Jack got up and walked to the window. Presently he returned and sat down again. I dreaded to hear what he was going to say, but he spoke with the same simplicity and gentleness.

"Geneviève lies before the Madonna in the marble room. The Madonna bends tenderly above her, and Geneviève smiles back into that calm face that never would have been except for her."

His voice broke, but he grasped my hand, saying, "Courage, Alec." Next morning he left for Ept to fulfil his trust.

IV

The same evening I took the keys and went into the house I had known so well. Everything was in order, but the silence was terrible. Though I went twice to the door of the marble room, I could not force myself to enter. It was beyond my strength. I went into the smoking-room and sat down before the spinet. A small lace handkerchief lay on the keys, and I turned away, choking. It was plain I could not stay, so I locked every door, every window, and the three front and back gates, and went away. Next morning Alcide packed my valise, and leaving him in charge of my apartments I took the Orient express for Constantinople. During the two years that I wandered through the East, at first, in our letters, we never mentioned Geneviève and Boris, but gradually their names crept in. I recollect particularly a passage in one of Jack's letters replying to one of mine.

"What you tell me of seeing Boris bending over you while you lay ill, and feeling his touch on your face, and hearing his voice of course troubles me. This that you describe must have happened a fortnight after he died. I say to myself that you were dreaming, that it was part of your delirium, but the explanation does not satisfy me, nor would it you."

Toward the end of the second year a letter came from Jack to me in India so unlike any thing that I had ever known of him that I decided to return at once to Paris. He wrote, "I am well and sell all my pictures as artists do, who have no need of money. I have not a care of my own, but I am more restless than if I had. I am unable to shake off a strange anxiety about you. It is not apprehension, it is rather a breathless expectancy, of what, God knows! I can only say it is wearing me out. Nights I dream always of you and Boris. I can never recall anything afterward, but I wake in the morning with my heart beating, and all day the excitement increases until I fall asleep at night to recall the same experience. I am quite exhausted by it, and have determined to break up this morbid condition. I must see you. Shall I go to Bombay or will you come to Paris?"

I telegraphed him to expect me by the next steamer.

When we met I thought he had changed very little; I, he insisted, looked in splendid health. It was good to hear his voice again, and as we sat and chatted about what life still held for us, we felt that it was pleasant to be alive in the bright spring weather.

We stayed in Paris together a week, and then I went for a week to Ept with him, but first of all we went to the cemetery at Sèvres, where Boris lay.

"Shall we place the 'Fates' in the little grove above him?" Jack asked, and I answered,

"I think only the 'Madonna' should watch over Boris' grave." But Jack was none the better for my home-coming. The dreams of which he could not retain even the least definite outline continued, and he said that at times the sense of breathless expectancy was suffocating.

"You see I do you harm and not good," I said. "Try a change without me." So he started alone for a ramble among the Channel Islands and I went back to Paris. I had not yet entered Boris' house, now mine, since my return, but I knew it must be done. It had been kept in order by Jack; there were servants there, so I gave up my own apartment and went there to live. Instead of the agitation I had feared, I found myself able to paint there tranquilly. I visited all the rooms—all but one. I could not bring myself to enter the marble room where Geneviève lay, and yet I felt the longing growing daily to look upon her face, to kneel beside her.

One April afternoon, I lay dreaming in the smoking-room, just as I had lain two years before, and mechanically I looked among the tawny Eastern rugs for the wolf-skin. At last I distinguished the pointed ears and flat cruel head, and I thought of my dream where I saw Geneviève lying beside it. The helmets still hung against the threadbare tapestry, among them the old Spanish morion which I remembered Geneviève had once put on when we were amusing ourselves with the ancient bits of mail. I turned my eyes to the spinet; every yellow key seemed eloquent of her caressing hand, and I rose, drawn by the strength of my life's passion to the sealed door of the marble room. The heavy doors swung inward under my trembling hands. Sunlight poured through the window, tipping with gold the wings of Cupid, and lingered like a nimbus over the brows of the Madonna. Her tender face bent in compassion over a marble form so exquisitely pure that I knelt and signed myself. Geneviève lay in the shadow under the Madonna, and yet, through her white arms, I saw the pale azure vein, and beneath her softly clasped hands the folds of her dress were tinged with rose, as if from some faint warm light within her breast.

Bending with a breaking heart I touched the marble drapery with my lips, then crept back into the silent house.

A maid came and brought me a letter, and I sat down in the little conservatory to read it; but as I was about to break the seal, seeing the girl lingering, I asked her what she wanted.

She stammered something about a white rabbit that had been caught in the house and asked what should be done with it. I told her to let it loose in the walled garden behind the house and opened my letter. It was from Jack, but so incoherent that I thought he must have lost his reason. It was nothing but a series of prayers to me not to leave the house until he could get back; he could not tell me why, there were the dreams, he said—he could explain nothing, but he was sure that I must not leave the house in the Rue Sainte-Cécile.

As I finished reading I raised my eyes and saw the same maidservant standing in the doorway holding a glass dish in which two gold fish were swimming: "Put them back into the tank and tell me what you mean by interrupting me," I said.

With a half suppressed whimper she emptied water and fish into an aquarium at the end of the conservatory, and turning to me asked my permission to leave my service. She said people were playing tricks on her, evidently with a design of getting her into trouble; the marble rabbit had been stolen and a live one had been brought into the house; the two beautiful marble fish were gone and she had just found those common live things flopping on the dining-room floor. I reassured her and sent her away saying I would look about myself. I went into the studio; there was nothing there but my canvasses and some casts, except the marble of the Easter Lily. I saw it on a table across the room. Then I strode angrily over to it. But the flower I lifted from the table was fresh and fragile and filled the air with perfume.

Then suddenly I comprehended and sprang through the hall-way to the marble room. The doors flew open, the sunlight streamed into my face and through it, in a heavenly glory, the Madonna smiled, as Geneviève lifted her flushed face from her marble couch, and opened her sleepy eyes.

The Yellow Sign

"Let the red dawn surmise
What we shall do,
When this blue starlight dies
And all is through."

I

There are so many things which are impossible to explain! Why should certain chords in music make me think of the brown and golden tints of autumn foliage? Why should the Mass of Sainte Cécile send my thoughts wandering among caverns whose walls blaze with ragged masses of virgin silver? What was it in the roar and turmoil of Broadway at six o'clock that flashed before my eyes the picture of a still Breton forest where sunlight filtered through spring foliage and Sylvia bent, half curiously, half tenderly, over a small green lizard, murmuring: "To think that this also is a little ward of God!"

When I first saw the watchman his back was toward me. I looked at him indifferently until he went into the church. I paid no more attention to him than I had to any other man who lounged through Washington Square that morning, and when I shut my window and turned back into my studio I had forgotten him. Late in the afternoon, the day being warm, I raised the window again and leaned out to get a sniff of air. A man was standing in the courtyard of the church, and I noticed him again with as little interest as I had that morning. I looked across the square to where the fountain was playing and then, with my mind filled with vague impressions of trees, asphalt drives, and the moving groups of nursemaids and holiday-makers, I started to walk back to my easel. As I turned, my listless glance included the man below in the churchyard. His face was toward me now, and with a perfectly involuntary movement I bent to see it. At the same moment he raised his head and looked at me. Instantly I thought of a coffin-worm. Whatever it was about the man that repelled me I did not know, but the impression of a plump white grave-worm was so intense and nauseating that I must have shown it in my expression, for he turned his puffy face away with a movement which made me think of a disturbed grub in a chestnut.

I went back to my easel and motioned the model to resume her pose. After working awhile I was satisfied that I was spoiling what I had done as rapidly as possible, and I took up a palette knife and scraped the color out again. The flesh tones were sallow and unhealthy, and I did not understand how I could have painted such sickly color into a study which before that had glowed with healthy tones.

I looked at Tessie. She had not changed, and the clear flush of health dyed her neck and cheeks as I frowned.

"Is it something I've done?" she said.

"No—I've made a mess of this arm, and for the life of me I can't see how I came to paint such mud as that into the canvas," I replied.

"Don't I pose well?" she insisted.

"Of course, perfectly."

"Then it's not my fault?"

"No, it's my own."

"I'm very sorry," she said.

I told her she could rest while I applied rag and turpentine to the plague spot on my canvas, and she went off to smoke a cigarette and look over the illustrations in the *Courier Français.*

I did not know whether it was something in the turpentine or a defect in the canvas, but the more I scrubbed the more that gangrene seemed to spread. I worked like a beaver to get it out, and yet the disease appeared to creep from limb to limb of the study before me. Alarmed I strove to arrest it, but now the color on the breast changed and the whole figure seemed to absorb the infection as a sponge soaks up water. Vigorously I plied palette knife, turpentine, and scraper, thinking all the time what a séance I should hold with Duval who had sold me the canvas; but soon I noticed it was not the canvas which was defective, nor yet the colors of Edward. "It must be the turpentine," I thought angrily, "or else my eyes have become so blurred and confused by the afternoon light that I can't see straight." I called Tessie, the model. She came and leaned over my chair blowing rings of smoke into the air.

"What *have* you been doing to it?" she exclaimed.

"Nothing," I growled, "it must be this turpentine!"

"What a horrible color it is now," she continued. "Do you think my flesh resembles green cheese?"

"No, I don't," I said angrily. "Did you ever know me to paint like that before?"

"No, indeed!"

"Well, then!"

"It must be the turpentine, or something," she admitted.

She slipped on a Japanese robe and walked to the window. I scraped and rubbed until I was tired and finally picked up my brushes and hurled them through the canvas with a forcible expression, the tone alone of which reached Tessie's ears.

Nevertheless she promptly began: "That's it! Swear and act silly and ruin your brushes. You've been three weeks on that study, and now look! What's the good of ripping the canvas? What creatures artists are!"

I felt about as much ashamed as I usually did after such an outbreak, and I turned the ruined canvas to the wall. Tessie helped me clean my brushes, and then danced away to dress. From the screen she regaled me with bits of advice concerning whole or partial loss of temper, until, thinking, perhaps, I had been tormented sufficiently, she came out to implore me to button her waist where she could not reach it on the shoulder.

"Everything went wrong from the time you came back from the window and talked about that horrid-looking man you saw in the churchyard," she announced.

"Yes, he probably bewitched the picture," I said yawning. I looked at my watch.

"It's after six, I know," said Tessie, adjusting her hat before the mirror.

"Yes," I replied, "I didn't mean to keep you so long." I leaned out of the window but recoiled with disgust, for the young man with the pasty face stood below in the churchyard. Tessie saw my gesture of disapproval and leaned from the window.

"Is that the man you don't like?" she whispered.

I nodded.

"I can't see his face, but he does look fat and soft. Someway or other," she continued, turning to look at me, "he reminds me of a dream,—an awful dream I once had. Or," she mused, looking down at her shapely shoes, "was it a dream after all?"

"How should I know?" I smiled.

Tessie smiled in reply.

"You were in it," she said, "so perhaps you might know something about it."

"Tessie! Tessie!" I protested, "don't you dare flatter by saying that you dream about me!"

"But I did," she insisted; "shall I tell you about it?"

Tessie leaned back on the open window-sill and began very seriously.

"One night last winter I was lying in bed thinking about nothing at all in particular. I had been posing for you and I was tired out, yet it seemed impossible for me to sleep. I heard the bells in the city ring, ten, eleven, and midnight. I must have fallen asleep about midnight because I don't remember hearing the bells after that. It seemed to me that I had scarcely closed my eyes when I dreamed that something impelled me to go to the window. I rose, and raising the sash leaned out. Twenty-fifth Street was deserted as far as I could see. I began to be afraid; everything outside seemed so—so black and uncomfortable. Then the sound of wheels in the distance came to my ears, and it seemed to me as though that was what I must wait for. Very slowly the wheels approached, and, finally, I could make out a vehicle moving along the street. It came nearer and nearer, and when it passed beneath my window I saw it was a hearse. Then, as I trembled with fear, the driver turned and looked straight at me. When I awoke I was standing by the open window shivering with cold, but the black-plumed hearse and the driver were gone. I dreamed this dream again in March last, and again awoke beside the open window. Last night the dream came again. You remember how it was raining; when I awoke, standing at the open window, my night-dress was soaked."

"But where did I come into the dream?" I asked.

"You—you were in the coffin; but you were not dead."

"In the coffin?"

"Yes."

"How did you know? Could you see me?"

"No; I only knew you were there."

"Had you been eating Welsh rarebits, or lobster salad?" I began laughing, but the girl interrupted me with a frightened cry.

"Hello! What's up?" I said, as she shrank into the embrasure by the window.

"The—the man below in the churchyard;—he drove the hearse."

"Nonsense," I said, but Tessie's eyes were wide with terror. I went to the window and looked out. The man was gone. "Come, Tessie," I urged, "don't be foolish. You have posed too long; you are nervous."

"Do you think I could forget that face?" she murmured. "Three times I saw the hearse pass below my window, and every time the driver turned and looked up at me. Oh, his face was so white and—and soft? It looked dead—it looked as if it had been dead a long time."

I induced the girl to sit down and swallow a glass of Marsala. Then I sat down beside her, and tried to give her some advice.

"Look here, Tessie," I said, "you go to the country for a week or two, and you'll have no more dreams about hearses. You pose all day, and when night comes your nerves are upset. You can't keep this up. Then again, instead of going to bed when your day's work is done, you run off to picnics at Sulzer's Park, or go to the Eldorado or Coney Island,[5] and when you come down here next morning you are fagged out. There was no real hearse. That was a soft-shell crab dream."

She smiled faintly.

"What about the man in the churchyard?"

"Oh, he's only an ordinary unhealthy, everyday creature."

"As true as my name is Tessie Reardon, I swear to you, Mr. Scott, that the face of the man below in the churchyard is the face of the man who drove the hearse!"

"What of it?" I said. "It's an honest trade."

"Then you think I *did* see the hearse?"

"Oh," I said diplomatically, "if you really did, it might not be unlikely that the man below drove it. There is nothing in that."

Tessie rose, unrolled her scented handkerchief and taking a bit of gum from a knot in the hem, placed it in her mouth. Then drawing on her gloves she offered me her hand, with a frank, "Good-night, Mr. Scott," and walked out.

II

The next morning, Thomas, the bellboy, brought me the *Herald* and a bit of news. The church next door had been sold. I thanked Heaven for it, not that it being a Catholic I had any repugnance for the congregation next door, but because my nerves were shattered by a blatant exhorter, whose every word echoed through the aisle of the church as if it had been my own rooms, and who insisted on his r's with a nasal persistence which revolted my every instinct. Then, too, there was a fiend in human shape, an organist, who reeled off some of the grand old hymns with an interpretation of his own, and I longed for the blood of a creature who could play the doxology with an amendment of minor chords which one hears only in a quartet of very young undergraduates. I believe the minister was a good man, but when he bellowed: "And the Lorrrd said unto Moses, the Lorrrd is a man of war; the Lorrrd is his name. My wrath shall wax hot and I will kill you with the sworrrd!" I wondered how many centuries of purgatory it would take to atone for such a sin.

"Who bought the property?" I asked Thomas.

"Nobody that I knows, sir. They do say the gent wot owns this 'ere 'Amilton flats was lookin' at it. 'E might be a bildin' more studios."

I walked to the window. The young man with the unhealthy face stood by the churchyard gate, and at the mere sight of him the same overwhelming repugnance took possession of me.

"By the way, Thomas," I said, "who is that fellow down there?"

Thomas sniffed. "That there worm, sir? 'E's night-watchman of the church, sir. 'E maikes me tired a-sittin' out all night on them steps and lookin' at you insultin' like. I'd a punched 'is 'ed, sir—beg pardon, sir—"

"Go on, Thomas."

"One night a comin' 'ome with 'Arry, the other English boy, I sees 'im a-sittin' there on them steps. We 'ad Molly and Jen with us, sir, the two girls on the tray service, an' 'e looks so insultin' at us that I up and sez: 'Wat you looking hat, you fat slug?'—beg pardon, sir, but that's 'ow I sez, sir. Then 'e don't say nothin' and I sez: 'Come out and I'll punch that puddin' 'ed.' Then I hopens the gate and goes in, but 'e don't say nothin', only looks insultin' like. Then I 'its 'im one, but ugh! 'is 'ed was that cold and mushy it ud sicken you to touch 'im."

"What did he do then?" I asked, curiously.

"'Im? Nawthin'."

"And you, Thomas?"

The young fellow flushed with embarrassment and smiled uneasily. "Mr. Scott, sir, I ain't no coward an' I can't make it out at all why I run. I was in the 5th Lawncers, sir, bugler at Tel-el-Kebir, an' was shot by the wells."

"You don't mean to say you ran away?"

"Yes, sir; I run."

"Why?"

"That's just what I want to know, sir. I grabbed Molly an' run, an' the rest was as frightened as I."

"But what were they frightened at?"

Thomas refused to answer for a while, but now my curiosity was aroused about the repulsive young man below and I pressed him. Three years' sojourn in America had not only modified Thomas' cockney dialect but had given him the American's fear of ridicule.

"You won't believe me, Mr. Scott, sir?"

"Yes, I will."

"You will lawf at me, sir?"

"Nonsense!"

He hesitated. "Well, sir, it's Gawd's truth that when I 'it 'im 'e grabbed me wrists, sir, and when I twisted 'is soft, mushy fist one of 'is fingers come off in me 'and."

The utter loathing and horror of Thomas' face must have been reflected in my own for he added:

"It's orful, an' now when I see 'im I just go away. 'E maikes me hill."

When Thomas had gone I went to the window. The man stood beside the church-railing with both hands on the gate, but I hastily retreated to my easel again, sickened and horrified, for I saw that the middle finger of his right hand was missing.

At nine o'clock Tessie appeared and vanished behind the screen with a merry "Good morning, Mr. Scott." When she had reappeared and taken her pose upon the model-stand I started a new canvas much to her delight. She remained silent as long as I was on the drawing, but as soon as the scrape of the charcoal ceased and I took up my fixative she began to chatter.

"Oh, I had such a lovely time last night. We went to Tony Pastor's."

"Who are 'we'?" I demanded.

"Oh, Maggie, you know, Mr. Whyte's model, and Pinkie McCormack—we call her Pinkie because she's got that beautiful red hair you artists like so much—and Lizzie Burke."

I sent a shower of spray from the fixative over the canvas, and said: "Well, go on."

"We saw Kelly and Baby Barnes the skirt-dancer and—and all the rest. I made a mash."

"Then you have gone back on me, Tessie?"

She laughed and shook her head.

"He's Lizzie Burke's brother, Ed. He's a perfect gen'l'man."

I felt constrained to give her some parental advice concerning mashing, which she took with a bright smile.

"Oh, I can take care of a strange mash," she said, examining her chewing gum, "but Ed is different. Lizzie is my best friend."

Then she related how Ed had come back from the stocking mill in Lowell, Massachusetts, to find her and Lizzie grown up, and what an accomplished young man he was, and how he thought nothing of squandering half a dollar for ice-cream and oysters to celebrate his entry as a clerk into the woollen department of Macy's. Before she finished I began to paint, and she resumed the pose, smiling and chattering like a sparrow. By noon I had the study fairly well rubbed in and Tessie came to look at it.

"That's better," she said.

I thought so too, and ate my lunch with a satisfied feeling that all was going well. Tessie spread her lunch on a drawing table opposite me and we drank our claret from the same bottle and lighted our cigarettes from the same match. I was very much attached to Tessie. I had watched her shoot up into a slender but exquisitely formed woman from a frail, awkward child. She had posed for me during the last three years, and among all my models she was my favorite. It would have troubled me very much indeed had she become "tough" or "fly," as the phrase goes, but I never noticed any deterioration of her manner, and felt at heart that she was all right. She and I never discussed morals at all, and I had no intention of doing so, partly because I had none myself, and partly because I knew she would do what she liked in spite of me. Still I did hope she would steer clear of complications, because I wished her well, and then also I had a selfish desire to retain the best model I had. I knew that mashing, as she termed it, had no significance with girls like Tessie, and that such things in America did not resemble in the least the same things in Paris. Yet having lived with my eyes open, I also knew that somebody would take Tessie away some day, in one manner or another, and though I professed to myself that marriage was nonsense, I sincerely hoped that, in this case, there would be a priest at the end of the vista. I am a Catholic. When I listen to high mass, when I sign myself, I feel that everything, including myself; is more cheerful, and when I confess, it does me good. A man who lives as much alone as I do, must confess to somebody. Then, again, Sylvia was Catholic, and it was reason enough for me. But I was speaking of Tessie, which is very different. Tessie also was Catholic and much more devout than I, so, taking it all in all, I had little fear for my pretty model until she should fall in love. But then I knew that fate alone would decide her future for her, and I prayed inwardly that fate would keep her away from men like me and throw into her path nothing but Ed Burkes and Jimmy McCormacks, bless her sweet face!

Tessie sat blowing rings of smoke up to the ceiling and tinkling the ice in her tumbler.

"Do you know that I also had a dream last night?" I observed.

"Not about that man," she laughed.

"Exactly. A dream similar to yours, only much worse."

It was foolish and thoughtless of me to say this, but you know how little tact the average painter has.

"I must have fallen asleep about 10 o'clock," I continued, "and after awhile I dreamt that I awoke. So plainly did I hear the midnight bells, the wind in the tree branches, and the whistle of steamers from the bay, that even now I can scarcely believe I was not awake. I seemed to be lying in a box which had a glass cover. Dimly I saw the street lamps as I passed, for I must tell you, Tessie, the box in which I reclined appeared to lie in a cushioned wagon which jolted me over a stony pavement. After a while I became impatient and tried to move but the box was too narrow. My hands were crossed on my breast so I could not raise them to help myself. I listened and then tried to call. My voice was gone. I could hear the trample of the horses attached to the wagon and even the breathing of the driver. Then another sound broke upon my ears like the raising of a window sash. I managed to turn my head a little, and found I could look, not only through the glass cover of my box, but also through the glass panes in the side of the covered vehicle. I saw houses, empty and silent, with neither light nor life about any of them excepting one. In that house a window was open on the first floor and a figure all in white stood looking down into the street. It was you."

Tessie had turned her face away from me and leaned on the table with her elbow.

"I could see your face," I resumed, "and it seemed to me to be very sorrowful. Then we passed on and turned into a narrow black lane. Presently the horses stopped. I waited and waited, closing my eyes with fear and impatience, but all was as silent as the grave. After what seemed to me hours, I began to feel uncomfortable. A sense that somebody was close to me made me unclose my eyes. Then I saw the white face of the hearse-driver looking at me through the coffin-lid—"

A sob from Tessie interrupted me. She was trembling like a leaf. I saw I had made an ass of myself and attempted to repair the damage.

"Why, Tess," I said, "I only told you this to show you what influence your story might have on another person's dreams. You don't suppose I really lay in a coffin, do you? What are you trembling for? Don't you see that your dream and my unreasonable dislike for that inoffensive watchman of the church simply set my brain working as soon as I fell asleep?"

She laid her head between her arms and sobbed as if her heart would break. What a precious triple donkey I had made of myself! But I was about to break my record. I went over and put my arm about her.

"Tessie, dear, forgive me," I said; "I had no business to frighten you with such nonsense. You are too sensible a girl, too good a Catholic to believe in dreams."

Her hand tightened on mine and her head fell back upon my shoulder, but she still trembled and I petted and comforted her.

"Come, Tess, open your eyes and smile."

Her eyes opened with a slow languid movement and met mine, but their expression was so queer that I hastened to reassure her again.

"It's all humbug, Tessie, you surely are not afraid that any harm will come to you because of that."

"No," she said, but her scarlet lips quivered.

"Then what's the matter? Are you afraid?"

"Yes. Not for myself."

"For me, then?" I demanded gayly.

"For you," she murmured in a voice almost inaudible, "I—I care for you."

At first I started to laugh, but when I understood her, a shock passed through me and I sat like one turned to stone. This was the crowning bit of idiocy I had committed. During the moment which elapsed between her reply and my answer I thought of a thousand responses to that innocent confession. I could pass it by with a laugh, I could misunderstand her and reassure her as to my health, I could simply point out that it was impossible she could love me. But my reply was quicker than my thoughts, and I might think and think now when it was too late, for I had kissed her on the mouth.

That evening I took my usual walk in Washington Park, pondering over the occurrences of the day. I was thoroughly committed. There was no back out now, and I stared the future straight in the face. I was not good, not even scrupulous, but I had no idea of deceiving either myself or Tessie. The one passion of my life lay buried in the sunlit forests of Brittany. Was it buried there forever? Hope cried "No!" For three years I had been listening to the voice of Hope, and for three years I had waited for a footstep on my threshold. Had Sylvia forgotten? "No!" cried Hope.

I said that I was not good. That is true, but still I was not exactly a comic opera villain. I had led an easy-going reckless life, taking what invited me of pleasure, deploring and sometimes bitterly regretting consequences. In one thing alone, except my painting, was I serious, and that was something which lay hidden if not lost in the Breton forests.

It was too late now for me to regret what had occurred during the day. Whatever it had been, pity, a sudden tenderness for sorrow, or the more brutal instinct of gratified vanity, it was all the same now, and unless I wished to bruise an innocent heart my path lay marked before me. The fire and strength, the depth of passion of a love which I had never even suspected, with all my imagined experience in the world, left me no alternative but to respond or send her away. Whether because I am so cowardly about giving pain to others, or whether it was that I have little of the gloomy Puritan in me, I do not know, but I shrank from disclaiming responsibility for that thoughtless kiss, and in fact had no time to do so before the gates of her heart opened and the flood poured forth. Others who habitually do their duty and find a sullen satisfaction in making themselves and everybody else unhappy, might have withstood it. I did not. I dared not. After the storm had abated I did tell her that she might better have loved Ed Burke and worn a plain gold ring, but she would not hear of it, and I thought perhaps that as long as she had decided to love somebody she could not marry, it had better be me. I, at least, could treat her with an intelligent affection, and whenever she became tired of her infatuation she could go none the worse for it. For I was decided on that point although I knew how hard it would be. I remember the usual termination of Platonic liaisons and thought how disgusted I had been whenever I heard of one. I knew I was undertaking a great deal for unscrupulous a man as I was, and I dreaded the future, but never for one moment did I doubt that she was safe with me. Had it been anybody but Tessie I should not have bothered my head about scruples. For it did not occur to me to sacrifice Tessie as I would have sacrificed a woman of the world. I looked the future squarely in the face and saw the several probable endings to the affair. She would either tire of the whole thing, or become so unhappy that I should have either to marry her or go away. If I married her we would be unhappy. I with a wife unsuited to me, and she with a husband unsuitable for any woman. For my past life could scarcely entitle me to marry. If I went away she might either fall ill, recover, and marry some Eddie Burke, or she might recklessly or deliberately go and do something foolish. On the other hand if she tired of me, then her whole life would be before her with beautiful vistas of Eddie Burkes and marriage rings and twins and Harlem flats and Heaven knows what. As I strolled along through the trees by the Washington Arch, I decided that she should find a substantial friend in me anyway and the future could take care of itself. Then I went into the house and put on my evening dress for the little faintly perfumed note on my dresser said, "Have a cab at the stage door at eleven," and the note was signed "Edith Carmichel, Metropolitan Theater."

I took supper that night, or rather we took supper, Miss Carmichel and I, at Solari's and the dawn was just beginning to gild the cross on the Memorial Church as I entered Washington Square after leaving Edith at the Brunswick. There was not a soul in the park as I passed among the trees and took the walk which leads from the Garibaldi statue to the Hamilton Apartment House, but as I passed the churchyard I saw a figure sitting on the stone steps. In spite of myself a chill crept over me at the sight of the white puffy face, and I hastened to pass. Then he said something which might have been addressed to me or might merely have been a mutter to himself, but a sudden furious anger flamed up within me that such a creature should address me. For an instant I felt like wheeling about and smashing my stick over his head, but I walked on, and entering the Hamilton went to my apartment. For some time I tossed about the bed trying to get the sound of his voice out of my ears, but could not. It filled my head, that muttering sound, like thick oily smoke from a fat-rendering vat or an odor of noisome decay. And as I lay and tossed about, the voice in my ears seemed more distinct, and I began to understand the words he had muttered. They came to me slowly as if I had forgotten them, and at last I could make some sense out of the sounds. It was this:

"Have you found the Yellow Sign?"

"Have you found the Yellow Sign?"

"Have you found the Yellow Sign?"

I was furious. What did he mean by that? Then with a curse upon him and his I rolled over and went to sleep, but when I awoke later I looked pale and haggard, for I had dreamed the dream of the night before and it troubled me more than I cared to think.

I dressed and went down into my studio. Tessie sat by the window, but as I came in she rose and put both arms around my neck for an innocent kiss. She looked so sweet and dainty that I kissed her again and then sat down before the easel.

"Hello! Where's the study I began yesterday?" I asked.

Tessie looked conscious, but did not answer. I began to hunt among the piles of canvases, saying, "Hurry up, Tess, and get ready; we must take advantage of the morning light."

When at last I gave up the search among the other canvases and turned to look around the room for the missing study I noticed Tessie standing by the screen with her clothes still on.

"What's the matter," I asked, "don't you feel well?"

"Yes."

"Then hurry."

"Do you want me to pose as—as I have always posed?"

Then I understood. Here was a new complication. I had lost, of course, the best nude model I had ever seen. I looked at Tessie. Her face was scarlet. Alas! Alas! We had eaten of the tree of knowledge, and Eden and native innocence were dreams of the past—I mean for her.

I suppose she noticed the disappointment on my face, for she said: "I will pose if you wish. The study is behind the screen here where I put it."

"No," I said, "we will begin something new;" and I went into my wardrobe and picked out a Moorish costume which fairly blazed with tinsel. It was a genuine costume, and Tessie retired to the screen with it enchanted. When she came forth again I was astonished. Her long black hair was bound above her forehead with a circlet of turquoises, and the ends curled about her glittering girdle. Her feet were encased in the embroidered pointed slippers and the skirt of her costume, curiously wrought with arabesques in silver, fell to her ankles. The deep metallic blue vest embroidered with silver and the short Mauresque jacket spangled and sewn with turquoises became her wonderfully. She came up to me and held up her face smiling. I slipped my hand into my pocket and drawing out a gold chain with a cross attached, dropped it over her head.

"It's yours, Tessie."

"Mine?" she faltered.

"Yours. Now go and pose." Then with a radiant smile she ran behind the screen and presently reappeared with a little box on which was written my name.

"I had intended to give it to you when I went home to-night," she said, "but I can't wait now."

I opened the box. On the pink cotton inside lay a clasp of black onyx, on which was inlaid a curious symbol or letter in gold. It was neither Arabic nor Chinese, nor as I found afterwards did it belong to any human script.

"It's all I had to give you for a keepsake," she said, timidly.

I was annoyed, but I told her how much I should prize it, and promised to wear it always. She fastened it on my coat beneath the lapel.

"How foolish, Tess, to go and buy me such a beautiful thing as this," I said.

"I did not buy it," she laughed.

Then she told me how she had found it one day while coming from the Aquarium in the Battery, how she had advertised it and watched the papers, but at last gave up all hopes of finding the owner.

"That was last winter," she said, "the very day I had the first horrid dream about the hearse."

I remembered my dream of the previous night but said nothing, and presently my charcoal was flying over a new canvas, and Tessie stood motionless on the model stand.

III

The day following was a disastrous one for me. While moving a framed canvas from one easel to another my foot slipped on the polished floor and I fell heavily on both wrists. There were so badly sprained that it was useless to attempt to hold a brush, and I was obliged to wander about the studio, glaring at unfinished drawings and sketches until despair seized me and I sat down to smoke and twiddle my thumbs with rage. The rain blew against the windows and rattled on the roof of the church, driving me into a nervous fit with its interminable patter. Tessie sat sewing by the window, and every now and then raised her head and looked at me with such innocent compassion that I began to feel ashamed of my irritation and looked about for something to occupy me. I had read all the papers and all the books in the library, but for the sake of something to do I went to the bookcases and shoved them open with my elbow. I knew every volume by its color and examined them all, passing slowly around the library and whistling to keep up my spirits.

I was turning to go into the dining-room when my eye fell upon a book bound in serpent skin, standing in a corner of the top shelf of the last bookcase. I did not remember it and from the floor could not decipher the pale lettering on the back, so I went to the smoking-room and called Tessie. She came in from the studio and climbed up to reach the book.

"What is it?" I asked.

"'The King in Yellow.'"

I was dumfounded. Who had placed it there? How came it in my rooms? I had long ago decided that I should never open that book, and nothing on earth could have persuaded me to buy it. Fearful lest curiosity might tempt me to open it, I had never even looked at it in book-stores. If I ever had had any curiosity to read it, the awful tragedy of young Castaigne, whom I knew, prevented me from exploring its wicked pages. I had always refused to listen to any description of it, and indeed, nobody ever ventured to discuss the second part aloud, so I had absolutely no knowledge of what those leaves might reveal. I stared at the poisonous mottled binding as I would at a snake.

"Don't touch it, Tessie," I said; "come down."

Of course my admonition was enough to arouse her curiosity, and before I could prevent it she took the book and, laughing, danced off into the studio with it. I called to her but she slipped away with a tormenting smile at my helpless hands, and I followed her with some impatience.

"Tessie!" I cried, entering the library, "listen, I am serious. Put that book away. I do not wish you to open it!" The library was empty. I went into both drawing-rooms, then into the bedrooms, laundry, kitchen, and finally returned to the library and began a systematic search. She had hidden herself so well that it was half an hour later when I discovered her crouching white and silent by the latticed window in the store-room above. At first glance I saw she had been punished for her foolishness. "The King in Yellow" lay at her feet, but the book was open at the second part. I looked at Tessie and saw it was too late. She had opened "The King in Yellow." Then I took her by the hand and led her into the studio. She seemed dazed, and when I told her to lie down on the sofa she obeyed me without a word. After a while she closed her eyes and her breathing became regular and deep, but I could not determine whether or not she slept. For a long while I sat silently beside her, but she neither stirred nor spoke, and at last I rose and entering the unused store-room took the book in my least injured hand. It seemed heavy as lead, but I carried it into the studio again; and sitting down on the rug beside the sofa, opened it and read it through from beginning to end.

When, faint with the excess of my emotions, I dropped the volume and leaned wearily back against the sofa, Tessie opened her eyes and looked at me.

We had been speaking for some time in a dull monotonous strain before I realized that we were discussing "The King in Yellow." Oh the sin of writing such words,—words which are clear as crystal, limpid and musical as bubbling springs, words which sparkle and glow like the poisoned diamonds of the Medicis! Oh the wickedness, the hopeless damnation of a soul who could fascinate and paralyze human creatures with such words,—words understood by the ignorant and wise alike, words which are more precious than jewels, more soothing than music, more awful than death!

We talked on, unmindful of the gathering shadows, and she was begging me to throw away the clasp of black onyx quaintly inlaid with what we now knew to be the Yellow Sign. I never shall know why I refused, though even at this hour, here in my bedroom as I write this confession, I should be glad to know what it was that prevented me from tearing the Yellow Sign from my breast and casting it into the fire. I am sure I wished to do so, and yet Tessie pleaded with me in vain. Night fell and the hours dragged on, but still we murmured to each other of the King and the Pallid Mask, and midnight sounded from the misty spires in the fog-wrapped city. We spoke of Hastur and of Cassilda, while outside the fog rolled against the blank window-panes as the cloud waves roll and break on the shores of Hali.

The house was very silent now and not a sound came up from the misty streets. Tessie lay among the cushions, her face a gray blot in the gloom, but her hands were clasped in mine and I knew that she knew and read my thoughts as I read hers, for we had understood the mystery of the Hyades and the Phantom of Truth was laid. Then as we answered each other, swiftly, silently, thought on thought, the shadows stirred in the gloom about us, and far in the distant streets we heard a sound. Nearer and nearer it came, the dull crunching wheels, nearer and yet nearer, and now, outside before the door it ceased, and I dragged myself to the window and saw a black-plumed hearse. The gate below opened and shut, and I crept shaking to my door and bolted it, but I knew no bolts, no locks, could keep that creature out who was coming for the Yellow Sign. And now I heard him moving very softly along the hall. Now he was at the door, and the bolts rotted at his touch. Now he had entered. With eyes starting from my head I peered into the darkness, but when he came into the room I did not see him. It was only when I felt him envelop me in his cold soft grasp that I cried out and struggled with deadly fury, but my hands were useless and he tore the onyx clasp from my coat and struck me full in the face. Then, as I fell, I heard Tessie's soft cry and her spirit fled: and even while falling I longed to follow her, for I knew that the King in Yellow had opened his tattered mantle and there was only God to cry to now.

I would tell more, but I cannot see what help it will be to the world. As for me I am past human help or hope. As I lie here, writing, careless even whether or not I die before I finish, I can see the doctor gathering up his powders and phials with a vague gesture to the good priest beside me, which I understand.

They will be very curious to know the tragedy—they of the outside world who write books and print millions of newspapers, but I shall write no more, and the father confessor will seal my last words with the seal of sanctity when his holy office is done. They of the outside world may send their creatures into wrecked homes and death-smitten firesides, and their newspapers will batten on blood and tears, but with me their spies must halt before the confessional. They know that Tessie is dead and that I am dying. They know how the people in the house, aroused by an infernal scream, rushed into my room and found one living and two dead, but they do not know what I shall tell them now; they do not know that the doctor said as he pointed to a horrible decomposed heap on the floor—the livid corpse of the watchman from the church: "I have no theory, no explanation. That man must have been dead for months!"

I think I am dying. I wish the priest would—

The Demoiselle d'Ys

"Mais je croy que je
 Suis descendu on puiz
 Tenebreux onquel disoit
 Heraclytus estre Verité cachée."

"There be three things which are too wonderful for me, yea, four which I know not:

"The way of an eagle in the air; the way of a serpent upon a rock; the way of a ship in the midst of the sea; and the way of a man with a maid."

I

The utter desolation of the scene began to have its effect; I sat down to face the situation and, if possible, recall to mind some landmark which might aid me in extricating myself from my present position. If I could only find the ocean again all would be clear, for I knew one could see the island of Groix from the cliffs.

I laid down my gun, and kneeling behind a rock lighted my pipe. Then I looked at my watch. It was nearly four o'clock. I might have wandered far from Kerselec since daybreak.

Standing the day before on the cliffs below Kerselec with Goulven, looking out over the sombre moors among which I had now lost my way, these downs had appeared to me level as a meadow, stretching to the horizon, and although I knew how deceptive is distance, I could not realize that what from Kerselec seemed to be mere grassy hollows were great valleys covered with gorse and heather, and what looked like scattered boulders were in reality enormous cliffs of granite.

"It's a bad place for a stranger," old Goulven had said; "you'd better take a guide;" and I had replied, "I shall not lose myself." Now I knew that I had lost myself, as I sat there smoking, with the sea-wind blowing in my face. On every side stretched the moorland, covered with flowering gorse and heath and granite boulders. There was not a tree in sight, much less a house. After a while, I picked up the gun, and turning my back on the sun tramped on again.

There was little use in following any of the brawling streams which every now and then crossed my path, for, instead of flowing into the sea, they ran inland to reedy pools in the hollows of the moors. I had followed several, but they all led me to swamps or silent little ponds from which the snipe rose peeping and wheeled away in an ecstasy of fright. I began to feel fatigued, and the gun galled my shoulder in spite of the double pads. The sun sank lower and lower, shining level across yellow gorse and the moorland pools.

As I walked my own gigantic shadow led me on, seeming to lengthen at every step. The gorse scraped against my leggings, crackled beneath my feet, showering the brown earth with blossoms, and the brake bowed and billowed along my path. From tufts of heath rabbits scurried away through the bracken, and among the swamp grass I heard the wild duck's drowsy quack. Once a fox stole across my path, and again, as I stooped to drink at a hurrying rill, a heron flapped heavily from the reeds beside me. I turned to look at the sun. It seemed to touch the edges of the plain. When at last I decided that it was useless to go on, and that I must make up my mind to spend at least one night on the moors, I threw myself down thoroughly fagged out. The evening sunlight slanted warm across my body, but the sea-winds began to rise, and I felt a chill strike through me from my wet shooting-boots. High overhead gulls were wheeling and tossing like bits of white paper; from some distant marsh a solitary curlew called. Little by little the sun sank into the plain, and the zenith flushed with the after-glow. I watched the sky change from palest gold to pink and then to smouldering fire. Clouds of midges danced above me, and high in the calm air a bat dipped and soared. My eyelids began to droop. Then as I shook off the drowsiness a sudden crash among the bracken roused me. I raised my eyes. A great bird hung quivering in the air above my face. For an instant I stared, incapable of motion; then something leaped past me in the ferns and the bird rose, wheeled, and pitched headlong into the brake.

I was on my feet in an instant peering through the gorse. There came the sound of a struggle from a bunch of heather close by, and then all was quiet. I stepped forward, my gun poised, but when I came to the heather the gun fell under my arm again, and I stood motionless in silent astonishment. A dead hare lay on the ground, and on the hare stood a magnificent falcon, one talon buried in the creature's neck, the other planted firmly on its limp flank. But what astonished me, was not the mere sight of a falcon sitting upon its prey. I had seen that more than once. It was that the falcon was fitted with a sort of leash about both talons, and from the leash hung a round bit of metal like a sleigh-bell. The bird turned its fierce yellow eyes on me, and then stooped and struck its curved beak into the quarry. At the same instant hurried steps sounded among the heather, and a girl sprang into the covert in front. Without a glance at me she walked up to the falcon, and passing her gloved hand under its breast, raised it from the quarry. Then she deftly slipped a small hood over the bird's head, and holding it out on her gauntlet, stooped and picked up the hare.

She passed a cord about the animal's legs and fastened the end of the thong to her girdle. Then she started to retrace her steps through the covert. As she passed me I raised my cap and she acknowledged my presence with a scarcely perceptible inclination. I had been so astonished, so lost in admiration of the scene before my eyes, that it had not occurred to me that here was my salvation. But as she moved away I recollected that unless I wanted to sleep on a windy moor that night I had better recover my speech without delay. At my first word she hesitated, and as I stepped before her I thought a look of fear came into her beautiful eyes. But as I humbly explained my unpleasant plight, her face flushed and she looked at me in wonder.

"Surely you did not come from Kerselec!" she repeated.

Her sweet voice had no trace of the Breton accent nor of any accent which I knew, and yet there was something in it I seemed to have heard before, something quaint and indefinable, like the theme of an old song.

I explained that I was an American, unacquainted with Finistère, shooting there for my own amusement.

"An American," she repeated in the same quaint musical tones. "I have never before seen an American."

For a moment she stood silent, then looking at me she said: "If you should walk all night you could not reach Kerselec now, even if you had a guide."

This was pleasant news.

"But," I began, "if I could only find a peasant's but where I might get something to eat, and shelter."

The falcon on her wrist fluttered and shook its head. The girl smoothed its glossy back and glanced at me.

"Look around," she said gently. "Can you see the end of these moors? Look, north, south, east, west. Can you see anything but moor-land and bracken?"

"No," I said.

"The moor is wild and desolate. It is easy to enter, but sometimes they who enter never leave it. There are no peasants' huts here."

"Well," I said "if you will tell me in which direction Kerselec lies, to-morrow it will take me no longer to go back than it has to come."

She looked at me again with an expression almost like pity.

"Ah," she said, "to come is easy and takes hours; to go is different— and may take centuries."

I stared at her in amazement but decided that I had misunderstood her. Then before I had time to speak she drew a whistle from her belt and sounded it.

"Sit down and rest," she said to me; "you have come a long distance and are tired."

She gathered up her pleated skirts and motioning me to follow picked her dainty way through the gorse to a flat rock among the ferns.

"They will be here directly," she said, and taking a seat at one end of the rock invited me to sit down on the other edge. The after-glow was beginning to fade in the sky and a single star twinkled faintly through the rosy haze. A long wavering triangle of water-fowl drifted southward over our heads and from the swamps around plover were calling.

"They are very beautiful—these moors," she said quietly.

"Beautiful, but cruel to strangers," I answered.

"Beautiful and cruel," she repeated dreamily, "beautiful and cruel."

"Like a woman," I said stupidly.

"Oh," she cried with a little catch in her breath and looked at me. Her dark eyes met mine and I thought she seemed angry or frightened.

"Like a woman," she repeated under her breath, "how cruel to say so!" Then after a pause, as though speaking aloud to herself, "how cruel for him to say that."

I don't know what sort of an apology I offered for my inane, though harmless speech, but I know that she seemed so troubled about it that I began to think I had said something very dreadful without knowing it, and remembered with horror the pitfalls and snares which the French language sets for foreigners. While I was trying to imagine what I might have said, a sound of voices came across the moor and the girl rose to her feet.

"No," she said, with a trace of a smile on her pale face, "I will not accept your apologies, Monsieur, but I must prove you wrong and that shall be my revenge. Look. Here come Hastur and Raoul."

Two men loomed up in the twilight. One had a sack across his shoulders and the other carried a hoop before him as a waiter carries a tray. The hoop was fastened with straps to his shoulders and around the edge of the circlet sat three hooded falcons fitted with tinkling bells. The girl stepped up to the falconer, and with a quick turn of her wrist transferred her falcon to the hoop where it quickly sidled off and nestled among its mates who shook their hooded heads and ruffled their feathers till the belled jesses tinkled again. The other man stepped forward and bowing respectfully took up the hare and dropped it into the game-sack.

"These are my piqueurs," said the girl turning to me with a gentle dignity. "Raoul is a good fauconnier and I shall some day make him grand veneur. Hastur is incomparable."

The two silent men saluted me respectfully.

"Did I not tell you, Monsieur, that I should prove you wrong?" she continued. "This then is my revenge, that you do me the courtesy of accepting food and shelter at my own house."

Before I could answer she spoke to the falconers who started instantly across the heath, and with a gracious gesture to me she followed. I don't know whether I made her understand how profoundly grateful I felt, but she seemed pleased to listen, as we walked over the dewy heather.

"Are you not very tired?" she asked.

I had clean forgotten my fatigue in her presence and I told her so.

"Don't you think your gallantry is a little old-fashioned," she said; and when I looked confused and humbled, she added quietly, "Oh, I like it, I like everything old-fashioned, and it is delightful to hear you say such pretty things."

The moorland around us was very still now under its ghostly sheet of mist. The plover had ceased their calling; the crickets and all the little creatures of the fields were silent as we passed, yet it seemed to me as if I could hear them beginning again far behind us. Well in advance the two tall falconers strode across the heather and the faint jingling of the hawk's bells came to our ears in distant murmuring chimes.

Suddenly a splendid hound dashed out of the mist in front, followed by another and another until half a dozen or more were bounding and leaping around the girl beside me. She caressed and quieted them with her gloved hand, speaking to them in quaint terms which I remembered to have seen in old French manuscripts.

Then the falcons on the circlet borne by the falconer ahead began to beat their wings and scream, and from somewhere out of sight the notes of a hunting-horn floated across the moor. The hounds sprang away before us and vanished in the twilight, the falcons flapped and squealed upon their perch and the girl taking up the song of the horn began to hum. Clear and mellow her voice sounded in the night air.

> "Chasseur, chasseur, chassez encore,
> Quittez Rosette et Jeanneton,
> Tonton, tonton, tontaine, tonton,
> Ou, pour, rabattre, dès l'aurore,
> Que les Amours soient de planton,
> Tonton, tontaine, tonton."

As I listened to her lovely voice a gray mass which rapidly grew more distinct loomed up in front, and the horn rang out joyously through the tumult of the hounds and falcons. A torch glimmered at a gate, a light streamed through an opening door, and we stepped upon a wooden bridge which trembled under our feet and rose creaking and straining behind us as we passed over the moat and into a small stone court, walled on every side. From an open doorway a man came and bending in salutation presented a cup to the girl beside me. She took the cup and touched it with her lips, then lowering it turned to me and said in a low voice, "I bid you welcome."

At that moment one of the falconers came with another cup, but before handing it to me, presented it to the girl, who tasted it. The falconer made a gesture to receive it, but she hesitated a moment and then stepping forward offered me the cup with her own hands. I felt this to be an act of extraordinary graciousness, but hardly knew what was expected of me, and did not raise it to my lips at once. The girl flushed crimson. I saw that I must act quickly.

"Mademoiselle," I faltered, "a stranger whom you have saved from dangers he may never realize, empties this cup to the gentlest and loveliest hostess of France."

"In His name," she murmured, crossing herself as I drained the cup. Then stepping into the doorway she turned to me with a pretty gesture and taking my hand in hers, led me into the house, saying again and again: "You are very welcome, indeed you are welcome to the Château d'Ys."

II

I awoke next morning with the music of the horn in my ears, and leaping out of the ancient bed, went to a curtained window where the sunlight filtered through little deep-set panes. The horn ceased as I looked into the court below.

A man who might have been brother to the two falconers of the night before stood in the midst of a pack of hounds. A curved horn was strapped over his back, and in his hand he held a long-lashed whip. The dogs whined and yelped, dancing around him in anticipation; there was the stamp of horses too in the walled yard.

"Mount!" cried a voice in Breton, and with a clatter of hoofs the two falconers, with falcons upon their wrists, rode into the courtyard among the hounds. Then I heard another voice which sent the blood throbbing

through my heart: "Piriou Louis, hunt the hounds well and spare neither spur nor whip. Thou Raoul and thou Gaston, see that the *epervier*
does not prove himself *niais,* and if it be best in your judgment, *faites
courtoisie à l'oiseau. Jardiner un oiseau* like the *mué* there on Hastur's
wrist is not difficult, but thou, Raoul, mayest not find it so simple to
govern that *hagard.* Twice last week he foamed *au vif* and lost the *bec-
cade* although he is used to the *leurre.* The bird acts like a stupid
branchier. Paître un hagard nest pas facile."

Was I dreaming? The old language of falconry which I had read in
yellow manuscripts—the old forgotten French of the middle ages was
sounding in my ears while the hounds bayed and the hawk's bells tinkled accompaniment to the stamping horses. She spoke again in the
sweet forgotten language:

"If you would rather attach the *longe* and leave thy *hagard au bloc,*
Raoul, I shall say nothing; for it were a pity to spoil so fair a day's sport
with an ill-trained *sors. Essimer abaisser,*—it is possibly the best way. *Ça
lui donnera des reins.* I was perhaps hasty with the bird. It takes time to
pass *à la filière* and the exercises *d'escap.*"

Then the falconer Raoul bowed in his stirrups and replied: "If it be
the pleasure of Mademoiselle, I shall keep the hawk."

"It is my wish," she answered. "Falconry I know, but you have yet to
give me many a lesson in *Autourserie,* my poor Raoul. Sieur Piriou
Louis, mount!"

The huntsman sprang into an archway and in an instant returned,
mounted upon a strong black horse, followed by a piqueur also mounted.

"Ah!" she cried joyously, "speed Glemarec René! speed! speed all!
Sound thy horn Sieur Piriou!"

The silvery music of the hunting-horn filled the courtyard, the
hounds sprang through the gateway and galloping hoof-beats plunged
out of the paved court; loud on the drawbridge, suddenly muffled, then
lost in the heather and bracken of the moors. Distant and more distant
sounded the horn, until it became so faint that the sudden carol of a
soaring lark drowned it in my ears. I heard the voice below responding
to some call from within the house.

"I do not regret the chase, I will go another time. Courtesy to the stranger, Pelagie, remember!"

And a feeble voice came quavering from within the house, *"Courtoisie."*

I stripped, and rubbed myself from head to foot in the huge earthen basin of icy water which stood upon the stone floor at the foot of my bed. Then I looked about for my clothes. They were gone, but on a settle near the door lay a heap of garments which I inspected with astonishment. As my clothes had vanished I was compelled to attire myself in the costume which had evidently been placed there for me to wear while my own clothes dried. Everything was there, cap, shoes, and hunting doublet of silvery gray homespun; but the close-fitting costume and seamless shoes belonged to another century, and I remembered the strange costumes of the three falconers in the courtyard. I was sure that it was not the modern dress of any portion of France or Brittany; but not until I was dressed and stood before a mirror between the windows did I realize that I was clothed much more like a young huntsman of the middle ages than like a Breton of that day. I hesitated and picked up the cap. Should I go down and present myself in that strange guise? There seemed to be no help for it, my own clothes were gone and there was no bell in the ancient chamber to call a servant, so I contented myself with removing a short hawk's feather from the cap, and opening the door went downstairs.

By the fireplace in the large room at the foot of the stairs an old Breton woman sat spinning with a distaff. She looked up at me when I appeared, and smiling frankly, wished me health in the Breton language, to which I laughingly replied in French. At the same moment my hostess appeared and returned my salutation with a grace and dignity that sent a thrill to my heart. Her lovely head with its dark curly hair was crowned with a headdress which set all doubts as to the epoch of my own costume at rest. Her slender figure was exquisitely set off in the homespun hunting-gown edged with silver, and on her gauntlet-covered wrist she bore one of her petted hawks. With perfect simplicity she took my hand and led me into the garden in the court, and seating herself before a table invited me very sweetly to sit beside her. Then she asked me in her soft quaint accent how I had passed the night and whether I was very much inconvenienced by wearing the clothes which old Pelagie had put there for me while I slept. I looked at my own clothes and shoes, drying in the sun by the garden-wall, and hated them. What horrors they were compared with the graceful costume which I now wore! I told her this laughing, but she agreed with me very seriously.

"We will throw them away," she said in a quiet voice. In my astonishment I attempted to explain that I not only could not think of accepting clothes from anybody, although for all I knew it might be the custom of hospitality in that part of the country, but that I should cut an impossible figure if I returned to France clothed as I was then.

She laughed and tossed her pretty head, saying something in old French which I did not understand, and the Pelagie trotted out with a tray on which stood two bowls of milk, a loaf of white bread, fruit, a platter of honeycomb, and a flagon of deep red wine. "You see I have not yet broken my fast because I wished you to eat with me. But I am very hungry," she smiled.

"I would rather die than forget one word of what you have said!" I blurted out while my cheeks burned. "She will think me mad," I added to myself, but she turned to me with sparking eyes.

"Ah!" she murmured. "Then Monsieur knows all that there is of chivalry—"

She crossed herself and broke bread—I sat and watched her white hands, not daring to raise my eyes to hers.

"Will you not eat," she asked; "why do you look so troubled?"

Ah, why? I knew it now. I knew I would give my life to touch with my lips those rosy palms—I understood now that from the moment when I looked into her dark eyes there on the moor last night I had loved her. My great and sudden passion held me speechless.

"Are you ill at ease?" she asked again.

Then like a man who pronounces his own doom I answered in a low voice: "Yes, I am ill at ease for love of you." And as she did not stir nor answer, the same power moved my lips in spite of me and I said, "I, who am unworthy of the lightest of your thoughts, I who abuse hospitality and repay your gently courtesy with bold presumption, I love you."

She leaned her head upon her hands, and answered softly, "I love you. Your words are very dear to me. I love you."

"Then I shall win you."

"Win me," she replied.

But all the time I had been sitting silent, my face turned toward her. She also silent, her sweet face resting on her upturned palm, sat facing me, and as her eyes looked into mine, I knew that neither she nor I had spoken human speech; but I knew that her soul had answered mine, and I drew myself up feeling youth and joyous love coursing through every vein. She, with a bright color in her lovely face, seemed as one awakened from a dream, and her eyes sought mine with a questioning glance which made me tremble with delight. We broke our fast, speaking of ourselves. I told her my name and she told me hers, the Demoiselle Jeanne d'Ys.

She spoke of her father and mother's death, and how the nineteen of her years had been passed in the little fortified farm alone with her nurse Pelagie. Glemarec René the piqueur, and the four falconers, Raoul, Gaston, Hastur, and the Sieur Piriou Louis, who had served her father. She had never been outside the moorland—never even had seen a human soul before, except the falconers and Pelagie. She did not know how she had heard of Kerselec; perhaps the falconers had spoken of it. She knew the legends of Loup Garou and Jeanne la Flamme from her nurse Pelagie. She embroidered and spun flax. Her hawks and hounds were her only distraction. When she had met me there on the moor she had been so frightened that she almost dropped at the sound of my voice. She had, it was true, seen ships at sea from the cliffs, but as far as the eye could reach the moors over which she galloped were destitute of any sign of human life. There was a legend which old Pelagie told, how anybody once lost in the unexplored moorland might never return, because the moors were enchanted. She did not know whether it was true, she never had thought about it until she met me. She did not know whether the falconers had even been outside or whether they could go if they would. The books in the house which Pelagie the nurse had taught her to read were hundreds of years old.

All this she told me with a sweet seriousness seldom seen in any one but children. My own name she found easy to pronounce and insisted, because my first name was Philip, I must have French blood in me. She did not seem curious to learn anything about the outside world, and I thought perhaps she considered it had forfeited her interest and respect from the stories of her nurse.

We were still sitting at the table and she was throwing grapes to the small field birds which came fearlessly to our very feet.

I began to speak in a vague way of going, but she would not hear of it, and before I knew it I had promised to stay a week and hunt with hawk and hound in their company. I also obtained permission to come again from Kerselec and visit her after my return.

"Why," she said innocently, "I do not know what I should do if you never came back;" and I, knowing that I had no right to awaken her with the sudden shock which the avowal of my own love would bring to her, sat silent, hardly daring to breathe.

"You will come very often?" she asked.

"Very often," I said.

"Every day?"

"Every day."

"Oh," she sighed, "I am very happy—come and see my hawks."

She rose and took my hand again with a childlike innocence of possession, and we walked through the garden and fruit trees to a grassy lawn which was bordered by a brook. Over the lawn were scattered fifteen or twenty stumps of trees—partially imbedded in the grass—and upon all of these except two sat falcons. They were attached to the stumps by thongs which were in turn fastened with steel rivets to their legs just above the talons. A little stream of pure spring water flowed in a winding course within easy distance of each perch.

The birds set up a clamor when the girl appeared, but she went from one to another caressing some, taking others for an instant upon her wrist, or stooping to adjust their jesses.

"Are they not pretty?" she said. "See, here is a falcon-gentil. We call it 'ignoble,' because it takes the quarry in direct chase. This is a blue falcon. In falconry we call it 'noble' because it rises over the quarry, and wheeling, drops upon it from above. This white bird is a gerfalcon from the north. It is also 'noble!' Here is a merlin, and this tiercelet is a falcon-heroner."

I asked her how she had learned the old language of falconry. She did not remember, but thought her father must have taught it to her when she was very young.

Then she led me away and showed me the young falcons still in the nest. "They are termed *niais* in falconry," she explained. "A *branchier* is the young bird which is just able to leave the nest and hop from branch to branch. A young bird which has not yet moulted is called a *sors,* and a *mué* is a hawk which has moulted in captivity. When we catch a wild falcon which has changed its plumage we term it a *hagard.* Raoul first taught me to dress a falcon. Shall I teach you how it is done?"

She seated herself on the bank of the stream among the falcons and I threw myself at her feet to listen.

Then the Demoiselle d'Ys held up one rosy-tipped finger and began very gravely,

"First one must catch the falcon."

"I am caught," I answered.

She laughed very prettily and told me my *dressage* would perhaps be difficult as I was noble.

"I am already tamed," I replied; "jessed and belled."

She laughed, delighted. "Oh, my brave falcon; then you will return at my call?"

"I am yours," I answered gravely.

She sat silent for a moment. Then the color heightened in her cheeks and she held up her finger again saying, "Listen; I wish to speak of falconry—"

"I listen, Countess Jeanne d'Ys."

But again she fell into the reverie, and her eyes seemed fixed on something beyond the summer clouds.

"Philip," she said at last.

"Jeanne," I whispered.

"That is all,—that is what I wished," she sighed,—"Philip and Jeanne."

She held her hand toward me and I touched it with my lips.

"Win me," she said, but this time it was the body and soul which spoke in unison.

After a while she began again: "Let us speak of falconry."

"Begin," I replied; "we have caught the falcon."

The Jeanne d'Ys took my hand in both of hers and told me how with infinite patience the young falcon was taught to perch upon the wrist, how little by little it became used to belled jesses and the *chaperon à cornette.*

"They must first have a good appetite," she said; "then little by little I reduce their nourishment which in falconry we call *pât.* When after many nights passed *au bloc* as these birds are now, I prevail upon the *hagard* to stay quietly on the wrist, then the bird is ready to be taught to come for its food. I fix the *pât* to the end of a thong or *leurre,* and teach the bird to come to me as soon as I begin to whirl the cord in circles about my head. At first I drop the *pât* when the falcon comes, and he eats the food on the ground. After a little he will learn to seize the *leurre* in motion as I whirl it around my head, or drag it over the ground. After this it is easy to teach the falcon to strike at game, always remembering to *'faire courtoisie à roiseau,'* that is, to allow the bird to taste the quarry."

A squeal from one of the falcons interrupted her, and she arose to adjust the *longe* which had become whipped about the *bloc,* but the bird still flapped its wings and screamed.

"What is the matter?" she said; "Philip, can you see?"

I looked around and at first saw nothing to cause the commotion which was now heightened by the screams and flapping of all the birds. Then my eye fell upon the flat rock beside the stream from which the girl had risen. A gray serpent was moving slowly across the surface of the bowlder, and the eyes in its flat triangular head sparkled like jet.

"A couleuvre," she said quietly.

"Is it harmless, is it not?" I asked.

She pointed to the black V-shaped figure on the neck.

"It is certain death," she said; "it is a viper."

We watched the reptile moving slowly over the smooth rock to where the sunlight fell in a broad warm patch.

I started forward to examine it, but she clung to arm crying, "Don't, Philip, I am afraid."

"For me?"

"For you, Philip,—I love you."

Then I took her in my arms and kissed her on the lips, but all I could say was: "Jeanne, Jeanne, Jeanne." And as she lay trembling on my breast, something struck my foot in the grass below, but I did not heed it. Then again something struck my ankle, and a sharp pain shot through me. I looked into the sweet face of Jeanne d'Ys and kissed her, and with all my strength lifted her in my arms and flung her from me. Then bending, I tore the viper from my ankle and set my heel upon its head. I remember feeling weak and numb,—I remember falling to the ground. Through my slowly glazing eyes I saw Jeanne's white face bending close to mine, and when the light in my eyes went out I still felt her arms about my neck, and her soft cheek against my drawn lips.

When I opened my eyes, I looked around in terror. Jeanne was gone. I saw the stream and the flat rock; I saw the crushed viper in the grass beside me, but the hawks and *blocs* had disappeared. I sprang to my feet. The garden, the fruit trees, the drawbridge and the walled court were gone. I stared stupidly at a heap of crumbling ruins, ivy-covered and gray, through which great trees had pushed their way. I crept forward, dragging my numbed foot, and as I moved, a falcon sailed from the tree-tops among the ruins, and soaring, mounting in narrowing circles, faded and vanished in the clouds above.

"Jeanne, Jeanne," I cried, but my voice died on my lips, and I fell on my knees among the weeds. And as God willed it, I, not knowing, had fallen kneeling before a crumbling shrine carved in stone for our Mother of Sorrows. I saw the sad face of the Virgin wrought in the cold stone. I saw the cross and thorns at her feet, and beneath it I read:

"PRAY FOR THE SOUL OF THE
DEMOISELLE JEANNE D'YS,
WHO DIED
IN HER YOUTH FOR LOVE OF
PHILIP, A STRANGER.
A.D. 1573."

But upon the icy slab lay a woman's glove still warm and fragrant.

The Maker of Moons

"I have heard what the Talkers were talking,—the talk
  Of the beginning and the end;
  But I do not talk of the beginning or the end."

I

Concerning Yue-Laou and the Xin I know nothing more than you shall know. I am miserably anxious to clear the matter up. Perhaps what I write may save the United States Government money and perhaps it may arouse the scientific world to action; at any rate it put an end to the terrible suspense of two people. Certainty is better suspense.

If the Government dares to disregard this warning and refuses to send a thoroughly equipped expedition at once, the people of the State may take swift vengeance on the whole region and leave a blackened devastated waste where to-day forest and flowering meadow land border the lake in the Cardinal Woods.

You already know part of the story; the New York papers have been full of alleged details. This much is true: Barris caught the "Shiner," red handed, or rather yellow handed, for his pockets and boots and dirty fists were stuffed with lumps of gold. I say gold, advisedly. You may call it what you please. You also know how Barris was—but unless I begin at the beginning of my experiences you will be none the wiser after all.

On the third of August of this present year I was standing in Tiffany's, chatting with George Godfrey of the designing department. On the glass counter between us lay a coiled serpent, an exquisite specimen of chiselled gold.

"No," replied Godfrey to my question, "it isn't my work; I wish it was. Why, man, it's a masterpiece!"

"Whose?" I asked.

"Now I should be very glad to know also," said Godfrey. "We bought it from an old jay who says he lives in the country somewhere about the Cardinal Woods. That's near Starlit Lake, I believe—"

"Lake of the Stars?" I suggested.

"Some call it Starlit Lake,—it's all the same. Well, my rustic Reuben says that he represents the sculptor of this snake for all practical and business purposes. He got his price too. We hope he'll bring us something more. We have sold this already to the Metropolitan Museum."

I was leaning idly on the glass case, watching the keen eyes of the artist in precious metals as he stooped over the gold serpent.

"A masterpiece!" he muttered to himself, fondling the glittering coil; "look at the texture! whew!" But I was not looking at the serpent. Something was moving,—crawling out of Godfrey's coat pocket,—the pocket nearest to me,—something soft and yellow with crab-like legs all covered with coarse yellow hair.

"What in Heaven's name," said I, "have you got in your pocket? It's crawling out—it's trying to creep up your coat, Godfrey!"

He turned quickly and dragged the creature out with his left hand.

I shrank back as he held the repulsive object dangling before me, and he laughed and placed it on the counter.

"Did you ever see anything like that?" he demanded.

"No," said I truthfully, "and I hope I never shall again. What is it?"

"I don't know. Ask them at the Natural History Museum—they can't tell you. The Smithsonian is all at sea too. It is, I believe, the connecting link between a sea-urchin, a spider, and the devil. It looks venomous but I can't find either fangs or mouth. Is it blind? These things may be eyes but they look as if they were painted. A Japanese sculptor might have produced such an impossible beast, but it is hard to believe that God did. It looks unfinished too. I have a mad idea that this creature is only one of the parts of some larger and more grotesque organism,—it looks so lonely, so hopelessly dependent, so cursedly unfinished. I'm going to use it as a model. If I don't out-Japanese the Japs my name isn't Godfrey."

The creature was moving slowly across the glass case towards me. I drew back.

"Godfrey," I said, "I would execute a man who executed any such work as you propose. What do you want to perpetuate such a reptile for? I can stand the Japanese grotesque but I can't stand that—spider—"

"It's a crab."

"Crab or spider or blind-worm—ugh! What do you want to do it for? It's a nightmare—it's unclean!"

I hated the thing. It was the first living creature that I had ever hated. For some time I had noticed a damp acrid odour in the air, and Godfrey said it came from the reptile.

"Then kill it and bury it," I said; "and by the way, where did it come from?"

"I don't know that either," laughed Godfrey; "I found it clinging to the box that this gold serpent was brought in. I suppose my old Reuben is responsible."

"If the Cardinal Woods are the lurking places for things like this," said I, "I am sorry that I am going to the Cardinal Woods."

"Are you?" asked Godfrey; "for the shooting?"

"Yes, with Barris and Pierpont. Why don't you kill that creature?"

"Go off on your shooting trip, and let me alone," laughed Godfrey.

I shuddered at the "crab," and bade Godfrey good-bye until December.

That night, Pierpont, Barris, and I sat chatting in the smoking-car of the Quebec Express when the long train pulled out of the Grand Central Depot. Old David had gone forward with the dogs; poor things, they hated to ride in the baggage car, but the Quebec and Northern road provides no sportsman's cars, and David and the three Gordon setters were in for an uncomfortable night.

Except for Pierpont, Barris, and myself, the car was empty. Barris, trim, stout, ruddy, and bronzed, sat drumming on the window ledge, puffing a short fragrant pipe. His gun-case lay beside him on the floor.

"When *I* have white hair and years of discretion," said Pierpont languidly, "I'll not flirt with pretty serving-maids; will you, Roy?"

"No," said I, looking at Barris.

"You mean the maid with the cap in the Pullman car?" asked Barris.

"Yes," said Pierpont.

I smiled, for I had seen it also.

Barris twisted his crisp grey moustache, and yawned.

"You children had better be toddling off to bed," he said. "That lady's-maid is a member of the Secret Service."

"Oh," said Pierpont, "one of your colleagues?"

"You might present us, you know," I said; "the journey is monotonous."

Barris had drawn a telegram from his pocket, and as he sat turning it over and over between his fingers he smiled. After a moment or two he handed it to Pierpont who read it with slightly raised eyebrows.

"It's rot,—I suppose it's cipher," he said; "I see it's signed by General Drummond—"

"Drummond, Chief of the Government Secret Service," said Barris.

"Something interesting?" I enquired, lighting a cigarette.

"Something so interesting," replied Barris, "that I'm going to look into it myself—"

"And break up our shooting trio—"

"No. Do you want to hear about it? Do you, Billy Pierpont?"

"Yes," replied that immaculate young man.

Barris rubbed the amber mouth-piece of his pipe on his handkerchief, cleared the stem with a bit of wire, puffed once or twice, and leaned back in his chair.

"Pierpont," he said, "do you remember that evening at the United States Club when General Miles, General Drummond, and I were examining that gold nugget that Captain Mahan had? You examined it also, I believe."

"I did," said Pierpont.

"Was it gold?" asked Barris, drumming on the window.

"It was," replied Pierpont.

"I saw it too," said I; "of course, it was gold."

"Professor La Grange saw it also," said Barris; "he said it was gold."

"Well?" said Pierpont.

"Well," said Barris, "it was not gold."

After a silence Pierpont asked what tests had been made.

"The usual tests," replied Barris. "The United States Mint is satisfied that it is gold, so is every jeweller who has seen it. But it is not gold,—and yet—it is gold."

Pierpont and I exchanged glances.

"Now," said I, "for Barris' usual coup-de-théâtre: what was the nugget?"

"Practically it was pure gold; but," said Barris, enjoying the situation intensely, "really it was not gold. Pierpont, what is gold?"

"Gold's an element, a metal—"

"Wrong! Billy Pierpont," said Barris coolly.

"Gold was an element when I went to school," said I.

"It has not been an element for two weeks," said Barris; "and, except General Drummond, Professor La Grange, and myself, you two youngsters are the only people, except one, in the world who know it,—or have known it."

"Do you mean to say that gold is a composite metal?" said Pierpont slowly.

"I do. La Grange has made it. He produced a scale of pure gold day before yesterday. That nugget was manufactured gold."

Could Barris be joking? Was this a colossal hoax? I looked at Pierpont. He muttered something about that settling the silver question, and turned his head to Barris, but there was that in Barris' face which forbade jesting, and Pierpont and I sat silently pondering.

"Don't ask me how it's made," said Barris, quietly; "I don't know. But I do know that somewhere in the region of the Cardinal Woods there is a gang of people who do know how gold is made, and who make it. You understand the danger this is to every civilized nation. It's got to be stopped of course. Drummond and I have decided that I am the man to stop it. Wherever and whoever these people are—these gold-makers,—they must be caught, every one of them,—caught or shot."

"Or shot," repeated Pierpont, who was owner of the Cross-Cut Gold Mine and found his income too small; "Professor La Grange will of course be prudent;—science need not know things that would upset the world!"

"Little Willy," said Barris laughing, "your income is safe."

"I suppose," said I, "some flaw in the nugget gave Professor La Grange the tip."

"Exactly. He cut the flaw out before sending the nugget to be tested. He worked on the flaw and separated gold into its three elements."

"He is a great man," said Pierpont, "but he will be the greatest man in the world if he can keep his discovery to himself."

"Who?" said Barris.

"Professor La Grange."

"Professor La Grange was shot through the heart two hours ago," replied Barris slowly.

II

We had been at the shooting box in the Cardinal Woods five days when a telegram was brought to Barris by a mounted messenger from the nearest telegraph station, Cardinal Springs, a hamlet on the lumber railroad which joins the Quebec and Northern at Three Rivers Junction, thirty miles below.

Pierpont and I were sitting out under the trees, loading some special shells as experiments; Barris stood beside us, bronzed, erect, holding his pipe carefully so that no sparks should drift into our powder box. The beat of hoofs over the grass aroused us, and when the lank messenger drew bridle before the door, Barris stepped forward and took the sealed telegram. When he had torn it open he went into the house and presently reappeared, reading something that he had written.

"This should go at once," he said, looking the messenger full in the face.

"At once, Colonel Barris," replied the shabby countryman.

Pierpont glanced up and I smiled at the messenger who was gathering his bridle and settling himself in his stirrups. Barris handed him the written reply and nodded good-bye: there was a thud of hoofs on the greensward, a jingle of bit and spur across the gravel, and the messenger was gone. Barris' pipe went out and he stepped to windward to relight it.

"It is queer," said I, "that your messenger—a battered native,—should speak like a Harvard man."

"He is a Harvard man," said Barris.

"And the plot thickens," said Pierpont; "are the Cardinal Woods full of your Secret Service men, Barris?"

"No," replied Barris, "but the telegraph stations are. How many ounces of shot are you using, Roy?"

I told him, holding up the adjustable steel measuring cup. He nodded. After a moment or two he sat down on a camp-stool beside us and picked up a crimper.

The Maker of Moons

"That telegram was from Drummond," he said; "the messenger was one of my men as you two bright little boys divined. Pooh! If he had spoken the Cardinal County dialect you wouldn't have known."

"His make-up was good," said Pierpont.

Barris twirled the crimper and looked at the pile of loaded shells. Then he picked up one and crimped it.

"Let 'em alone," said Pierpont, "you crimp too tight."

"Does his little gun kick when the shells are crimped too tight?" enquired Barris tenderly; "well, he shall crimp his own shells then,—where's his little man?"

"His little man" was a weird English importation, stiff, very carefully scrubbed, tangled in his aspirates, named Howlett. As valet, gilly, gunbearer, and crimper, he aided Pierpont to endure the ennui of existence, by doing for him everything except breathing. Lately, however, Barris' taunts had driven Pierpont to do a few things for himself. To his astonishment he found that cleaning his own gun was not a bore, so he timidly loaded a shell or two, was much pleased with himself, loaded some more, crimped them, and went to breakfast with an appetite. So when Barris asked where "his little man" was, Pierpont did not reply but dug a cupful of shot from the bag and poured it solemnly into the half filled shell.

Old David came out with the dogs and of course there was a pow-wow when "Voyou," my Gordon, wagged his splendid tail across the loading table and sent a dozen unstopped cartridges rolling over the grass, vomiting powder and shot.

"Give the dogs a mile or two," said I; "we will shoot over the Sweet Fern Covert about four o'clock, David."

"Two guns, David," added Baths.

"Are you not going?" asked Pierpont, looking up, as David disappeared with the dogs.

"Bigger game," said Barris shortly. He picked up a mug of ale from the tray which Howlett had just set down beside us and took a long pull. We did the same, silently. Pierpont set his mug on the turf beside him and returned to his loading.

We spoke of the murder of Professor La Grange, of how it had been concealed by the authorities in New York at Drummond's request, of the certainty that it was one of the gang of gold-makers who had done it, and of the possible alertness of the gang.

"Oh, they know that Drummond will be after them sooner or later," said Barris, "but they don't know that the mills of the gods have already begun to grind. Those smart New York papers builded better than they knew when their ferret-eyed reporter poked his red nose into the house on 58th Street and sneaked off with a column on his cuffs about the 'suicide' of Professor La Grange. Billy Pierpont, my revolver is hanging in your room; I'll take yours too—"

"Help yourself," said Pierpont.

"I shall be gone over night," continued Barris; "my poncho and some bread and meat are all I shall take except the 'barkers.'"

"Will they bark to-night?" I asked.

"No, I trust not for several weeks yet. I shall nose about a bit. Roy, did it ever strike you how queer it is that this wonderfully beautiful country should contain no inhabitants?"

"It's like those splendid stretches of pools and rapids which one finds on every trout river and in which one never finds a fish," suggested Pierpont.

"Exactly,—and Heaven alone knows why," said Barris; "I suppose this country is shunned by human beings for the same mysterious reasons."

"The shooting is the better for it," I observed.

"The shooting is good," said Barris, "have you noticed the snipe on the meadow by the lake? Why it's brown with them! That's a wonderful meadow."

"It's a natural one," said Pierpont, "no human being ever cleared that land."

"Then it's supernatural," said Barris; "Pierpont, do you want to come with me?"

Pierpont's handsome face flushed as he answered slowly, "It's awfully good of you,—if I may."

"Bosh," said I, piqued because he had asked Pierpont, "what use is little Willy without his man?"

"True," said Barris gravely, "you can't take Howlett, you know."

Pierpont muttered something which ended in "d—n."

"Then," said I, "there will be but one gun on the Sweet Fern Covert this afternoon. Very well, I wish you joy of your cold supper and colder bed. Take your night-gown, Willy, and don't sleep on the damp ground."

"Let Pierpont alone," retorted Barris, "you shall go next time, Roy."

"Oh, all right,—you mean when there's shooting going on?"

"And I?" demanded Pierpont, grieved.

"You too, my son; stop quarrelling! Will you ask Howlett to pack our kits—lightly mind you,—no bottles,—they clink."

"My flask doesn't," said Pierpont, and went off to get ready for a night's stalking of dangerous men.

"It is strange," said I, "that nobody ever settles in this region. How many people live in Cardinal Springs, Barris?"

"Twenty counting the telegraph operator and not counting the lumbermen; they are always changing and shifting. I have six men among them."

"Where have you no men? In the Four Hundred?"

"I have men there also,—chums of Billy's only he doesn't know it. David tells me that there was a strong flight of woodcock last night. You ought to pick up some this afternoon."

Then we chatted about alder-cover and swamp until Pierpont came out of the house and it was time to part.

"Au revoir," said Barris, buckling on his kit, "come along, Pierpont, and don't walk in the damp grass."

"If you are not back by to-morrow noon," said I, "I will take Howlett and David and hunt you up. You say your course is due north?"

"Due north," replied Barris, consulting his compass.

"There is a trail for two miles and a spotted lead for two more," said Pierpont.

"Which we won't use for various reasons," added Barris pleasantly; "don't worry, Roy, and keep your confounded expedition out of the way; there's no danger."

He knew, of course, what he was talking about and I held my peace.

When the tip end of Pierpont's shooting coat had disappeared in the Long Covert, I found myself standing alone with Howlett. He bore my gaze for a moment and then politely lowered his eyes.

"Howlett," said I, "take these shells and implements to the gun room, and drop nothing. Did Voyou come to any harm in the briers this morning?"

"No 'arm, Mr. Cardenhe, sir," said Howlett.

"Then be careful not to drop anything else," said I, and walked away leaving him decorously puzzled. For he had dropped no cartridges. Poor Howlett!

III

About four o'clock that afternoon I met David and the dogs at the spinney which leads into the Sweet Fern Covert. The three setters, Voyou, Gamin, and Mioche, were in fine feather,—David had killed a woodcock and a brace of grouse over them that morning,—and they were thrashing about the spinney at short range when I came up, gun under arm and pipe lighted.

"What's the prospect, David," I asked, trying to keep my feet in the tangle of wagging, whining dogs; "hello, what's amiss with Mioche?"

"A brier in his foot sir; I drew it and stopped the wound but I guess the gravel's got in. If you have no objection, sir, I might take him back with me."

"It's safer," I said; "take Gamin too, I only want one dog this afternoon. What is the situation?"

"Fair sir; the grouse lie within a quarter of a mile of the oak second growth. The woodcock are mostly on the alders. I saw any number of snipe on the meadows. There's something else in by the lake,—I can't just tell what, but the wood-duck set up a clatter when I was in the thicket and they come dashing through the wood as if a dozen foxes was snappin' at their tail feathers."

"Probably a fox," I said; "leash those dogs,—they must learn to stand it. I'll be back by dinner time."

"There is one more thing sir," said David, lingering with his gun under his arm.

"Well," said I.

"I saw a man in the woods by the Oak Covert,—at least I think I did."

"A lumberman?"

"I think not sir—at least,—do they have Chinamen among them?"

"Chinese? No. You didn't see a Chinaman in the woods here?"

"I—I think I did sir,—I can't say positively. He was gone when I ran into the covert."

"Did the dogs notice it?"

"I can't say—exactly. They acted queer like. Gamin here lay down an' whined—it may have been colic—and Mioche whimpered,—perhaps it was the brier."

"And Voyou?"

"Voyou, he was most remarkable sir, and the hair on his back stood up, I did see a groundhog makin' for a tree near by."

"Then no wonder Voyou bristled. David, your Chinaman was a stump or tussock. Take the dogs now."

"I guess it was sir; good afternoon sir," said David, and walked away with the Gordons leaving me alone with Voyou in the spinney.

I looked at the dog and he looked at me.

"Voyou!"

The dog sat down and danced with his fore feet, his beautiful brown eyes sparkling.

"You're a fraud," I said; "which shall it be, the alders or the upland? Upland? Good!—now for the grouse,—heel, my friend, and show your miraculous self-restraint."

Voyou wheeled into my tracks and followed close, nobly refusing to notice the impudent chipmunks and the thousand and one alluring and important smells which an ordinary dog would have lost no time in investigating.

The brown and yellow autumn woods were crisp with drifting heaps of leaves and twigs that crackled under foot as we turned from the spinney into the forest. Every silent little stream hurrying toward the lake was gay with painted leaves afloat, scarlet maple or yellow oak. Spots of sunlight fell upon the pools, searching the brown depths, illuminating the gravel bottom where shoals of minnows swam to and fro, and to and fro again, busy with the purpose of their little lives. The crickets were chirping in the long brittle grass on the edge of the woods, but we left them far behind in the silence of the deeper forest.

"Now!" said I to Voyou.

The dog sprang to the front, circled once, zigzagged through the ferns around us and, all in a moment, stiffened stock still, rigid as sculp-tured bronze. I stepped forward, raising my gun, two paces, three paces, ten perhaps, before a great cock-grouse blundered up from the brake and burst through the thicket fringe toward the deeper growth. There was a flash and puff from my gun, a crash of echoes among the low wooded cliffs, and through the faint veil of smoke something dark dropped from mid-air amid a cloud of feathers, brown as the brown leaves under foot.

"Fetch!"

Up from the ground sprang Voyou, and in a moment he came gal-loping back, neck arched, tail stiff but waving, holding tenderly in his pink mouth a mass of mottled bronzed feathers. Very gravely he laid the bird at my feet and crouched close beside it, his silky ears across his paws, his muzzle on the ground.

I dropped the grouse into my pocket, held for a moment a silent ca-ressing communion with Voyou, then swung my gun under my arm and motioned the dog on.

It must have been five o'clock when I walked into a little opening in the woods and sat down to breathe. Voyou came and sat down in front of me.

"Well?" I enquired.

Voyou gravely presented one paw which I took.

"We will never get back in time for dinner," said I, "so we might as well take it easy. It's all your fault, you know. Is there a brier in your foot?—let's see,—there! It's out my friend and you are free to nose about and lick it. If you loll your tongue out you'll get it all over twigs and moss. Can't you lie down and try to pant less? No, there is no use in sniffing and looking at that fern patch, for we are going to smoke a little, doze a little, and go home by moonlight. Think what a big dinner we will have! Think of Howlett's despair when we are not in time! Think of all the stories you will have to tell to Gamin and Mioche! Think what a good dog you have been! There—you are tired old chap; take forty winks with me."

Voyou was a little tired. He stretched out on the leaves at my feet but whether or not he really slept I could not be certain, until his hind legs twitched and I knew he was dreaming of mighty deeds.

Now I may have taken forty winks, but the sun seemed to be no lower when I sat up and unclosed my lids. Voyou raised his head, saw in my eyes that I was not going yet, thumped his tail half a dozen times on the dried leaves, and settled back with a sigh.

I looked lazily around, and for the first time noticed what a wonderfully beautiful spot I had chosen for a nap. It was an oval glade in the heart of the forest, level and carpeted with green grass. The trees that surrounded it were gigantic; they formed one towering circular wall of verdure, blotting out all except the turquoise blue of the sky-oval above. And now I noticed that in the centre of the greensward lay a pool of water, crystal clear, glimmering like a mirror in the meadow grass, beside a block of granite. It scarcely seemed possible that the symmetry of tree and lawn and lucent pool could have been one of nature's accidents. I had never before seen this glade nor had I ever heard it spoken of by either Pierpont or Barris. It was a marvel, this diamond clear basin, regular and graceful as a Roman fountain, set in the gem of turf. And these great trees,—they also belonged, not in America but in some legend-haunted forest of France, where moss-grown marbles stand neglected in dim glades, and the twilight of the forest shelters fairies and slender shapes from shadow-land.

I lay and watched the sunlight showering the tangled thicket where masses of crimson Cardinal-flowers glowed, or where one long dusty sunbeam tipped the edge of the floating leaves in the pool, turning them to palest gilt. There were birds too, passing through the dim avenues of trees like jets of flame, the gorgeous Cardinal-Bird in his deep stained crimson robe,—the bird that gave to the woods, to the village fifteen miles away, to the whole country, the name of Cardinal.

I rolled over on my back and looked up at the sky. How pale,—paler than a robin's egg,—it was. I seemed to be lying at the bottom of a well, walled with verdure, high towering on every side. And, as I lay, all about me the air became sweet scented. Sweeter and sweeter and more penetrating grew the perfume, and I wondered what stray breeze, blowing over acres of lilies, could have brought it. But there was no breeze; the air was still. A gilded fly alighted on my hand,—a honey-fly. It was as troubled as I by the scented silence.

Then, behind me, my dog growled.

I sat quite still at first, hardly breathing, but my eyes were fixed on a shape that moved along the edge of the pool among the meadow grasses. The dog had ceased growling and was now staring, alert and trembling.

At last I rose and walked rapidly down to the pool, my dog following close to heel.

The figure, a woman's, turned slowly toward us.

IV

She was standing still when I approached the pool. The forest around us was so silent that when I spoke the sound of my own voice startled me. "No," she said,—and her voice was smooth as flowing water, "I have not lost my way. Will he come to me, your beautiful dog?"

Before I could speak, Voyou crept to her and laid his silky head against her knees.

"But surely," said I, "you did not come here alone."

"Alone? I did come alone."

"But the nearest settlement is Cardinal, probably nineteen miles from where we are standing."

"I do not know Cardinal," she said.

"Ste. Croix in Canada is forty miles at least,—how did you come into the Cardinal Woods?" I asked amazed.

"Into the woods?" she repeated a little impatiently.

"Yes."

She did not answer at first but stood caressing Voyou with gentle phrase and gesture.

"Your beautiful dog I am fond of but I am not fond of being questioned," she said quietly. "My name is Ysonde and I came to the fountain here to see your dog."

I was properly quenched. After a moment or two I did say that in another hour it would be growing dusky, but she neither replied nor looked at me.

"This," I ventured, "is a beautiful pool,—you call it a fountain,—a delicious fountain: I have never before seen it. It is hard to imagine that nature did all this."

"Is it?" she said.

"Don't you think so?" I asked.

"I haven't thought; I wish when you go you would leave me your dog."

"My—my dog?"

"If you don't mind," she said sweetly, and looked at me for the first time in the face.

For an instant our glances met, then she grew grave, and I saw that her eyes were fixed on my forehead. Suddenly she rose and drew nearer, looking intently at my forehead. There was a faint mark there, a tiny crescent, just over my eyebrow. It was a birthmark.

"Is that a scar?" she demanded drawing nearer.

"That crescent shaped mark? No."

"No? Are you sure?" she insisted.

"Perfectly," I replied, astonished.

"A—a birthmark?"

"Yes,—may I ask why?"

As she drew away from me, I saw that the color had fled from her cheeks. For a second she clasped both hands over her eyes as if to shut out my face, then slowly dropping her hands, she sat down on a long square block of stone which half encircled the basin, and on which to my amazement I saw carving. Voyou went to her again and laid his head in her lap.

"What is your name?" she asked at length.

"Roy Cardenhe."

"Mine is Ysonde. I carved these dragon-flies on the stone, these fishes and shells and butterflies you see."

"You! They are wonderfully delicate,—but those are not American dragon-flies—"

"No—they are more beautiful. See, I have my hammer and chisel with me."

She drew from a queer pouch at her side a small hammer and chisel and held them toward me.

"You are very talented," I said, "where did you study?"

"I? I never studied,—I knew how. I saw things and cut them out of scone. Do you like them? Some time I will show you other things that I have done. If I had a great lump of bronze I could make your dog, beautiful as he is."

Her hammer fell into the fountain and I leaned over and plunged my arm into the water to find it.

"It is there, shining on the sand," she said, leaning over the pool with me.

"Where," said I, looking at our reflected faces in the water. For it was only in the water that I had dared, as yet, to look her long in the face.

The pool mirrored the exquisite oval of her head, the heavy hair, the eyes. I heard the silken rustle of her girdle, I caught the flash of a white arm, and the hammer was drawn up dripping with spray.

The troubled surface of the pool grew calm and again I saw her eyes reflected.

"Listen," she said in a low voice, "do you think you will come again to my fountain?"

"I will come," I said. My voice was dull; the noise of water filled my ears.

Then a swift shadow sped across the pool; I rubbed my eyes. Where her reflected face had bent beside mine there was nothing mirrored but the rosy evening sky with one pale star glimmering. I drew myself up and turned. She was gone. I saw the faint star twinkling above me in the afterglow, I saw the tall trees motionless in the still evening air, I saw my dog slumbering at my feet.

The sweet scent in the air had faded, leaving in my nostrils the heavy odor of fern and forest mould. A blind fear seized me, and I caught up my gun and sprang into the darkening woods. The dog followed me, crashing through the undergrowth at my side. Duller and duller grew the light, but I strode on, the sweat pouring from my face and hair, my mind a chaos. How I reached the spinney I can hardly tell. As I turned up the path I caught a glimpse of a human face peering at me from the darkening thicket,—a horrible human face, yellow and drawn with high-boned cheeks and narrow eyes.

Involuntarily I halted; the dog at my heels snarled. Then I sprang straight at it, floundering blindly through the thicket, but the night had fallen swiftly and I found myself panting and struggling in a maze of twisted shrubbery and twining vines, unable to see the very undergrowth that ensnared me.

It was a pale face, and a scratched one that I carried to a late dinner that night. Howlett served me, dumb reproach in his eyes, for the soup had been standing and the grouse was juiceless.

David brought the dogs in after they had had their supper, and I drew my chair before the blaze and set my ale on a table beside me. The dogs curled up at my feet, blinking gravely at the sparks that snapped and flew in eddying showers from the heavy birch logs.

"David," said I, "did you say you saw a Chinaman today?"

"I did sir."

"What do you think about it now?"

"I may have been mistaken sir—"

"But you think not. What sort of whiskey did you put in my flask today?"

"The usual sir."

"Is there much gone?"

"About three swallows sir, as usual."

"You don't suppose there could have been any mistake about that whiskey,—no medicine could have gotten into it for instance."

David smiled and said, "No sir."

"Well," said I, "I have had an extraordinary dream."

When I said "dream," I felt comforted and reassured. I had scarcely dared to say it before, even to myself.

"An extraordinary dream," I repeated; "I fell asleep in the woods about five o'clock, in that pretty glade where the fountain—I mean the pool is. You know the place?"

"I do not sir."

I described it minutely, twice, but David shook his head.

"Carved stone did you say sir? I never chanced on it. You don't mean the New Spring—"

"No, no! This glade is way beyond that. Is it possible that any people inhabit the forest between here and the Canada line?"

"Nobody short of Ste. Croix; at least I have no knowledge of any."

"Of course," said I, "when I thought I saw a Chinaman, it was imagination. Of course I had been more impressed than I was aware of by your adventure. Of course you saw no Chinaman, David."

"Probably not sir," replied David dubiously.

I sent him off to bed, saying I should keep the dogs with me all night; and when he was gone, I took a good long draught of ale, "just to shame the devil," as Pierpont said, and lighted a cigar. Then I thought of Barris and Pierpont, and their cold bed, for I knew they would not dare build a fire, and, in spite of the hot chimney corner and the crackling blaze, I shivered in sympathy.

"I'll tell Barris and Pierpont the whole story and take them to see the carved stone and the fountain," I thought to myself; "what a marvelous dream it was—Ysonde,—if it was a dream."

Then I went to the mirror and examined the faint white mark above my eyebrow.

V

About eight o'clock next morning, as I sat listlessly eyeing my coffee cup which Howlett was filling, Gamin and Mioche set up a howl, and in a moment more I heard Barris' step on the porch.

"Hello, Roy," said Pierpont, stamping into the dining room, "I want my breakfast by jingo! Where's Howlett,—none of your *café au lait* for me,—I want a chop and some eggs. Look at that dog, he'll wag the hinge off his tail in a moment—"

"Pierpont," said I, "this loquacity is astonishing but welcome. Where's Barris? You are soaked from neck to ankle."

Pierpont sat down and tore off his stiff muddy leggings.

"Barris is telephoning to Cardinal Springs,—I believe he wants some of his men,—down! Gamin, you idiot! Howlett, three eggs poached and more toast,—what was I saying? Oh, about Barris; he's struck something or other which he hopes will locate these gold-making fellows. I had a jolly time,—he'll tell you about it."

"Billy! Billy!" I said in pleased amazement, "you are learning to talk! Dear me! You load your own shells and you carry your own gun and you fire it yourself—hello! Here's Barris all over mud. You fellows really ought to change your rig—whew! what a frightful odor!"

"It's probably this," said Barris tossing something onto the hearth where it shuddered for a moment and then began to writhe; "I found it in the woods by the lake. Do you know what it can be, Roy?"

To my disgust I saw it was another of those spidery wormy crablike creatures that Godfrey had in Tiffany's.

"I thought I recognized that acrid odor," I said; "for the love of the Saints take it away from the breakfast table, Barris!"

"But what is it?" he persisted, unslinging his field-glass and revolver.

"I'll tell you what I know after breakfast," I replied firmly. "Howlett, get a broom and sweep that thing into the road.—What are you laughing at, Pierpont?"

Howlett swept the repulsive creature out and Barris and Pierpont went to change their dew-soaked clothes for dryer raiment. David came to take the dogs for an airing and in a few minutes Barris reappeared and sat down in his place at the head of the table.

"Well," said I, "is there a story to tell?"

"Yes, not much. They are near the lake on the other side of the woods,—I mean these gold-makers. I shall collar one of them this evening. I haven't located the main gang with any certainty,—shove the toast rack this way will you, Roy,—no, I am not at all certain, but I've nailed one anyway. Pierpont was a great help, really,—and, what do you think, Roy? He wants to join the Secret Service!"

"Little Willy!"

"Exactly. Oh I'll dissuade him. What sort of a reptile was that I brought in? Did Howlett sweep it away?"

"He can sweep it back again for all I care," I said indifferently. "I've finished my breakfast."

"No," said Barris, hastily swallowing his coffee, "it's of no importance; you can tell me about the beast—"

"Serve you right if I had it brought in on toast," I returned.

Pierpont came in radiant, fresh from the bath.

"Go on with your story, Roy," he said; and I told them about Godfrey and his reptile pet.

"Now what in the name of common sense can Godfrey find interesting that creature?" I ended, tossing my cigarette into the fireplace.

"It's Japanese, don't you think?" said Pierpont.

"No," said Barris, "it is not artistically grotesque, it's vulgar and horrible,—it looks cheap and unfinished—"

"Unfinished,—exactly," said I, "like an American humorist—"

"Yes," said Pierpont, "cheap. What about that gold serpent?"

"Oh, the Metropolitan Museum bought it; you must see it, it's marvellous."

Barris and Pierpont had lighted their cigarettes and, after a moment, we all rose and strolled out to the lawn, where chairs and hammocks were placed under the maple trees.

David passed, gun under arm, dogs heeling.

"Three guns on the meadows at four this afternoon," said Pierpont.

"Roy," said Barris as David bowed and started on, "what did you do yesterday?"

This was the question that I had been expecting. All night long I had dreamed of Ysonde and the glade in the woods, where, at the bottom of the crystal fountain, I saw the reflection of her eyes. All the morning while bathing and dressing I had been persuading myself that the dream was not worth recounting and that a search for the glade and the imaginary stone carving would be ridiculous. But now, as Barris asked the question, I suddenly decided to tell him the whole story.

"See here, you fellows," I said abruptly, "I am going to tell you something queer. You can laugh as much as you please too, but first I want to ask Barris a question or two. You have been in China, Barris?"

"Yes," said Barris, looking straight into my eyes.

"Would a Chinaman be likely to turn lumberman?"

"Have you seen a Chinaman?" he asked in a quiet voice.

"I don't know; David and I both imagined we did."

Barris and Pierpont exchanged glances.

"Have you seen one also?" I demanded, turning to include Pierpont.

"No," said Barris slowly; "but I know that there is, or has been, a Chinaman in these woods."

"The devil!" said I.

"Yes," said Barris gravely; "the devil, if you like,—a devil,—a member of the Kuen-Yuin."

I drew my chair close to the hammock where Pierpont lay at full length, holding out to me a ball of pure gold.

"Well?" said I, examining the engraving on its surface, which represented a mass of twisted creatures,—dragons, I supposed.

"Well," repeated Barris, extending his hand to take the golden ball, "this globe of gold engraved with reptiles and Chinese hieroglyphics is the symbol of the Kuen-Yuin."

"Where did you get it?" I asked, feeling that something startling was impending.

"Pierpont found it by the lake at sunrise this morning. It is the symbol of the Kuen-Yuin," he repeated, "the terrible Kuen-Yuin, the sorcerers of China, and the most murderously diabolical sect on earth."

We puffed our cigarettes in silence until Barris rose, and began to pace backward and forward among the trees, twisting his grey moustache.

"The Kuen-Yuin are sorcerers," he said, pausing before the hammock where Pierpont lay watching him; "I mean exactly what I say,—sorcerers. I've seen them,—I've seen them at their devilish business, and I repeat to you solemnly, that as there are angels above, there is a race of devils on earth, and they are sorcerers. Bah!" he cried, "talk to me of Indian magic and Yogis and all that clap-trap! Why, Roy, I tell you that the Kuen-Yuin have absolute control of a hundred millions of people, mind and body, body and soul. Do you know what goes on in the interior of China? Does Europe know,—could any human being conceive of the condition of that gigantic hell-pit? You read the papers, you hear diplomatic twaddle about Li-Hung-Chang and the Emperor, you see accounts of battles on sea and land, and you know that Japan has raised a toy tempest along the jagged edge of the great unknown. But you never before heard of the Kuen-Yuin; no, nor has any European except a stray missionary or two, and yet I tell you that when the fires from this pit of hell have eaten through the continent to the coast, the explosion will inundate half a world,—and God help the other half."

Pierpont's cigarette went out; he lighted another, and looked hard at Barris.

"But," resumed Barris quietly, "'sufficient unto the day,' you know,—I didn't intend to say as much as I did,—it would do no good,—even you and Pierpont will forget it,—it seems so impossible and so far away,—like the burning out of the sun. What I want to discuss is the possibility or probability of a Chinaman,—a member of the Kuen-Yuin, being here, at this moment, in the forest."

"If he is," said Pierpont, "possibly the gold-makers owe their discovery to him."

"I do not doubt it for a second," said Barris earnestly.

I took the little golden globe in my hand, and examined the characters engraved upon it.

"Barris," said Pierpont, "I can't believe in sorcery while I am wearing one of Sanford's shooting suits in the pocket of which rests an uncut volume of the 'Duchess.'"

"Neither can I," I said, "for I read the *Evening Post,* and I know Mr. Godkin would not allow it. Hello! What's the matter with this gold ball?"

"What is the matter?" said Barris grimly.

"Why—why—it's changing color—purple, no, crimson—no, it's green I mean—good Heavens! these dragons are twisting under my fingers—"

"Impossible!" muttered Pierpont, leaning over me; "those are not dragons—"

"No!" I cried excitedly; "they are pictures of that reptile that Barris brought back—see—see how they crawl and turn—"

"Drop it!" commanded Barris; and I threw the ball on the turf. In an instant we had all knelt down on the grass beside it, but the globe was again golden, grotesquely wrought with dragons and strange signs.

Pierpont, a little red in the face, picked it up, and handed it to Barris. He placed it on a chair, and sat down beside me.

"Whew!" said I, wiping the perspiration from my face, "how did you play us that trick, Barris?"

"Trick?" said Barris contemptuously.

I looked at Pierpont, and my heart sank. If this was not a trick, what was it? Pierpont returned my glance and colored, but all he said was, "It's devilish queer," and Barris answered, "Yes, devilish." Then Barris asked me again to tell my story, and I did, beginning from the time I met David in the spinney to the moment when I sprang into the darkening thicket where that yellow mask had grinned like a phantom skull.

"Shall we try to find the fountain?" I asked after a pause.

"Yes,—and—er—the lady," suggested Pierpont vaguely.

"Don't be an ass," I said a little impatiently, "you need not come, you know."

"Oh, I'll come," said Pierpont, "unless you think I am indiscreet—"

"Shut up, Pierpont," said Barris, "this thing is serious; I never heard of such a glade or such a fountain, but it's true that nobody knows this forest thoroughly. It's worth while trying for; Roy, can you find your way back to it?"

"Easily," I answered; "when shall we go?"

"It will knock our snipe shooting on the head," said Pierpont, "but then when one has the opportunity of finding a live dream-lady—"

I rose, deeply offended, but Pierpont was not very penitent and his laughter was irresistible.

"The lady's yours by right of discovery," he said. "I'll promise not to infringe on your dreams,—I'll dream about other ladies—"

"Come, come," said I, "I'll have Howlett put you to bed in a minute. Barris, if you are ready,—we can get back to dinner—"

Barris had risen and was gazing at me earnestly.

"What's the matter?" I asked nervously, for I saw that his eyes were fixed on my forehead, and I thought of Ysonde and the white crescent scar.

"Is that a birthmark?" said Barris.

"Yes—why, Barris?"

"Nothing,—an interesting coincidence—"

"What!—for Heaven's sake!"

"The scar,—or rather the birthmark. It is the print of the dragon's claw,—the crescent symbol of Yue-Laou—"

"And who the devil is Yue-Laou?" I said crossly.

"Yue-Laou,—the Moon Maker, Dzil-Nbu of the Kuen-Yuin;—it's Chinese mythology, but it is believed that Yue-Laou has returned to rule the Kuen-Yuin—"

"The conversation," interrupted Pierpont, "smacks of peacock's feathers and yellow-jackets. The chicken-pox has left its card on Roy, and Barris is guying us. Come on, you fellows, and make your call on the dream-lady. Barris, I hear galloping; here come your men."

Two mud splashed riders clattered up to the porch and dismounted at a motion from Barris. I noticed that both of them carried repeating rifles and heavy Colt's revolvers.

They followed Barris, deferentially, into the dining-room, and presently we heard the tinkle of plates and bottles and the low hum of Barris' musical voice.

Half an hour later they came out again, saluted Pierpont and me, and galloped away in the direction of the Canadian frontier. Ten minutes passed, and, as Barris did not appear, we rose and went into the house, to find him. He was sitting silently before the table, watching the small golden globe, now glowing with scarlet and orange fire, brilliant as a live coal. Howlett, mouth ajar, and eyes starting from the sockets, stood petrified behind him.

"Are you coming," asked Pierpont, a little startled. Barris did not answer. The globe slowly turned to pale gold again,—but the face that Barris raised to ours was white as a sheet. Then he stood up, and smiled with an effort which was painful to us all.

"Give me a pencil and a bit of paper," he said.

Howlett brought it. Barris went to the window and wrote rapidly. He folded the paper, placed it in the top drawer of his desk, locked the drawer, handed me the key, and motioned us to precede him.

When again we stood under the maples, he turned to me with an impenetrable expression. "You will know when to use the key," he said: "Come, Pierpont, we must try to find Roy's fountain."

VI

At two o'clock that afternoon, at Barris' suggestion, we gave up the search for the fountain in the glade and cut across the forest to the spinney where David and Howlett were waiting with our guns and the three dogs.

Pierpont guyed me unmercifully about the "dream-lady" as he called her, and, but for the significant coincidence of Ysonde's and Barris' questions concerning the white scar on my forehead, I should long ago have been perfectly persuaded that I had dreamed the whole thing. As it was, I had no explanation to offer. We had not been able to find the glade although fifty times I came to landmarks which convinced me that we were just about to enter it. Barris was quiet, scarcely uttering a word to either of us during the entire search. I had never before seen him depressed in spirits. However, when we came in sight of the spinney where a cold bit of grouse and a bottle of Burgundy awaited each, Barris seemed to recover his habitual good humor.

"Here's to the dream-lady!" said Pierpont, raising his glass and standing up.

I did not like it. Even if she was only a dream, it irritated me to hear Pierpont's mocking voice. Perhaps Barris understood,—I don't know, but he bade Pierpont drink his wine without further noise, and that young man obeyed with a childlike confidence which almost made Barris smile.

"What about the snipe, David," I asked; "the meadows should be in good condition."

"There is not a snipe on the meadows, sir," said David solemnly.

"Impossible," exclaimed Barris, "they can't have left."

"They have sir," said David in a sepulchral voice which I hardly recognized. We all three looked at the old man curiously, waiting for his explanation of this disappointing but sensational report.

David looked at Howlett and Howlett examined the sky.

"I was going," began the old man, with his eyes fastened on Howlett, "I was going along by the spinney with the dogs when I heard a noise in the covert and I seen Howlett come walkin' very fast toward me. In fact," continued David, "I may say he was runnin'. Was you runnin', Howlett?"

Howlett said "Yes," with a decorous cough.

"I beg pardon," said David, "but I'd rather Howlett told the rest. He saw things which I did not."

"Go on, Howlett," commanded Pierpont, much interested.

Howlett coughed again behind his large red hand.

"What David says is true sir," he began; "I h'observed the dogs at a distance 'ow they was a workin' sir, and David stood a lightin' of 's pipe be'ind the spotted beech when I see a 'ead pop up in the covert 'oldin a stick like 'e was h'aimin' at the dogs sir"—

"A head holding a stick?" said Pierpont severely.

"The 'ead 'ad 'ands, sir," explained Howlett, "'ands that' 'eld a painted stick,—like that, sir. 'Owlett, thinks I to meself, this 'ere's queer, so I jumps in an' runs, but the beggar 'e seen me an' w'en I comes alongside of David, 'e was gone. ''Ello 'Owlett,' sez David, 'what the 'ell'—I beg pardon, sir,—''ow did you come 'ere,' sez 'e very loud. 'Run!' sez I, 'the Chinaman is harryin' the dawgs!' 'For Gawd's sake wot Chinaman?' sez David, h'aimin' is gun at every bush. Then I thinks I see 'im an' we run an' run, the dawgs a boundin' close to heel sir, but we don't see no Chinaman."

"I'll tell the rest," said David, as Howlett coughed and stepped in a modest corner behind the dogs.

"Go on," said Barns in a strange voice.

"Well sir, when Howlett and I stopped chasin', we was on the cliff overlooking the south meadow. I noticed that there was hundreds of birds there, mostly yellow-legs and plover, and Howlett seen them too. Then before I could say a word to Howlett, something out in the lake gave a splash—a splash as if the whole cliff had fallen into the water. I was that scared that I jumped straight into the bush and Howlett he sat down quick, and all those snipe wheeled up—there was hundreds,—all a squeelin' with fright, and the wood-duck came bowlin' over the meadows as if the old Nick was behind."

David paused and glanced meditatively at the dogs.

"Go on," said Barris in the same strained voice.

"Nothing more sir. The snipe did not come back."

"But that splash in the lake?"

"I don't know what it was sir."

"A salmon? A salmon couldn't have frightened the duck and the snipe that way?"

"No—oh no, sir. If fifty salmon had jumped they couldn't have made that splash. Couldn't they, Howlett?"

"No 'ow," said Howlett.

"Roy," said Barris at length, "what David tells us settles the snipe shooting for to-day. I am going to take Pierpont up to the house. Howlett and David will follow with the dogs,—I have something to say to them. If you care to come, come along; if not, go and shoot a brace of grouse for dinner and be back by eight if you want to see what Pierpont and I discovered last night."

David whistled Gamin and Mioche to heel and followed Howlett and his hamper toward the house. I called Voyou to my side, picked up my gun and turned to Barris.

"I will be back by eight," I said; "you are expecting to catch one of the gold-makers, are you not?"

"Yes," said Barns listlessly.

Pierpont began to speak about the Chinaman but Barris motioned him to follow, and, nodding to me, took the path that Howlett and David had followed toward the house. When they disappeared I tucked my gun under my arm and turned sharply into the forest, Voyou trotting close to my heels.

In spite of myself the continued apparition of the Chinaman made me nervous. If he troubled me again I had fully decided to get the drop on him and find out what he was doing in the Cardinal Woods. If he could give no satisfactory account of himself I would march him in to Barris as a gold-making suspect,—I would march him in anyway, I thought, and rid the forest of his ugly face. I wondered what it was that David had heard in the lake. It must have been a big fish, a salmon, I thought; probably David's and Howlett's nerves were overwrought after their Celestial chase.

A whine from the dog broke the thread of my meditation and I raised my head. Then I stopped short in my tracks.

The lost glade lay straight before me.

Already the dog had bounded into it, across the velvet turf to the carved stone where a slim figure sat. I saw my dog lay his silky head lovingly against her silken kirtle; I saw her face bend above him, and I caught my breath and slowly entered the sun-lit glade.

Half timidly she held out one white hand.

"Now that you have come," she said, "I can show you more of my work. I told you that I could do other things besides these dragon-flies and moths carved here in stone. Why do you stare at me so? Are you ill?"

"Ysonde," I stammered.

"Yes," she said, with a faint color under her eyes.

"I—I never expected to see you again," I blurted out, "—you—I—I— thought I had dreamed—"

"Dreamed, of me? Perhaps you did, is that strange?"

"Strange? N—no—but—where did you go when—when we were leaning over the fountain together? I saw your face,—your face reflected beside mine and then—then suddenly I saw the blue sky and only a star twinkling."

"It was because you fell asleep," she said, "was it not?"

"I—asleep?"

"You slept—I thought you were very tired and I went back—"

"Back?—where?"

"Back to my home where I carve my beautiful images; see, here is one I brought to show you to-day."

I took the sculptured creature that she held toward me, a massive golden lizard with frail claw-spread wings of gold so thin that the sunlight burned through and fell on the ground in flaming gilded patches.

"Good Heavens!" I exclaimed, "this is astounding! Where did you learn to do such work? Ysonde, such a thing is beyond price!"

"Oh, I hope so," she said earnestly, "I can't bear to sell my work, but my step-father takes it and sends it away. This is the second thing I have done and yesterday he said I must give it to him. I suppose he is poor."

"I don't see how he can be poor if he gives you gold to model in," I said, astonished.

"Gold!" she exclaimed, "gold! He has a room full of gold! He makes it."

I sat down on the turf at her feet completely unnerved.

"Why do you look at me so?" she asked, a little troubled.

"Where does your step-father live?" I said at last.

"Here."

"Here!"

"In the woods near the lake. You could never find our house."

"A house!"

"Of course. Did you think I lived in a tree? How silly. I live with my step-father in a beautiful house,—a small house, but very beautiful. He makes his gold there but the men who carry it away never come to the house, for they don't know where it is and if they did they could not get in. My step-father carries the gold in lumps to a canvas satchel. When the satchel is full he takes it out into the woods where the men live and I don't know what they do with it. I wish he could sell the gold and become rich for then I could go back to Yian where all the gardens are sweet and the river flows under the thousand bridges."

"Where is this city?" I asked faintly.

"Yian? I don't know. It is sweet with perfume and the sound of silver bells all day long. Yesterday I carried a blossom of dried lotus buds from Yian, in my breast, and all the woods were fragrant. Did you smell it?"

"Yes."

"I wondered, last night, whether you did. How beautiful your dog is; I love him. Yesterday I thought most about your dog but last night—"

"Last night," I repeated below my breath.

"I thought of you. Why do you wear the dragon-claw?"

I raised my hand impulsively to my forehead, covering the scar.

"What do you know of the dragon-claw?" I muttered.

"It is the symbol of Yue-Laou, and Yue-Laou rules the Kuen-Yuin, my step-father says. My step-father tells me everything that I know. We lived in Yian until I was sixteen years old. I am eighteen now; that is two years we have lived in the forest. Look!—see those scarlet birds! What are they? There are birds of the same color in Yian."

"Where is Yian, Ysonde?" I asked with deadly calmness.

"Yian? I don't know."

"But you have lived there?"

"Yes, a very long time."

"Is it across the ocean, Ysonde?"

"It is across seven oceans and the great river which is longer than from the earth to the moon."

"Who told you that?"

"Who? My step-father; he tells me everything."

"Will you tell me his name, Ysonde?"

"I don't know it, he is my step-father, that is all."

"And what is your name?"

"You know it, Ysonde."

"Yes, but what other name."

"That is all, Ysonde. Have you two names? Why do you look at me so impatiently?"

"Does your step-father make gold? Have you seen him make it?"

"Oh yes. He made it also in Yian and I loved to watch the sparks at night whirling like golden bees. Yian is lovely,—if it is all like our garden and the gardens around. I can see the thousand bridges from my garden and the white mountain beyond—"

"And the people—tell me of the people, Ysonde!" I urged gently.

"The people of Yian? I could see them in swarms like ants—oh! many, many millions crossing and recrossing the thousand bridges."

"But how did they look? Did they dress as I do?"

"I don't know. They were very far away, moving specks on the thousand bridges. For sixteen years I saw them every day from my garden but I never went out of my garden into the streets of Yian, for my step-father forbade me."

"You never saw a living creature near by in Yian?" I asked in despair.

"My birds, oh such tall, wise-looking birds, all over grey and rose color."

She leaned over the gleaming water and drew her polished hand across the surface.

"Why do you ask me these questions," she murmured; "are you pleased?"

"Tell me about your step-father," I insisted. "Does he look as I do? Does he dress, does he speak as I do? Is he American?"

"American? I don't know. He does not dress as you do and he does not look as you do. He is old, very, very old. He speaks sometimes as you do, sometimes as they do in Yian. I speak also in both manners."

"Then speak as they do in Yian," I urged impatiently, "speak as— why, Ysonde! why are you crying? Have I hurt you?—I did not intend,—I did not dream of your caring! There Ysonde, forgive me,—see, I beg you on my knees here at your feet."

I stopped, my eyes fastened on a small golden ball which hung from her waist by a golden chain. I saw it trembling against her thigh, I saw it change color, now crimson, now purple, now flaming scarlet. It was the symbol of the Kuen-Yuin.

She bent over me and laid her fingers gently on my arm.

"Why do you ask me such things?" she said, while the tears glistened on her lashes. "It hurts me here,—" she pressed her hand to her breast,—"it pains.—I don't know why. Ah, now your eyes are hard and cold again; you are looking at the golden globe which hangs from my waist. Do you wish to know also what that is?"

"Yes," I muttered, my eyes fixed on the infernal color flames which subsided as I spoke, leaving the ball a pale gilt again.

"It is the symbol of the Kuen-Yuin," she said in a trembling voice; "why do you ask?"

"Is it yours?"

"Y—yes."

"Where did you get it?" I cried harshly.

"My—my step-fa—"

Then she pushed me away from her with all the strength of her slender wrists and covered her face.

If I slipped my arm about her and drew her to me,—if I kissed away the tears that fell slowly between her fingers,—if I told her how I loved her—how it cut me to the heart to see her unhappy,—after all that is my own business. When she smiled through her tears, the pure love and sweetness in her eyes lifted my soul higher than the high moon vaguely glimmering through the sun-lit blue above. My happiness was so sudden, so fierce and overwhelming that I only knelt there, her fingers clasped in mine, my eyes raised to the blue vault and the glimmering moon. Then something in the long grass beside me moved close to my knees and a damp acrid odor filled my nostrils.

"Ysonde!" I cried, but the touch of her hand was already gone and my two clenched fists were cold and damp with dew.

"Ysonde!" I called again, my tongue stiff with fright;—but I called as one awaking from a dream—a horrid dream, for my nostrils quivered with the damp acrid odor and I felt the crab-reptile clinging to my knee. Why had the night fallen so swiftly,—and where was I—where?—stiff, chilled, torn, and bleeding, lying flung like a corpse over my own threshold with Voyou licking my face and Barris stooping above me in the light of a lamp that flared and smoked in the night breeze like a torch. Faugh! the choking stench of the lamp aroused me and I cried out:

"Ysonde!"

"What the devil's the matter with him?" muttered Pierpont, lifting me in his arms like a child, "has he been stabbed, Barris?"

VII

In a few minutes I was able to stand and walk stiffly into my bedroom where Howlett had a hot bath ready and a hotter tumbler of Scotch. Pierpont sponged the blood from my throat where it had coagulated. The cut was slight, almost invisible, a mere puncture from a thorn. A shampoo cleared my mind, and a cold plunge and alcohol friction did the rest.

"Now," said Pierpont, "swallow your hot Scotch and lie down. Do you want a broiled woodcock? Good, I fancy you are coming about."

Barris and Pierpont watched me as I sat on the edge of the bed, solemnly chewing on the woodcock's wishbone and sipping my Bordeaux, very much at my ease.

Pierpont sighed his relief.

"So," he said pleasantly, "it was a mere case of ten dollars or ten days. I thought you had been stabbed—"

"I was not intoxicated," I replied, serenely picking up a bit of celery.

"Only jagged?" enquired Pierpont, full of sympathy.

"Nonsense," said Barris, "let him alone. Want some more celery, Roy?—it will make you sleep."

"I don't want to sleep," I answered; "when are you and Pierpont going catch your gold-maker?"

Barris looked at his watch and closed it with a snap.

"In an hour; you don't propose to go with us?"

"But I do,—toss me a cup of coffee, Pierpont, will you,—that's just what I propose to do. Howlett, bring the new box of Panatellas,—the mild imported;—and leave the decanter. Now Barris, I'll be dressing, and you and Pierpont keep still and listen to what I have to say. Is that door shut tight?"

Barris locked it and sat down.

"Thanks," said I. "Barris, where is the city of Yian?"

An expression akin to terror flashed into Barris' eyes and I saw him stop breathing for a moment.

"There is no such city," he said at length, "have I been talking in my sleep?"

"It is a city," I continued, calmly, "where the river winds under the thousand bridges, where the gardens are sweet scented and the air is filled with the music of silver bells—"

"Stop!" gasped Barris, and rose trembling from his chair. He had grown ten years older.

"Roy," interposed Pierpont coolly, "what the deuce are you harrying Barris for?"

I looked at Barris and he looked at me. After a second or two he sat down again.

"Go on, Roy," he said.

"I must," I answered, "for now I am certain that I have not dreamed."

I told them everything; but, even as I told it, the whole thing seemed so vague, so unreal, that at times I stopped with the hot blood tingling in my ears, for it seemed impossible that sensible men, in the year of our Lord 1896, could seriously discuss such matters.

I feared Pierpont, but he did not even smile. As for Barris, he sat with his handsome head sunk on his breast, his unlighted pipe clasped tight in both hands.

When I had finished, Pierpont turned slowly and looked at Barris. Twice he moved his lips as if about to ask something and then remained mute.

"Yian is a city," said Barris, speaking dreamily; "was that why you wished to know, Pierpont?"

We nodded silently.

"Yian is a city," repeated Barris, "where the great river winds under the thousand bridges,—where the gardens are sweet scented, and the air is filled with the music of silver bells."

My lips formed the question, "Where is this city?"

"It lies," said Barris, almost querulously, "across the seven oceans and the river which is longer than from the earth to the moon."

"What do you mean?" said Pierpont.

"Ah," said Barris, rousing himself with an effort and raising his sunken eyes, "I am using the allegories of another land; let it pass. Have I not told you of the Kuen-Yuin? Yian is the centre of the Kuen-Yuin. It lies hidden in that gigantic shadow called China, vague and vast as the midnight Heavens,—a continent unknown, impenetrable."

"Impenetrable," repeated Pierpont below his breath.

"I have seen it," said Barns dreamily. "I have seen the dead plains of Black Cathay and I have crossed the mountains of Death, whose summits are above the atmosphere. I have seen the shadow of Xangi cast across Abaddon. Better to die a million miles from Yezd and Ater Quedah than to have seen the white water-lotus close in the shadow of Xangi! I have slept among the ruins of Xaindu where the winds never cease and the Wulwulleh is wailed by the dead."

"And Yian," I urged gently.

There was an unearthly look on his face as he turned slowly toward me. "Yian,—I have lived there—and loved there. When the breath of my body shall cease, when the dragon's claw shall fade from my arm,"—he tore up his sleeve, and we saw a white crescent shining above his elbow,—"when the light of my eyes has faded forever, then, even then I shall not forget the city of Yian. Why, it is my home,—mine! The river and the thousand bridges, the white peak beyond, the sweet-scented gardens, the lilies, the pleasant noise of the summer wind laden with bee music and the music of bells,—all these are mine. Do you think because the Kuen-Yuin feared the dragon's claw on my arm that my work with them is ended? Do you think that because Yue-Laou could give, that I acknowledge his right to take away? Is he Xangi in whose shadow the white water-lotus dares not raise its head? No! No!" he cried violently, "it was not from Yue-Laou, the sorcerer, the Maker of Moons, that my happiness came! It was real, it was not a shadow to vanish like a tinted bubble! Can a sorcerer create and give a man the woman he loves? Is Yue-Laou as great as Xangi then? Xangi is God. In His own time, in His infinite goodness and mercy He will bring me again to the woman I love. And I know she waits for me at God's feet."

In the strained silence that followed I could hear my heart's double beat and I saw Pierpont's face, blanched and pitiful. Barris shook himself and raised his head. The change in his ruddy face frightened me.

"Heed!" he said, with a terrible glance at me; "the print of the dragon's claw is on your forehead and Yue-Laou knows it. If you must love, then love like a man, for you will suffer like a soul in hell, in the end. What is her name again?"

"Ysonde," I answered simply.

VIII

At nine o'clock that night we caught one of the gold-makers. I do not know how Barris had laid his trap; all I saw of the affair can be told in minute or two.

We were posted on the Cardinal road about a mile below the house, Pierpont and I with drawn revolvers on one side, under a butter-nut tree, Barris on the other, a Winchester across his knees.

I had just asked Pierpont the hour, and he was feeling for his watch when far up the road we heard the sound of a galloping horse, nearer, nearer, clattering, thundering past. Then Barris' rifle spat flame and the dark mass, horse and rider, crashed into the dust. Pierpont had the half stunned horseman by the collar in a second,—the horse was stone dead,—and, as we lighted a pine knot to examine the fellow, Barris' two riders galloped up and drew bridle beside us.

"Hm!" said Barris with a scowl, "it's the 'Shiner,' or I'm a moon-shiner."

We crowded curiously around to see the "Shiner." He was red-headed, fat and filthy, and his little red eyes burned in his head like the eyes of an angry pig.

Barris went through his pockets methodically while Pierpont held him and I held the torch. The Shiner was a gold mine; pockets, shirt, bootlegs, hat, even his dirty fists, clutched tight and bleeding, were bursting with lumps of soft yellow gold. Barris dropped this "moonshine gold," as we had come to call it, into the pockets of his shooting-coat, and withdrew to question the prisoner. He came back again in a few minutes and motioned his mounted men to take the Shiner in charge. We watched them, rifle on thigh, walking their horses slowly away into the darkness, the Shiner, tightly bound, shuffling sullenly between them.

"Who is the Shiner?" asked Pierpont, slipping the revolver into his pocket again.

"A moonshiner, counterfeiter, forger, and highwayman," said Barris, "and probably a murderer. Drummond will be glad to see him, and I think it likely he will be persuaded to confess to him what he refuses to confess to me."

"Wouldn't he talk?" I asked.

"Not a syllable. Pierpont, there is nothing more for you to do."

"For me to do? Are you not coming back with us, Barris?"

"No," said Barris.

We walked along the dark road in silence for a while, I wondering what Barris intended to do, but he said nothing more until we reached our own verandah. Here he held out his hand, first to Pierpont, then to me, saying good-bye as though he were going on a long journey.

"How soon will you be back?" I called out to him as he turned away toward the gate. He came across the lawn again and again took our hands with a quiet affection that I had never imagined him capable of.

"I am going," he said, "to put an end to his gold-making to-night. I know that you fellows have never suspected what I was about on my little solitary evening strolls after dinner. I will tell you. Already I have unobtrusively killed four of these gold-makers,—my men put them under ground just below the new wash-out at the four mile stone. There are three left alive,—the Shiner whom we have, another criminal named 'Yellow,' or 'Yaller' in the vernacular, and the third—"

"The third," repeated Pierpont, excitedly.

"The third I have never yet seen. But I know who and what he is,—I know; and if he is of human flesh and blood, his blood will flow to-night."

As he spoke a slight noise across the turf attracted my attention. A mounted man was advancing silently in the starlight over the spongy meadowland. When he came nearer Barris struck a match, and we saw that he bore a corpse across his saddle bow.

"Yaller, Colonel Barris," said the man, touching his slouched hat in salute. This grim introduction to the corpse made me shudder, and, after a moment's examination of the stiff, wide-eyed dead man, I drew back.

"Identified," said Barris, "take him to the four mile post and carry his effects to Washington,—under seal, mind, Johnstone."

Away cantered the rider with his ghastly burden, and Barris took our hands once more for the last time. Then he went away, gaily, with a jest on his lips, and Pierpont and I turned back into the house.

For an hour we sat moodily smoking in the hall before the fire, saying little until Pierpont burst out with: "I wish Barris had taken one of us with him to-night!"

The same thought had been running in my mind, but I said: "Barris knows what he's about."

This observation neither comforted us nor opened the lane to further conversation, and after a few minutes Pierpont said good night and called for Howlett and hot water. When he had been warmly tucked away by Howlett, I turned out all but one lamp, sent the dogs away with David and dismissed Howlett for the night.

I was not inclined to retire for I knew I could not sleep. There was a book lying open on the table beside the fire and I opened it and read a page or two, but my mind was fixed on other things.

The window shades were raised and I looked out at the star-set firmament. There was no moon that night but the sky was dusted all over with sparkling stars and a pale radiance, brighter even than moonlight, fell over meadow and wood. Far away in the forest I heard the voice of the wind, a soft warm wind that whispered a name, Ysonde.

"Listen," sighed the voice of the wind, and "listen" echoed the swaying trees with every little leaf a-quiver. I listened.

Where the long grasses trembled with the cricket's cadence I heard her name, Ysonde; I heard it in the rustling woodbine where grey moths hovered; I heard it in the drip, drip, drip of the dew from the porch. The silent meadow brook whispered her name, the rippling woodland streams repeated it, Ysonde, Ysonde, until all earth and sky were filled with the soft thrill, Ysonde, Ysonde, Ysonde.

A night-thrush sang in a thicket by the porch and I stole to the verandah to listen. After a while it began again, a little further on. I ventured out into the road. Again I heard it far away in the forest and I followed it, for I knew it was singing of Ysonde.

When I came to the path that leaves the main road and enters the Sweet-Fern Covert below the spinney, I hesitated; but the beauty of the night lured me on and the night-thrushes called me from every thicket. In the starry radiance, shrubs, grasses, field flowers, stood out distinctly, for there was no moon to cast shadows. Meadow and brook, grove and stream, were illuminated by the pale glow. Like great lamps lighted the planets hung from the high domed sky and through their mysterious rays the fixed stars, calm, serene, stared from the heavens like eyes.

I waded on waist deep through fields of dewy golden-rod, through late clover and wild-oat wastes, through crimson fruited sweetbrier, blueberry, and wild plum, until the low whisper of the Wier Brook warned me that the path had ended.

But I would not stop, for the night air was heavy with the perfume of water-lilies and far away, across the low wooded cliffs and the wet meadow-land beyond, there was a distant gleam of silver, and I heard the murmur of sleepy waterfowl. I would go to the lake. The way was clear except for the dense young growth and the snares of the moose-bush.

The night-thrushes had ceased but I did not want for the company of living creatures. Slender, quick darting forms crossed my path at intervals, sleek mink, that fled like shadows at my step, wiry weasels and fat muskrats, hurrying onward to some tryst or killing.

I never had seen so many little woodland creatures on the move at night. I began to wonder where they all were going so fast, why they all hurried on in the same direction. Now I passed a hare hopping through the brushwood, now a rabbit scurrying by, flag hoisted. As I entered the beech second-growth two foxes glided by me; a little further on a doe crashed out of the underbrush, and close behind her stole a lynx, eyes shining like coals.

He neither paid attention to the doe nor to me, but loped away toward the north.

The lynx was in flight.

"From what?" I asked myself, wondering. There was no forest fire, no cyclone, no flood.

If Barris had passed that way could he have stirred up this sudden exodus? Impossible; even a regiment in the forest could scarcely have put to rout these frightened creatures.

"What on earth," thought I, turning to watch the headlong flight of a fisher-cat, "what on earth has started the beasts out at this time of night?"

I looked up into the sky. The placid glow of the fixed stars comforted me and I stepped on through the narrow spruce belt that leads down to the borders of the Lake of the Stars.

Wild cranberry and moose-bush entwined my feet, dewy branches spattered me with moisture, and the thick spruce needles scraped my face as I threaded my way over mossy logs and deep spongy tussocks down to the level gravel of the lake shore.

Although there was no wind the little waves were hurrying in from the lake and I heard them splashing among the pebbles. In the pale star glow thousands of water-lilies lifted their half-closed chalices toward the sky.

I threw myself full length upon the shore, and, chin on hand, looked out across the lake.

Splash, splash, came the waves along the shore, higher, nearer, until a film of water, thin and glittering as a knife blade, crept up to my elbows. I could not understand it; the lake was rising, but there had been no rain. All along the shore the water was running up; I heard the waves among the sedge grass; the weeds at my side were awash in the ripples. The lilies rocked on the tiny waves, every wet pad rising on the swells, sinking, rising again until the whole lake was glimmering with undulating blossoms. How sweet and deep was the fragrance from the lilies. And now the water was ebbing, slowly, and the waves receded, shrinking from the shore rim until the white pebbles appeared again, shining like froth on a brimming glass.

No animal swimming out in the darkness along the shore, no heavy salmon surging, could have set the whole shore aflood as though the wash from a great boat were rolling in. Could it have been the overflow, through the Weir Brook, of some cloud-burst far back in the forest? This was the only way I could account for it, and yet when I had crossed the Wier Brook I had not noticed that it was swollen.

And as I lay there thinking, a faint breeze sprang up and I saw the surface of the lake whiten with lifted lily pads.

All around me the alders were sighing; I heard the forest behind me stir; the crossed branches rubbing softly, bark against bark. Something—it may have been an owl—sailed out of the night, dipped, soared, and was again engulfed, and far across the water I heard its faint cry, Ysonde.

Then first, for my heart was full, I cast myself down upon my face, calling on her name. My eyes were wet when I raised my head,—for the spray from the shore was drifting in again,—and my heart beat heavily;

"No more, no more." But my heart lied, for even as I raised my face to the calm stars, I saw her standing still, close beside me; and very gently I spoke her name, Ysonde. She held out both hands.

"I was lonely," she said, "and I went to the glade, but the forest is full of frightened creatures and they frightened me. Has anything happened in the woods? The deer are running toward the heights."

Her hand still lay in mine as we moved along the shore, and the lapping of the water on rock and shallow was no lower than our voices.

"Why did you leave me without a word, there at the fountain in the glade?" she said.

"I leave you!—"

"Indeed you did, running swiftly with your dog, plunging through thickets and brush,—oh—you frightened me."

"Did I leave you so?"

"Yes—after—"

"After?"

"You had kissed me—"

Then we leaned down together and looked into the black water set with stars, just as we had bent together over the fountain in the glade.

"Do you remember?" I asked.

"Yes. See, the water is inlaid with silver stars,—everywhere white lilies floating and the stars below, deep, deep down."

"What is the flower you hold in your hand?"

"White water-lotus."

"Tell me about Yue-Laou, Dzil-Nbu of the Kuen-Yuin," I whispered, lifting her head so I could see her eyes.

"Would it please you to hear?"

"Yes, Ysonde."

"All that I know is yours, now, as I am yours, all that I am. Bend closer. Is it of Yue-Laou you would know? Yue-Laou is Dzil-Nbu of the Kuen-Yuin. He lived in the Moon. He is old—very, very old, and once, before he came to rule the Kuen-Yuin, he was the old man who unites with a silken cord all predestined couples, after which nothing can prevent their union. But all that is changed since he came to rule the KuenYuin. Now he has perverted the Xin,—the good genii of China,—and has fashioned from their warped bodies a monster which he calls the Xin. This monster is horrible, for it not only lives in its own body, but it has thousands of loathsome satellites,—living creatures without mouths, blind, that move when the Xin moves, like a mandarin and his escort. They are part of the Xin although they are not attached. Yet if one of these satellites is injured the Xin writhes with agony. It is fearful— this huge living bulk and these creatures spread out like severed fingers that wriggle around a hideous hand."

"Who told you this?"

"My step-father."

"Do you believe it?"

"Yes. I have seen one of the Xin's creatures."

"Where, Ysonde?"

"Here in the woods."

"Then you believe there is a Xin here?"

"There must be,—perhaps in the lake—"

"Oh, Xins inhabit lakes?"

"Yes, and the seven seas. I am not afraid here."

"Why?"

"Because I wear the symbol of the Kuen-Yuin."

"Then I am not safe," I smiled.

"Yes you are, for I hold you in my arms. Shall I tell you more about the Xin? When the Xin is about to do to death a man, the Yeth-hounds gallop through the night—"

"What are the Yeth-hounds, Ysonde?"

"The Yeth-hounds are dogs without heads. They are the spirits of murdered children, which pass through the woods at night, making a wailing noise."

"Do you believe this?"

"Yes, for I have worn the yellow lotus—"

"The yellow lotus—"

"Yellow is the symbol of faith—"

"Where?"

"In Yian," she said faintly.

After a while I said, "Ysonde, you know there is a God?"

"God and Xangi are one."

"Have you ever heard of Christ?"

"No," she answered softly.

The wind began again among the tree tops. I felt her hands closing in mine.

"Ysonde," I asked again, "do you believe in sorcerers?"

"Yes, the Kuen-Yuin are sorcerers; Yue-Laou is a sorcerer."

"Have you seen sorcery?"

"Yes, the reptile satellite of the Xin—"

"Anything else?"

"My charm,—the golden ball, the symbol of the Kuen-Yuin. Have you seen it change,—have you seen the reptiles writhe—?"

"Yes," I said shortly, and then remained silent, for a sudden shiver of apprehension had seized me. Barris also had spoken gravely, ominously of the sorcerers, the Kuen-Yuin, and I had seen with my own eyes the graven reptiles turning and twisting on the glowing globe.

"Still," said I aloud, "God lives and sorcery is but a name."

"Ah," murmured Ysonde, drawing closer to me, "they say, in Yian, the Kuen-Yuin live; God is but a name."

"They lie," I whispered fiercely.

"Be careful," she pleaded, "they may hear you. Remember that you have the mark of the dragon's claw on your brow."

"What of it?" I asked, thinking also of the white mark on Barris' arm.

"Ah don't you know that those who are marked with the dragon's claw are followed by Yue-Laou, for good or for evil,—and the evil means death if you offend him?"

"Do you believe that!" I asked impatiently.

"I know it," she sighed.

"Who told you all this? Your step-father? What in Heaven's name is he then,—a Chinaman!"

"I don't know; he is not like you."

"Have—have you told him anything about me?"

"He knows about you—no, I have told him nothing,—ah what is this—see—it is a cord, a cord of silk about your neck—and about mine!"

"Where did that come from?" I asked astonished.

"It must be—it must be Yue-Laou who binds me to you,—it is as my step-father said—he said Yue-Laou would bind us—"

"Nonsense," I said almost roughly, and seized the silken cord, but to my amazement it melted in my hand like smoke.

"What is all this damnable jugglery!" I whispered angrily, but my anger vanished as the words were spoken, and a convulsive shudder shook me to the feet. Standing on the shore of the lake, a stone's throw away, was a figure, twisted and bent,—a little old man, blowing sparks from a live coal which he held in his naked hand. The coal glowed with increasing radiance, lighting up the skull-like face above it, and threw a red glow over the sands at his feet. But the face!—the ghastly Chinese face on which the light flickered,—and the snaky slitted eyes, sparkling as the coal glowed hotter. Coal! It was not a coal but a golden globe staining the night with crimson flames,—it was the symbol of the Kuen-Yuin.

"See! See!" gasped Ysonde, trembling violently, "see the moon rising from between his fingers! Oh I thought it was my step-father and it is Yue-Laou the Maker of Moons—no! no! it is my step-father—ah God! they are the same!"

Frozen with terror I stumbled to my knees, groping for my revolver which bulged in my coat pocket; but something held me—something which bound me like a web in a thousand strong silky meshes. I struggled and turned but the web grew tighter; it was over us—all around us, drawing, pressing us into each other's arms until we lay side by side, bound hand and body and foot, palpitating, panting like a pair of netted pigeons.

And the creature on the shore below! What was my horror to see a moon, huge, silvery, rise like a bubble from between his fingers, mount higher, higher into the still air and hang aloft in the midnight sky, while another moon rose from his fingers, and another and yet another until the vast span of Heaven was set with moons and the earth sparkled like a diamond in the white glare.

A great wind began to blow from the east and it bore to our ears a long mournful howl,—a cry so unearthly that for a moment our hearts stopped.

"The Yeth-hounds!" sobbed Ysonde, "do you hear!—they are passing through the forest! The Xin is near!"

Then all around us in the dry sedge grasses came a rustle as if some small animals were creeping, and a damp acrid odor filled the air. I knew the smell, I saw the spidery crablike creatures swarm out around me and drag their soft yellow hairy bodies across the shrinking grasses. They passed, hundreds of them, poisoning the air, tumbling, writhing, crawling with their blind mouthless heads raised. Birds, half asleep and confused by the darkness, fluttered away before them in helpless fright, rabbits sprang from their forms, weasels glided away like flying shadows. What remained of the forest creatures rose and fled from the loathsome invasion; I heard the squeak of a terrified hare, the snort of stampeding deer, and the lumbering gallop of a bear; and all the time I was choking, half suffocated by the poisoned air.

Then, as I struggled to free myself from the silken snare about me, I cast a glance of deadly fear at the sorcerer below, and at the same moment I saw him turn in his tracks.

"Halt!" cried a voice from the bushes.

"Barris!" I shouted, half leaping up in my agony.

I saw the sorcerer spring forward, I heard the bang! bang! bang! of a revolver, and, as the sorcerer fell on the water's edge, I saw Barris jump out into the white glare and fire again, once, twice, three times, into the writhing figure at his feet.

Then an awful thing occurred. Up out of the black lake reared a shadow, a nameless shapeless mass, headless, sightless, gigantic, gaping from end to end.

A great wave struck Barris and he fell, another washed him up on the pebbles, another whirled him back into the water and then,—and then the thing fell over him,—and I fainted.

This, then, is all that I know concerning Yue-Laou and the Xin. I do not fear the ridicule of scientists or of the press for I have told the truth. Barris is gone and the thing that killed him is alive to-day in the Lake of the Stars while the spider-like satellites roam through the Cardinal Woods. The game has fled, the forests around the lake are empty of any living creatures save the reptiles that creep when the Xin moves in the depths of the lake.

General Drummond knows what he has lost in Barris, and we, Pierpont and I, know what we have lost also. His will we found in the drawer, the key of which he had handed me. It was wrapped in a bit of paper on which was written:

"Yue-Laou the sorcerer is here in the Cardinal Woods. I must kill him or he will kill me. He made and gave to me the woman I loved,—he made her,—I saw him,—he made her out of a white water-lotus bud. When our child was born, he came again before me and demanded from me the woman I loved. Then, when I refused, he went away, and that night my wife and child vanished from my side, and I found upon her pillow a white lotus bud. Roy, the woman of your dream, Ysonde, may be my child. God help you if you love her for Yue-Laou will give,—and take away, as though he were Xangi, which is God. I will kill Yue-Laou before I leave this forest,—or he will kill me.

"Franklyn Barris."

Now the world knows what Barris thought of the Kuen-Yuin and of Yue-Laou. I see that the newspapers are just becoming excited over the glimpses that Li-Hung-Chang has afforded them of Black Cathay and the demons of the Kuen-Yuin. The Kuen-Yuin are on the move.

Pierpont and I have dismantled the shooting box in the Cardinal Woods. We hold ourselves ready at a moment's notice to join and lead the first Government party to drag the Lake of Stars and cleanse the forest of the crab reptiles. But it will be necessary that a large force assembles, and a well-armed force, for we never have found the body of Yue-Laou, and, living or dead, I fear him. Is he living?

Pierpont, who found Ysonde and myself lying unconscious on the lake shore, the morning after, saw no trace of corpse or blood on the sands. He may have fallen into the lake, but I fear and Ysonde fears that he is alive. We never were able to find either her dwelling place or the glade and the fountain again. The only thing that remains to her of her former life is the gold serpent in the Metropolitan Museum and her golden globe, the symbol of the Kuen-Yuin; but the latter no longer changes color.

David and the dogs are waiting for me in the court yard as I write. Pierpont is in the gun room loading shells, and Howlett brings him mug after mug of my ale from the wood. Ysonde bends over my desk,—I feel her hand on my arm, and she is saying, "Don't you think you have done enough to-day, dear? How can you write such silly nonsense without a shadow of truth or foundation?"

A Pleasant Evening

"Et pis, doucett'ment on s'endort,
 On fait sa carne, on fait sa sorgue,
 On ronfle, et, comme tin tuyau d'orgue,
 L'tuyau s'met a ronfler pus fort. . . ."

ARISTIDE BRUANT.

I

As I stepped upon the platform of a Broadway cable-car at Forty-second Street, somebody said: "Hello, Hilton, Jamison's looking for you."

"Hello, Curtis," I replied, "what does Jamison want?"

"He wants to know what you've been doing all the week," said Curtis, hanging desperately to the railing as the car lurched forward; "he says you seem to think that the *Manhattan Illustrated Weekly* was created for the sole purpose of providing salary and vacations for you."

"The shifty old tom-cat!" I said, indignantly, "he knows well enough where I've been. Vacation! Does he think the State Camp in June is a snap?"

"Oh," said Curtis, "you've been to Peekskill?"

"I should say so," I replied, my wrath rising as I thought of my assignment.

"Hot?" inquired Curtis, dreamily.

"One hundred and three in the shade," I answered. "Jamison wanted three full pages and three half pages, all for process work, and a lot of line drawings into the bargain. I could have faked them—I wish I had. I was fool enough to hustle and break my neck to get some honest drawings, and that's the thanks I get!"

"Did you have a camera?"

151

"No. I will next time—I'll waste no more conscientious work on Jamison," I said sulkily.

"It doesn't pay," said Curtis. "When I have military work assigned me, I don't do the dashing sketch-artist act, you bet; I go to my studio, light my pipe, pull out a lot of old *Illustrated London News,* select several suitable battle scenes by Caton Woodville—and use 'em too."

The car shot around the neck-breaking curve at Fourteenth Street.

"Yes," continued Curtis, as the car stopped in front of the Morton House for a moment, then plunged forward again amid a furious clanging of gongs, "it doesn't pay to do decent work for the fat-headed men who run the *Manhattan Illustrated.* They don't appreciate it."

"I think the public does," I said, "but I'm sure Jamison doesn't. It would serve him right if I did what most of you fellows do—take a lot of Caton Woodville's and Thulstrup's drawings, change the uniforms, 'chic' a figure or two, and turn in a drawing labelled 'from life.' I'm sick of this sort of thing anyway. Almost every day this week I've been chasing myself over that tropical camp, or galloping in the wake of those batteries. I've got a full page of the 'camp by moonlight,' full pages of 'artillery drill' and 'light battery in action,' and a dozen smaller drawings that cost me more groans and perspiration than Jamison ever knew in all his lymphatic life!"

"Jamison's got wheels," said Curtis,—"more wheels than there are bicycles in Harlem. He wants you to do a full page by Saturday."

"A what?" I exclaimed, aghast.

"Yes he does—he was going to send Jim Crawford, but Jim expects to go to California for the winter fair, and you've got to do it."

"What is it?" I demanded savagely.

"The animals in Central Park," chuckled Curtis.

I was furious. The animals! Indeed! I'd show Jamison that I was entitled to some consideration! This was Thursday; that gave me a day and a half to finish a full-page drawing for the paper, and, after my work at the State Camp I felt that I was entitled to a little rest. Anyway I objected to the subject. I intended to tell Jamison so—I intended to tell him firmly. However, many of the things that we often intended to tell Jamison were never told. He was a peculiar man, fat-faced, thin-lipped, gentle-voiced, mild-mannered, and soft in his movements as a pussy-cat. Just why our firmness should give way when we were actually in his presence, I have never quite been able to determine. He said very little—so did we, although we often entered his presence with other intentions.

The truth was that the *Manhattan Illustrated Weekly* was the best paying, best illustrated paper in America, and we young fellows were not anxious to be cast adrift. Jamison's knowledge of art was probably as extensive as the knowledge of any "Art editor" in the city. Of course that was saying nothing, but the fact merited careful consideration on our part, and we gave it much consideration.

This time, however, I decided to let Jamison know that drawings are not produced by the yard, and that I was neither a floor-walker nor a hand-me-down. I would stand up for my rights; I'd tell old Jamison a few things to set the wheels under his silk hat spinning, and if he attempted any of his pussy-cat ways on me, I'd give him a few plain facts that would curl what hair he had left.

Glowing with a splendid indignation I jumped off the car at the City Hall, followed by Curtis, and a few minutes later entered the office of the *Manhattan Illustrated News.*

"Mr. Jamison would like to see you, sir," said one of the compositors as I passed into the long hallway. I threw my drawings on the table and passed a handkerchief over my forehead.

"Mr. Jamison would like to see you, sir," said a small freckle-faced boy with a smudge of ink on his nose.

"I know it," I said, and started to remove my gloves.

"Mr. Jamison would like to see you, sir," said a lank messenger who was carrying a bundle of proofs to the floor below.

"The deuce take Jamison," I said to myself. I started toward the dark passage that leads to the abode of Jamison, running over in my mind the neat and sarcastic speech which I had been composing during the last ten minutes.

Jamison looked up and nodded softly as I entered the room. I forgot my speech.

"Mr. Hilton," he said, "we want a full page of the Zoo before it is removed to Bronx Park. Saturday afternoon at three o'clock the drawing must be in the engraver's hands. Did you have a pleasant week in camp?"

"It was hot," I muttered, furious to find that I could not remember my little speech.

"The weather," said Jamison, with soft courtesy, "is oppressive everywhere. Are your drawings in, Mr. Hilton?"

"Yes. It was infernally hot and I worked like a nigger—"

"I suppose you were quite overcome. Is that why you took a two days' trip to the Catskills? I trust the mountain air restored you—but—was it prudent to go to Cranston's for the cotillion Tuesday? Dancing in such uncomfortable weather is really unwise. Good-morning, Mr. Hilton, remember the engraver should have your drawings on Saturday by three."

I walked out, half hypnotized, half enraged. Curtis grinned at me as I passed—I could have boxed his ears.

"Why the mischief should I lose my tongue whenever that old tom-cat purrs!" I asked myself as I entered the elevator and was shot down to the first floor. "I'll not put up with this sort of thing much longer—how in the name of all that's foxy did he know that I went to the mountains? I suppose he thinks I'm lazy because I don't wish to be boiled to death. How did he know about the dance at Cranston's? Old cat!"

The roar and turmoil of machinery and busy men filled my ears as I tossed the avenue and turned into the City Hall Park.

From the staff on the tower the flag drooped in the warm sunshine with scarcely a breeze to lift its crimson bars. Overhead stretched a splendid cloudless sky, deep, deep blue, thrilling, scintillating in the gemmed rays of the sun.

Pigeons wheeled and circled about the roof of the grey Post Office or dropped out of the blue above to flutter around the fountain in the square.

On the steps of the City Hall the unlovely politician lounged, exploring his heavy under jaw with wooden toothpick, twisting his drooping black moustache, or distributing tobacco juice over marble steps and close-clipped grass.

My eyes wandered from these human vermin to the calm scornful face of Nathan Hale, on his pedestal, and then to the grey-coated Park policeman whose occupation was to keep little children from the cool grass.

A young man with thin hands and blue circles under his eyes was slumbering on a bench by the fountain, and the policeman walked over to him and struck him on the soles of his shoes with a short club.

The young man rose mechanically, stared about, dazed by the sun, shivered, and limped away. I saw him sit down on the steps of the white marble building, and I went over and spoke to him. He neither looked at me, nor did he notice the coin I offered.

"You're sick," I said, "you had better go to the hospital."

"Where?" he asked vacantly—"I've been, but they wouldn't receive me."

He stooped and tied the bit of string that held what remained of his shoe to his foot.

"You are French," I said.

"Yes."

"Have you no friends? Have you been to the French Consul?"

"The Consul!" he replied; "no, I haven't been to the French Consul."

After a moment I said, "You speak like a gentleman."

He rose to his feet and stood very straight, looking me, for the first time, directly in the eyes.

"Who are you?" I asked abruptly.

"An outcast," he said, without emotion, and limped off thrusting his hands into his ragged pockets.

"Huh!" said the Park policeman who had come up behind me in time to hear my question and the vagabond's answer; "don't you know who that hobo is?—An' you a newspaper man!"

"Who is he, Cusick?" I demanded, watching the thin shabby figure moving across Broadway toward the river.

"On the level you don't know, Mr. Hilton?" repeated Cusick, suspiciously.

"No, I don't; I never before laid eyes on him."

"Why," said the sparrow policeman, "that's 'Soger Charlie';—you remember—that French officer what sold secrets to the Dutch Emperor."

"And was to have been shot? I remember now, four years ago—and he escaped—you mean to say that is the man?"

"Everybody knows it," sniffed Cusick, "I'd a-thought you newspaper gents would have knowed it first."

"What was his name?" I asked after a moment's thought.

"Soger Charlie—"

"I mean his name at home."

"Oh, some French dago name. No Frenchman will speak to him here; sometimes they curse him and kick him. I guess he's dyin' by inches."

I remembered the case now. Two young French cavalry officers were arrested, charged with selling plans of fortifications and other military secrets to the Germans. On the eve of their conviction, one of them, Heaven only knows how, escaped and turned up in New York. The other was duly shot. The affair had made some noise, because both young men were of good families. It was a painful episode, and I had hastened to forget it. Now that it was recalled to my mind, I remembered the newspaper accounts of the case, but I had forgotten the names of the miserable young men.

"Sold his country," observed Cusick, watching a group of children out of the corner of his eyes—"you can't trust no Frenchman nor dagoes nor Dutchmen either. I guess Yankees are about the only white men."

I looked at the noble face of Nathan Hale and nodded.

"Nothin' sneaky about us, eh, Mr. Hilton?"

I thought of Benedict Arnold and looked at my boots.

Then the policeman said, "Well, solong, Mr. Hilton," and went away to frighten a pasty-faced little girl who had climbed upon the railing and was leaning down to sniff the fragrant grass.

"Cheese it, de cop!" cried her shrill-voiced friends, and the whole bevy of small ragamuffins scuttled away across the square.

With a feeling of depression I turned and walked toward Broadway, where the long yellow cable-cars swept up and down, and the din of gongs and the deafening rumble of heavy trucks echoed from the marble walls of the Court House to the granite mass of the Post Office.

Throngs of hurrying busy people passed up town and down town, slim sober-faced clerks, trim cold-eyed brokers, here and there a red-necked politician linking arms with some favourite heeler, here and there a City Hall lawyer, sallow-faced and saturnine. Sometimes a fireman, in his severe blue uniform, passed through the crowd, sometimes a blue-coated policeman, mopping his clipped hair, holding his helmet in his white-gloved hand. There were women too, pale-faced shop girls with pretty eyes, tall blonde girls who might be typewriters and might not, and many, many older women whose business in that part of the city no human being could venture to guess, but who hurried up town and down town, all occupied with something that gave to the whole restless throng a common likeness—the expression of one who hastens toward a hopeless goal.

I knew some of those who passed me. There was little Jocelyn of the *Mail and Express;* there was Hood, who had more money than he wanted and was going to have less than he wanted when he left Wall Street; there was Colonel Tidmouse of the 45th Infantry, N.G.S.N.Y., probably coming from the office of the *Army and Navy Journal,* and there was Dick Harding who wrote the best stories of New York life that have been printed. People said his hat no longer fitted,—especially people who also wrote stories of New York life and whose hats threatened to fit as long as they lived.

I looked at the statue of Nathan Hale, then at the human stream that flowed around his pedestal.

"Quand même," I muttered and walked out into Broadway, signalling to the gripman of an uptown cable-car.

II

I passed into the Park by the Fifth Avenue and 59th Street gate; I could never bring myself to enter it through the gate that is guarded by the hideous pigmy statue of Thorwaldsen.

The afternoon sun poured into the windows of the New Netherlands Hotel, setting every orange-curtained pane a-glitter, and tipping the wings of the bronze dragons with flame.

Gorgeous masses of flowers blazed in the sunshine from the grey terraces of the Savoy, from the high grilled court of the Vanderbilt palace, and from the balconies of the Plaza opposite.

The white marble façade of the Metropolitan Club was a grateful relief in the universal glare, and I kept my eyes on it until I had crossed the dusty street and entered the shade of the trees.

Before I came to the Zoo I smelled it. Next week it was to be removed to the fresh cool woods and meadows in Bronx Park, far from the stifling air of the city, far from the infernal noise of the Fifth Avenue omnibuses.

A noble stag stared at me from his enclosure among the trees as I passed down the winding asphalt walk. "Never mind, old fellow," said I, "you will be splashing about in the Bronx River next week and cropping maple shoots to your heart's content."

On I went, past herds of staring deer, past great lumbering elk, and moose, and long-faced African antelopes, until I came to the dens of the great carnivora.

The tigers sprawled in the sunshine, blinking and licking their paws; the lions slept in the shade or squatted on their haunches, yawning gravely. A slim panther travelled to and fro behind her barred cage, pausing at times to peer wistfully out into the free sunny world. My heart ached for caged wild things, and I walked on, glancing up now and then to encounter the blank stare of a tiger or the mean shifty eyes of some ill-smelling hyena.

Across the meadow I could see the elephants swaying and swinging their great heads, the sober bison solemnly slobbering over their cuds, the sarcastic countenances of camels, the wicked little zebras, and a lot more animals of the camel and llama tribe, all resembling each other, all equally ridiculous, stupid, deadly uninteresting.

Somewhere behind the old arsenal an eagle was screaming, probably a Yankee eagle; I heard the "tchug! tchug!" of a blowing hippopotamus, the squeal of a falcon, and the snarling yap! of quarrelling wolves.

"A pleasant place for a hot day!" I pondered bitterly, and I thought some things about Jamison that I shall not insert in this volume. But I lighted a cigarette to deaden the aroma from the hyenas, unclasped my etching block, sharpened my pencil, and fell to work on a family group of hippopotami.

They may have taken me for a photographer, for they all wore smiles as if "welcoming a friend," and my sketch block presented a series of wide open jaws, behind which shapeless bulky bodies vanished in alarming perspective.

The alligators were easy; they looked to me as though they had not moved since the founding of the Zoo, but I had a bad time with the big bison, who persistently turned his tail to me, looking stolidly around his flank to see how I stood it. So I pretended to be absorbed in the antics of two bear cubs, and the dreary old bison fell into the trap, for I made some good sketches of him and laughed in his face as I closed the book.

There was a bench by the abode of the eagles, and I sat down on it to draw the vultures and condors, motionless as mummies among the piled rocks. Gradually I enlarged the sketch, bringing in the gravel plaza, the steps leading up to Fifth Avenue, the sleepy park policeman in front of the arsenal—and a slim, white-browed girl, dressed in shabby black, who stood silently in the shade of the willow trees.

After a while I found that the sketch, instead of being a study of the eagles, was in reality a composition in which the girl in black occupied the principal point of interest. Unwittingly I had subordinated everything else to her, the brooding vultures, the trees and walks, and the half indicated groups of sun-warmed loungers.

She stood very still, her pallid face bent, her thin white hands loosely clasped before her. "Rather dejected reverie," I thought, "probably she's out of work." Then I caught a glimpse of a sparkling diamond ring on the slender third finger of her left hand.

"She'll not starve with such a stone as that about her," I said to myself, looking curiously at her dark eyes and sensitive mouth. They were both beautiful, eyes and mouth—beautiful, but touched with pain.

After a while I rose and walked back to make a sketch or two of the lions and tigers. I avoided the monkeys—I can't stand them, and they never seem funny to me, poor dwarfish, degraded caricatures of all that is ignoble in ourselves.

"I've enough now," I thought; "I'll go home and manufacture a full page that will probably please Jamison." So I strapped the elastic band around my sketching block, replaced pencil and rubber in my waistcoat pocket, and strolled off toward the Mall to smoke a cigarette in the evening glow before going back to my studio to work until midnight, up to the chin in charcoal grey and Chinese white.

Across the long meadow I could see the roofs of the city faintly looming above the trees. A mist of amethyst, ever deepening, hung low on the horizon, and through it, steeple and dome, roof and tower, and the tall chimneys where thin fillets of smoke curled idly, were transformed into pinnacles of beryl and flaming minarets, swimming in filmy haze. Slowly the enchantment deepened; all that was ugly and shabby and mean had fallen away from the distant city, and now it towered into the evening sky, splendid, gilded, magnificent, purified in the fierce furnace of the setting sun.

The red disk was half hidden now; the tracery of trees, feathery willow and budding birch, darkened against the glow; the fiery rays shot far across the meadow, gilding the dead leaves, staining with soft crimson the dark moist tree trunks around me.

Far across the meadow a shepherd passed in the wake of a huddling flock, his dog at his heels, faint moving blots of grey.

A squirrel sat up on the gravel walk in front of me, ran a few feet, and sat up again, so close that I could see the palpitation of his sleek flanks.

Somewhere in the grass a hidden field insect was rehearsing last summer's solos; I heard the tap! tap! tat-tat-t-t-tat! of a woodpecker among the branches overhead and the querulous note of a sleepy robin.

The twilight deepened; out of the city the music of bells floated over wood and meadow; faint mellow whistles sounded from the river craft along the north shore, and the distant thunder of a gun announced the close of a June day.

The end of my cigarette began to glimmer with a redder light; shepherd and flock were blotted out in the dusk, and I only knew they were still moving when the sheep bells tinkled faintly.

Then suddenly that strange uneasiness that all have known—that half-awakened sense of having seen it all before, of having been through it all, came over me, and I raised my head and slowly turned.

A figure was seated at my side. My mind was struggling with the instinct to remember. Something so vague and yet so familiar—something that eluded thought yet challenged it, something—God knows what! troubled me. And now, as I looked, without interest, at the dark figure beside me, an apprehension, totally involuntary, an impatience to understand, came upon me, and I sighed and turned restlessly again to the fading west.

I thought I heard my sigh re-echoed—I scarcely heeded; and in a moment I sighed again, dropping my burned-out cigarette on the gravel beneath my feet.

"Did you speak to me?" said some one in a low voice, so close that I swung around rather sharply.

"No," I said after a moment's silence.

It was a woman. I could not see her face clearly, but I saw on her clasped hands, which lay listlessly in her lap, the sparkle of a great diamond. I knew her at once. It did not need a glance at the shabby dress of black, the white face, a pallid spot in the twilight, to tell me that I had her picture in my sketch-book.

"Do—do you mind if I speak to you?" she asked timidly. The hopeless sadness in her voice touched me, and I said: "Why, no, of course not. Can I do anything for you?"

"Yes," she said, brightening a little, "if you—you only would."

"I will if I can," said I, cheerfully; "what is it? Out of ready cash?"

"No, not that," she said, shrinking back.

I begged her pardon, a little surprised, and withdrew my hand from my change pocket.

"It is only—only that I wish you to take these,"—she drew a thin packet from her breast,—"these two letters."

"I?" I asked astonished.

"Yes, if you will."

"But what am I to do with them?" I demanded.

"I can't tell you; I only know that I must give them to you. Will you take them?"

"Oh, yes, I'll take them," I laughed, "am I to read them?" I added to myself, "It's some clever begging trick."

"No," she answered slowly, "you are not to read them; you are to give them to somebody."

"To whom? Anybody?"

"No, not to anybody. You will know whom to give them to when the time comes."

"Then I am to keep them until further instructions?"

"Your own heart will instruct you," she said, in a scarcely audible voice. She held the thin packet toward me, and to humor her I took it. It was wet.

"The letters fell into the sea," she said; "there was a photograph which should have gone with them but the salt water washed it blank. Will you care if I ask you something else?"

"I? Oh, no."

"Then give me the picture that you made of me to-day."

I laughed again, and demanded how she knew I had drawn her.

"Is it like me?" she said.

"I think it is very like you," I answered truthfully.

"Will you not give it to me?"

Now it was on the tip of my tongue to refuse, but I reflected that I had enough sketches for a full page without that one, so I handed it to her, nodded that she was welcome, and stood up. She rose also, the diamond flashing on her finger.

"You are sure that you are not in want?" I asked, with a tinge of good-natured sarcasm.

"Hark!" she whispered; "listen!—do you hear the bells of the convent!"

I looked out into the misty night.

"There are no bells sounding," I said, "and anyway there are no convent bells here. We are in New York, mademoiselle"—I had noticed her French accent—"we are in Protestant Yankee-land, and the bells that ring are much less mellow than the bells of France."

I turned pleasantly to say good-night. She was gone.

III

"Have you ever drawn a picture of a corpse?" inquired Jamison next morning as I walked into his private room with a sketch of the proposed full page of the Zoo.

"No, and I don't want to," I replied, sullenly.

"Let me see your Central Park page," said Jamison in his gentle voice, and I displayed it. It was about worthless as an artistic production, but it pleased Jamison, as I knew it would.

"Can you finish it by this afternoon?" he asked, looking up at me with persuasive eyes.

"Oh, I suppose so," I said, wearily; "anything else, Mr. Jamison?"

"The corpse," he replied, "I want a sketch by to-morrow—finished."

"What corpse?" I demanded, controlling my indignation as I met Jamison's soft eyes.

There was a mute duel of glances. Jamison passed his hand across his forehead with a slight lifting of the eyebrows.

"I shall want it as soon as possible," he said in his caressing voice.

What I thought was, "Damned purring pussy-cat!" What I said was, "Where is this corpse?"

"In the Morgue—have you read the morning papers? No? Ah,—as you very rightly observe you are too busy to read the morning papers. Young men must learn industry first, of course, of course. What you are to do is this: the San Francisco police have sent out an alarm regarding the disappearance of a Miss Tufft—the millionaire's daughter, you know. To-day a body was brought to the Morgue here in New York, and it has been identified as the missing young lady,—by a diamond ring. Now I am convinced that it isn't, and I'll show you why, Mr. Hilton."

He picked up a pen and made a sketch of a ring on a margin of that morning's *Tribune.*

"That is the description of her ring as sent on from San Francisco. You notice the diamond is set in the centre of the ring where the two gold serpents' *tails* cross!

"Now the ring on the finger of the woman in the Morgue is like this," and he rapidly sketched another ring where the diamond rested in the *fangs* of the two gold serpents.

"That is the difference," he said in his pleasant, even voice.

"Rings like that are not uncommon," said I, remembering that I had seen such a ring on the finger of the white-faced girl in the Park the evening before. Then a sudden thought took shape—perhaps that was the girl whose body lay in the Morgue!

"Well," said Jamison, looking up at me, "what are you thinking about?"

"Nothing," I answered, but the whole scene was before my eyes, the vultures brooding among the rocks, the shabby black dress, and the pallid face,—and the ring, glittering on that slim white hand!

"Nothing," I repeated, "when shall I go, Mr. Jamison? Do you want a portrait—or what?"

"Portrait,—careful drawing of the ring, and,—er—a centre piece of the Morgue at night. Might as well give people the horrors while we're about it."

"But," said I, "the policy of this paper—"

"Never mind, Mr. Hilton," purred Jamison, "I am able to direct the policy of this paper."

"I don't doubt you are," I said angrily.

"I am," he repeated, undisturbed and smiling; "you see this Tufft case interests society. I am—er—also interested."

He held out to me a morning paper and pointed to a heading.

I read: "Miss Tufft Dead! Her Fiancé was Mr. Jamison, the well known Editor."

"What!" I cried in horrified amazement. But Jamison had left the room, and I heard him chatting and laughing softly with some visitors in the press-room outside.

I flung down the paper and walked out.

"The cold-blooded toad!" I exclaimed again and again;—"making capital out of his fiancée's disappearance! Well, I—I'm d—nd! I knew he was a bloodless, heartless grip-penny, but I never thought—I never imagined—" Words failed me.

Scarcely conscious of what I did I drew a *Herald* from my pocket and saw the column entitled: "Miss Tufft Found! Identified by a Ring. Wild Grief of Mr. Jamison, her Fiance."

That was enough. I went out into the street and sat down in City Hall Park. And, as I sat there, a terrible resolution came to me; I would draw that dead girl's face in such a way that it would chill Jamison's sluggish blood, I would crowd the black shadows of the Morgue with forms and ghastly faces, and every face should bear something in it of Jamison. Oh, I'd rouse him from his cold snaky apathy! I'd confront him with Death in such an awful form, that, passionless, base, inhuman as he was, he'd shrink from it as he would from a dagger thrust. Of course I'd lose my place, but that did not bother me, for I had decided to resign anyway, not having a taste for the society of human reptiles. And, as I sat there in the sunny park, furious, trying to plan a picture whose sombre horror should leave in his mind an ineffaceable scar, I suddenly thought of the pale black-robed girl in Central Park. Could it be her poor slender body that lay among the shadows of the grim Morgue! If ever brooding despair was stamped on any face, I had seen its print on hers when she spoke to me in the Park and gave me the letters. The letters! I had not thought of them since, but now I drew them from my pocket and looked at the addresses.

"Curious," I thought, "the letters are still damp; they smell of salt water too."

I looked at the address again, written in the long fine hand of an educated woman who had been bred in a French convent. Both letters bore the same address, in French:

> "Captain d'Yniol.
> (Kindness of a Stranger.)"

"Captain d'Yniol," I repeated aloud—"confound it, I've heard that name! Now, where the deuce—where in the name of all that's queer—" Somebody who had sat down on the bench beside me placed a heavy hand on my shoulder.

It was the Frenchman, "Soger Charlie."

"You spoke my name," he said in apathetic tones.

"Your name!"

"Captain d'Yniol," he repeated; "it is my name."

I recognized him in spite of the black goggles he was wearing, and, at the same moment, it flashed into my mind that d'Yniol was the name of the traitor who had escaped. Ah, I remembered now!

"I am Captain d'Yniol," he said again, and I saw his fingers closing on my coat sleeve.

It may have been my involuntary movement of recoil,—I don't know,—but the fellow dropped my coat and sat straight up on the bench.

"I am Captain d'Yniol," he said for the third time, "charged with treason and under sentence of death."

"And innocent!" I muttered, before I was even conscious of having spoken. What was it that wrung those involuntary words from my lips, I shall never know, perhaps—but it was I, not he, who trembled, seized with a strange agitation, and it was I, not he, whose hand was stretched forth impulsively, touching his.

Without a tremor he took my hand, pressed it almost imperceptibly, and dropped it. Then I held both letters toward him, and, as he nei-ther looked at them nor at me, I placed them in his hand. Then he started.

"Read them," I said, "they are for you."

"Letters!" he gasped in a voice that sounded like nothing human.

"Yes, they are for you,—I know it now—"

"Letters!—letters directed to *me?*"

"Can you not see?" I cried.

Then he raised one frail hand and drew the goggles from his eyes, and, as I looked, I saw two tiny white specks exactly in the centre of both pupils.

"Blind!" I faltered.

"I have been unable to read for two years," he said.

After a moment he placed the tip of one finger on the letters.

"They are wet," I said; "shall—would you like to have me read them?" For a long time he sat silently in the sunshine, fumbling with his cane, and I watched him without speaking. At last he said, "Read, Mon-sieur," and I took the letters and broke the seals.

The first letter contained a sheet of paper, damp and discoloured, on which a few lines were written:

"My darling, I knew you were innocent—" Here the writing ended, but, in the blur beneath, I read: "Paris shall know—France shall know, for at last I have the proofs and I am coming to find you, my soldier, and to place them in your own dear brave hands. They know, now, at the War Ministry—they have a copy of the traitor's confession—but they dare not make it public—they dare not withstand the popular astonish-ment and rage. Therefore I sail on Monday from Cherbourg by the Green Cross Line, to bring you back to your own again, where you will stand before all the world, without fear, without reproach."

"ALINE."

"This—this is terrible!" I stammered; "can God live and see such things done!"

But with his thin hand he gripped my arm again, bidding me read the other letter; and I shuddered at the menace in his voice.

Then, with his sightless eyes on me, I drew the other letter from the wet, stained envelope. And before I was aware—before I understood the purport of what I saw, I had read aloud these half effaced lines:

"The *Lorient* is sinking—an iceberg—mid-ocean—goodbye—you are innocent—I love—"

"The *Lorient!*" I cried; "it was the French steamer that was never heard from—the *Lorient* of the Green Cross Line! I had forgotten—I—"

The loud crash of a revolver stunned me; my ears rang and ached with it as I shrank back from a ragged dusty figure that collapsed on the bench beside me, shuddered a moment, and tumbled to the asphalt at my feet.

The trampling of the eager hard-eyed crowd, the dust and taint of powder in the hot air, the harsh alarm of the ambulance clattering up Mail Street,—these I remember, as I knelt there, helplessly holding the dead man's hands in mine.

"Soger Charlie," mused the sparrow policeman, "shot his-self, didn't he, Mr. Hilton? You seen him, sir,—blowed the top of his head off, didn't he, Mr. Hilton?"

"Soger Charlie," they repeated, "a French dago what shot his-self;" and the words echoed in my ears long after the ambulance rattled away, and the increasing throng dispersed, sullenly, as a couple of policemen cleared a space around the pool of thick blood on the asphalt.

They wanted me as a witness, and I gave my card to one of the policemen who knew me. The rabble transferred its fascinated stare to me, and I turned away and pushed a path between frightened shop girls and ill-smelling loafers, until I lost myself in the human torrent of Broadway.

The torrent took me with it where it flowed—East? West?—I did not notice nor care, but I passed on through the throng, listless, deadly weary of attempting so solve God's justice—striving to understand His purpose—His laws—His judgments which are "true and righteous altogether."

IV

"More to be desired are they than gold, yea, than much fine gold. Sweeter also than honey and the honey-comb!"

I turned sharply toward the speaker who shambled at my elbow. His sunken eyes were dull and lustreless, his bloodless face gleamed pallid as a death mask above the blood-red jersey—the emblem of the soldiers of Christ.

I don't know why I stopped, lingering, but, as he passed, I said, "Brother, I also was meditating upon God's wisdom and His testimonies."

The pale fanatic shot a glance at me, hesitated, and fell into my own pace, walking by my side. Under the peak of his Salvation Army cap his eyes shone in the shadow with a strange light.

"Tell me more," I said, sinking my voice below the roar of traffic, the clang! clang! of the cable-cars, and the noise of feet on the worn pavements—"tell me of His testimonies."

"Moreover by them is Thy servant warned and in keeping of them there is great reward. Who can understand His errors? Cleanse Thou me from secret faults. Keep back Thy servant also from presumptuous sins. Let them not have dominion over me. Then shall I be upright and I shall be innocent from the great transgression. Let the words of my mouth and the meditation of my heart be acceptable in Thy sight, O Lord! My strength and my Redeemer!"

"It is Holy Scripture that you quote," I said; "I also can read that when I choose. But it cannot clear for me the reasons—it cannot make understand—"

"What?" he asked, and muttered to himself.

"That, for instance," I replied, pointing to a cripple, who had been born deaf and dumb and horridly misshapen,—a wretched diseased lump on the sidewalk below St. Paul's Churchyard,—a sore-eyed thing that mouthed and mowed and rattled pennies in a tin cup as though the sound of copper could stem the human pack that passed hot on the scent of gold.

Then the man who shambled beside me turned and looked long and earnestly into my eyes. And after a moment a dull recollection stirred within me—a vague something that seemed like the awakening memory of a past, long, long forgotten, dim, dark, too subtle, too frail, too indefinite—ah! the old feeling that all men have known—the old strange uneasiness, that useless struggle to remember when and where it all occurred before.

And the man's head sank on his crimson jersey, and he muttered, muttered to himself of God and love and compassion, until I saw that the fierce heat of the city had touched his brain, and I went away and left him prating of mysteries that none but such as he dare name.

So I passed on through dust and heat; and the hot breath of men reached my cheek and eager eyes looked into mine. Eyes, eyes,—that met my own and looked through them, beyond—far beyond to where gold glittered amid the mirage of eternal hope. Gold! It was in the air where the soft sunlight gilded the floating moats, it was under foot in the dust that the sun made gilt, it glimmered from every window pane where the long red beams struck golden sparks above the gasping gold-hunting hordes of Wall Street.

High, high, in the deepening sky the tall buildings towered, and the breeze from the bay lifted the sun-dyed flags of commerce until they waved above the turmoil of the hives below—waved courage and hope and strength to those who lusted after gold.

The sun dipped low behind Castle William as I turned listlessly into the Battery, and the long straight shadows of the trees stretched away over greensward and asphalt walk.

Already the electric lights were glimmering among the foliage although the bay shimmered like polished brass and the topsails of the ships glowed with a deeper hue, where the red sun rays fall athwart the rigging.

Old men tottered along the sea-wall, tapping the asphalt with worn canes, old women crept to and fro in the coming twilight,—old women who carried baskets that gaped for charity or bulged with mouldy stuffs,—food, clothing?—I could not tell; I did not care to know.

The heavy thunder from the parapets of Castle William died away over the placid bay, the last red arm of the sun shot up out of the sea, and wavered and faded into the sombre tones of the afterglow. Then came the night, timidly at first, touching sky and water with grey fingers, folding the foliage into soft massed shapes, creeping onward, onward, more swiftly now, until colour and form had gone from all the earth and the world was a world of shadows.

And, as I sat there on the dusky sea-wall, gradually the bitter thoughts faded and I looked out into the calm night with something of that peace that comes to all when day is ended.

The death at my very elbow of the poor blind wretch in the Park had left a shock, but now my nerves relaxed their tension and I began to think about it all,—about the letters and the strange woman who had given them to me. I wondered where she had found them,—whether they really were carried by some vagrant current in to the shore from the wreck of the fated *Lorient.*

Nothing but these letters had human eyes encountered from the Lorient, although we believed that fire or berg had been her portion; for there had been no storms when the *Lorient* steamed away from Cherbourg.

And what of the pale-faced girl in black who had given these letters to me, saying that my own heart would teach me where to place them?

I felt in my pockets for the letters where I had thrust them all crumpled and wet. They were there, and I decided to turn them over to the police. Then I thought of Cusick and the City Hall Park and these set my mind running on Jamison and my own work,—ah! I had forgotten that,—I had forgotten that I had sworn to stir Jamison's cold, sluggish blood! Trading on his fiancée's reported suicide,—or murder! True, he had told me that he was satisfied that the body at the Morgue was not Miss Tufft's because the ring did not correspond with his fiancée's ring. But what sort of a man was that!—to go crawling and nosing about morgues and graves for a full-page illustration which might sell a few extra thousand papers. I had never known he was such a man. It was strange too—for that was not the sort of illustration that the *Weekly* used; it was against all precedent—against the whole policy of the paper. He would lose a hundred subscribers where he would gain one by such work.

"The callous brute!" I muttered to myself, "I'll wake him up—I'll—"

I sat straight up on the bench and looked steadily at a figure which was moving toward me under the spluttering electric light.

It was the woman I had met in the Park.

She came straight up to me, her pale face gleaming like marble in the dark, her slim hands outstretched.

"I have been looking for you all day—all day," she said, in the same low thrilling tones,—"I want the letters back; have you them here?"

"Yes," I said, "I have them here,—take them in Heaven's name; they have done enough evil for one day!"

She took the letters from my hand; I saw the ring, made of the double serpents, flashing on her slim finger, and I stepped closer, and looked her in the eyes.

"Who are you?" I asked.

"I? My name is of no importance to you," she answered.

"You are right," I said, "I do not care to know your name. That ring of yours—"

"What of my ring?" she murmured.

"Nothing,—a dead woman lying in the Morgue wears such a ring. Do you know what your letters have done? No? Well I read them to a miserable wretch and he blew his brains out!"

"You read them to a man!"

"I did. He killed himself."

"Who was that man?"

"Captain d'Yniol—"

With something between a sob and a laugh she seized my hand and covered it with kisses, and I, astonished and angry, pulled my hand away from her cold lips and sat down on the bench.

"You needn't thank me," I said sharply; "if I had known that,—but no matter. Perhaps after all the poor devil is better off somewhere in other regions with his sweetheart who was drowned,—yes, I imagine he is. He was blind and ill,—and broken-hearted."

"Blind?" she asked gently.

"Yes. Did you know him?"

"I knew him."

"And his sweetheart, Aline?"

"Aline," she repeated softly,—"she is dead. I come to thank you in her name."

"For what?—for his death?"

"Ah, yes, for that."

"Where did you get those letters?" I asked her, suddenly.

She did not answer, but stood fingering the wet letters.

Before I could speak again she moved away into the shadows of the trees, lightly, silently, and far down the dark walk I saw her diamond flashing.

Grimly brooding, I rose and passed through the Battery to the steps of the Elevated Road. These I climbed, bought my ticket, and stepped out to the damp platform. When a train came I crowded in with the rest, still pondering on my vengeance, feeling and believing that I was to scourge the conscience of the man who speculated on death.

And at last the train stopped at 28th Street, and I hurried out and down the steps and away to the Morgue.

When I entered the Morgue, Skelton, the keeper, was standing before a slab that glistened faintly under the wretched gas jets. He heard my footsteps, and turned around to see who was coming. Then he nodded, saying: "Mr. Hilton, just take a look at this here stiff—I'll be back in a moment—this is the one that all the papers take to be Miss Tufft,—but they're all off, because this stiff has been here now for two weeks."

I drew out my sketching-block and pencils.

"Which is it, Skelton?" I asked, fumbling for my rubber.

"This one, Mr. Hilton, the girl what's smilin'. Picked up off Sandy Hook, too. Looks as if she was asleep, eh?"

"What's she got in her hand—clenched tight? Oh,—a letter. Turn up the gas, Skelton, I want to see her face."

The old man turned the gas jet, and the flame blazed and whistled in the damp, fetid air. Then suddenly my eyes fell on the dead.

Rigid, scarcely breathing, I stared at the ring, made of two twisted serpents set with a great diamond,—I saw the wet letters crushed in her slender hand,—I looked, and—God help me!—I looked upon the dead face of the girl with whom I had been speaking on the Battery!

"Dead for a month at least," said Skelton, calmly.

Then, as I felt my senses leaving me, I screamed out, and at the same instant somebody from behind seized my shoulder and shook me savagely—shook me until I opened my eyes again and gasped and coughed.

"Now then, young feller!" said a Park policeman bending over me, "if you go to sleep on a bench, somebody 'll lift your watch!"

I turned, rubbing my eyes desperately.

Then it was all a dream—and no shrinking girl had come to me with damp letters,—I had not gone to the office—there was no such person as Miss Tufft,—Jamison was not an unfeeling villain,—no, indeed!—he treated us all much better than we deserved, and he was kind and generous too. And the ghastly suicide! Thank God that also was a myth,—and the Morgue and the Battery at night where that pale-faced girl had—ugh!

I felt for my sketch-block, found it; turned the pages of all the animals that I had sketched, the hippopotami, the buffalo, the tigers—ah! where was that sketch in which I had made the woman in shabby black the principal figure, with the brooding vultures all around and the crowd in the sunshine—? It was gone.

I hunted everywhere, in every pocket. It was gone.

At last I rose and moved along the narrow asphalt path in the falling twilight.

And as I turned into the broader walk, I was aware of a group, a policeman holding a lantern, some gardeners, and a knot of loungers gathered about something,—a dark mass on the ground.

"Found 'em just so," one of the gardeners was saying, "better not touch 'em until the coroner comes."

The policeman shifted his bull's-eye a little; the rays fell on two faces, on two bodies, half supported against a park bench. On the finger of the girl glittered a splendid diamond, set between the fangs of two gold serpents. The man had shot himself; he clasped two wet letters in his hand. The girl's clothing and hair were wringing wet, and her face was the face of a drowned person.

"Well, sir," said the policeman, looking at me; "you seem to know these two people—by your looks—"

"I never saw them before," I gasped, and walked on, trembling in every nerve.

For among the folds of her shabby black dress I had noticed the end of a paper,—my sketch that I had missed!

Pompe Funèbre

In the days when the keepers of the house shall tremble.

When I first saw the sexton he was standing motionless behind a stone. Presently he moved on again, pausing at times, and turning right and left with that nervous, jerky motion that always chills me.

His path lay across the blighted moss and withered leaves scattered in moist layers along the bank of the little brown stream, and I, wondering what his errand might be, followed, passing silently over the rotting forest mould. Once or twice he heard me, for I saw him stop short, a blot of black and orange in the sombre woods; but he always started on again, hurrying at times as though the dead might grow impatient.

For the sexton that I followed through the November forest was one of those small creatures that God has sent to bury little things that die alone in the world. Undertaker, sexton, mute, and gravedigger in one, this thing, robed in black and orange, buries all things that die unheeded by the world. And so they call it—this little beetle in black and orange—the "sexton."

How he hurried! I looked up into the gray sky where ashen branches, interlaced, swayed in unfelt winds, and I heard the dry leaves rattle in the tree tops, and the thud of acorns on the mould. A sombre bird peered at me from a heap of brush, then ran pattering over the leaves.

The sexton had reached a bit of broken ground, and was scuffling over sticks and gulleys toward a brown tuft of withered grass above. I dared not help him; besides, I could not bring myself to touch him, he was so horribly absorbed in his errand.

I halted for a moment. The eagerness of this live creature to find his dead and handle it; the odour of death and decay in this little forest world, where I had waited for spring when Lys moved among the flowering gorse, singing like a throstle in the wind—all this troubled me, and I lagged behind.

The sexton scrambled over the dead grass, raising his seared eyes at every wave of wind. The wind brought sadness with it, the scent of lifeless trees, the vague rustle of gorse buds, yellow and dry as paper flowers.

Along the stream, rotting water plants, scorched and frost-blighted, lay massed above the mud. I saw their pallid stems swaying like worms in the listless current.

The sexton had reached a mouldering stump, and now he seemed undecided. I sat down on a fallen tree, moist and bleached, that crumbled under my touch, leaving a stale odour in the air. Overhead a crow rose heavily and flapped out into the moorland; the wind rattled the stark blackthorns; a single drop of rain touched my cheek. I looked into the stream for some sign of life; there was nothing, except a shapeless creature that might have been a blindworm, lying belly upward on the mud bottom. I touched it with a stick. It was stiff and dead.

The wind among the sham paperlike gorse buds filled the woods with a silken rustle. I put out my hand and touched a yellow blossom; it felt like an immortelle on a funeral pillow.

The sexton had moved on again; something, perhaps a musty spider's web, had stuck to one leg, and he dragged it as he laboured on through the wood. Some little field mouse torn by weasel or kestrel, some crushed mole, some tiny dead pile of fur or feather, lay not far off, stricken by God or man or brother creature. And the sexton knew it—how, God knows! But he knew it, and hurried on to his tryst with the dead.

His path now lay along the edge of a tidal inlet from the Groix River. I looked down at the gray water through the leafless branches, and I saw a small snake, head raised, swim from a submerged clot of weeds into the shadow of a rock. There was a curlew, too, somewhere in the black swamp, whose dreary, persistent call cursed the silence.

I wondered when the sexton would fly; for he could fly if he chose; it is only when the dead are near, very near, that he creeps. The soiled mess of cobweb still stuck to him, and his progress was impeded by it. Once I saw a small brown and white spider, striped like a zebra, running swiftly in his tracks, but the sexton turned and raised his two clubbed forelegs in a horrid imploring attitude that still had something of men-ace under it. The spider backed away and sidled under a stone.

When anything that is dying—sick and close to death—falls upon the face of the earth, something moves in the blue above, floating like a moat; then another, then others. These specks that grow out of the fath-omless azure vault are jewelled flies. They come to wait for Death.

The sexton also arranges rendezvous with Death, but never waits; Death must arrive the first.

When the heavy clover is ablaze with painted wings, when bees hum and blunder among the white-thorn, or pass by like swift singing bullets, the sexton snaps open his black and orange wings and hums across the clover with the bees. Death in a scented garden, the tokens of the plague on a fair young breast, the gray flag of fear in the face of one who reels into the arms of Destruction, the sexton scrambling in the lap of spring, folding his sleek wings, unfolding them to ape the buzz of bees, passing over sweet clover tops to the putrid flesh that summons him—these things must be and will be to the end.

The sexton was running now—running fast, trailing the cobweb over twigs and mud. The edge of the wood was near, for I could see the win-ter wheat, like green scenery in a theatre, stretching for miles across the cliffs, crude as painted grass. And as I crept through the brittle forest fringe, I saw a figure lying face downward in the wheat—a girl's slender form, limp, motionless.

The sexton darted under her breast.

Then I threw myself down beside her, crying, "Lys! Lys!" And as I cried, the icy rain burst out across the moors, and the trees dashed their stark limbs together till the whole spectral forest tossed and danced, and the wind roared among the cliffs.

And through the Dance of Death Lys trembled in my arms, and sobbed and clung to me, murmuring that the Purple Emperor was dead; but the wind tore the words from her white lips, and flung them out across the sea, where the winter lightning lashed the stark heights of Groix.

Then the fear of death was stilled in my soul, and I raised her from the ground, holding her close.

And I saw the sexton, just beyond us, hurry across the ground and seek shelter under a little dead skylark, stiff-winged, muddy, lying alone in the rain.

In the storm, above us, a bird hovered singing through the rain. It passed us twice, still singing, and as it passed again we saw the shadow it cast upon the world was whiter than snow.

The Messenger

All-wise,
Hast thou seen all there is to see with thy two eyes?
Dost thou know all there is to know, and so,
Omniscient,
Darest thou still to say thy brother lies?

R. W. C.

I

"The bullet entered here," said Max Fortin, and he placed his middle finger over a smooth hole exactly in the centre of the forehead. I sat down upon a mound of dry seaweed and unslung my fowling piece. The little chemist cautiously felt the edges of the shot-hole, first with his middle finger, then with his thumb.

"Let me see the skull again," said I.

Max Fortin picked it up from the sod.

"It's like all the others," he observed. I nodded, without offering to take it from him. After a moment he thoughtfully replaced it upon the grass at my feet.

"It's like all the others," he repeated, wiping his glasses on his handkerchief. "I thought you might care to see one of the skulls, so I brought this over from the gravel pit. The men from Bannalec are digging yet. They ought to stop."

"How many skulls are there altogether?" I inquired.

"They found thirty-eight skulls; there are thirty-nine noted in the list. They lie piled up in the gravel pit on the edge of Le Bihan's wheat field. The men are at work yet. Le Bihan is going to stop them."

"Let's go over," said I; and I picked up my gun and started across the cliffs, Fortin on one side, Môme on the other.

179

"Who has the list?" I asked, lighting my pipe. "You say there is a list?"

"The list was found rolled up in a brass cylinder," said the little chemist. He added: "You should not smoke here. You know that if a single spark drifted into the wheat—"

"Ah, but I have a cover to my pipe," said I, smiling.

Fortin watched me as I closed the pepper-box arrangement over the glowing bowl of the pipe. Then he continued:

"The list was made out on thick yellow paper; the brass tube has preserved it. It is as fresh to-day as it was in 1760. You shall see it."

"Is that the date?"

"The list is dated 'April, 1760.' The Brigadier Durand has it. It is not written in French."

"Not written in French!" I exclaimed.

"No," replied Fortin solemnly, "it is written in Breton."

"But," I protested, "the Breton language was never written or printed in 1760."

"Except by priests," said the chemist.

"I have heard of but one priest who ever wrote the Breton language," I began.

Fortin stole a glance at my face.

"You mean—the Black Priest?" he asked.

I nodded.

Fortin opened his mouth to speak again, hesitated, and finally shut his teeth obstinately over the wheat stem that he was chewing.

"And the Black Priest?" I suggested encouragingly. But I knew it was useless; for it is easier to move the stars from their courses than to make an obstinate Breton talk. We walked on for a minute or two in silence.

"Where is the Brigadier Durand?" I asked, motioning Môme to come out of the wheat, which he was trampling as though it were heather. As I spoke we came in sight of the farther edge of the wheat field and the dark, wet mass of cliffs beyond.

"Durand is down there—you can see him; he stands just behind the Mayor of St. Gildas."

"I see," said I; and we struck straight down, following a sun-baked cattle path across the heather.

When we reached the edge of the wheat field, Le Bihan, the Mayor of St. Gildas, called to me, and I tucked my gun under my arm and skirted the wheat to where he stood.

"Thirty-eight skulls," he said in his thin, high-pitched voice; "there is but one more, and I am opposed to further search. I suppose Fortin told you?"

I shook hands with him, and returned the salute of the Brigadier Durand.

"I am opposed to further search," repeated Le Bihan, nervously picking at the mass of silver buttons which covered the front of his velvet and broadcloth jacket like a breastplate of scale armour.

Durand pursed up his lips, twisted his tremendous mustache, and hooked his thumbs in his sabre belt.

"As for me," he said, "I am in favour of further search."

"Further search for what—for the thirty-ninth skull?" I asked.

Le Bihan nodded. Durand frowned at the sunlit sea, rocking like a bowl of molten gold from the cliffs to the horizon. I followed his eyes. On the dark glistening cliffs, silhouetted against the glare of the sea, sat a cormorant, black, motionless, its horrible head raised toward heaven.

"Where is that list, Durand?" I asked.

The gendarme rummaged in his despatch pouch and produced a brass cylinder about a foot long. Very gravely he unscrewed the head and dumped out a scroll of thick yellow paper closely covered with writing on both sides. At a nod from Le Bihan he handed me the scroll. But I could make nothing of the coarse writing, now faded to a dull brown.

"Come, come, Le Bihan," I said impatiently, "translate it, won't you? You and Max Fortin make a lot of mystery out of nothing, it seems."

Le Bihan went to the edge of the pit where the three Bannalec men were digging, gave an order or two in Breton, and turned to me.

As I came to the edge of the pit the Bannalec men were removing a square piece of sailcloth from what appeared to be a pile of cobblestones.

"Look!" said Le Bihan shrilly. I looked. The pile below was a heap of skulls. After a moment I clambered down the gravel sides of the pit and walked over to the men of Bannalec. They saluted me gravely, leaning on their picks and shovels, and wiping their sweating faces with sunburned hands.

"How many?" said I in Breton.

"Thirty-eight," they replied.

I glanced around. Beyond the heap of skulls lay two piles of human bones. Beside these was a mound of broken, rusted bits of iron and steel. Looking closer, I saw that this mound was composed of rusty bayonets, sabre blades, scythe blades, with here and there a tarnished buckle attached to a bit of leather hard as iron.

I picked up a couple of buttons and a belt plate. The buttons bore the royal arms of England; the belt plate was emblazoned with the English arms, and also with the number "27."

"I have heard my grandfather speak of the terrible English regiment, the 27th Foot, which landed and stormed the fort up there," said one of the Bannalec men.

"Oh!" said I; "then these are the bones of English soldiers?"

"Yes," said the men of Bannalec.

Le Bihan was calling to me from the edge of the pit above, and I handed the belt plate and buttons to the men and climbed the side of the excavation.

"Well," said I, trying to prevent Wine from leaping up and licking my face as I emerged from the pit, "I suppose you know what these bones are. What are you going to do with them?"

"There was a man," said Le Bihan angrily, "an Englishman, who passed here in a dog-cart on his way to Quimper about an hour ago, and what do you suppose he wished to do?"

"Buy the relics?" I asked, smiling.

"Exactly—the pig!" piped the mayor of St. Gildas. "Jean Marie Tregunc, who found the bones, was standing there where Max Fortin stands, and do you know what he answered? He spat upon the ground, and said: 'Pig of an Englishman, do you take me for a desecrator of graves?'"

I knew Tregunc, a sober, blue-eyed Breton, who lived from one year's end to the other without being able to afford a single bit of meat for a meal. "How much did the Englishman offer Tregunc?" I asked.

"Two hundred francs for the skulls alone."

I thought of the relic hunters and the relic buyers on the battlefields of our civil war.

"Seventeen hundred and sixty is long ago," I said.

"Respect for the dead can never die," said Fortin.

"And the English soldiers came here to kill your fathers and burn your homes," I continued.

"They were murderers and thieves, but—they are dead," said Tregunc, coming up from the beach below, his long sea rake balanced on his dripping jersey.

"How much do you earn every year, Jean Marie?" I asked, turning to shake hands with him.

"Two hundred and twenty francs, monsieur."

"Forty-five dollars a year," I said. "Bah! you are worth more, Jean. Will you take care of my garden for me? My wife wished me to ask you. I think it would be worth one hundred francs a month to you and to me. Come on, Le Bihan—come along, Fortin—and you, Durand. I want somebody to translate that list into French for me."

Tregunc stood gazing at me, his blue eyes dilated.

"You may begin at once," I said, smiling, "If the salary suits you?"

"It suits," said Tregunc, fumbling for his pipe in a silly way that annoyed Le Bihan.

"Then go and begin your work," cried the mayor impatiently; and Tregunc started across the moors toward St. Gildas, taking off his velvet-ribboned cap to me and gripping his sea rake very hard.

"You offer him more than my salary," said the mayor, after a moment's contemplation of his silver buttons.

"Pooh!" said I, "what do you do for your salary except play dominoes with Max Fortin at the Groix Inn?"

Le Bihan turned red, but Durand rattled his sabre and winked at Max Fortin, and I slipped my arm through the arm of the sulky magistrate, laughing.

"There's a shady spot under the cliff," I said; "come on, Le Bihan, and read me what is in the scroll."

In a few moments we reached the shadow of the cliff; and I threw myself upon the turf, chin on hand, to listen.

The gendarme, Durand, also sat down, twisting his mustache into needlelike points. Fortin leaned against the cliff, polishing his glasses and examining us with vague, near-sighted eyes; and Le Bihan, the mayor, planted himself in our midst, rolling up the scroll and tucking it under his arm.

"First of all," he began in a shrill voice, "I am going to light my pipe, and while lighting it I shall tell you what I have heard about the attack on the fort yonder. My father told me; his father told him."

He jerked his head in the direction of the ruined fort, a small, square stone structure on the sea cliff, now nothing but crumbling walls. Then he slowly produced a tobacco pouch, a bit of flint and tinder, and a long-stemmed pipe fitted with a microscopical bowl of baked clay. To fill such a pipe requires ten minutes' close attention. To smoke it to a finish takes but four puffs. It is very Breton, this Breton pipe. It is the crystallization of everything Breton.

"Go on," said I, lighting a cigarette.

"The fort," said the mayor, "was built by Louis XIV, and was dismantled twice by the English. Louis XV restored it in 1739. In 1760 it was carried by assault by the English. They came across from the island of Groix—three shiploads—and they stormed the fort and sacked St. Julien yonder, and they started to burn St. Gildas—you can see the marks of their bullets on my house yet; but the men of Bannalec and the men of Lorient fell upon them with pike and scythe and blunderbuss, and those who did not run away lie there below in the gravel pit now—thirty-eight of them."

"And the thirty-ninth skull?" I asked, finishing my cigarette.

The mayor had succeeded in filling his pipe, and now he began to put his tobacco pouch away.

"The thirty-ninth skull," he mumbled, holding the pipestem between his defective teeth—"the thirty-ninth skull is no business of mine. I have told the Bannalec men to cease digging."

"But what is—whose is the missing skull?" I persisted curiously.

The mayor was busy trying to strike a spark to his tinder. Presently he set it aglow, applied it to his pipe, took the prescribed four puffs, knocked the ashes out of the bowl, and gravely replaced the pipe in his pocket.

"The missing skull?" he asked.

"Yes," said I impatiently.

The mayor slowly unrolled the scroll and began to read, translating from the Breton into French. And this is what he read:

"'ON THE CLIFFS OF ST. GILDAS,
"'*April 13, 1760.*

"'On this day, by order of the Count of Soisic, general in chief of the Breton forces now lying in Kerselec Forest, the bodies of thirty-eight English soldiers of the 27th, 50th, and 72d regiments of Foot were buried in this spot, together with their arms and equipments.'"

The mayor paused and glanced at me reflectively.

"Go on, Le Bihan," I said.

"With them," continued the mayor, turning the scroll and reading on the other side, "was buried the body of that vile traitor who betrayed the fort to the English. The manner of his death was as follows: By order of the most noble Count of Soisic, the traitor was first branded upon the forehead with the brand of an arrowhead. The iron burned through the flesh, and was pressed heavily so that the brand should even burn into the bone of the skull. The traitor was then led out and bidden to kneel. He admitted having guided the English from the island of Groix. Although a priest and a Frenchman, he had violated his priestly office to aid him in discovering the password to the fort. This password he extorted during confession from a young Breton girl who was in the habit of rowing across from the island of Groix to visit her husband in the fort. When the fort fell, this young girl, crazed by the death of her husband, sought the Count of Soisic and told how the priest had forced her to confess to him all she knew about the fort. The priest was arrested at St. Gildas as he was about to cross the river to Lorient. When arrested he cursed the girl, Marie Trevec—"

"What!" I exclaimed, "Marie Trevec!"

"Marie Trevec," repeated Le Bihan; "the priest cursed Marie Trevec, and all her family and descendants. He was shot as he knelt, having a mask of leather over his face, because the Bretons who composed the squad of execution refused to fire at a priest unless his face was concealed. The priest was l'Abbé Sorgue, commonly known as the Black Priest on account of his dark face and swarthy eyebrows. He was buried with a stake through his heart."

Le Bihan paused, hesitated, looked at me, and handed the manuscript back to Durand. The gendarme took it and slipped it into the brass cylinder.

"So," said I, "the thirty-ninth skull is the skull of the Black Priest."

"Yes," said Fortin. "I hope they won't find it."

"I have forbidden them to proceed," said the mayor querulously. "You heard me, Max Fortin."

I rose and picked up my gun. Môme came and pushed his head into my hand.

"That's a fine dog," observed Durand, also rising.

"Why don't you wish to find his skull?" I asked Le Bihan. "It would be curious to see whether the arrow brand really burned into the bone."

"There is something in that scroll that I didn't read to you," said the mayor grimly. "Do you wish to know what it is?"

"Of course," I replied in surprise.

"Give me the scroll again, Durand," he said; then he read from the bottom: "I, l'Abbé Sorgue, forced to write the above by my executioners, have written it in my own blood; and with it I leave my curse. My curse on St. Gildas, on Marie Trevec, and on her descendants. I will come back to St. Gildas when my remains are disturbed. Woe to that Englishman whom my branded skull shall touch!"

"What rot!" I said. "Do you believe it was really written in his own blood?"

"I am going to test it," said Fortin, "at the request of Monsieur le Maire. I am not anxious for the job, however."

"See," said Le Bihan, holding out the scroll to me, "it is signed, 'l'Abbé Sorgue.'"

I glanced curiously over the paper.

"It must be the Black Priest," I said. "He was the only man who wrote in the Breton language. This is a wonderfully interesting discovery, for now, at last, the mystery of the Black Priest's disappearance is cleared up. You will, of course, send this scroll to Paris, Le Bihan?"

"No," said the mayor obstinately, "it shall be buried in the pit below where the rest of the Black Priest lies."

I looked at him and recognised that argument would be useless. But still I said, "It will be a loss to history, Monsieur Le Bihan."

"All the worse for history, then," said the enlightened mayor of St. Gildas.

We had sauntered back to the gravel pit while speaking. The men of Bannalec were carrying the bones of the English soldiers toward the St. Gildas cemetery, on the cliffs to the east, where already a knot of white-coiffed women stood in attitudes of prayer; and I saw the sombre robe of a priest among the crosses of the little graveyard.

"They were thieves and assassins; they are dead now," muttered Max Fortin.

"Respect the dead," repeated the Mayor of St. Gildas, looking after the Bannalec men.

"It was written in that scroll that Marie Trevec, of Groix Island, was cursed by the priest—she and her descendants," I said, touching Le Bihan on the arm. "There was a Marie Trevec who married an Yves Trevec of St. Gildas—"

"It is the same," said Le Bihan, looking at me obliquely.

"Oh!" said I; "then they were ancestors of my wife."

"Do you fear the curse?" asked Le Bihan.

"What?" I laughed.

"There was the case of the Purple Emperor," said Max Fortin timidly.

Startled for a moment, I faced him, then shrugged my shoulders and kicked at a smooth bit of rock which lay near the edge of the pit, almost embedded in gravel.

"Do you suppose the Purple Emperor drank himself crazy because he was descended from Marie Trevec?" I asked contemptuously.

"Of course not," said Max Fortin hastily.

"Of course not," piped the mayor. "I only— Hello! What's that you're kicking?"

"What?" said I, glancing down, at the same time involuntarily giving another kick. The smooth bit of rock dislodged itself and rolled out of the loosened gravel at my feet.

"The thirty-ninth skull!" I exclaimed. "By jingo, it's the noddle of the Black Priest! See! there is the arrowhead branded on the front!"

The mayor stepped back. Max Fortin also retreated. There was a pause, during which I looked at them, and they looked anywhere but at me.

"I don't like it," said the mayor at last, in a husky, high voice. "I don't like it! The scroll says he will come back to St. Gildas when his remains are disturbed. I—I don't like it, Monsieur Darrel—"

"Bosh!" said I; "the poor wicked devil is where he can't get out. For Heaven's sake, Le Bihan, what is this stuff you are talking in the year of grace 1896?"

The mayor gave me a look.

"And he says 'Englishman.' You are an Englishman, Monsieur Darrel," he announced.

"You know better. You know I'm an American."

"It's all the same," said the Mayor of St. Gildas, obstinately.

"No, it isn't!" I answered, much exasperated, and deliberately pushed the skull till it rolled into the bottom of the gravel pit below.

"Cover it up," said I; "bury the scroll with it too, if you insist, but I think you ought to send it to Paris. Don't look so gloomy, Fortin, unless you believe in were-wolves and ghosts. Hey! what the—what the devil's the matter with you, anyway? What are you staring at, Le Bihan?"

"Come, come," muttered the mayor in a low, tremulous voice, "it's time we got out of this. Did you see? Did you see, Fortin?"

"I saw," whispered Max Fortin, pallid with fright.

The two men were almost running across the sunny pasture now, and I hastened after them, demanding to know what was the matter.

"Matter!" chattered the mayor, gasping with exasperation and terror. "The skull is rolling uphill again!" and he burst into a terrified gallop. Max Fortin followed close behind.

I watched them stampeding across the pasture, then turned toward the gravel pit, mystified, incredulous. The skull was lying on the edge of the pit, exactly where it had been before I pushed it over the edge. For a second I stared at it; a singular chilly feeling crept up my spinal column, and I turned and walked away, sweat starting from the root of every hair on my head. Before I had gone twenty paces the absurdity of the whole thing struck me. I halted, hot with shame and annoyance, and retraced my steps.

There lay the skull.

"I rolled a stone down instead of the skull," I muttered to myself. Then with the butt of my gun I pushed the skull over the edge of the pit and watched it roll to the bottom; and as it struck the bottom of the pit,

Môme, my dog, suddenly whipped his tail between his legs, whimpered, and made off across the moor.

"Môme!" I shouted, angry and astonished; but the dog only fled the faster, and I ceased calling from sheer surprise.

"What the mischief is the matter with that dog!" I thought. He had never before played me such a trick.

Mechanically I glanced into the pit, but I could not see the skull. I looked down. The skull lay at my feet again, touching them.

"Good heavens!" I stammered, and struck at it blindly with my gun-stock. The ghastly thing flew into the air, whirling over and over, and rolled again down the sides of the pit to the bottom. Breathlessly I stared at it, then, confused and scarcely comprehending, I stepped back from the pit, still facing it, one, ten, twenty paces, my eyes almost starting from my head, as though I expected to see the thing roll up from the bottom of the pit under my very gaze. At last I turned my back to the pit and strode out across the gorse-covered moorland toward my home. As I reached the road that winds from St. Gildas to St. Julien I gave one last hasty glance at the pit over my shoulder. The sun shone hot on the sod about the excavation. There was something white and bare and round on the turf at the edge of the pit. It might have been a stone; there were plenty of them lying about.

II

When I entered my garden I saw Môme sprawling on the stone door-step. He eyed me sideways and flopped his tail.

"Are you not mortified, you idiot dog?" I said, looking about the upper windows for Lys.

Môme rolled over on his back and raised one deprecating forepaw, as though to ward off calamity.

"Don't act as though I was in the habit of beating you to death," I said, disgusted. I had never in my life raised whip to the brute. "But you are a fool dog," I continued. "No, you needn't come to be babied and wept over; Lys can do that, if she insists, but I am ashamed of you, and you can go the devil."

Môme slunk off into the house, and I followed, mounting directly to my wife's boudoir. It was empty.

"Where has she gone?" I said, looking hard at Môme, who had followed me. "Oh! I see you don't know. Don't pretend you do. Come off that lounge! Do you think Lys wants tan-coloured hairs all over her lounge?"

I rang the bell for Catherine and 'Fine, but they didn't know where "madame" had gone; so I went into my room, bathed, exchanged my somewhat grimy shooting clothes for a suit of warm, soft knickerbockers, and, after lingering some extra moments over my toilet—for I was particular, now that I had married Lys—I went down to the garden and took a chair out under the fig-trees.

"Where can she be?" I wondered. Môme came sneaking out to be comforted, and I forgave him for Lys's sake, whereupon he frisked.

"You bounding cur," said I, "now what on earth started you off across the moor? If you do it again I'll push you along with a charge of dust shot."

As yet I had scarcely dared think about the ghastly hallucination of which I had been a victim, but now I faced it squarely, flushing a little with mortification at the thought of my hasty retreat from the gravel pit.

"To think," I said aloud, "that those old woman's tales of Max Fortin and Le Bihan should have actually made me see what didn't exist at all! I lost my nerve like a schoolboy in a dark bedroom." For I knew now that I had mistaken a round stone for a skull each time, and had pushed a couple of big pebbles into the pit instead of the skull itself.

"By jingo!" said I, "I'm nervous; my liver must be in a devil of a condition if I see such things when I'm awake! Lys will know what to give me."

I felt mortified and irritated and sulky, and thought disgustedly of Le Bihan and Max Fortin.

But after a while I ceased speculating, dismissed the mayor, the chemist, and the skull from my mind, and smoked pensively, watching the sun low dipping in the western ocean. As the twilight fell for a moment over ocean and moorland, a wistful, restless happiness filled my heart, the happiness that all men know—all men who have loved.

Slowly the purple mist crept out over the sea; the cliffs darkened; the forest was shrouded.

Suddenly the sky above burned with the afterglow, and the world was alight again.

Cloud after cloud caught the rose dye; the cliffs were tinted with it; moor and pasture, heather and forest burned and pulsated with the gentle flush. I saw the gulls turning and tossing above the sand bar, their snowy wings tipped with pink; I saw the sea swallows sheering the surface of the still river, stained to its placid depths with warm reflections of the clouds. The twitter of drowsy hedge birds broke out in the stillness; a salmon rolled its shining side above tide-water.

The interminable monotone of the ocean intensified the silence. I sat motionless, holding my breath as one who listens to the first low rumour of an organ. All at once the pure whistle of a nightingale cut the silence, and the first moonbeam silvered the wastes of mist-hung waters.

I raised my head.

Lys stood before me in the garden.

When we had kissed each other, we linked arms and moved up and down the gravel walks, watching the moonbeams sparkle on the sand bar as the tide ebbed and ebbed. The broad beds of white pinks about us were atremble with hovering white moths; the October roses hung all abloom, perfuming the salt wind.

"Sweetheart," I said, "where is Yvonne? Has she promised to spend Christmas with us?"

"Yes, Dick; she drove me down from Plougat this afternoon. She sent her love to you. I am not jealous. What did you shoot?"

"A hare and four partridges. They are in the gun room. I told Catherine not to touch them until you had seen them."

Now I suppose I knew that Lys could not be particularly enthusiastic over game or guns; but she pretended she was, and always scornfully denied that it was for my sake and not for the pure love of sport. So she dragged me off to inspect the rather meagre game bag, and she paid me pretty compliments and gave a little cry of delight and pity as I lifted the enormous hare out of the sack by his ears.

"He'll eat no more of our lettuce," I said, attempting to justify the assassination.

"Unhappy little bunny—and what a beauty! O Dick, you are a splendid shot, are you not?"

I evaded the question and hauled out a partridge.

"Poor little dead things!" said Lys in a whisper; "it seems a pity—doesn't it, Dick? But then you are so clever—"

"We'll have them broiled," I said guardedly; "tell Catherine."

Catherine came in to take away the game, and presently 'Fine Lelocard, Lys's maid, announced dinner, and Lys tripped away to her boudoir.

I stood an instant contemplating her blissfully, thinking, "My boy, you're the happiest fellow in the world—you're in love with your wife!"

I walked into the dining room, beamed at the plates, walked out again; met Tregunc in the hallway, beamed on him; glanced into the kitchen, beamed at Catherine, and went up stairs, still beaming.

Before I could knock at Lys's door it opened, and Lys came hastily out. When she saw me she gave a little cry of relief, and nestled close to my breast.

"There is something peering in at my window," she said.

"What!" I cried angrily.

"A man, I think, disguised as a priest, and he has a mask on. He must have climbed up by the bay tree."

I was down the stairs and out of doors in no time. The moonlit garden was absolutely deserted. Tregunc came up, and together we searched the hedge and shrubbery around the house and out to the road.

"Jean Marie," said I at length, "loose my bulldog—he knows you—and take your supper on the porch where you can watch. My wife says the fellow is disguised as a priest, and wears a mask."

Tregunc showed his white teeth in a smile. "He will not care to venture in here again, I think, Monsieur Darrel."

I went back and found Lys seated quietly at the table.

"The soup is ready, dear," she said. "Don't worry; it was only some foolish lout from Bannalec. No one in St. Gildas or St. Julien would do such a thing."

I was too much exasperated to reply at first, but Lys treated it as a stupid joke, and after a while I began to look at it in that light.

Lys told me about Yvonne, and reminded me of my promise to have Herbert Stuart down to meet her.

"You wicked diplomat!" I protested. "Herbert is in Paris, and hard at work for the Salon."

"Don't you think he might spare a week to flirt with the prettiest girl in Finistère?" inquired Lys innocently.

"Prettiest girl! Not much!" I said.

"Who is, then?" urged Lys.

I laughed a trifle sheepishly.

"I suppose you mean me, Dick," said Lys, colouring up.

"Now I bore you, don't I?"

"Bore me? Ah, no, Dick."

After coffee and cigarettes were served I spoke about Tregunc, and Lys approved.

"Poor Jean! he will be glad, won't he? What a dear fellow you are!"

"Nonsense," said I; "we need a gardener; you said so yourself, Lys."

But Lys leaned over and kissed me, and then bent down and hugged Môme, who whistled through his nose in sentimental appreciation.

"I am a very happy woman," said Lys.

"Môme was a very bad dog to-day," I observed.

"Poor Môme!" said Lys, smiling.

When dinner was over and Môme lay snoring before the blaze—for the October nights are often chilly in Finistère—Lys curled up in the chimney corner with her embroidery, and gave me a swift glance from under her drooping lashes.

"You look like a schoolgirl, Lys," I said teasingly. "I don't believe you are sixteen yet."

She pushed back her heavy burnished hair thoughtfully. Her wrist was as white as surf foam.

"Have we been married four years? I don't believe it," I said.

She gave me another swift glance and touched the embroidery on her knee, smiling faintly.

"I see," said I, also smiling at the embroidered garment. "Do you think it will fit?"

"Fit?" repeated Lys. Then she laughed.

"And," I persisted, "are you perfectly sure that you—er—we shall need it?"

"Perfectly," said Lys. A delicate colour touched her cheeks and neck. She held up the little garment, all fluffy with misty lace and wrought with quaint embroidery.

"It is very gorgeous," said I; "don't use your eyes too much, dearest. May I smoke a pipe?"

"Of course," she said, selecting a skein of pale blue silk.

For a while I sat and smoked in silence, watching her slender fingers among the tinted silks and thread of gold.

Presently she spoke: "What did you say your crest is, Dick?"

"My crest? Oh, something or other rampant on a something or other—"

"Dick!"

"Dearest?"

"Don't be flippant."

"But I really forget. It's an ordinary crest; everybody in New York has them. No family should be without 'em."

"You are disagreeable, Dick. Send Josephine upstairs for my album."

"Are you going to put that crest on the—the—whatever it is?"

"I am; and my own crest, too."

I thought of the Purple Emperor and wondered a little.

"You didn't know I had one, did you?" she smiled.

"What is it?" I replied evasively.

"You shall see. Ring for Josephine."

I rang, and, when 'Fine appeared, Lys gave her some orders in a low voice, and Josephine trotted away, bobbing her white-coiffed head with a "Bien, madame!"

After a few minutes she returned, bearing a tattered, musty volume, from which the gold and blue had mostly disappeared.

I took the book in my hands and examined the ancient emblazoned covers.

"Lilies!" I exclaimed.

"Fleur-de-lis," said my wife demurely.

"Oh!" said I, astonished, and opened the book.

"You have never before seen this book?" asked Lys, with a touch of malice in her eyes.

"You know I haven't. Hello! What's this? Oho! So there should be a *de* before Trevec? Lys de Trevec? Then why in the world did the Purple Emperor—"

"Dick!" cried Lys.

"All right," said I. "Shall I read about the Sieur de Trevec who rode to Saladin's tent alone to seek for medicine for St. Louis? or shall I read about—what is it? Oh, here it is, all down in black and white—about the Marquis de Trevec who drowned himself before Alva's eyes rather than surrender the banner of the fleur-de-lis to Spain? It's all written here. But, dear, how about that soldier named Trevec who was killed in the old fort on the cliff yonder?"

"He dropped the *de,* and the Trevecs since then have been Republicans," said Lys—"all except me."

"That's quite right," said I; "it is time that we Republicans should agree upon some feudal system. My dear, I drink to the king!" and I raised my wine-glass and looked at Lys.

"To the king," said Lys, flushing. She smoothed out the tiny garment on her knees; she touched the glass with her lips; her eyes were very sweet. I drained the glass to the king.

After a silence I said: "I will tell the king stories. His Majesty shall be amused."

"His Majesty," repeated Lys softly.

"Or hers," I laughed. "Who knows?"

"Who knows?" murmured Lys, with a gentle sigh.

"I know some stores about Jack the Giant-Killer," I announced. "Do you, Lys?"

"I? No, not about a giant-killer, but I know all about the were-wolf, and Jeanne-la-Flamme, and the Man in Purple Tatters, and—O dear me! I know lots more."

"You are very wise," said I. "I shall teach his Majesty English."

"And I Breton," cried Lys jealously.

"I shall bring playthings to the king," said I—"big green lizards from the gorse, little gray mullets to swim in glass globes, baby rabbits from the forest of Kerselec—"

"And I," said Lys, "will bring the first primrose, the first branch of aubepine, the first jonquil, to the king—my king."

"Our king," said I; and there was peace in Finistère.

I lay back, idly turning the leaves of the curious old volume.

"I am looking," said I, "for the crest."

"The crest, dear? It is a priest's head with an arrow-shaped mark on the forehead, on a field—"

I sat up and stared at my wife.

"Dick, whatever is the matter?" she smiled. "The story is there in that book. Do you care to read it? No? Shall I tell it to you? Well, then: It happened in the third crusade. There was a monk whom men called the Black Priest. He turned apostate, and sold himself to the enemies of Christ. A Sieur de Trevec burst into the Saracen camp, at the head of only one hundred lances, and carried the Black Priest away out of the very midst of their army."

"So that is how you come by the crest," I said quietly; but I thought of the branded skull in the gravel pit, and wondered.

"Yes," said Lys. "The Sieur de Trevec cut the Black Priest's head off, but first he branded him with an arrow mark on the forehead. The book says it was a pious action, and that the Sieur de Trevec got great merit by it. But I think it was cruel, the branding," she sighed.

"Did you ever hear of any other Black Priest?"

"Yes. There was one in the last century, here in St. Gildas. He cast a white shadow in the sun. He wrote in the Breton language. Chronicles, too, I believe. I never saw them. His name was the same as that of the old chronicler, and of the other priest, Jacques Sorgue. Some said he was a lineal descendant of the traitor. Of course the first Black Priest was bad enough for anything. But if he did have a child, it need not have been the ancestor of the last Jacques Sorgue. They say this one was a holy man. They say he was so good he was not allowed to die, but was caught up to heaven one day," added Lys, with believing eyes.

I smiled.

"But he disappeared," persisted Lys.

"I'm afraid his journey was in another direction," I said jestingly, and thoughtlessly told her the story of the morning. I had utterly forgotten the masked man at her window, but before I finished I remembered him fast enough, and realized what I had done as I saw her face whiten.

"Lys," I urged tenderly, "that was only some clumsy clown's trick. You said so yourself. You are not superstitious, my dear?"

Her eyes were on mine. She slowly drew the little gold cross from her bosom and kissed it. But her lips trembled as they pressed the symbol of faith.

III

About nine o'clock the next morning I walked into the Groix Inn and sat down at the long discoloured oaken table, nodding good-day to Marianne Bruyère, who in turn bobbed her white coiffe at me.

"My clever Bannalec maid," said I, "what is good for a stirrup-cup at the Groix Inn?"

"Schist?" she inquired in Breton.

"With a dash of red wine, then," I replied.

She brought the delicious Quimperlé cider, and I poured a little Bordeaux into it. Marianne watched me with laughing black eyes.

"What makes your cheeks so red, Marianne?" I asked. "Has Jean Marie been here?"

"We are to be married, Monsieur Darrel," she laughed.

"Ah! Since when has Jean Marie Tregunc lost his head?"

"His head? Oh, Monsieur Darrel—his heart, you mean!"

"So I do," said I. "Jean Marie is a practical fellow."

"It is all due to your kindness—" began the girl, but I raised my hand and held up the glass.

"It's due to himself. To your happiness, Marianne," and I took a hearty draught of the schist. "Now," said I, "tell me where I can find Le Bihan and Max Fortin."

"Monsieur Le Bihan and Monsieur Fortin are above in the broad room. I believe they are examining the Red Admiral's effects."

"To send them to Paris? Oh, I know. May I go up, Marianne?"

"And God go with you," smiled the girl.

When I knocked at the door of the broad room above little Max Fortin opened it. Dust covered his spectacles and nose; his hat, with the tiny velvet ribbons fluttering, was all awry.

"Come in, Monsieur Darrel," he said; "the mayor and I are packing up the effects of the Purple Emperor and of the poor Red Admiral."

"The collections?" I asked, entering the room. "You must be very careful in packing those butterfly cases; the slightest jar might break wings and antennae, you know."

Le Bihan shook hands with me and pointed to the great pile of boxes.

"They're all cork lined," he said, "but Fortin and I are putting felt around each box. The Entomological Society of Paris pays the freight."

The combined collections of the Red Admiral and the Purple Emperor made a magnificent display.

I lifted and inspected case after case set with gorgeous butterflies and moths, each specimen carefully labelled with the name in Latin. There were cases filled with crimson tiger moths all aflame with colour; cases devoted to the common yellow butterflies; symphonies in orange and pale yellow; cases of soft gray and dun-coloured sphinx moths; and cases of garish nettle-bred butterflies of the numerous family of *Vanessa.*

All alone in a great case by itself was pinned the purple emperor, the *Apatura Iris,* that fatal specimen that had given the Purple Emperor his name and quietus.

I remembered the butterfly, and stood looking at it with bent eyebrows. Le Bihan glanced up from the floor where he was nailing down the lid of a box full of cases.

"It is settled, then," said he, "that madame, your wife, gives the Purple Emperor's entire collection to the city of Paris?"

I nodded.

"Without accepting anything for it?"

"It is a gift," I said.

"Including the purple emperor there in the case? That butterfly is worth a great deal of money," persisted Le Bihan.

"You don't suppose that we would wish to sell that specimen, do you?" I answered a trifle sharply.

"If I were you I should destroy it," said the mayor in his high-pitched voice.

"That would be nonsense," said I—"like your burying the brass cylinder and scroll yesterday."

"It was not nonsense," said Le Bihan doggedly, "and I should prefer not to discuss the subject of the scroll."

I looked at Max Fortin, who immediately avoided my eyes.

"You are a pair of superstitious old women," said I, digging my hands into my pockets; "you swallow every nursery tale that is invented."

"What of it?" said Le Bihan sulkily; "there's more truth than lies in most of 'em."

"Oh!" I sneered, "does the Mayor of St. Gildas and St. Julien believe in the Loup-garou?"

"No, not in the Loup-garou."

"In what, then—Jeanne-la-Flamme?"

"That," said Le Bihan with conviction, "is history."

"The devil it is!" said I; "and perhaps, monsieur the mayor, your faith in giants is unimpaired?"

"There were giants—everybody knows it," growled Max Fortin. "And you a chemist!" I observed scornfully.

"Listen, Monsieur Darrel," squeaked Le Bihan; "you know yourself that the Purple Emperor was a scientific man. Now suppose I should tell you that he always refused to include in his collection a Death's Messenger?"

"A what?" I exclaimed.

"You know what I mean—that moth that flies by night; some call it the Death's Head, but in St. Gildas we call it 'Death's Messenger.'"

"Oh!" said I, "you mean that big sphinx moth that is commonly known as the 'death's-head moth.' Why the mischief should the people here call it death's messenger?"

"For hundreds of years it has been known as death's messenger in St. Gildas," said Max Fortin. "Even Froissart speaks of it in his commentaries on Jacques Sorgue's Chronicles. The book is in your library."

"Sorgue? And who was Jacques Sorgue? I never read his book."

"Jacques Sorgue was the son of some unfrocked priest—I forget. It was during the crusades."

"Good Heavens!" I burst out, "I've been hearing of nothing but crusades and priests and death and sorcery ever since I kicked that skull into the gravel pit, and I am tired of it, I tell you frankly. One would think we lived in the dark ages. Do you know what year of our Lord it is, Le Bihan?"

"Eighteen hundred and ninety-six," replied the mayor.

"And yet you two hulking men are afraid of a death's-head moth."

"I don't care to have one fly into the window," said Max Fortin; "it means evil to the house and the people in it."

"God alone knows why he marked one of his creatures with a yellow death's head on the back," observed Le Bihan piously, "but I take it that he meant it as a warning; and I propose to profit by it," he added triumphantly.

"See here, Le Bihan," I said; "by a stretch of imagination one can make out a skull on the thorax of a certain big sphinx moth. What of it?"

"It is a bad thing to touch," said the mayor, wagging his head.

"It squeaks when handled," added Max Fortin.

"Some creatures squeak all the time," I observed, looking hard at Le Bihan.

"Pigs," added the mayor.

"Yes, and asses," I replied. "Listen, Le Bihan: do you mean to tell me that you saw that skull roll uphill yesterday?"

The mayor shut his mouth tightly and picked up his hammer.

"Don't be obstinate," I said; "I asked you a question."

"And I refuse to answer," snapped Le Bihan. "Fortin saw what I saw; let him talk about it."

I looked searchingly at the little chemist.

"I don't say that I saw it actually roll up out of the pit, all by itself," said Fortin with a shiver, "but—but then, how did it come up out of the pit, if it didn't roll up all by itself?"

"It didn't come up at all; that was a yellow cobblestone that you mistook for the skull again," I replied. "You were nervous, Max."

"A—a very curious cobblestone, Monsieur Darrel," said Fortin.

"I also was a victim to the same hallucination," I continued, "and I regret to say that I took the trouble to roll two innocent cobblestones into the gravel pit, imagining each time that it was the skull I was rolling."

"It was," observed Le Bihan with a morose shrug.

"It just shows," said I, ignoring the mayor's remark, "how easy it is to fix up a train of coincidences so that the result seems to savour of the supernatural. Now, last night my wife imagined that she saw a priest in a mask peer in at her window—"

Fortin and Le Bihan scrambled hastily from their knees, dropping hammer and nails.

"W-h-a-t—what's that?" demanded the mayor.

I repeated what I had said. Max Fortin turned livid.

"My God!" muttered Le Bihan, "the Black Priest is in St. Gildas!"

"D-don't you—you know the old prophecy?" stammered Fortin; "Froissart quotes it from Jacques Sorgue:

> 'When the Black Priest rises from the dead,
> St. Gildas folk shall shriek in bed;
> When the Black Priest rises from his grave,
> May the good God St. Gildas save!'"

"Aristide Le Bihan," I said angrily, "and you, Max Fortin, I've got enough of this nonsense! Some foolish lout from Bannalec has been in St. Gildas playing tricks to frighten old fools like you. If you have nothing better to talk about than nursery legends I'll wait until you come to your senses. Good-morning." And I walked out, more disturbed than I cared to acknowledge to myself.

The day had become misty and overcast. Heavy, wet clouds hung in the east. I heard the surf thundering against the cliffs, and the gray gulls squealed as they tossed and turned high in the sky. The tide was creeping across the river sands, higher, higher, and I saw the seaweed floating on the beach, and the *lançons* springing from the foam, silvery thread-like flashes in the gloom. Curlew were flying up the river in twos and threes; the timid sea swallows skimmed across the moors toward some quiet, lonely pool, safe from the coming tempest. In every hedge field birds were gathering, huddling together, twittering restlessly.

When I reached the cliffs I sat down, resting my chin on my clenched hands. Already a vast curtain of rain, sweeping across the ocean miles away, hid the island of Groix. To the east, behind the white semaphore on the hills, black clouds crowded up over the horizon. After a little the thunder boomed, dull, distant, and slender skeins of lightning unravelled across the crest of the coming storm. Under the cliff at my feet the surf rushed foaming over the shore, and the *lançons* jumped and skipped and quivered until they seemed to be but the reflections of the meshed lightning.

I turned to the east. It was raining over Groix, it was raining at Sainte Barbe, it was raining now at the semaphore. High in the storm whirl a few gulls pitched; a nearer cloud trailed veils of rain in its wake; the sky was spattered with lightning; the thunder boomed.

As I rose to go, a cold raindrop fell upon the back of my hand, and another, and yet another on my face. I gave a last glance at the sea, where the waves were bursting into strange white shapes that seemed to fling out menacing arms toward me. Then something moved on the cliff, something black as the black rock it clutched—a filthy cormorant, craning its hideous head at the sky.

Slowly I plodded homeward across the sombre moorland, where the gorse stems glimmered with a dull metallic green, and the heather, no longer, violet and purple, hung drenched and dun-coloured among the dreary rocks. The wet turf creaked under my heavy boots, the black-thorn scraped and grated against knee and elbow. Over all lay a strange light, pallid, ghastly, where the sea spray whirled across the landscape and drove into my face until it grew numb with the cold. In broad bands, rank after rank, billow on billow, the rain burst out across the endless moors, and yet there was no wind to drive it at such a pace.

Lys stood at the door as I turned into the garden, motioning me to hasten; and then for the first time I became conscious that I was soaked to the skin.

"How ever in the world did you come to stay out when such a storm threatened?" she said. "Oh, you are dripping! Go quickly and change; I have laid your warm underwear on the bed, Dick."

I kissed my wife, and went upstairs to change my dripping clothes for something more comfortable.

When I returned to the morning room there was a driftwood fire on the hearth, and Lys sat in the chimney corner embroidering.

"Catherine tells me that the fishing fleet from Lorient is out. Do you think they are in danger, dear?" asked Lys, raising her blue eyes to mine as I entered.

"There is no wind, and there will be no sea," said I, looking out of the window. Far across the moor I could see the black cliffs looming in the mist.

"How it rains!" murmured Lys; "come to the fire, Dick."

I threw myself on the fur rug, my hands in my pockets, my head on Lys's knees.

"Tell me a story," I said. "I feel like a boy of ten."

Lys raised a finger to her scarlet lips. I always waited for her to do that.

"Will you be very still, then?" she said.

"Still as death."

"Death," echoed a voice, very softly.

"Did you speak, Lys?" I asked, turning so that I could see her face.

"No; did you, Dick?"

"Who said 'death'?" I asked, startled.

"Death," echoed a voice, softly.

I sprang up and looked about. Lys rose too, her needles and embroidery falling to the floor. She seemed about to faint, leaning heavily on me, and I led her to the window and opened it a little way to give her air. As I did so the chain lightning split the zenith, the thunder crashed, and a sheet of rain swept into the room, driving with it something that fluttered—something that flapped, and squeaked, and beat upon the rug with soft, moist wings.

We bent over it together, Lys clinging to me, and we saw that it was a death's-head moth drenched with rain.

The dark day passed slowly as we sat beside the fire, hand in hand, her head against my breast, speaking of sorrow and mystery and death. For Lys believed that there were things on earth that none might understand, things that must be nameless forever and ever, until God rolls up the scroll of life and all is ended. We spoke of hope and fear and faith, and the mystery of the saints; we spoke of the beginning and the end, of the shadow of sin, of omens, and of love. The moth still lay on the floor, quivering its sombre wings in the warmth of the fire, the skull and ribs clearly etched upon its neck and body.

"If it is a messenger of death to this house," I said, "why should we fear, Lys?"

"Death should be welcome to those who love God," murmured Lys, and she drew the cross from her breast and kissed it.

"The moth might die if I threw it out into the storm," I said after a silence.

"Let it remain," sighed Lys.

Late that night my wife lay sleeping, and I sat beside her bed and read in the Chronicle of Jacques Sorgue. I shaded the candle, but Lys grew restless, and finally I took the book down into the morning room, where the ashes of the fire rustled and whitened on the hearth.

The death's-head moth lay on the rug before the fire where I had left it. At first I thought it was dead, but, when I looked closer I saw a lambent fire in its amber eyes. The straight white shadow it cast across the floor wavered as the candle flickered.

The pages of the Chronicle of Jacques Sorgue were damp and sticky; the illuminated gold and blue initials left flakes of azure and gilt where my hand brushed them.

"It is not paper at all; it is thin parchment," I said to myself; and I held the discoloured page close to the candle flame and read, translating laboriously:

> "I, Jacques Sorgue, saw all these things. And I saw the Black Mass celebrated in the chapel of St. Gildas-on-the-Cliff. And it was said by the Abbé Sorgue, my kinsman: for which deadly sin the apostate priest was seized by the most noble Marquis of Plougastel and by him condemned to be burned with hot irons, until his seared soul quit its body and fly to its master the devil. But when the Black Priest lay in the crypt of Plougastel, his master Satan came at night and set him free, and carried him across land and sea to Mahmoud, which is Soldan or Saladin. And I, Jacques Sorgue, travelling afterward by sea, beheld with my own eyes my kinsman, the Black Priest of St. Gildas, borne along in the air upon a vast black wing, which was the wing of his master Satan. And this was seen also by two men of the crew."

I turned the page. The wings of the moth on the floor began to quiver. I read on and on, my eyes blurring under the shifting candle flame. I read of battles and of saints, and I learned how the great Soldan made his pact with Satan, and then I came to the Sieur de Trevec, and read how he seized the Black Priest in the midst of Saladin's tents and carried him away and cut off his head, first branding him on the forehead. "And before he suffered," said the Chronicle, "he cursed the Sieur de Trevec and his descendants, and he said he would surely return to St. Gildas. 'For the violence you do to me, I will do violence to you. For the evil I suffer at your hands, I will work evil on you and your descendants. Woe to your children, Sieur de Trevec!'" There was a whirr, a beating of strong wings, and my candle flashed up as in a sudden breeze. A humming filled the room; the great moth darted hither and thither, beating, buzzing, on ceiling and wall. I flung down my book and stepped forward. Now it lay fluttering upon the window sill, and for a moment I had it under my hand, but the thing squeaked and I shrank back. Then suddenly it darted across the candle flame; the light flared and went out, and at the same moment a shadow moved in the darkness outside. I raised my eyes to the window. A masked face was peering in at me.

Quick as thought I whipped out my revolver and fired every cartridge, but the face advanced beyond the window, the glass melting away before it like mist, and through the smoke of my revolver I saw something creep swiftly into the room. Then I tried to cry out, but the thing was at my throat, and I fell backward among the ashes of the hearth.

When my eyes unclosed I was lying on the hearth, my head among the cold ashes. Slowly I got on my knees, rose painfully, and groped my way to a chair. On the floor lay my revolver, shining in the pale light of early morning. My mind clearing by degrees, I looked, shuddering, at the window. The glass was unbroken. I stooped stiffly, picked up my revolver and opened the cylinder. Every cartridge had been fired. Mechanically I closed the cylinder and placed the revolver in my pocket. The book, the Chronicles of Jacques Sorgue, lay on the table beside me, and as I started to close it I glanced at the page. It was all splashed with rain, and the lettering had run, so that the page was merely a confused blur of gold and red and black. As I stumbled toward the door I cast a fearful glance over my shoulder. The death's-head moth crawled shivering on the rug.

IV

The sun was about three hours high. I must have slept, for I was aroused by the sudden gallop of horses under our window. People were shouting and calling in the road. I sprang up and opened the sash. Le Bihan was there, an image of helplessness, and Max Fortin stood beside him, polishing his glasses. Some gendarmes had just arrived from Quimperlé, and I could hear them around the corner of the house, stamping, and rattling their sabres and carbines, as they led their horses into my stable.

Lys sat up, murmuring half-sleepy, half-anxious questions.

"I don't know," I answered. "I am going out to see what it means."

"It is like the day they came to arrest you," Lys said, giving me a troubled look. But I kissed her, and laughed at her until she smiled too. Then I flung on coat and cap and hurried down the stairs.

The first person I saw standing in the road was the Brigadier Durand.

"Hello!" said I, "have you come to arrest me again? What the devil is all this fuss about, anyway?"

"We were telegraphed for an hour ago," said Durand briskly, "and for a sufficient reason, I think. Look there, Monsieur Darrel!"

He pointed to the ground almost under my feet.

"Good heavens!" I cried, "where did that puddle of blood come from?"

"That's what I want to know, Monsieur Darrel. Max Fortin found it at daybreak. See, it's splashed all over the grass, too. A trail of it leads into your garden, across the flower beds to your very window, the one that opens from the morning room. There is another trail leading from this spot across the road to the cliffs, then to the gravel pit, and thence across the moor to the forest of Kerselec. We are going to mount in a minute and search the bosquets. Will you join us? Bon Dieu! but the fellow bled like an ox. Max Fortin says it's human blood, or I should not have believed it."

The little chemist of Quimperlé came up at that moment, rubbing his glasses with a coloured handkerchief.

"Yes, it is human blood," he said, "but one thing puzzles me: the corpuscles are yellow. I never saw any human blood before with yellow corpuscles. But your English Doctor Thompson asserts that he has—"

"Well, it's human blood, anyway—isn't it?" insisted Durand, impatiently.

"Ye-es," admitted Max Fortin.

"Then it's my business to trail it," said the big gendarme, and he called his men and gave the order to mount.

"Did you hear anything last night?" asked Durand of me.

"I heard the rain. I wonder the rain did not wash away these traces."

"They must have come after the rain ceased. See this thick splash, how it lies over and weighs down the wet grass blades. Pah!"

It was a heavy, evil-looking clot, and I stepped back from it, my throat closing in disgust.

"My theory," said the brigadier, "is this: Some of those Biribi fishermen, probably the Icelanders, got an extra glass of cognac into their hides and quarrelled on the road. Some of them were slashed, and staggered to your house. But there is only one trail, and yet—and yet, how could all that blood come from only one person? Well, the wounded man, let us say, staggered first to your house and then back here, and he wandered off, drunk and dying, God knows where. That's my theory."

"A very good one," said I calmly. And you are going to trail him?"

"Yes."

"When?"

"At once. Will you come?"

"Not now. I'll gallop over by-and-by. You are going to the edge of the Kerselec forest?"

"Yes; you will hear us calling. Are you coming, Max Fortin? And you, Le Bihan? Good; take the dog-cart."

The big gendarme tramped around the corner to the stable and presently returned mounted on a strong gray horse; his sabre shone on his saddle; his pale yellow and white facings were spotless. The little crowd of white-coiffed women with their children fell back, as Durand touched spurs and clattered away followed by his two troopers. Soon after Le Bihan and Max Fortin also departed in the mayor's dingy dog-cart.

"Are you coming?" piped Le Bihan shrilly.

"In a quarter of an hour," I replied, and went back to the house.

When I opened the door of the morning room the death's-head moth was beating its strong wings against the window. For a second I hesitated, then walked over and opened the sash. The creature fluttered out, whirred over the flower beds a moment, then darted across the moorland toward the sea. I called the servants together and questioned them. Josephine, Catherine, Jean Marie Tregunc, not one of them had heard the slightest disturbance during the night. Then I told Jean Marie to saddle my horse, and while I was speaking Lys came down.

"Dearest," I began, going to her.

"You must tell me everything you know, Dick," she interrupted, looking me earnestly in the face.

"But there is nothing to tell—only a drunken brawl, and some one wounded."

"And you are going to ride—where, Dick?"

"Well, over to the edge of Kerselec forest. Durand and the mayor, and Max Fortin, have gone on, following a—a trail."

"What trail?"

"Some blood."

"Where did they find it?"

"Out in the road there." Lys crossed herself.

"Does it come near our house?"

"Yes."

"How near?"

"It comes up to the morning-room window," said I, giving in.

Her hand on my arm grew heavy. "I dreamed last night—"

"So did I—" but I thought of the empty cartridges in my revolver, and stopped.

"I dreamed that you were in great danger, and I could not move hand or foot to save you; but you had your revolver, and I called out to you to fire—"

"I did fire!" I cried excitedly.

"You—you fired?"

I took her in my arms. "My darling," I said, "something strange has happened—something that I cannot understand as yet. But, of course, there is an explanation. Last night I thought I fired at the Black Priest."

"Ah!" gasped Lys.

"Is that what you dreamed?"

"Yes, yes, that was it! I begged you to fire—"

"And I did."

Her heart was beating against my breast. I held her close in silence.

"Dick," she said at length, "perhaps you killed the—the thing."

"If it was human I did not miss," I answered grimly. "And it was human," I went on, pulling myself together, ashamed of having so nearly gone to pieces. "Of course it was human! The whole affair is plain enough. Not a drunken brawl, as Durand thinks; it was a drunken lout's practical joke, for which he has suffered. I suppose I must have filled him pretty full of bullets, and he has crawled away to die in Kerselec forest. It's a terrible affair; I'm sorry I fired so hastily; but that idiot Le Bihan and Max Fortin have been working on my nerves till I am as hysterical as a schoolgirl," I ended angrily.

"You fired—but the window glass was not shattered," said Lys in a low voice.

"Well, the window was open, then. And as for the—the rest—I've got nervous indigestion, and a doctor will settle the Black Priest for me, Lys."

I glanced out of the window at Tregunc waiting with my horse at the gate.

"Dearest, I think I had better go to join Durand and the others."

"I will go too."

"Oh, no!"

"Yes, Dick."

"Don't, Lys."

"I shall suffer every moment you are away."

"The ride is too fatiguing, and we can't tell what unpleasant sight you may come upon. Lys, you don't really think there is anything supernatural in this affair?"

"Dick," she answered gently, "I am a Bretonne." With both arms around my neck, my wife said, "Death is the gift of God. I do not fear it when we are together. But alone—oh, my husband, I should fear a God who could take you away from me!"

We kissed each other soberly, simply, like two children. Then Lys hurried away to change her gown, and I paced up and down the garden waiting for her.

She came, drawing on her slender gauntlets. I swung her into the saddle, gave a hasty order to Jean Marie, and mounted.

Now, to quail under thoughts of terror on a morning like this, with Lys in the saddle beside me, no matter what had happened or might happen, was impossible. Moreover, Môme came sneaking after us. I asked Tregunc to catch him, for I was afraid he might be brained by our horses' hoofs if he followed, but the wily puppy dodged and bolted after Lys, who was trotting along the high-road. "Never mind," I thought; "if he's hit he'll live, for he has no brains to lose."

Lys was waiting for me in the road beside the Shrine of Our Lady of

St. Gildas when I joined her. She crossed herself, I doffed my cap, then we shook out our bridles and galloped toward the forest of Kerselec.

We said very little as we rode. I always loved to watch Lys in the saddle. Her exquisite figure and lovely face were the incarnation of youth and grace; her curling hair glistened like threaded gold.

Out of the corner of my eye I saw the spoiled puppy Môme come bounding cheerfully alongside, oblivious of our horses' heels. Our road swung close to the cliffs. A filthy cormorant rose from the black rocks and flapped heavily across our path. Lys's horse reared, but she pulled him down, and pointed at the bird with her riding crop.

"I see," said I; "it seems to be going our way. Curious to see a cormorant in a forest, isn't it?"

"It is a bad sign," said Lys. "You know that Morbihan proverb: 'When the cormorant turns from the sea, Death laughs in the forest, and wise woodsmen build boats.'"

"I wish," said I sincerely, "that there were fewer proverbs in Brittany."

We were in sight of the forest now; across the gorse I could see the sparkle of gendarmes' trappings, and the glitter of Le Bihan's silver-buttoned jacket. The hedge was low and we took it without difficulty, and trotted across the moor to where Le Bihan and Durand stood gesticulating.

They bowed ceremoniously to Lys as we rode up.

"The trail is horrible—it is a river," said the mayor in his squeaky voice. "Monsieur Darrel, I think perhaps madame would scarcely care to come any nearer."

Lys drew bridle and looked at me.

"It is horrible!" said Durand, walking up beside me; "it looks as though a bleeding regiment had passed this way. The trail winds and winds about there in the thickets; we lose it at times, but we always find it again. I can't understand how one man—no, nor twenty—could bleed like that!"

A halloo, answered by another, sounded from the depths of the forest.

"It's my men; they are following the trail," muttered the brigadier. "God alone knows what is at the end!"

"Shall we gallop back, Lys?" I asked.

"No; let us ride along the western edge of the woods and dismount. The sun is so hot now, and I should like to rest for a moment," she said.

"The western forest is clear of anything disagreeable," said Durand.

"Very well," I answered; "call me, Le Bihan, if you find anything."

Lys wheeled her mare, and I followed across the springy heather, Môme trotting cheerfully in the rear.

We entered the sunny woods about a quarter of a kilometre from where we left Durand. I took Lys from her horse, flung both bridles over a limb, and, giving my wife my arm, aided her to a flat mossy rock which overhung a shallow brook gurgling among the beech trees. Lys sat down and drew off her gauntlets. Moine pushed his head into her lap, received an undeserved caress, and came doubtfully toward me. I was weak enough to condone his offence, but I made him lie down at my feet, greatly to his disgust.

I rested my head on Lys's knees, looking up at the sky through the crossed branches of the trees.

"I suppose I have killed him," I said. "It shocks me terribly, Lys."

"You could not have known, dear. He may have been a robber, and—if—not— Did—have you ever fired your revolver since that day four years ago, when the Red Admiral's son tried to kill you? But I know you have not."

"No," said I, wondering. "It's a fact, I have not. Why?"

"And don't you remember that I asked you to let me load it for you the day when Yves went off, swearing to kill you and his father?"

"Yes, I do remember. Well?"

"Well, I—I took the cartridges first to St. Gildas chapel and dipped them in holy water. You must not laugh, Dick," said Lys gently, laying her cool hands on my lips.

"Laugh, my darling!"

Overhead the October sky was pale amethyst, and the sunlight burned like orange flame through the yellow leaves of beech and oak. Gnats and midges danced and wavered overhead; a spider dropped from a twig halfway to the ground and hung suspended on the end of his gossamer thread.

"Are you sleepy, dear?" asked Lys, bending over me.

"I am—a little; I scarcely slept two hours last night," I answered. "You may sleep, if you wish," said Lys, and touched my eyes caressingly.

"Is my head heavy on your knees?"

"No, Dick."

I was already in a half doze; still I heard the brook babbling under the beeches and the humming of forest flies overhead. Presently even these were stilled.

The next thing I knew I was sitting bolt upright, my ears ringing with a scream, and I saw Lys cowering beside me, covering her white face with both hands.

As I sprang to my feet she cried again and clung to my knees. I saw my dog rush growling into a thicket, then I heard him whimper, and he came backing out, whining, ears flat, tail down. I stooped and disengaged Lys's hand.

"Don't go, Dick!" she cried. "O God, it's the Black Priest!"

In a moment I had leaped across the brook and pushed my way into the thicket. It was empty. I stared about me; I scanned every tree trunk, every bush. Suddenly I saw him. He was seated on a fallen log, his head resting in his hands, his rusty black robe gathered around him. For a moment my hair stirred under my cap; sweat started on my forehead and cheekbone; then I recovered my reason, and understood that the man was human and was probably wounded to death. Ay, to death; for there, at my feet, lay the wet trail of blood, over leaves and stones, down into the little hollow, across to the figure in black resting silently under the trees.

I saw that he could not escape even if he had the strength, for before him, almost at his very feet, lay a deep, shining swamp.

As I stepped forward my foot broke a twig. At the sound the figure started a little, then its head fell forward again. Its face was masked. Walking up to the man, I bade him tell where he was wounded. Durand and the others broke through the thicket at the same moment and hurried to my side.

"Who are you who hide a masked face in a priest's robe?" said the gendarme loudly.

There was no answer.

"See—see the stiff blood all over his robe!" muttered Le Bihan to Fortin.

"He will not speak," said I.

"He may be too badly wounded," whispered Le Bihan.

"I saw him raise his head," I said; "my wife saw him creep up here."

Durand stepped forward and touched the figure.

"Speak!" he said.

"Speak!" quavered Fortin.

Durand waited a moment, then with a sudden upward movement he stripped off the mask and threw back the man's head. We were looking into the eye sockets of a skull. Durand stood rigid; the mayor shrieked. The skeleton burst out from its rotting robes and collapsed on the ground before us. From between the staring ribs and the grinning teeth spurted a torrent of black blood, showering the shrinking grasses; then the thing shuddered, and fell over into the black ooze of the bog. Little bubbles of iridescent air appeared from the mud; the bones were slowly engulfed, and, as the last fragments sank out of sight, up from the depths and along the bank crept a creature, shiny, shivering, quivering its wings.

It was a death's-head moth.

I wish I had time to tell you how Lys outgrew superstitions—for she never knew the truth about the affair, and she never will know, since she has promised not to read this book. I wish I might tell you about the king and his coronation, and how the coronation robe fitted. I wish that I were able to write how Yvonne and Herbert Stuart rode to a boar hunt in Quimperlé, and how the hounds raced the quarry right through the town, overturning three gendarmes, the notary, and an old woman. But I am becoming garrulous, and Lys is calling me to come and hear the king say that he is sleepy. And his Highness shall not be kept waiting.

The Harbor-Master

I

Because it all seems so improbable—so horribly impossible to me now, sitting here safe and sane in my own library—I hesitate to record an episode which already appears to me less horrible than grotesque. Yet, unless this story is written now, I know I shall never have the courage to tell the truth about the matter—not from fear of ridicule, but because I myself shall soon cease to credit what I now know to be true. Yet scarcely a month has elapsed since I heard the stealthy purring of what I believed to be the shoaling undertow—scarcely a month ago, with my own eyes, I saw that which, even now, I am beginning to believe never existed. As for the harbor-master—and the blow I am now striking at the old order of things— But of that I shall not speak now, or later; I shall try to tell the story simply and truthfully, and let my friends testify as to my probity and the publishers of this book corroborate them.

On the 29th of February I resigned my position under the government and left Washington to accept an offer from Professor Farrago—whose name he kindly permits me to use—and on the first day of April I entered upon my new and congenial duties as general superintendent of the waterfowl department connected with Zoological Gardens then in course of erection at Bronx Park, New York.

For a week I followed the routine, examining the new foundations, studying the architect's plans, following the surveyors through the Bronx thickets, suggesting arrangements for water-courses and pools destined to be included in the enclosures for swans, geese, pelicans, herons, and such of the waders and swimmers as we might expect to acclimate in Bronx Park.

It was at that time the policy of the trustees and officers of the Zoological Gardens neither to employ collectors nor to send out expeditions in search of specimens. The society decided to depend upon voluntary contributions, and I was always busy, part of the day, in dictating answers to correspondents who wrote offering their services as hunters of big game, collectors of all sorts of fauna, trappers, snarers, and also to those who offered specimens for sale, usually at exorbitant rates.

To the proprietors of five-legged kittens, mangy lynxes, moth-eaten coyotes, and dancing bears I returned courteous but uncompromising refusals—of course, first submitting all such letters, together with my replies, to Professor Farrago.

One day toward the end of May, however, just as I was leaving Bronx Park to return to town, Professor Lesard, of the reptilian department, called out to me that Professor Farrago wanted to see me a moment; so I put my pipe into my pocket again and retraced my steps to the temporary, wooden building occupied by Professor Farrago, general superintendent of the Zoological Gardens. The professor, who was sitting at his desk before a pile of letters and replies submitted for approval by me, pushed his glasses down and looked over them at me with whimsical smile that suggested amusement, impatience, annoyance, and perhaps a faint trace of apology.

"Now, here's a letter," he said, with a deliberate gesture toward a sheet of paper impaled on a file—"a letter that I suppose you remember." He disengaged the sheet of paper and handed it to me.

"Oh yes," I replied, with a shrug; "of course the man is mistaken—or—"

"Or what?" demanded Professor Farrago, tranquilly, wiping his glasses.

"—Or a liar," I replied

After a silence he leaned back in his chair and bade me read the letter to him again, and I did so with a contemptuous tolerance for the writer, who must have been either a very innocent victim or a very stupid swindler. I said as much to Professor Farrago, but, to my surprise, he appeared to waver.

"I suppose," he said, with his near-sighted, embarrassed smile, "that nine hundred and ninety-nine men in a thousand would throw that letter aside and condemn the writer as a liar or a fool?"

"In my opinion," said I, "he's one or the other."

"He isn't—in mine," said the professor, placidly.

"What!" I exclaimed. "Here is a man living all alone on a strip of rock and sand between the wilderness and the sea, who wants you to send somebody to take charge of a bird that doesn't exist!"

"How do you know," asked Professor Farrago, "that the bird in question does not exist?"

"It is generally accepted," I replied, sarcastically, "that the great auk has been extinct for years. Therefore I may be pardoned for doubting that our correspondent possesses a pair of them alive."

"Oh, you young fellows," said the professor smiling wearily, "you embark on a theory for destinations that don't exist."

He leaned back in his chair, his amused eyes searching space for the imagery that made him smile.

"Like swimming squirrels, you navigate with the help of Heaven and a stiff breeze, but you never land where you hope to—do you?"

Rather red in the face, I said: "Don't you believe the great auk to be extinct?"

"Audubon saw the great auk."

"Who has seen a single specimen since?"

"Nobody—except our correspondent here," he replied, laughing.

I laughed, too, considering the interview at an end, but the professor went on, coolly:

"Whatever it is that our correspondent has—and I am daring to believe that it *is* the great auk itself—I want you to secure it for the society."

When my astonishment subsided my first conscious sentiment was one of pity. Clearly, Professor Farrago was on the verge of dotage—ah, what a loss to the world!

I believe now that Professor Farrago perfectly interpreted my thoughts, but he betrayed neither resentment nor impatience. I drew a chair up beside his desk—there was nothing to do but to obey, and this fool's errand was none of my conceiving.

Together we made out a list of articles necessary for me and itemized the expenses I might incur, and I set a date for my return, allowing no margin for a successful termination to the expedition.

"Never mind that," said the professor. "What I want you to do is to get those birds here safely. Now, how many men will you take?"

"None," I replied, bluntly; "it's a useless expense, unless there is something to bring back. If there is I'll write you, you may be sure."

"Very well," said Professor Farrago, good-humoredly, "you shall have all the assistance you may require. Can you leave to-night?"

The old gentleman was certainly prompt. I nodded, half-sulkily, aware of his amusement.

"So," I said, picking up my hat, "I am to start north to find a place called Black Harbor, where there is a man named Halyard who possesses, among other household utensils, two extinct great auks—"

We were both laughing by this time. I asked him why on earth he credited the assertion of a man he had never before heard of.

"I suppose," he replied, with the same half-apologetic, half-humorous smile, "it is instinct. I feel, somehow, that this man Halyard *has* got an auk—perhaps two. I can't get away from the idea that we are on the eve of acquiring the rarest of living creatures. It's odd for a scientist to talk as I do; doubtless you're shocked—admit it, now!"

But I was not shocked; on the contrary, I was conscious that the same strange hope that Professor Farrago cherished was beginning, in spite of me, to stir my pulses, too.

"If he has—" I began, then stopped.

The professor and I looked hard at each other in silence.

"Go on," he said, encouragingly.

But I had nothing more to say, for the prospect of beholding with my own eyes a living specimen of the great auk produced a series of conflicting emotions within me which rendered speech profanely superfluous.

As I took my leave Professor Farrago came to the door of the temporary, wooden office and handed me the letter written by the man Halyard. I folded it and put it into my pocket, as Halyard might require it for my own identification.

"How much does he want for the pair?" I asked.

"Ten thousand dollars. Don't demur—if the birds are really—"

"I know," I said, hastily, not daring to hope too much.

"One thing more," said Professor Farrago, gravely; "you know, in that last paragraph of his letter, Halyard speaks of something else in the way of specimens—an undiscovered species of amphibious biped—just read that paragraph again, will you?"

I drew the letter from my pocket and read as he directed:

"When you have seen the two living specimens of the great auk, and have satisfied yourself that I tell the truth, you may be wise enough to listen without prejudice to a statement I shall make concerning the existence of the strangest creature ever fashioned. I will merely say, at this time, that the creature referred to is an amphibious biped and inhabits the ocean near this coast. More I cannot say, for I personally have not seen the animal, but I have a witness who has, and there are many who affirm that they have seen the creature. You will naturally say that my statement amounts to nothing; but when your representative arrives, if he be free from prejudice, I expect his reports to you concerning this sea-biped will confirm the solemn statements of a witness I know to be unimpeachable.

"Yours truly, Burton Halyard.

"BLACK HARBOR"

"Well," I said, after a moment's thought, "here goes for the wild-goose chase."

"Wild auk, you mean," said Professor Farrago, shaking hands with me. "You will start to-night, won't you?"

"Yes, but Heaven knows how I'm every going to land in this man Halyard's door-yard. Good-bye!"

"About that sea-biped—" began Professor Farrago, shyly.

"Oh, don't!" I said; "I can swallow the auks, feathers and claws, but if this fellow Halyard is hinting he's seen an amphibious creature resembling a man—"

"—Or a woman," said the professor, cautiously.

I retired, disgusted, my faith shaken in the mental vigor of Professor Farrago.

II

The three days' voyage by boat and rail was irksome. I bought my kit at Sainte Croix, on the Central Pacific Railroad, and on June 1st I began the last stage of my journey via the Sainte Isole broad-gauge, arriving in the wilderness by daylight. A tedious forced march by blazed trail, freshly spotted on the wrong side, of course, brought me to the northern terminus of the rusting, narrow-gauge lumber railway which runs from the heart of the hushed pine wilderness to the sea.

Already a long train of battered flat-cars, piled with sluice-props and roughly hewn sleepers, was moving slowly off into the brooding forest gloom, when I came in sight of the track; but I developed a gratifying and unexpected burst of speed, shouting all the while. The train stopped; I swung myself aboard the last car, where a pleasant young fellow was sitting on the rear brake, chewing spruce and reading a letter.

"Come aboard, sir," he said, looking up with a smile; "I guess you're the man in a hurry."

"I'm looking for a man named Halyard," I said, dropping rifle and knapsack on the fresh-cut, fragrant pile of pine. "Are you Halyard?"

"No, I'm Francis Lee, bossing the mica pit at Port-of-Waves," he replied, "but this letter is from Halyard, asking me to look out for a man in a hurry from Bronx Park, New York."

"I'm that man," said I, filling my pipe and offering him a share of the weed of peace, and we sat side by side smoking very amiably, until a signal from the locomotive sent him forward and I was left alone, lounging at ease, head pillowed on both arms, watching the blue sky flying through the branches overhead.

Long before we came in sight of the ocean I smelled it; the fresh, salt aroma stole into my senses, drowsy with the heated odor of pine and hemlock, and I sat up, peering ahead into the dusky sea of pines.

Fresher and fresher came the wind from the sea, in puffs, in mild, sweet breezes, in steady, freshening currents, blowing the feathery crowns of the pines, setting the balsam's blue tufts rocking.

Lee wandered back over the long line of flats, balancing himself nonchalantly as the cars swung around a sharp curve, where water dripped from a newly propped sluice that suddenly emerged from the depths of the forest to run parallel to the railroad track.

"Built it this spring," he said, surveying his handiwork, which seemed to undulate as the cars swept past. "It runs to the cover—or ought to—" He stopped abruptly with a thoughtful glance at me.

"So you're going over to Halyard's?" he continued, as though answering a question asked by himself.

I nodded.

"You've never been there—of course?"

"No," I said, "and I'm not likely to go again."

I would have told him why I was going if I had not already begun to feel ashamed of my idiotic errand.

"I guess you're going to look at those birds of his," continued Lee, placidly.

"I guess I am," I said, sulkily, glancing askance to see whether he was smiling.

But he only asked me, quite seriously, whether a great auk was really a very rare bird; and I told him that the last one ever seen had been found dead off Labrador in January, 1870. Then I asked him whether these birds of Halyard's were really great auks, and he replied, somewhat indifferently, that he supposed they were—at least, nobody had ever before seen such birds near Port-of-Waves.

"There's something else," he said, running a pine-sliver through his pipestem—"something that interests us all here more than auks, big or little. I suppose I might as well speak of it, as you are bound to hear about it sooner or later."

He hesitated, and I could see that he was embarrassed, searching for the exact words to convey his meaning.

"If," said I, "you have anything in this region more important to science than the great auk, I should be very glad to know about it."

Perhaps there was the faintest tinge of sarcasm in my voice, for he shot a sharp glance at me and then turned slightly. After a moment, however, he put his pipe into his pocket, laid hold of the brake with both hands, vaulted to his perch aloft, and glanced down at me.

"Did you ever hear of the harbor-master?" he asked, maliciously.

"Which harbor-master?" I inquired.

"You'll know before long," he observed, with a satisfied glance into perspective.

This rather extraordinary observation puzzled me. I waited for him to resume, and, as he did not, I asked him what he meant.

"If I knew," he said, "I'd tell you. But, come to think of it, I'd be a fool to go into details with a scientific man. You'll hear about the harbor-master—perhaps you will see the harbor-master. In that event I should be glad to converse with you on the subject."

I could not help laughing at his prim and precise manner, and, after a moment, he also laughed, saying:

"It hurts a man's vanity to know he knows a thing that somebody else knows he doesn't know. I'm damned if I say another word about the harbor-master until you've been to Halyard's!"

"A harbor-master," I persisted, "is an official who superintends the mooring of ships—isn't he?"

But he refused to be tempted into conversation, and we lounged silently on the lumber until a long, thin whistle from the locomotive and a rush of stinging salt-wind brought us to our feet. Through the trees I could see the bluish-black ocean, stretching out beyond black headlands to meet the clouds; a great wind was roaring among the trees as the train slowly came to a standstill on the edge of the primeval forest.

Lee jumped to the ground and aided me with my rifle and pack, and then the train began to back away along a curved side-track which, Lee said, led to the mica-pit and company stores.

"Now what will you do?" he asked, pleasantly. "I can give you a good dinner and a decent bed to-night if you like—and I'm sure Mrs. Lee would be very glad to have you stop with us as long as you choose."

I thanked him, but said that I was anxious to reach Halyard's before dark, and he very kindly led me along the cliffs and pointed out the path.

"This man Halyard," he said, "is an invalid. He lives at a cove called Black Harbor, and all his truck goes through to him over the company's road. We receive it here, and send a pack-mule through once a month. I've met him; he's a bad-tempered hypochondriac, a cynic at heart, and a man whose word is never doubted. If he says he has a great auk, you may be satisfied he has."

My heart was beating with excitement at the prospect; I looked out across the wooded headlands and tangled stretches of dune and hollow, trying to realize what it might mean to me, to Professor Farrago, to the world, if I should lead back to New York a live auk.

"He's a crank," said Lee; "frankly, I don't like him. If you find it unpleasant there, come back to us."

"Does Halyard live alone?" I asked.

"Yes—except for a professional trained nurse—poor thing!"

"A man?"

"No," said Lee, disgustedly.

Presently he gave me a peculiar glance; hesitated, and finally said: "Ask Halyard to tell you about his nurse and—the harbor-master. Goodbye—I'm due at the quarry. Come and stay with us whenever you care to; you will find a welcome at Port-of-Waves."

We shook hands and parted on the cliff, he turning back into the forest along the railway, I starting northward, pack slung, rifle over my shoulder. Once I met a group of quarrymen, faces burned brick-red, scarred hands swinging as they walked. And, as I passed them with a nod, turning, I saw that they also had turned to look after me, and I caught a word or two of their conversation, whirled back to me on the sea-wind.

They were speaking of the harbor-master.

III

Toward sunset I came out on a sheer granite cliff where the sea-birds were whirling and clamoring, and the great breakers dashed, rolling in double-thundered reverberations on the sun-dyed, crimson sands below the rock.

Across the half-moon of beach towered another cliff, and, behind this, I saw a column of smoke rising in the still air. It certainly came from Halyard's chimney, although the opposite cliff prevented me from seeing the house itself.

I rested a moment to refill my pipe, then resumed rifle and pack, and cautiously started to skirt the cliffs. I had descended half-way toward the beach, and was examining the cliff opposite, when something on the very top of the rock arrested my attention—a man darkly outlined against the sky. The next moment, however, I knew it could not be a man, for the object suddenly glided over the face of the cliff and slid down the sheer, smooth face like a lizard. Before I could get a square look at it, the thing crawled into the surf—or, at least, it seemed to—but the whole episode occurred so suddenly, so unexpectedly, that I was not sure I had seen anything at all.

However, I was curious enough to climb the cliff on the land side and make my way toward the spot where I imagined I saw the man. Of course, there was nothing there—not a trace of a human being, I mean. Something had been there—a sea-otter, possibly—for the remains of a freshly killed fish lay on the rock, eaten to the back-bone and tail.

The next moment, below me, I saw the house, a freshly painted, trim, flimsy structure, modern, and very much out of harmony with the splendid savagery surrounding it. It struck a nasty, cheap note in the noble, gray monotony of headland and sea.

The descent was easy enough. I crossed the crescent beach, hard as pink marble, and found a little trodden path among the rocks, that led to the front porch of the house.

There were two people on the porch—I heard their voices before I saw them—and when I set my foot upon the wooden steps, I saw one of them, a woman, rise from her chair and step hastily toward me.

"Come back!" cried the other, a man with a smooth-shaven, deeply lined face, and a pair of angry, blue eyes; and the woman stepped back quietly, acknowledging my lifted hat with a silent inclination.

The man, who was reclining in an invalid's rolling-chair, clapped both large, pale hands to the wheels and pushed himself out along the porch. He had shawls pinned about him, an untidy, drab-colored hat on his head, and, when he looked down at me, he scowled.

"I know who you are," he said, in his acid voice; "you're one of the Zoological men from Bronx Park. You look like it, anyway."

"It is easy to recognize you from your reputation," I replied, irritated at his discourtesy.

"Really," he replied, with something between a sneer and a laugh, "I'm obliged for your frankness. You're after my great auks, are you not?"

"Nothing else would have tempted me into this place," I replied, sincerely.

"Thank Heaven for that," he said. "Sit down a moment; you've interrupted us." Then, turning to the young woman, who wore the neat gown and tiny cap of a professional nurse, he bade her resume what she had been saying. She did so, with a deprecating glance at me, which made the old man sneer again.

"It happened so suddenly," she said, in her low voice, "that I had no chance to get back. The boat was drifting in the cove; I sat in the stern, reading, both oars shipped, and the tiller swinging. Then I heard a scratching under the boat, but thought it might be seaweed—and, next moment, came those soft thumpings, like the sound of a big fish rubbing its nose against a float."

Halyard clutched the wheels of his chair and stared at the girl in grim displeasure.

"Didn't you know enough to be frightened?" he demanded.

"No—not then," she said, coloring faintly; "but when, after a few moments, I looked up and saw the harbor-master running up and down the beach, I was horribly frightened."

"Really?" said Halyard, sarcastically; "it was about time." Then, turning to me, he rasped out: "And that young lady was obliged to row all the way to Port-of-Waves and call to Lee's quarrymen to take her boat in."

Completely mystified, I looked from Halyard to the girl, not in the least comprehending what all this meant.

"That will do," said Halyard, ungraciously, which curt phrase was apparently the usual dismissal for the nurse.

She rose, and I rose, and she passed me with an inclination, stepping noiselessly into the house.

"I want beef-tea!" bawled Halyard after her; then he gave me an unamiable glance.

"I was a well-bred man," he sneered; "I'm a Harvard graduate, too, but I live as I like, and I do what I like, and I say what I like."

"You certainly are not reticent," I said, disgusted.

"Why should I be?" he rasped; "I pay that young woman for my irritability; it's a bargain between us."

"In your domestic affairs," I said, "there is nothing that interests me. I came to see those auks."

"You probably believe them to be razor-billed auks," he said, contemptuously. "But they're not; they're great auks."

I suggested that he permit me to examine them, and he replied, indifferently, that they were in a pen in his backyard, and that I was free to step around the house when I cared to.

I laid my rifle and pack on the veranda, and hastened off with mixed emotions, among which hope no longer predominated. No man

in his senses would keep two such precious prizes in a pen in his backyard, I argued, and I was perfectly prepared to find anything from a puf-
fin to a penguin in that pen.

I shall never forget, as long as I live, my stupor of amazement when
I came to the wire-covered enclosure. Not only were there two great
auks in the pen, alive, breathing, squatting in bulky majesty on their
seaweed bed, but one of them was gravely contemplating two newly
hatched chicks, all bill and feet, which nestled sedately at the edge of a
puddle of salt-water, where some small fish were swimming.

For a while excitement blinded, nay, deafened me. I tried to realize
that I was gazing upon the last individuals of an all but extinct race—the
sole survivors of the gigantic auk, which, for thirty years, has been ac-
counted an extinct creature.

I believe that I did not move muscle nor limb until the sun had
gone down and the crowding darkness blurred my straining eyes and
blotted the great, silent, bright-eyed birds from sight.

Even then I could not tear myself away from the enclosure; I listened
to the strange, drowsy note of the male bird, the fainter responses of the
female, the thin plaints of the chicks, huddling under her breast; I heard
their flipper-like, embryotic wings beating sleepily as the birds stretched
and yawned their beaks and clacked them, preparing for slumber.

"If you please," came a soft voice from the door, "Mr. Halyard
awaits your company to dinner."

IV

I dined well—or, rather, I might have enjoyed my dinner if Mr. Halyard
had been eliminated; and the feast consisted exclusively of a joint of
beef, the pretty nurse, and myself. She was exceedingly attractive—with a
disturbing fashion of lowering her head and raising her dark eyes when
spoken to.

As for Halyard, he was unspeakable, bundled up in his snuffy shawls,
and making uncouth noises over his gruel. But it is only just to say that his
table was worth sitting down to and his wine was sound as a bell.

"Yah!" he snapped, "I'm sick of this cursed soup—and I'll trouble
you to fill my glass—"

"It is dangerous for you to touch claret," said the pretty nurse.

"I may as well die at dinner as anywhere," he observed.

"Certainly," said I, cheerfully passing the decanter, but he did not appear overpleased with the attention.

"I can't smoke, either," he snarled, hitching the shawls around until he looked like Richard the Third.

However, he was good enough to shove a box of cigars at me, and I took one and stood up, as the pretty nurse slipped past and vanished into the little parlor beyond.

We sat there for a while without speaking. He picked irritably at the bread-crumbs on the cloth, never glancing in my direction; and I, tired from my long foot-tour, lay back in my chair, silently appreciating one of the best cigars I ever smoked.

"Well," he rasped out at length, "what do you think of my auks— and my veracity?"

I told him that both were unimpeachable.

"Didn't they call me a swindler down there at your museum?" he demanded.

I admitted that I had heard the term applied. Then I made a clean breast of the matter, telling him that it was I who had doubted; that my chief, Professor Farrago, had sent me against my will, and that I was ready and glad to admit that he, Mr. Halyard, was a benefactor of the human race.

"Bosh!" he said. "What good does a confounded wobbly, bandy-toed bird do to the human race?"

But he was pleased, nevertheless; and presently he asked me, not unamiably, to punish his claret again.

"I'm done for," he said; "good things to eat and drink are no good to me. Some day I'll get mad enough to have a fit, and then—"

He paused to yawn.

"Then," he continued, "that little nurse of mine will drink up my claret and go back to civilization, where people are polite."

Somehow or other, in spite of the fact that Halyard was an old pig, what he said touched me. There was certainly not much left in life for him—as he regarded life.

"I'm going to leave her this house," he said, arranging his shawls. "She doesn't know it. I'm going to leave her my money, too. She doesn't know that. Good Lord! What kind of a woman can she be to stand my bad temper for a few dollars a month!"

"I think," said I, "that it's partly because she's poor, partly because she's sorry for you."

He looked up with a ghastly smile.

"You think she really is sorry?"

Before I could answer he went on: "I'm no mawkish sentimentalist, and I won't allow anybody to be sorry for me—do you hear?"

"Oh, I'm not sorry for you!" I said, hastily, and, for the first time since I had seen him, he laughed heartily, without a sneer.

We both seemed to feel better after that; I drank his wine and smoked his cigars, and he appeared to take a certain grim pleasure in watching me. "There's no fool like a young fool," he observed, presently.

As I had no doubt he referred to me, I paid him no attention.

After fidgeting with his shawls, he gave me an oblique scowl and asked me my age.

"Twenty-four," I replied.

"Sort of a tadpole, aren't you?" he said.

As I took no offence, he repeated the remark.

"Oh, come," said I, "there's no use in trying to irritate me. I see through you; a row acts like a cocktail on you—but you'll have to stick to gruel in my company."

"I call that impudence!" he rasped out, wrathfully.

"I don't care what you call it," I replied, undisturbed, "I am not going to be worried by you. Anyway," I ended, "it is my opinion that you could be very good company if you chose."

The proposition appeared to take his breath away—at least, he said nothing more; and I finished my cigar in peace and tossed the stump into a saucer.

"Now," said I, "what price do you set upon your birds, Mr. Halyard?"

"Ten thousand dollars," he snapped, with an evil smile.

"You will receive a certified check when the birds are delivered," I said, quietly.

"You don't mean to say you agree to that outrageous bargain—and I won't take a cent less, either—Good Lord!—haven't you any spirit left?" he cried, half rising from his pile of shawls.

His piteous eagerness for a dispute sent me into laughter impossible to control, and he eyed me, mouth open, animosity rising visibly.

Then he seized the wheels of his invalid chair and trundled away, too mad to speak; and I strolled out into the parlor, still laughing.

The pretty nurse was there, sewing under a hanging lamp.

"If I am not indiscreet—" I began.

"Indiscretion is the better part of valor," said she, dropping her head but raising her eyes.

So I sat down with a frivolous smile peculiar to the appreciated.

"Doubtless," said I, "you are hemming a 'kerchief."

"Doubtless I am not," she said; "this is a night-cap for Mr. Halyard."

A mental vision of Halyard in a night-cap, very mad, nearly set me laughing again.

"Like the King of Yvetot, he wears his crown in bed," I said, flippantly.

"The King of Yvetot might have made that remark," she observed, re-threading her needle.

It is unpleasant to be reproved. How large and red and hot a man's ears feel.

To cool them, I strolled out to the porch; and, after a while, the pretty nurse came out, too, and sat down in a chair not far away. She probably regretted her lost opportunity to be flirted with.

"I have so little company—it is a great relief to see somebody from the world," she said. "If you can be agreeable, I wish you would."

The idea that she had come out to see me was so agreeable that I remained speechless until she said: "Do tell me what people are doing in New York."

So I seated myself on the steps and talked about the portion of the world inhabited by me, while she sat sewing in the dull light that straggled out from the parlor windows.

She had a certain coquetry of her own, using the usual methods with an individuality that was certainly fetching. For instance, when she lost her needle—and, another time, when we both, on hands and knees, hunted for her thimble.

However, directions for these pastimes may be found in contemporary classics.

I was as entertaining as I could be—perhaps not quite as entertaining as a young man usually thinks he is. However, we got on very well together until I asked her tenderly who the harbor-master might be, whom they all discussed so mysteriously.

"I do not care to speak about it," she said, with a primness of which I had not suspected her capable.

Of course I could scarcely pursue the subject after that—and, indeed, I did not intend to—so I began to tell her how I fancied I had seen a man on the cliff that afternoon, and how the creature slid over the sheer rock like a snake.

To my amazement, she asked me to kindly discontinue the account of my adventures, in an icy tone, which left no room for protest.

"It was only a sea-otter," I tried to explain, thinking perhaps she did not care for snake stories.

But the explanation did not appear to interest her, and I was mortified to observe that my impression upon her was anything but pleasant.

"She doesn't seem to like me and my stories," thought I, "but she is too young, perhaps, to appreciate them."

So I forgave her—for she was even prettier than I had thought her at first—and I took my leave, saying that Mr. Halyard would doubtless direct me to my room.

Halyard was in his library, cleaning a revolver, when I entered.

"Your room is next to mine," he said; "pleasant dreams, and kindly refrain from snoring."

"May I venture an absurd hope that you will do the same?" I replied, politely.

That maddened him, so I hastily withdrew.

I had been asleep for at least two hours when a movement by my bedside and a light in my eyes awakened me. I sat bolt upright in bed, blinking at Halyard, who, clad in a dressing-gown and wearing a nightcap, had wheeled himself into my room with one hand, while with the other he solemnly waved a candle over my head.

"I'm so cursed lonely," he said—"come, there's a good fellow—talk to me in your own original, impudent way."

I objected strenuously, but he looked so worn and thin, so lonely and bad-tempered, so lovelessly grotesque, that I got out of bed and passed a spongeful of cold water over my head.

Then I returned to bed and propped the pillows up for a back-rest, ready to quarrel with him if it might bring some little pleasure into his morbid existence.

"No," he said, amiably, "I'm too worried to quarrel, but I'm much obliged for your kindly offer. I want to tell you something."

"What?" I asked, suspiciously.

"I want to ask you if you ever saw a man with gills like a fish?"

"Gills?" I repeated.

"Yes, gills! Did you?"

"No," I replied, angrily, "and neither did you."

"No, I never did," he said, in a curiously placid voice, "but there's a man with gills like a fish who lives in the ocean out there. Oh, you needn't look that way—nobody ever thinks of doubting my word, and I tell you that there's a man—or a thing that looks like a man—as big as you are, too—all slate-colored—with nasty red gills like a fish!—and I've a witness to prove what I say!"

"Who?" I asked, sarcastically.

"The witness? My nurse."

"Oh! She saw a slate-colored man with gills?"

"Yes, she did. So did Francis Lee, superintendent of the Mica Quarry Company at Port-of-Waves. So have a dozen men who work in the quarry. Oh, you needn't laugh, young man. It's an old story here, and anybody can tell you about the harbor-master."

"The harbor-master!" I exclaimed.

"Yes, that slate-colored thing with gills, that looks like a man—and—by Heaven! *is* a man—that's the harbor-master. Ask any quarryman at Port-of-Waves what it is that comes purring around their boats at the wharf and unties painters and changes the mooring of every cat-boat in the cove at night! Ask Francis Lee what it was he saw running and leaping up and down the shoal at sunset last Friday! Ask anybody along the coast what sort of a thing moves about the cliffs like a man and slides over them into the sea like an otter—"

"I saw it do that!" I burst out.

"Oh, did you? Well, *what was it?*"

Something kept me silent, although a dozen explanations flew to my lips.

After a pause, Halyard said: "You saw the harbor-master, that's what you saw!"

I looked at him without a word.

"Don't mistake me," he said, pettishly; "I don't think that the harbor-master is a spirit or a sprite or a hobgoblin, or any sort of damned rot. Neither do I believe it to be an optical illusion."

"What do you think it is?" I asked.

"I think it's a man—I think it's a branch of the human race—that's what I think. Let me tell you something: the deepest spot in the Atlantic Ocean is a trifle over five miles deep—and I suppose you know that this place lies only about a quarter of a mile off this headland. The British exploring vessel, *Gull,* Captain Marotte, discovered and sounded it, I believe. Anyway, it's there, and it's my belief that the profound depths are inhabited by the remnants of the last race of amphibious human beings!"

This was childish; I did not bother to reply.

"Believe it or not, as you will," he said, angrily; "one thing I know, and that is this: the harbor-master has taken to hanging around my cove, and he is attracted by my nurse! I won't have it! I'll blow his fishy gills out of his head if I ever get a shot at him! I don't care whether it's homicide or not—anyway, it's a new kind of murder and it attracts me!"

I gazed at him incredulously, but he was working himself into a passion, and I did not choose to say what I thought.

"Yes, this slate-colored thing with gills goes purring and grinning and spitting about after my nurse—when she walks, when she rows, when she sits on the beach! Gad! It drives me nearly frantic. I won't tolerate it, I tell you!"

"No," said I, "I wouldn't either." And I rolled over in bed convulsed with laughter.

The next moment I heard my door slam. I smothered my mirth and rose to close the window, for the land-wind blew cold from the forest, and a drizzle was sweeping the carpet as far as my bed.

That luminous glare which sometimes lingers after the stars go out, threw a trembling, nebulous radiance over sand and cove. I heard the seething currents under the breakers' softened thunder—louder than I ever heard it. Then, as I closed my window, I saw a man standing, ankle-deep, in the surf, all alone there in the night. But—was it a man? For the figure suddenly began running over the beach on all fours like a beetle, waving its limbs like feelers. Before I could throw open the window again it darted into the surf, and, when I leaned out into the chilling drizzle, I saw nothing save the flat ebb crawling on the coast—I heard nothing save the purring of bubbles on seething sands.

V

It took me a week to perfect my arrangements for transporting the great auks, by water, to Port-of-Waves, where a lumber schooner was to be sent from Petite Sainte Isole, chartered by me for a voyage to New York.

I had constructed a cage made of osiers, in which my auks were to squat until they arrived at Bronx Park. My telegrams to Professor Farrago were brief. One merely said "Victory!" Another explained that I wanted no assistance; and a third read: "Schooner chartered. Arrive New York July 1st. Send furniture-van to foot of Bluff Street."

My week as a guest of Mr. Halyard proved interesting. I wrangled with that invalid to his heart's content, I worked all day on my osier cage, I hunted the thimble in the moonlight with the pretty nurse. We sometimes found it.

As for the thing they called the harbor-master, I saw it a dozen times, but always either at night or so far away and so close to the sea that of course no trace of it remained when I reached the spot, rifle in hand.

I had quite made up my mind that the so-called harbor-master was a demented darky—wandered from, Heaven knows where—perhaps shipwrecked and gone mad from his sufferings. Still, it was far from pleasant to know that the creature was strongly attracted by the pretty nurse.

She, however, persisted in regarding the harbor-master as a sea-creature; she earnestly affirmed that it had gills, like a fish's gills, that it had a soft, fleshy hole for a mouth, and its eyes were luminous and lid-less and fixed.

"Besides," she said, with a shudder, "it's all slate color, like a por-poise, and it looks as wet as a sheet of India-rubber in a dissecting-room."

The day before I was to set sail with my auks in a cat-boat bound for Port-of-Waves, Halyard trundled up to me in his chair and announced his intention of going with me.

"Going where?" I asked.

"To Port-of-Waves and then to New York," he replied, tranquilly.

I was doubtful, and my lack of cordiality hurt his feelings.

"Oh, of course, if you need the sea-voyage—" I began.

"I don't; I need you," he said, savagely; "I need the stimulus of our daily quarrel. I never disagreed so pleasantly with anybody in my life; it agrees with me; I am a hundred per cent. better than I was last week."

I was inclined to resent this, but something in the deep-lined face of the invalid softened me. Besides, I had taken a hearty liking to the old pig.

"I don't want any mawkish sentiment about it," he said, observing me closely; "I won't permit anybody to feel sorry for me—do you under-stand?"

"I'll trouble you to use a different tone in addressing me," I replied, hotly; "I'll feel sorry for you if I choose to!" And our usual quarrel pro-ceeded, to his deep satisfaction.

By six o'clock next evening I had Halyard's luggage stowed away in the cat-boat, and the pretty nurse's effects corded down, with the newly hatched auk-chicks in a hat-box on top. She and I placed the osier cage aboard, securing it firmly, and then, throwing tablecloths over the auks' heads, we led those simple and dignified birds down the path and across the plank at the little wooden pier. Together we locked up the house, while Halyard stormed at us both and wheeled himself furiously up and down the beach below. At the last moment she forgot her thimble. But we found it, I forget where.

"Come on!" shouted Halyard, waving his shawls furiously; "what the devil are you doing up there?"

He received our explanation with a sniff, and we trundled him aboard without further ceremony.

"Don't run me across the plank like a streamer trunk!" he shouted, as I shot him dexterously into the cock-pit. But the wind was dying anyway, and I had no time to dispute with him then.

The sun was setting above the pine-clad ridge as our sail flapped and partly filled, and I cast off, and began a long tack, east by south, to avoid the spouting rocks on our starboard bow.

The sea-birds rose in clouds as we swung across the shoal, the black surf-ducks scuttered out to sea, the gulls tossed their sun-tipped wings in the ocean, riding the rollers like bits of froth.

Already we were sailing slowly out across that great hole in the ocean, five miles deep, the most profound sounding ever taken in the Atlantic. The presence of great heights or great depths, seen or unseen, always impresses the human mind—perhaps oppresses it. We were very silent; the sunlight stain on cliff and beach deepened to crimson, then faded into sombre purple bloom that lingered long after the rose-tint died out in the zenith.

Our progress was slow; at times, although the sail filled with the rising land breeze, we scarcely seemed to move at all.

"Of course," said the pretty nurse, "we couldn't be aground in the deepest hole in the Atlantic."

"Scarcely," said Halyard, sarcastically, "unless we're grounded on a whale."

"What's that soft thumping?" I asked. "Have we run afoul of a barrel or log?"

It was almost too dark to see, but I leaned over the rail and swept the water with my hand.

Instantly something smooth glided under it, like the back of a great fish, and I jerked my hand back to the tiller. At the same moment the whole surface of the water seemed to purr, with a sound like the breaking of froth in a champagne-glass.

"What's the matter with you?" asked Halyard, sharply.

"A fish came up under my hand," I said; "a porpoise or something—"

With a low cry, the pretty nurse clasped my arm in both her hands.

"Listen!" she whispered. "It's purring around the boat."

"What the devil's purring?" shouted Halyard. "I won't have anything purring around me!"

At that moment, to my amazement, I saw that the boat had stopped entirely, although the sail was full and the small pennant fluttered from the mast-head. Something, too, was tugging at the rudder, twisting and jerking it until the tiller strained and creaked in my hand. All at once it snapped; the tiller swung useless and the boat whirled around, heeling in the stiffening wind, and drove shoreward.

It was then that I, ducking to escape the boom, caught a glimpse of something ahead—something that a sudden wave seemed to toss on deck and leave there, wet and flapping—a man with round, fixed, fishy eyes, and soft, slaty skin.

But the horror of the thing were the two gills that swelled and re-laxed spasmodically, emitting a rasping, purring sound—two gasping, blood-red gills, all fluted and scalloped and distended.

Frozen with amazement and repugnance, I stared at the creature; I felt the hair stirring on my head and the icy sweat on my forehead.

"It's the harbor-master!" screamed Halyard.

The harbor-master had gathered himself into a wet lump, squatting motionless in the bows under the mast; his lidless eyes were phospho-rescent, like the eyes of living codfish. After a while I felt that either fright or disgust was going to strangle me where I sat, but it was only the arms of the pretty nurse clasped around me in a frenzy of terror.

There was not a fire-arm aboard that we could get at. Halyard's hand crept backward where a steel shod boat-hook lay, and I also made a clutch at it. The next moment I had it in my hand, and staggered for-ward, but the boat was already tumbling shoreward among the breakers, and the next I knew the harbor-master ran at me like a colossal rat, just as the boat rolled over and over through the surf; spilling freight and passengers among the seaweed-covered rocks.

When I came to myself I was thrashing about knee-deep in a rocky pool, blinded by the water and half suffocated, while under my feet, like a stranded porpoise, the harbor-master made the water boil in his ef-forts to upset me. But his limbs seemed soft and boneless; he had no nails, no teeth, and he bounced and thumped and flapped and splashed like a fish, while I rained blows on him with the boat-hook that sounded like blows on a football. And all the while his gills were blowing out and frothing, and purring, and his lidless eyes looked into mine, until, nauseated and trembling, I dragged myself back to the beach, where already the pretty nurse alternately wrung her hands and her petticoats in ornamental despair.

Beyond the cove, Halyard was bobbing up and down, afloat in his invalid's chair, trying to steer shoreward. He was the maddest man I ever saw.

"Have you killed that rubber-headed thing yet?" he roared.

"I can't kill it," I shouted, breathlessly. "I might as well try to kill a football!"

"Can't you punch a hole in it?" he bawled. "If I can only get at him—"

His words were drowned in a thunderous splashing, a roar of great, broad flippers beating the sea, and I saw the gigantic forms of my two great auks, followed by their chicks, blundering past in a shower of spray, driving headlong out into the ocean.

"Oh, Lord!" I said. "I can't stand that," and, for the first time in my life, I fainted peacefully—and appropriately—at the feet of the pretty nurse.

It is within the range of possibility that this story may be doubted. It doesn't matter; nothing can add to the despair of a man who has lost two great auks.

As for Halyard, nothing affects him—except his involuntary sea-bath, and that did him so much good that he writes me from the South that he's going on a walking-tour through Switzerland—if I'll join him. I might have joined him if he had not married the pretty nurse. I wonder whether— But, of course, this is no place for speculation.

In regard to the harbor-master, you may believe it or not, as you choose. But if you hear of any great auks being found, kindly throw a tablecloth over their heads and notify the authorities at the new Zoological Gardens in Bronx Park, New York. The reward is ten thousand dollars.

The Carpet of Belshazzar

We all were glad to see him; on his return he had found us all his friends. Nobody had spoken to him about his abrupt departure from New York; nobody had mentioned Westover; nothing connected with that episode was even hinted at by any of us, I believe, during his short sojourn among us. It was he himself who spoke of it first.

Of course during his absence we had followed his career; many among us had read and tried to understand what he had written in his three world-famous volumes, "Occult Philosophy," "The Weight of Human Souls," and "The Interstellar Laws of Psychic Phenomena."

It seemed, at times, here to us in America, that it was impossible that the idle man we had known so well could have become the great Psychic Scientist who had written these three astounding works—who now occupied the Chair of Psychical Philosophy in the great University of Trebizond—the man who was the confidential adviser of the Shah of Persia, the mentor of the Ameer of Afghanistan, the inspirer of the greatest diplomat of all the East—the late Akhound of Swat.

As he sat there in his immaculate evening dress, bronzed, youthful looking, presiding so quietly at the little dinner which he had given to us as a half-formal, half-intimate leave-taking before he sailed, it seemed to us incredible that this man, now on his return journey to Trebizond via Lhassa, could be the beloved and dreaded arbiter of Asiatic politics—the one white man in all the Orient who had ever been wholly respected, and absolutely feared by the temporal and spiritual heads of nations, religions, clans, and sects.

That, of course, he was what is popularly known as an adept, we supposed. What his wisdom, his insight, his amazing knowledge of the occult might include, we preferred, rather uncomfortably, not to conjecture.

There is, naturally, in all of us a childlike desire to hear of marvels; there is also a stronger and more childish desire to see miracles performed.

I am quite sure that we all hoped he might perhaps care to do something for us—merely to convince us. And at first, I know that many among us, seated there in the private room at the Lenox Club, felt a trifle ill at ease and a little in awe of this man with whom we were at such close quarters.

There was nothing particularly remarkable about the dinner; it was the usual excellent affair one might expect at the Lenox; the wines perfect, the service flawless.

And now, smoking our cigars, lounging in groups over the flower-laden table, we fell into the old, intimate, easy channels of conversation, chatting of past days, of our hopes and ambitions.

And our host, quiet, self-contained, pushed back his chair, looking somewhat curiously, I thought, from one to the other. And I thought, too, as his pleasant bronzed features changed from a faint smile to a graver expression, and then reverted to the smile for a moment, that he seemed to see something in each of us that was perhaps hidden from ourselves—that, as his eyes swept us, he was not only capable of reading much of what was not understood by us, but also something in the hidden future which awaited each of us.

So strongly did this idea begin to take hold of me that it began to make me uneasy. I felt, too, that others among us harbored that same idea—for the conversation was less accented now, and intermittent; voices had fallen to a lower, quieter pitch; and after a little nobody spoke.

Then I saw that we all were looking straight at our host, as though under some subtle and fascinated compulsion.

He sat very still; his composure appeared a trifle forced, as though he had voicelessly summoned us to concentrate upon him our attention, and was now searching for the exact words for some statement which he had meant to make to us all.

After a moment a slight flush crept over his handsome face. He said:

"You fellows are very good to come here and let me take leave of you so pleasantly. You have been very kind to me since I have come again among you. The sort of friendship that asks nothing but takes a man for granted is a good sort. Helmer,"—he looked at the sculptor Helmer—"I shall see you soon again." We all turned in surprise to Helmer, who seemed as surprised as we were. "I shall see you sooner than you expect ... Smith!"—he smiled at J. Abingdon Smith, 3d— "some day you will uproot a Tree of Dreams, but not the dream, Smith; that will become very real when you awake—as true"—and he turned to the man on his left—"as true as a dream which you shall dream under the Sign of Venus."

We sat there breathless, expectant. He was doing something after all; he was prophesying, in a curious sort of manner, probably speaking in symbols. And though we could not understand, we listened while the little shivers fluttered our pulses.

Then he looked at Edgerton, smiling; and Edgerton flushed up and looked back at him, almost defiantly.

"Edgerton," he said, "don't worry too much. What is not to be settled in court can sometimes be settled—*ex curia*." And to the young man on his right: "Doctor, don't overwork. If you do you will learn a stranger truth than is locked up among the molecules and atoms in your laboratory!"

Then he leaned across the table and laid one hand on Leeds's shoulder. "I congratulate you," he said, smiling; "you've got a good-natured ghost following you about. But he'll leave you if you turn idle. And don't be afraid, my boy."

"I'm not afraid," said young Leeds, rather pallid, but straightening up in his chair.

Our host laughed; then his face changed, and he raised his eyes to Shannon:

"Where is Harrod?" he asked slowly.

"At Bar Harbor," replied Shannon, "I believe."

"I thought so. And—remember one thing—there is a certain law which governs the validity of a check drawn to a man's order when that check has been signed by a man no longer living. But, Shannon, the intention is the important thing in such a matter."

"What, exactly, do you mean?" asked Shannon, astonished.

But our host had already turned to Escourt:

"Captain," he said, "you sail—when?"

"I have no sailing orders," laughed Escourt.

"Not yet?" Our host looked quietly at the young officer. "Well, it isn't the length of a voyage that counts, Escourt—nor the size of the troopship. No, you will anchor, some day, in a smaller craft than you started in, in the Port of the Golden Pool."

Escourt, still smiling, waited; but our host sat silent, head bent, one hand on the edge of the tablecloth.

"Not one of you," he said, without raising his eyes, "not one among you but who shall come face to face with what you still consider miracles. . . . Even Hildreth, yonder"—Hildreth jumped—"even Hildreth shall learn the Swastika."

"Swa—swat? What—what?" stammered Hildreth.

"Nothing to alarm you," smiled the other; then again the swift shadow fell across his face.

"Not one man among you who has not proven his friendship for me," he said, looking up and around. And to me he added: "You must prove it still further by telling fearlessly to the world what there will be to tell after I have gone, and after my words have been proven—the words I have spoken here to-night—and which no one among you understands. . . . But you all will understand them. And when the last man among you has understood"—turning again to me—"you must bear witness to the world, bear witness in printed page and over your own signature. Do you promise?"

"Yes," I said.

Then very quietly he looked around the table, and leaned forward, regarding each man in turn.

"I think," he said, "that it is time you understood exactly the facts about which you have forborne to question me. And I mean to tell you before we part; I mean to tell you the truth concerning Westover and—all that happened. . . . And when you know these facts, then you may begin to surmise why I went to Trebizond, why I remain, and—and—*what miracle of happiness I have found there—for the third time reincarnated.*"

He leaned back in his chair; his clear eyes became fixed and dreamy. Then he began to speak, in a low voice, as though to himself:

Time, and the funeral of Time, alas!—and the Old Year's passing-bell! Whistles from city and river, deep horns sounding from the foggy docks; and under my window a voice and a song—ah! that young voice in the street below calling me through the falling snow!

If it be true that Time makes all hurts well, I do not know; and "a thousand years in Thy sight is but as yesterday when it is passed, and as a watch in the night"; a thousand years! And this also is true; the flames of love make hot the furnace of Abaddon.

We were in the gallery as usual, Geraldine and I—the gallery where the carpets of the East were hung along the shadowy walls. For lately it was my pleasure to acquire rare rugs, and it was my profession to furnish expert opinion upon the age and origin of Oriental carpets, and to read and interpret the histories of forgotten emperors and the mysteries of long-forgotten gods from the colors and intricate flowery labyrinths tied in silk or wool to the warps of some dead sultan's lustrous tapestry.

Here in the long sky gallery hung my own rugs against the arabesque incrusted-ivory panels—Tabriz, Shiraz, Sehna, and Saruk—a somber blaze of color shot with fire—all rare, some priceless; Turkish Kulah, softly silky as a golden lion's hide, Persian Sehna, shimmering with rose and violet lights, fiercely brilliant rugs from Samarkand, superbly flowered, secreting deep in every floral thicket traceries of the ancient Mongol conqueror; Feraghans glowing like jewel-sewn velvets set with the Herati and the lotus—symbols of Egypt or of China, as you please to interpret the oldest pattern in the world.

Far in the gallery's amber-tinted gloom the red of Ispahan dominated, subduing fiery vistas to smoldering harmony through which, like a vast sapphire set in opals, glimmered the superb lost Persian blue.

There was one other rug, an Eighur, the famous so-called "Babilu," or "Carpet of Belshazzar"; but it hung alone in imperial magnificence behind the locked doors of a marble room, which it seemed to fill with a soft luster of its own, radiating from the mystic "Tree of Heaven" woven in its center.

We were, as I say, in this gallery; Geraldine poring over an illuminated volume on cuneiform inscriptions, I, with pad and pencil, idly shifting and reshifting the Kufic key to the ancient cipher, which always left me stranded where I had begun with the stately repetition:

"King of Kings—
King of Kings—
King of Kings—"

As for Westover, my cousin, he was, as usual, in the laboratory fussing with his venomous extracts—an occupation which, to my dismay, he had taken up within the year, working, as he explained, on the theory that every poison has its antidote. Yet it seemed to me that he was more anxious to invent some new and subtle toxic than to devise the remedy.

From where I sat I could not see him, but the crystalline tinkle of his glass retorts and bottles distracted my attention from the penciled calculations. Without moving my head, I glanced across the room at Geraldine. She looked up immediately, raising her level eyebrows in mute inquiry as though I had moved or spoken; then, realizing that I had not, she bent above the book once more, the warm color stealing to her cheeks.

Within the year a wordless intimacy had grown up between us; we never understood it, never acknowledged it, and at times it disconcerted us.

I sat silent, tracing with my pencil series after series of futile Kufic combinations with the cuneiforms, but ever the first turn of the ancient key creaked in my ears,

"King of Kings—
King of Kings—"

until the triverbal reiteration wore on my nerves.

Geraldine leaned back abruptly, closing her book.

"I'm tired and nervous," she said. "You may wear out your eyes and temper if you choose—and you're doing the latter, for I'm as restless as an eel. Besides, I'm lonely, and I'm going back to the East—if you'll come, too."

I laughed, understanding what she meant by the "East."

"Will you come with me?" she insisted.

"Yes," I said, "whenever you are ready."

She sprang to her feet, scattering the illuminated pages over the floor, and stood an instant facing me, tall, dark-eyed, smiling, brushing back the lustrous hair from her cheeks.

"Where is Jim?" she asked—although we both knew.

"In the laboratory," I replied mechanically.

Still busy with her hair, she regarded me dreamily out of those dark, sweet eyes of hers.

"It would be wonderful," she mused, "if Jim should find an antidote to death; but I wish it were not necessary to kill so many little helpless creatures. Did you hear that pitiful sound in there yesterday? Was it something he was killing?"

"I don't know," I said. And after a silence: "What are you going to do?"

She shook her head vaguely and leaned against the window, looking out into the rain.

"Shall we go back to our inscriptions?" I suggested.

She shook her head again. After a while she turned away from the window, stifling a dainty yawn, and stretched out, languidly straightening up to the full height of her young body.

"I feel stupid," she said; "I'm tired of cryptograms and the pages of dusty books. I'm tired of the rain, too. The languor of April is in me. I'm homesick for lands I never knew. So come back to the East with me, Dick."

She held out her hand to me with a confident little smile; and knowing what she meant, I acquiesced in her caprice, and conducted her solemnly to the piano, leaving her before it.

She stood there for a space, musing, her lovely head bent; then, still standing, she struck a sequence of chords—chords pulsating with color; and through them flashed strange little trills like threads of tinsel.

"This is an Eighur carpet I am dreaming of," she murmured, as the music swelled, glowing as tints and hues glow in the old dyes of the East.

Wave on wave of color seemed to spread from the keys under her fingers; she looked back at me over her shoulder with a warning nod.

"I shall begin to weave very soon. Khiounnou horsemen may appear and frighten me for a moment—but I shall finish. Listen! I am at the loom."

Seating herself, she developed out of the flowing, somber harmony a monotonous minor theme, suddenly checked by a distant rattle like the clatter of nomad lances on painted stirrups; then she picked up the thread of the melody again, dropped it, breathless for a moment's quivering silence, resumed it, twisting it into delicate arabesques, threading it across the dull, rich harmonies, at first slowly, then faster, faster, swift as the flying fingers of a nomad maid tying fretted silver in a Ghiordes knot. The whirring tempo was the cadence of the loom; soft feathery notes flew like carded wool; thicker, duller, softer grew the fabric, dense, silky, heavily lustrous.

Suddenly she broke the thread off short, the whole fabric falling with a muffled shock.

"Why did you do that?" I demanded wrathfully.

"The rug is woven; the weaver is dead," she said.

"Oh, go on, Geraldine," I insisted; "don't stop half way in a thing like that. It's the East—it's the real East, I tell you. How you do it—you who have never seen the East—Heaven only knows!"

"U Allah Aalem," she murmured; "it's in me." Then she looked back at me, laughing. "Centuries ago you and I heard that music along the Arax—or I sang it among the Tcherkess roses for you, perhaps—perhaps in the gardens of Trebizond."

"That might explain it," I said gravely. Lately she had found pleasure in a fancy that she and I had lived together in the East, centuries since, and that we were soon to return forever.

"You and I," she mused, touching the keys lightly—"and Jim, of course," she added.

"Of course," I said.

She dropped her head, striking chord on chord with nervous precision; and hanging in the wake of every ringing harmony a frail melody floated like the Chinese cloud band in a Kirman tapestry.

"What's that air?" I asked, fascinated.

"I don't know; it sounds pagan, doesn't it?—like the wicked beauty of Babylon. Do you hear how it beats on and on like the rhythm of naked feet—little, delicate, naked feet ablaze with gems—the feet of Herodiade perhaps—thud—thud—tching!—don't you hear them, Dick? And now listen to those silky, flowery trills! They're Asiatic; ancient Cathay is awaking—camel bells in the hazar of the Golden Emperor! Hark!—now you hear trumpets, don't you? Well, of course that must be the Mongols marching with the Prince of the Vanguard. Hark! How savagely the brutal Afghan theme breaks in with its fierce trampling and the staccato echo of Tekke drums! It's frightening me out of the East. I think we had better come home, Dick," she added, mischievously running into the latest popular street song.

"How on earth could you do that!" I exclaimed wrathfully. "You're a futile mixture of feather brain and genius!"

But where was the genius hidden under that laughing and exquisite mask confronting me? Suddenly the delicate mask became grave.

"Let me laugh when I can, Dick," she said. "It is not often I laugh."

I was silent.

"Of course you may be horrid if you choose," she observed with a shrug, running a brilliantly inane series of trills from end to end of the keyboard. "But it's no use scolding, for I won't study, I won't compose, I won't 'try to do something,' and I won't be serious. I'm shallow, I'm frivolous, I've the soul of a Trebizond dancing girl, and I like it. Now what are you going to do?"

"I'm going out," I said ungraciously.

"Oh—alone?"

"Not if you'll come. It's stopped raining. Will you come? Oh, get your hat, Geraldine, and stop that torment of idiotic trills!"

"If Jim doesn't mind, I think I'll go and sit in the laboratory with him," she observed carelessly.

I looked at her without comment.

"I have a curious idea," she continued, "that he might like to have me around to-day while he is working."

I stared at her, but there was no bitterness in her tranquil smile as she leaned forward, resting her elbows on the polished rosewood case.

"So I won't go with you, Dick," she said slowly.

One of those intervals of restless silence, which within the year we had learned to dread, menaced us now. Mute, motionless, I watched the soft color deepening in her face, then, impatient, roused myself and walked over to the laboratory. Westover looked up as I pushed aside the screen.

"Will you drive with us?" I asked. "The sun's out."

He declined, peering at me through his glass mask.

"Come on, Jim," I urged. "You've inhaled enough poison for one day. Take off your mask and wash your hands and drive us out to High Bridge. I'll telephone to the stable if you say the word, and they'll hook up the new four. Is it a go?"

"No," he said coldly, and turned on his heel, lifting a test tube to the light.

He was more taciturn and a trifle uglier than usual. I watched him for a moment warming the test tube over a burner, then without further parley replaced the screen, closed the double glass doors, and walked back to Geraldine.

"Doesn't Jim care to come?" she asked.

I said that her husband appeared to be absorbed in his work.

"Very well," she said, with airy composure; "trot along, Dicky—and if you see a bunch of jonquils growing on Fifth Avenue, you may pick them for me—or for that pretty girl you met at Lakewood—"

"I'll send you a bunch as big as a bushel."

"A bushel of flowers is as compromising as a declaration," she said. "Send them to her."

"There's only one way to settle it," I said; "I'll send them to the loveliest girl in the world—shall I?"

She assented, laughing uncertainly.

"I think I'll pay Jim a little call," she said, rising from the piano and walking slowly toward the laboratory.

A few moments later as I passed down the broad stairway I heard Westover's penetrating voice: "Let that glass tube alone, Geraldine! Why the devil can't you keep your hands off things when you come in here?"

I lingered for a while in the hallway, thinking that she might change her mind and come down, for she had left the laboratory to her husband, and I heard her moving about in her own apartment. She did not come, and after a little while I left the house, a sense of apprehension depressing me.

The asphalt of Fifth Avenue was still wet with the first warm rain of April, but the sun glittered on window and pavement and flashed along the polished panels of carriages crowding the avenue from curb to curb. A breath of spring had set the sparrows chattering and chirping; the movement of the throng, the bright gowns, the fresh faces of young girls, and the endless façades of glass reflecting it—all were pleasant to me, a man sensitive to impressions.

And so in the pale sunshine I sauntered on through the throng, now idling curiously by some shop window whither a display of jewels or curios attracted me, now strolling on again content with the soft color in sky and sunlight.

I found a florist whose shop windows were filled with thickets of fragrant, fragile spring flowers; and every little scented blossom that I touched, choosing the freshest, nodded to the voiceless cadence of a name repeated—and: "Geraldine! Geraldine!" they nodded, so confidently, so sweetly, that what was I to do but send them to her?

And so I sauntered on again, threading the throng, half-minded to turn back, yet ever tempted on by idleness, until above me the twin spires of the cathedral glimmered, all silvered in the shimmering blue.

Halting, undecided, I presently became aware of an old man, his withered hands crossed before him, standing quite patiently under the cathedral terrace. Before him on the sidewalk rested a basket draped with a brilliant rug or two and heaped with tawdry rubbish—scarlet fezzes, slippers of spangled leather, tasseled charms of gilt, flimsy striped fabrics—all the worthless flummery known as "Oriental" to the good peoples of the West.

Few stopped to look; no one bought. As I passed him his dimmed gaze met mine; all the wistfulness of the very poor, all the mystery of the very, very old, was in his eyes. Moved by impulse, perhaps, I spoke to him in a low voice, using the Turkish language.

A dull animation came into his misty eyes.

"Allahou Ekber," he muttered, in a trembling voice; "it is sweet to hear your words, my son."

"Mussulman," I said, "who are you who recite the Tekbir here under the spires of a Roman church?"

"Is there harm in bearing witness to the glory of God here under the minarets of your cathedral?" he asked humbly.

"Spire and minaret are one to Him," I said. "Who are you, Mussulman?"

"My name is Khassar," he said; "my nation Eighur; my fort is the Issig-Kul; Baïon-Aoul my clan. I am an Eighur Turk, a Khodja; and I am able to write the Turkish language in Arabic and in Eighur-Mongol characters."

"Reverend father," I said, full of astonishment and pity, "how should a Khodja of the Baïon-Aoul come to this? Even the Tekrin horseman halts at the sea."

"It is written," he said feebly, "that we belong to God and we return to Him."

Troubled, I stood there on the sidewalk, oblivious to the knot of idlers around us, curious to hear two men so different conversing in a common tongue.

I wished to give him something, yet did not venture to humiliate him without pretense of buying.

"Here is my card," I said, "on which is written my name and where I live. Bring me these rugs to-night, ata. I wish to buy."

"You do not desire them," he said, shaking his head. "You know the East; you understand these rugs; you know they are worthless, acid-washed, singed, rubbed with pumice, smoked—every vile Armenian practice used! You know the dyes are aniline; that they are loosely tied, hastily and flimsily woven by Armenian dogs and sons of dogs. You mean kindness; you have done me enough by speaking to me."

He passed his trembling hand over his ragged beard.

"You who know carpets and love them," he quavered; "listen attentively. I have a strip to show—not here—but I could bring it."

"Bring it," I said gently.

He fumbled in the pocket of his tattered coat and presently brought to light a scrap of paper on which was scrawled some Persian characters.

"It is such a carpet as I have never seen," he said; "there is nothing in our history or our traditions to teach us the meaning of this carpet—nothing save that it is an Eighur rug inscribed in Persian and in an unknown script. I have traced the characters in a single cartouche. Read, my son."

And I read, translating freely:

"Ten thousand thousand stars shine down on Babylon. The desert well reflects but one."

"I will bring the carpet," he said, after a silence. "I do not know its value; it has no beauty any longer; only the ghost of ancient splendor remains in the thin knots clinging to warp and weft. And it is old, my son, older than tradition. Upon it there is not one sign to teach us the mystery of its meaning."

He peered at me with his old, sad eyes, earnestly.

"I will bring it," he said. "Go with Ali, thou fair comrade of Hassan."

"May the Blessed Companions intervene for you," I said.

And so we parted, gravely and with circumstance, I to stroll homeward, touched, musing curiously upon this carpet of which a nomad Mussulman could make nothing. The Persian verse from the cartouche interested me, too, the refrain lingering persistently in my memory:

> *"Ten thousand thousand stars shine down on Babylon. The desert well reflects but one."*

Never before, save on the imperial carpet known as Belshazzar's Rug, had I encountered any inscription mentioning Babylon. So, at the first glance, the nomad's rug should have some value. But speculation was facile—surely I ought to have learned that if unnumbered disappointments could teach me anything.

Thinking of these things, I passed along the noble avenue, retracing my steps to the big dusky house standing alone, with two old trees to guard it—relics, like the mansion, of the great city's infancy—the last old dwelling left marooned amid the arid wastes of commerce. Here my cousin and his wife lived with me in winter; I with them at their Lenox home in summer.

A brougham or two at the curb before the house warned me of clients waiting or of visitors for Geraldine—doubtless the latter, for it was now past five.

Under the circumstances I went in to second Geraldine—for Westover never troubled himself to be civil to her friends.

There were people there, and tea—and a pretty, wordless welcome from Geraldine.

The violet-tinted April dusk brought candlelight; people went away and others came; then, one by one, they left, and we were alone, Geraldine and I—and the new moon shining through the frail curtains. For a long time we talked together, aimlessly, of this and that which mattered nothing to anybody. A maid entered to draw the curtains. When she left, Geraldine laughed and picked up a cluster of yellow jonquils.

"Your courage failed you, after all," she said; "the loveliest woman in the world must go without my flowers to-night."

"She has them," I retorted.

"Do you mean me, Dick?" she said under her breath.

"Did you doubt it?"

She bowed her head. Silence, ever waiting to ensnare us, crept like a shadow in between us. And I would not have it.

"An old man is to bring a rug to-night," I said abruptly.

Geraldine stirred in her armchair, repeating in a low voice:

"Ten thousand thousand stars shine down on Babylon. The desert well reflects but one. Abaddon none."

Bolt upright in my chair I listened, incredulous of my own ears.

"Where on earth did you hear that?" I demanded.

"I read it on Belshazzar's Rug in cuneiform with the Kufic key," she answered, watching me.

"You—all alone—interpreted that?" I asked, astounded.

"Yes. It is the cuneiform inscription in the gold cartouche."

Profound astonishment left me silent. She lay back in her chair with a little laugh of pure excitement.

"After you went out," she said, "I was horribly lonely, and I thought of you, and then I thought about the work you loved—the cuneiforms—and—as Jim did not seem to need me in the laboratory—I thought to myself: 'Suppose—suppose by luck I could unravel the inscription on the gold cartouche! Dick would be the happiest man in the world.' And then—your—your flowers came, and I sat for a while alone with them. Then, on impulse, I jumped up and took the Kufic tables and all the combinations that you and I had tried together, and I slipped upstairs to the marble room and knelt down before Belshazzar's Rug. O Dick! the Tree of Heaven seemed to quiver in every jeweled branch and leaf!—it was only the draught from the closing door that moved the rug, but the mystic tree swayed there as the folds of the carpet moved, and I seemed to feel the mystery of the Prophet's Paradise stealing into me, penetrating me like the incense of forbidden wine—and I—I felt very Eastern and very pagan, kneeling there.

"It was strange, too; the intricate Kufic key seemed to be falling into place of its own impulse, symbol after symbol promising a linked symmetry of sense, until, almost before I was conscious of the miracle, it had been wrought there in the marble room; and my eyes were opened; and I, kneeling before the Tree of Heaven, read quite clearly what is written in the gold cartouche on the great carpet of Belshazzar. Dick! I prayed so hard that I might read it. And I have read it—for you!"

In the eloquence of her emotion she had risen, holding out both hands to me; I caught them, crushing them to my lips.

Ominous pulsating silence grew between us; her fingers relaxed and her hands fell from my lips. The stillness, intense, absolute, became a tension, a growing resistless force pressing us apart, slowly, inexorably driving me back step by step against the silk-hung wall, which I reached for, groping, steadying myself.

Never before had we been so swayed, so thrilled; never before had we been so reckless of the peril. Over us a magic snare had fallen, and we had evaded it—an unseen and delicate web, enmeshing us, drawing us together limb to limb, body to body, soul to soul, there on the kindling edges of destruction.

She sank back into the deep seat by the window, her white hands tightening on the gilded foliation of the chair's carved arms. And I saw how pale her face was and how her dark eyes were fixed steadily upon the floor as though destruction was a pit whose edge lay at her feet.

Presently I became aware that the world outside the curtained windows was moving still—had perhaps never halted on its way to wait upon our fate. And, crossing the room, I raised the shade and saw the new moon, low in the sky, kneeling amid the watching stars. Yellow rays from a street lamp illuminated the old trees' foliage, edging with palest fire the tracery of new-born leaves, tufting each stem and twig, exquisite, delicately formal as the leafy labyrinths of the Tree of Heaven spreading above the flowery field of Belshazzar's Rug.

Khassar the nomad had come and gone, and his rug hung in the marble room, pale as the tinted shadow cast by the great carpet of Belshazzar.

The nomad's rug was clean but very ancient, and so worn, so time-eaten to the very warp, that the Kherdeh was all but obliterated in the metnih. But outside of that, between the outside band and the ara, or central line, there were traces of ancient glory and dimmed outlines of design; and I saw the twelve cartouches inscribed alternately in Persian and in cuneiform characters. There, too, were the worn remains of floral thickets haunted of beast and bird, intricate allegories, chronicles in color and symbol, every leaf, every blossom, every creature fraught with mystic meaning; and there also, still faintly to be made out, the shadowy foliage of the Tree of Heaven.

"How much did you pay for that ghost of a rug?" demanded Westover, who had followed me upstairs after dressing for dinner.

When I told him he shrugged his shoulders, but made no comment. A moment later Geraldine entered, and his small eyes, no longer furtive, were fixed and dull.

"They say in the East," I remarked, "that when all color is gone from an Eighur rug a lost soul takes it for its abode. Eighur women are supposed to have souls occasionally, and to lose them now and then."

"There are plenty of lost souls in town," observed Westover; "no doubt you'll have your choice of tenants for your carpet—or," he added, staring at space, "if you like I'll provide you."

I did not understand his remark, but it left a vaguely sinister impression. Geraldine, standing between us, her white fingers linked behind her, looked up at me very gravely.

"Do you know," she said, "that I am convinced that I wove that rug some centuries ago?"

"I have no doubt of it," I replied, smiling.

"Do you doubt it, Jim?" she asked gayly.

He did not reply.

"As a matter of fact," I said, "it was always believed that a young girl who dared to weave the Tree of Heaven into an Eighur carpet died when her task was ended—her entire physical and spiritual vitality entering into the sacred tree and infusing it with mystic splendor."

"Oh, I died as you say," observed Geraldine gravely.

"I don't see that you infused much physical or spiritual splendor into that rug," observed Westover.

"I must die again, you know, Jim, and bring all its vanished beauty back," she said gayly. "Shall I, Dick?—and leave you a priceless carpet as my bequest and monument?"

Westover turned on his heel, fidgeting with his collar. Recently his neck had grown fat behind the ears.

A few moments later dinner was announced.

We lingered late over dinner, I remember. Jim drank heavily—a habit which both Geraldine and I had long since left unnoticed, she shrinking from the sullen rebuff certain to follow even a playful protest, I understanding the utter hopelessness of interference. His mind, already shaken, would one day shatter, and the dreadful price be paid.

As he sat there sousing walnuts in port, in his altered features and swollen hands I seemed to divine something malicious and patient and powerful—that indescribable physical menace one feels in the inert brooding eye of the mentally and spiritually crippled.

When Geraldine rose he stood up unsteadily. After she had gone he lighted a cigar and turned his bloodshot eyes on me.

"Is that wine expensive?" he demanded, pointing to Geraldine's half-empty glass.

"Rather," I said.

He picked up the glass, examined it, sniffing at the contents.

"It's poor claret," he said. "Taste it. It's pure poison, I tell you."

"I'm sorry," I said indifferently.

Again he sniffed it. "Faugh!" he sneered, and threw it into the fireplace behind him. Then he got on his feet, heavily, muttering to himself, and stumbled off through the drawing-room.

For a while I sat there amid the shaded candles, staring at space. But I could not read the future pictured there amid the empty chairs and the flowers, already drooping in each crystal vase.

When at length I roused myself and went upstairs, passing her apartment I heard her singing to herself, and I wondered that she could.

I paused on the gallery stairway to listen; and she could not have heard my footsteps on the thick deep carpeting, yet she came to the door and opened it, looking up at me where I stood.

"You are going to the marble room. May I come and help you?" she asked sweetly. And as I was silent, she said again: "Let me be happy, won't you, Dick? Let me be where you are."

"Have I ever avoided you, Geraldine?"

I descended the steps, she laid her hand lightly on my arm, and together we mounted the stairway toward the gallery.

"I was singing a Hillah tent song when you passed," she said, "partly because I was lonely, and partly"—she hesitated, looking around at me— "partly because I've come to the conclusion, Dick, that I was once at Belshazzar's feast in Cadimirra—for there's a great deal of wickedness in me—you'd never believe it, would you?"

She smiled at me so innocently, so adorably, that I laughed outright.

"I've heard that the maids of Babilu-Ki had a bowing acquaintance with the devil," I said. "Even an Eighur girl nodded pleasantly to Erlik now and then—according to the chronicles of the Tekrins."

"Oh, they surely did," she said. And, "Thank you, Dick," she added, as we reached the gallery; "when I am an old woman you must help me up the steep places."

"It is you who help me," I said lightly.

She stood, resting her arm on the table while I gathered up the mass of papers containing our cuneiform combinations and the Kufic key.

"All that is useless," she said suddenly. Her manner and smile had altered.

I looked up in surprise, and at the same instant she pushed the papers from beneath my hands.

"The memory of things forgotten centuries ago has returned to me," she said feverishly. "I am a pagan again. It was Istar who first taught my hands to weave and my fingers to tie the Sehna knot. I wove that carpet; what I have woven there I can read. Why do you laugh? Will you believe me if I translate the mystery of each inscription as easily as I read the gold cartouche? Come; we shall never need those papers again."

What new caprice was this? She was smiling, almost fixedly, and I thought that there was something in her overflushed face and in the star-like brilliancy of her eyes not quite normal. At the same moment the electric lights in the laboratory went out. Westover was evidently in there. I waited, expecting him to appear, but he did not. Again I reached for the papers, but Geraldine scattered them with a quick sweep of her hand.

"Won't you believe me? Won't you let me try?" she repeated almost impatiently.

With a quick movement she bent forward past me and shut off the lights in the gallery where we stood. Another second, and the lights in the marble room broke out fiercely; and there, full in the dazzling glory, I saw the great carpet of Belshazzar hanging, and beside it the Eighur rug—a pallid shadow on the wall.

Geraldine, hands clasped to her scarlet mouth, dark eyes fixed, moved forward slowly, opalescent tints flashing on her smooth bare arms and shoulders, her head a delicate silhouette against the glare.

I followed, pausing at her side, and we stood silently before the miracle, the great folds gently stirring in some unfelt current; and I saw the upper branches of the Tree of Heaven sway, and a thousand leaves, all glistening, quiver and subside.

"One can almost hear the rustling of the leaves," I whispered.

"I hear more than that," she murmured. "I hear my soul bidding me good-by."

She smiled dreamily, turning to the faded Eighur carpet, and stepping back one pace, dropped her left arm, clasping my hand in hers.

"It was I who wove that carpet—I, maid of the Issig-Kul—and it was you, beloved of Hassan, who inspired it."

"What are you saying, Geraldine?" I began uneasily; "where did you ever hear my name linked with the name of Hassan?"

Her palm was burning hot, her eyes too bright. The fever of caprice possessed her, and her imagination was running riot.

There was a silence, through which a distant sound penetrated—the faint ring of glass somewhere in the laboratory. Westover was tying on his crystal mask.

She heard it, too, and she turned, looking me full in the eyes.

"Dick," she said, "he has slain my body. My soul is bidding me good-by."

"It is my own that he is dragging to destruction, not yours," I muttered.

But she only clasped my hand tighter, the fixed smile stamped on her lips.

"Listen," she whispered, raising her arm. "This is what is written in the rose cartouche on the Eighur carpet that I made:

'Roses of Babylon: Ashes of roses in Abaddon.'

Love and its awful penalty, Dick—and the warning I wove, coffined in cryptogram! Listen again. The cartouche below was once topaz—for I wove it—I!

'All Paradise the cost:
Warp and weft for souls so lost.'

—Mine, Dick, mine!—lost in loving as I loved, centuries since. I have no soul; I have never had any since I lost it then. It is there, tenanting the phantom of an Eighur carpet. Do you not understand? There is my faded monument and refuge—that magic-woven sanctuary—that hiding place from hell!"

Her little feverish fingers tightened convulsively in mine; the color flamed in her cheeks. Suddenly she crushed our clasped hands to her heart, and I felt it leaping madly.

"Geraldine," I stammered, "what is all this ghastly nonsense? Are you ill?"

"Listen! Listen!" she whispered; "the next cartouche was blue—the lost Persian blue! I know; why should I not know—I who wove it centuries ago? And thus it reads, O thou whom I loved to my destruction—thou whom I love!

'Time and the Guest
Shall meet me twice—once East, once West.'

"Ah, prophetess was I by Istar's favor—seeing I died for love. Do you not understand, Dick? Time and the Guest!—the Guest is Death—the Guest we all must entertain one day—and I twice—once in the East, once here in the West—here, now!"

"Geraldine, are you mad?" I whispered; "look at me!—turn and look at me, I say!"

But she shivered in my arms, whispering that she was ransoming her soul and mine. A distant sound broke from the laboratory, and we listened.

"Hush, beloved," she said breathlessly; "the last cartouche is black! And this is written there:

'Soul, lotus-sealed,
Receive—thy—Paradise—'"

Her voice died out; a terrible pallor struck her face; she swayed where she stood, the smile frozen on her bloodless lips.

As I caught her to me, her head fell straight back and her body sank a dead weight in my arms. Then a dreadful thing occurred; the faded ancient tapestry glowed out like a live ember, kindling from end to end, brighter, fiercer, flaming into living fire; and the phantom Tree of Heaven, flashing, superbly jeweled, burst into magnificent florescence.

Blinded, almost stupefied, I staggered back, but the straining cry died in my throat as a voice is strangled in dreadful dreams.

Again I strove to shout. The rug, glowing like a living ember, slowly faded before my eyes. Suddenly the last spark went out in a shower of whitening ashes.

Again I strove to cry out: "Jim! Jim!" but my lips stiffened with horror as I listened. For he was somewhere there in the darkness, laughing.

"It was in her wine," he chuckled—"and I saw her kiss the glass and look at you!—and you, there, staring at nothing! Stare at it now!"

And again: "Do you think I have never watched her?—and you? Now she's in hell, and we'll race for her on even terms once more."

Silence: a low, insane laugh, cut by a report and the crash of glass as he fell, shattering his masked face upon the floor.

After a long while I spoke, listening intently. Then I took up my burden.

And there was no sound save the soft stirring of her silken gown as I bore her through the darkness, my cold lips pressed to hers.

He has never returned to America, but now that the time has come for me to fulfill my part, I do so, setting down what I know and what occult information I have received in letters from him, of the strange fate which overtook, separately, each and every man present at that farewell dinner at the Lenox Club.

My own fate is stranger still—to record these facts and take my position as his historian and his disciple.

The Sign of Venus

In the card room the game, which had started from a chance suggestion, bid fair to develop into an all-night séance: the young foreign diplomat had shed his coat and lighted a fresh cigar; somebody threw a handkerchief over the face of the clock, and a sleepy club servant took reserve orders for two dozen siphons and other details.

"That lets me out," said Hetherford, rising from his chair with a nod at the dealer. He tossed his cards on the table, settled side obligations with the man on his left, yawned, and put on his hat.

Somebody remonstrated: "It's only two o'clock, Hetherford; you have no white man's burden sitting up for you at home."

But Hetherford shook his head, smiling.

So a servant removed his chair, another man cut in, the dealer dealt cards all around. Presently from somewhere in the smoke haze came a voice, "Hearts." And a quiet voice retorted, "I double it."

Hetherford lingered a moment, then turned on his heel, sauntered out across the hallway and down the stairs into the court, refusing with a sign the offered cab.

Breathing deeply, yawning once or twice, he looked up at the stars. The night air refreshed him; he stood a moment, thoughtfully contemplating his half-smoked cigar, then tossed it away and stepped out into the street.

The street was quiet and deserted; darkened brownstone mansions stared at him through somber windows as he passed; his footsteps echoed across the pavement like the sound of footsteps following.

His progress was leisurely; the dreary monotony of the house fronts soothed him. He whistled a few bars of a commonplace tune, crossed the deserted avenue under the electric lamps, and entered the dimly lighted beyond.

Here all was silence; the doors of many houses were boarded up—sign that their tenants had migrated to the country. No shadowy cat fled along the iron railings at his approach; no night watchman prowled in deserted dooryards or peered at him from obscurity.

Strolling at ease, thoughts nowhere, he had traversed half the block, when an opening door and a glimmer of light across the sidewalk attracted his attention.

As he approached the house from whence the light came, a figure suddenly appeared on the stoop—a girl in a white ball gown—hastily ascending the stone steps. Gaslight from the doorway tinted her bared arms and shoulders. She bent her graceful head and gazed earnestly at Hetherford.

"I beg your pardon," she almost whispered; "might I ask you to help me?"

Hetherford stopped and wheeled short.

"I—I really beg your pardon," she said, "but I am in such distress. Could I ask you to find me a cab?"

"A cab!" he repeated uncertainly; "why, yes—I will with pleasure—" He turned and looked up and down the deserted street, slowly lifting his hand to his short mustache. "If you are in a hurry," he said, "I had better go to the nearest stables—"

"But there is something more," she said, in a tremulous voice; "could you get me a wrap—a cloak—anything to throw over my gown?"

He looked up at her, bewildered. "Why, I don't believe I—" he began, then fell silent before her troubled gaze. "I'll do anything I can for you," he said abruptly. "I have a raincoat at the club—if your need is urgent—"

"It is urgent; but there is something else—something more urgent, more difficult for me to ask you. I must go to Willow Brook—I must go now, to-night! And I—I have no money."

"Do you mean Willow Brook in Westchester?" he asked, astonished. "There is no train at this hour of the morning!"

"Then—then what am I to do?" she faltered. "I cannot stay another moment in that house."

After a silence he said: "Are you afraid of anybody in that house?"

"There is nobody in the house," she said with a shudder; "my mother is in Westchester; all the household are there. I—I came back—a few moments ago—unexpectedly—" She stammered and winced under his keen scrutiny; then the pallor of utter despair came into her cheeks, and she hid her white face in her hands.

Hetherford watched her for a moment.

"I don't exactly understand," he said gently, "but I'll do anything I can for you. I'll go to the club and get my raincoat; I'll go to the stables and get a cab; I haven't any money with me, but it would take only a few minutes for me to drive to the club and get some. . . . Please don't be distressed; I'll do anything you desire."

She dropped her arms with a hopeless gesture.

"But you say there is no train!"

"You could drive to the house of some of your friends—"

"No, no! Oh, my friends must never know of this!"

"I see," he said gravely.

"No, you don't see," she said unsteadily. "The truth is that I am almost frightened to death."

"Can you not tell me what has frightened you so?"

"If I tried to tell you, you would think me mad—you would indeed—"

"Try," he said soothingly.

"Why—why, it startled me to find myself in this house," she began. "You see, I didn't expect to come here; I didn't really want to come here," she added piteously. "Oh, it is simply dreadful to come—like this!" She glanced fearfully over her shoulder at the lighted doorway above, then turned to Hetherford as though dazed.

"Tell me," he said in a quiet voice.

"Yes—I'll tell you. At first it was all dark—but I must have known I was in my own room, for I felt around on the dresser for the matches and lighted a candle. And when I saw that it was truly my own room, and when I caught sight of my own face in the mirror, it terrified me—" She pressed her fingers to her cheeks with a shudder. "Then I ran downstairs and lighted the gas in the hall and peered into the mirror; and I saw a face there—a face like my own—"

Pale, voiceless, she leaned on the bronze balustrade, fair head drooping, lids closed.

Presently, eyes still closed, she said: "You will not leave me alone here—will you—" Her voice died to a whisper.

"No—of course not," he replied slowly.

There was an interval of silence; she passed her hand across her eyes and raised her head, looking up at the stars.

"You see," she murmured, "I dare not be alone; I *dare* not lose touch with the living. I suppose you think me mad, but I am not; I am only stunned. Please stay with me."

"Of course," he said in a soothing voice. "Everything will come out all right—"

"Are you sure?"

"Perfectly. I don't quite know what to say—how to reassure you and offer you any help—"

He fell silent, standing there on the sidewalk, worrying his short mustache. The situation was a new one to him.

"Suppose," he suggested, "that you try to take a little rest. I'll sit down on the steps—"

She looked at him in wide-eyed alarm. "Do you mean that I should go into that house—alone!"

"Well—you oughtn't to stand on the steps all night. It is nearly three o'clock. You are frightened and nervous. Really you must go in and—"

"Then you must come, too," she said desperately. "This nightmare is more than I can endure alone. I'm not a coward; none of my race is. But I need a living being near me. Will you come?"

He bowed. She turned, hastily gathering her filmy gown, and mounted the shadowy steps without a sound; and he followed leisurely, even perhaps warily, every sense alert.

He was prepared to see the end of this encounter—see it through to an explanation if it took all summer. Of the situation, however, and of her, he had so far ventured no theory. The type of woman and the situation were perfectly new to him. He was aware that anything might happen in New York, and, closing the heavy front door, he was ready for it.

The hall gas jets were burning brightly, and in the darkened drawing-room he could distinguish the heavy outlines of furniture cased in dust coverings.

She asked him to strike a match and light the sconces in the draw-ing-room, and he did so, curiosity now thoroughly aroused.

As the gas flared up, shrouded pictures and furniture sprang into view surrounding him, and in the dusk of the room beyond he saw a ray of light glimmering on the foliated carving of a gilded harp.

Slowly he turned to the girl beside him. A warm shadow dimmed her delicate features, yet they were the loveliest he had ever looked upon.

Suddenly he understood the mute message of her eyes: "My impru-dence places me at your mercy."

"Your helplessness places me at yours," he said aloud, scarcely con-scious that he had spoken.

At that a bright flush transfigured her. "I trusted you the moment saw you," she said impulsively. "Do you mind sitting there opposite me? shall take this chair—rather near you—"

She sank into an armchair; and, touched and a trifle amused, he seated himself, at a little nod from her, awaiting her further pleasure.

She lay there for a minute or two without speaking, rounded arms resting on the gilt arms of the chair, eyes thoughtfully studying him.

"I've simply got to tell you everything," she said at length. "It can do no harm, I think," he replied pleasantly.

"No; no harm. The harm has been done. Yet, with you sitting there so near me, I am not frightened now. It is curious," she mused, "that I should feel no apprehension now. And yet—and yet—"

She leaned toward him, dropping her linked fingers in her lap.

"Tell me, did you ever hear of the Sign of Venus?—the *Signum Veneris?*" she asked.

"I've heard of it—yes," he replied, surprised. And as she said noth-ing, he went on: "The distinguished gentleman who occupies the chair of Applied Psychics at the university lectures on the Sign of Venus, I be-lieve."

"Did you attend the lectures?" she asked calmly.

He said he had not, smiling a trifle.

"I did."

"They were probably amusing," he ventured.

"Not very. Psychic phenomena bored me; I went during Lent. Psychic phenomena—" She hesitated, embarrassed at his amusement. "I suppose you laugh at that sort of thing."

"No, I don't laugh at it. Queer things occur, they say. All I know is that I myself have never seen anything happen that could not be explained by natural laws."

"I have," she said.

He bent his head in polite acquiescence.

"I went to the lectures," she said. "I am not very intellectual; nothing he said interested me very much—which was, of course, suitable for a Lenten amusement."

She leaned a little nearer, small hands tightly interlaced on her knee.

"His lecture on the Sign of Venus was the last." She lifted a white finger, drawing the imaginary *Signum Veneris* in the air. Hetherford nodded gravely.

"The lecture," she continued, "ended with an explanation of the Sign of Venus—how, contemplating it by starlight, one might pass into that physical unconsciousness which leaves the mind free to control the soul."

She held out her left hand toward him. On a stretched finger a ring glistened, mounted with the Sign of Venus blazing in brilliants.

"I had this made specially," she said; "not that I had any particular desire to test it—no curiosity. It never occurred to me that here in New York one could—could—"

"What?" asked Hetherford dryly.

"—could leave one's own body at will."

"I don't believe it could be accomplished in New York," he said with great gravity. "And that's a pretty safe conclusion to come to, is it not?"

She dropped her eyes, silent for a moment, resting her delicate chin on the palm of her hand. Then she lifted her eyes to him calmly, and the direct beauty of her gaze disturbed him.

"No, it is not a safe conclusion to come to. Listen to me. Last night they gave a dance at the Willow Brook Hunt. It was nearly two o'clock this morning when I left the club house and started home across the lawn with my mother and the maid—"

"But how on earth could—" he began, then begged her pardon and waited.

She continued serenely: "The night was warm and lovely, and it was clear starlight. When I entered my room I sent the maid away and sat down by the open window. The scent of the flowers and the beauty of the night made me restless; I went downstairs, unbolted the door, and slipped out through the garden to the pergola. My hammock hung there, and I lay down in it, looking out at the stars."

She drew the ring from her finger, holding it out for him to see.

"The starlight caught the gems on the Sign of Venus," she said under her breath; "that was the beginning. And then—I don't know why—as I lay there idly turning the ring on my finger, I found myself saying, 'I must go to New York: I must leave my body here asleep in the hammock and go to my own room in Fifty-eighth Street.'"

A curious little chill passed over Hetherford.

"I said it again and again—I don't know why. I remember the ring glittered; I remember it grew brighter and brighter. And then—and then! I found myself upstairs in the dark, groping over the dresser for the matches."

Again that faint chill touched Hetherford.

"I was stupefied for a moment," she said tremulously; "then I suspected what I had done, and it frightened me. And when I lighted the candle, and saw it was truly my own room—and when I caught sight of my own face in the mirror—terror seized me; it was like a glimpse of something taken unawares. For, do you know that although in the glass I saw my own face, the face was not looking back at me." She dropped her head, crushing the ring in both hands. "The reflected face was far lovelier than mine; and it was mine, I think, yet it was not looking at me, and it moved when I did not move. I wonder—I wonder—"

The tension was too much. "If that be so," he said, steadying his voice—"if you saw a face in your mirror, the face was your own." He made an impatient gesture, rising to his feet at the same moment. "All that you have told me can be explained," he said.

"How can it? At this very moment I am asleep in my hammock."

"We will deal with that later," he said, smiling down at her. "Where is there a looking-glass?"

"There is one in the hallway." She rose, slipping the ring on her finger, and led the way to where an oval gilt mirror hung partly covered with dust cloths.

He cast aside the coverings. "Now look into the glass," he said gayly.

She raised her head and faced the mirror for an instant.

"Come here," she whispered; and he stepped behind her, looking over her shoulder.

In the glass, as though reflected, he saw her face, but *the face was is profile!*

A shiver passed over him from head to foot.

"Did I not tell you?" she whispered. "Look! See, the other face is moving, while I am still!"

"There's something wrong about the glass, of course," he muttered; "it's defective."

"But who is that in the glass?"

"It is you—your profile. I don't exactly understand. Good Lord! It's turning away from us!"

She shrank against the wall, wide-eyed, breathing rapidly.

"There is no use in our being frightened," he said, scarcely knowing what he uttered. "This is Fifty-eighth Street, New York, 1903." He shook his shoulders, squaring them, and forced a smile. "Don't be frightened; there's an explanation for all this. You are not asleep in Westchester; you are here in your own house. You mustn't tremble so. Give me your hand a moment."

She laid her hand in his obediently; it shook like a leaf. He held it firmly, touching the fluttering pulse.

"You are certainly no spirit," he said, smiling; "your hand is warm and yielding. Ghosts don't have hands like that, you know."

Her fingers lay in his, quite passive now, but the pulse quickened.

"The explanation of it all is this," he said. "You have had a temporary suspension of consciousness, during which time you, without being aware of what you were doing, came to town from Willow Brook. You believe you went to the dance at the Hunt Club, but probably you did not. Instead, during a lapse of consciousness, you went to the station, took a train to town, came straight to your own house—" He hesitated.

"Yes," she said, "I have a key to the door. Here it is." She drew it from the bosom of her gown; he took it triumphantly.

"You simply awoke to consciousness while you were groping for the matches. That is all there is to it; and you need not be frightened at all!" he announced.

"No, not frightened," she said, shaking her head; "only—only I wonder how I can get back. I've tried to fix my mind on my ring—on the Sign of Venus—I cannot seem to—"

"But that's nonsense!" he protested cheerfully. "That ring has nothing to do with the matter."

"But it brought me here! Truly I am asleep in my hammock. Won't you believe it?"

"No; and you mustn't, either," he said impatiently. "Why, just now I explained to you—"

"I know," she said, looking down at the ring on her hand; "but you are wrong—truly you are."

"I am not wrong," he said, laughing. "It was only a dream—the dance, the return, the hammock—all these were parts of a dream so intensely real that you cannot shake it off at once."

"Then—then *who* was that we saw in the mirror?"

"Let us try it again," he said confidently. She suffered him to lead her again to the mirror; again they peered into its glimmering depths, heads close together.

A second's breathless silence, then she caught his hand in both of hers with a low cry; for the strange profile was slowly turning toward them a face of amazing beauty—her own face transfigured, radiantly glorified.

"My soul!" she gasped, and would have fallen at his feet had he not held her and supported her to the stairs, where she sank down, hiding her face in her arms.

As for him, he was terribly shaken; he strove to speak, to reason with her, with himself, but a stupor chained body and mind, and he only leaned there on the newel post, vaguely aware of his own helplessness.

Far away in the night the bells of a church began striking the hour— one, two, three, four. Presently the distant rattle of a wagon sounded. The city stirred in its slumbers.

He found himself bending beside her, her passive hands in his once more, and he was saying: "As a matter of fact, all this is quite capable of an explanation. Don't be distressed—please don't be frightened or sad. We've both had some sort of hallucination, that's all—really that is all."

"I am not frightened now," she said dreamily. "I am quite sure that— that I am not dead. I am only asleep in my hammock. When I awake—"

Again, in spite of himself, he shivered.

"Will you do one more thing for me?" she asked.

"Yes—a million."

"Only one. It is unreasonable, it is perhaps silly—and I have no right to ask—"

"Ask it," he begged.

"Then—then, will you go to Willow Brook? Now?"

"Now?" he repeated blankly.

"Yes." She looked down at him with the shadow of a smile touching lips and eyes. "I am asleep in the hammock; I sleep very, very soundly— and very, very late into the morning. They may not find me there for a long while. So would you mind going to Willow Brook to awaken me?"

"I—I—but you do not expect me to leave you here and find you in Westchester!" he stammered.

"You need not go," she said quietly. "If you will telephone to the house and ask somebody to go out to the pergola—"

"No," he said, "I will go; I will go anywhere on earth for you."

He stood up, his senses in a whirl. She rose, too, leaning lightly on the balustrade.

"Thank you," she said sweetly. "When you awake me, give me this." She held out the *Signum Veneris;* and he took it, and bending his head slowly raised it to his lips.

It was almost morning when he entered his own house. In a dull trance he dressed, turned again to the stairs, and crept out into the shadowy street.

People began to pass him; an early electric tram whizzed up Forty-second Street as he entered the railway station. Presently he found himself in a car, clutching his ticket in one hand, her ring in the other.

"It is I who am mad, not she," he muttered as the train glided from the station, through the long yard, dim in morning mist, where green and crimson lanterns still sparkled faintly.

Again he pressed the *Signum Veneris* to his lips. "It is I who am mad—love mad!" he whispered as the far treble warning of the whistle aroused him and sent him stumbling out into the soft fresh morning air.

The rising sun smote him full in the eyes as he came in sight of the club house among the still green trees, and the dew on the lawn flashed like the gems of the *Signum Veneris* on the ring he held so tightly.

Across the club house lawn stood another house, circled with gardens in full bloom; and to the left, among young trees, the white columns of a pergola glistened, tinted with rose from the early sun.

There was not a soul astir as he crossed the lawn and entered the garden, brushing the dew from overweighted blossoms as he passed.

Suddenly, at a turn in the path, he came upon the pergola, and saw a brilliant hammock hanging in the shadow.

Over the hammock's fringe something light and fluffy fell in folds like the billowy frills of a ball gown. He stumbled forward, dazed, incredulous, and stood trembling for an instant.

Then, speechless, he sank down beside her, and dropped the ring into the palm of her half-closed and unconscious hand.

A ray of sunlight fell across her hair; slowly her blue eyes unclosed, smiling divinely.

And in her partly open palm the Sign of Venus glimmered like dew silvering a budding rose.

The Ladies of the Lake

At the suggestion of several hundred thousand ladies desiring to revel and possibly riot in the saturnalia of equal franchise, the unnamed lakes in that vast and little known region in Alaska bounded by the Ylanqui River and the Thunder Mountains were now being inexorably named after women.

It was a beautiful thought. Already several exquisite, lonely bits of water, gem-set among the eternal peaks, mirrors for cloud and soaring eagle, a glass for the moon as keystone to the towering arch of stars, had been irrevocably labelled.

Already there was Lake Amelia Jones, Lake Sadie Dingleheimer, Lake Maggie McFadden, and Lake Mrs. Gladys Doolittle Batt.

I longed to see these lakes under the glamour of their newly added beauty.

Imagine, therefore, my surprise and happiness when I received the following communication from my revered and beloved chief, Professor Farrago, dated from the Smithsonian Institute, Washington, whither he had been summoned in haste to examine and pronounce upon the identity of a very small bird supposed to be a specimen of that rare and almost extinct creature, the two-toed titmouse, *Mustitta duototus,* to be scientifically exact, as I invariably strive to be.

The important letter in question was as follows:

> To
> Percy Smith, B.S., D.F., etc., etc.,
> Curator, Department of Anthropology,
> Administration Building,
> Bronx Park, N.Y.
>
> *My Dear Mr. Smith:*
> Several very important and determined ladies, recently

honoured by the Government in having a number of lakes in Alaska named after them, have decided to make a pilgrimage to that region, inspired by a characteristic desire to gaze upon the lakes named after them individually.

They request information upon the following points:

1st. Are the waters of the lakes in that locality sufficiently clear for a lady to do her hair by? In that event, the expedition will not burden itself with looking-glasses.

2nd. Are there any hotels? (You need merely say, no. I have tried to explain to them that it is, for the most part, an unexplored wilderness, but they insist upon further information from you.)

3rd. If there are hotels, is there also running water to be had? (You may tell them that there is plenty of running water.)

4th. What are the summer outdoor amusements? (You may inform them that there is plenty of bathing, boating, fishing, and an abundance of shade trees. Also, excellent mountain-climbing to be had in the vicinity. You need not mention the pastimes of "Hunt the Flea" or "Dodge the Skeeter.")

I am not by nature cruel, Mr. Smith, but when these ladies informed me that they had decided to penetrate that howling and unexplored wilderness without being burdened or interfered with by any member of my sex, for one horrid and criminal moment I hoped they would. Because in that event none of them would ever come back.

However, in my heart milder and more humane sentiments prevailed. I pointed out to them the peril of their undertaking, the dangers of an unexplored region, the necessity of masculine guidance and support.

My earnestness and solicitude were, I admit, prompted partly by a desire to utilize this expensively projected expedition as a vehicle for the accumulation of scientific data.

As soon as I heard of it I conceived the plan of attaching two members of our Bronx Park scientific staff to the expedition—you, and Mr. Brown.

But no sooner did these determined ladies hear of it than they repelled the suggestion with indignation.

Now, the matter stands as follows: These ladies don't want any man in the expedition; but they have at last realized that they've got to take a guide or two. And there are no feminine guides in Alaska.

Therefore, considering the immense and vital importance of such an opportunity to explore and report upon this unknown region at somebody else's expense, I suggest that you and Brown meet these ladies at Lake Mrs. Susan W. Pillsbury, which lies on the edge of the region to be explored; that you, without actually perjuring yourselves too horribly, convey to them the misleading impression that you are the promised guides provided for them by a cowed and avuncular Government; and that you take these fearsome ladies about and let them gaze at their reflections in the various lakes named after them; and that, while the expedition lasts, you secretly make such observations, notes, reports, and collections of the flora and fauna of the region as your opportunities may permit.

No time is to be lost. If, at Lake Susan W. Pillsbury, you find regular guides awaiting these ladies, you will bribe these guides to go away and you yourselves will then impersonate the guides. I know of no other way for you to explore this region, as all our available resources at Bronx Park have already been spent in painting appropriate scenery to line the cages of the mammalia, and also in the present exceedingly expensive expedition in search of the polka-dotted boom-bock, which is supposed to inhabit the jungle beyond Lake Niggerplug.

My most solemn and sincere wishes accompany you. Bless you!

FARRAGO.

II

This, then, is how it came about that "Kitten" Brown and I were seated, one midgeful morning in July, by the pellucid waters of Lake Susan W. Pillsbury, gnawing sections from a greasily fried trout, upon which I had attempted culinary operations.

Brown's baptismal name was William; but the unfortunate young man was once discovered indiscreetly embracing a pretty assistant in the Administration Building at Bronx, and, furthermore, was overheard to address her as "Kitten."

So Kitten Brown it was for him in future. After he had fought all the younger members of the scientific staff in turn, he gradually became resigned to this annoying *nom d'amour.*

Lightly but thoroughly equipped for scientific field research, we had arrived at the rendezvous in time to bribe the two guides engaged by the Government to go back to their own firesides.

A week later the formidable expedition of representative ladies arrived; and now they were sitting on the shore of Lake Susan W. Pillsbury, at a little distance from us, trying to keep the midges from their features and attempting to eat the fare provided for them by me.

I myself couldn't eat it. No wonder they murmured. But hunger goaded them to attack the greasy mess of trout and fried cornmeal.

Kitten was saying to me:

"Our medicine chest isn't very extensive. I hope they brought their own. If they didn't, some among us will never again see New York."

I stole a furtive glance at the unfortunate women. There was one among them—but let me first enumerate their heavy artillery:

There was the Reverend Dr. Amelia Jones, blond, adipose, and close to the four-score mark. She stepped high in the Equal Franchise ranks. Nobody had ever had the temerity to answer her back.

There was Miss Sadie Dingleheimer, fifty, emaciated, anemic, and gauntly glittering with thick-lensed eye-glasses. She was the President of the National Prophylactic Club, whatever that may be.

There was Miss Margaret McFadden, a Titian, profusely toothed, muscular, and President of the Hair Dressers' Union of the United States.

There was Mrs. Gladys Doolittle Batt, a grass one—Batt being represented as a vanishing point—President of the National Eugenic and Purity League; tall, gnarled, sinuously powerful, and prone to emotional attacks. The attacks were directed toward others.

These, then, composed the heavy artillery. The artillery of the light brigade consisted only of a single piece. Her name was Angelica White, a delegate from the Trained Nurses' Association of America. The nurses had been too busy with their business to attend such picnics, so one had been selected by lot to represent the busy Association on this expedition.

Angelica White was a tall, fair, yellow-haired girl of twenty-two or three, with violet-blue eyes and red lips, and a way of smiling a little when spoken to—but let that pass. I mean only to be scientifically minute. A passion for fact has ever obsessed me. I have little literary ability and less desire to sully my pen with that degraded form of letters known as fiction. Once in my life my mania for accuracy involved me lyrically. It was a short poem, but an earnest one:

> Truth is mighty and must prevail,
> Otherwise it were inadvisable to tell the tale.

I bestowed it upon the New York *Evening Post,* but declined remuneration. My message belonged to the world. I don't mean the newspaper.

Her eyes, then, were tinted with that indefinable and agreeable nuance which modifies blue to a lilac or violet hue.

Watching her askance, I was deeply sorry that my cooking seemed to pain her.

"Guide!" said Mrs. Doolittle Batt, in that remarkable, booming voice of hers.

"Ma'am!" said Kitten Brown and I with spontaneous alacrity, leaping from the ground as though shot at.

"This cooking," she said, with an ominous stare at us, "is atrocious. Don't you know how to cook?"

I said with a smiling attempt at ease:

"There are various ways of cooking food for the several species of mammalia which all-wise Providence—"

"Do you think you're cooking for wild-cats?" she demanded. Our smiles faded.

"It's my opinion that you're incompetent," remarked the Reverend Dr. Jones, slapping at midges with a hand that might have rocked all the cradles of the nation, but had not rocked any.

"We're not getting our money's worth," said Miss Dingleheimer, "even if the Government does pay your salaries."

I looked appealingly from one stony face to another. In Miss McFadden's eye there was the sombre glint of battle. She said:

"If you can guide us no better than you cook, God save us all this day week!" And she hurled the contents of her tin plate into Lake Susan W. Pillsbury.

Mrs. Doolittle Batt arose:

"Come," she said; "it is time we started. What is the name of the first lake we may hope to encounter?"

We knew no more than did they, but we said that Lake Gladys Doolittle Batt was the first, hoping to placate that fearsome woman.

"Come on, then!" she cried, picking up her carved and varnished mountain staff.

Miss Dingleheimer had brought one, too, from the Catskills.

So Kitten Brown and I loaded our mule, set him in motion, and drove him forward into the unknown.

Where we were going we had not the slightest idea; the margin of the lake was easy travelling, so easy that we never noticed that we had already gone around the lake three times, until Mrs. Batt recognized the fact and turned on us furiously.

I didn't know how to explain it, except to say feebly that I was doing it as a sort of preliminary canter to harden and inure the ladies.

"We don't need hardening!" she snarled. "Do you understand that!"

I comprehended that at once. But I forced a sickly smile and skipped forward in the wake of my mule, with something of the same abandon which characterizes the flight of an unwelcome dog.

In the terrified ear of Kitten I voiced my doubts concerning the prospects of a pleasant journey.

We marched in the following order: Arthur, the heavily laden mule, led; then came Kitten Brown and myself, all hung over with stew-pans shot-guns, rifles, cartridge-belts, ponchos, and the toilet reticules of the ladies; then marched the Reverend Dr. Jones, and, in order, filing behind her, Miss Dingleheimer, Mrs. Batt, Miss McFadden, and Miss White—the latter in her trained nurse's costume and wearing a red cross on her sleeve—an idea of Mrs. Batt, who believed in emergency methods.

Mrs. Batt also bore a banner, much interfered with by the foliage, bearing the inscription:

EQUAL RIGHTS!
EUGENICS OR EXTERMINATION!

After a while she shouted:

"Guide! Here, you may carry this banner for a while! I'm tired."

Kitten and I took turns with it after that. It was hard work, particularly as one by one in turn they came up and hung their parasols and shopping reticules all over us. We plodded forward like a pair of moving department stores, not daring to shift our burdens to Arthur, because we had already stuffed into the panniers of that simple and dignified animal all our collecting boxes, cyanide jars, butterfly nets, note-books, reels of piano wire, thermometers, barometers, hydrometers, stereometers, aeronoids, adnoids—everything, in fact, that guides are not supposed to pack into the woods, but which we had smuggled unbeknown to those misguided ones we guided.

And, to make room for our scientific paraphernalia, we had been obliged to do a thing so mean, so inexpressibly low, that I blush to relate it. But facts are facts; we discarded nearly a ton of feminine impedimenta. There was fancy work of all sorts in the making or in the raw—materials for knitting, embroidering, tatting, sewing, hemming, stitching, drawn-work, lace-making, crocheting.

Also we disposed of almost half a ton of toilet necessities—powder, perfumery, cosmetics, hot-water bags, slippers, negligees, novels, magazines, bon-bons, chewing-gum, hat-boxes, gloves, stockings, underwear.

We left enough apparel for each lady to change once. They'd have to do some scrubbing now. Science can not be halted by hatpins; cosmos can not be side-tracked by cosmetics.

Toward sunset we came upon a small, crystal clear pond, set between the bases of several lofty mountains. I was ready to drop with fatigue, but I nerved myself, drew a deep, exultant breath, and with one of those fine, sweeping gestures, I cried:

"Lake Mrs. Gladys Doolittle Batt! Eureka! At last! Excelsior!"

There was a profound silence behind me. I turned, striving to mask my apprehension with a smile. The ladies were regarding the pond in surprise. I admit that it was a pond, not a lake.

Injecting into my voice the last remnants of glee which I could summon, I shouted, "Eureka!" and began to caper about as though the size and beauty of the pond had affected me with irrepressible enthusiasm, hoping by my emotion to stampede the convention.

The cold voice of Mrs. Doolittle Batt checked my transports:

"Is that puddle named after me?" she demanded.

"M-ma'am?" I stammered.

"If that wretched frog-pond has been christened with my name, somebody is going to get into trouble," she said ominously.

A profound silence ensued. Arthur patiently switched at flies. As for me, I looked up at the majestic pines, gazed upon the lofty and eternal hills, then ventured a sneaking glance all around me. But I could discover no avenue of escape in case Mrs. Batt should charge me.

"I had been informed," she began dangerously, "that the majestic body of water, which I understood had been honoured with my name, was twelve miles long and three miles wide. *This* appears to be a puddle!"

"B-b-but it's very p-pretty," I protested feebly. "It's quite round and clear, and it's nearly a quarter of a mile in d-diameter—"

"Mind your business!" retorted Mrs. Doolittle Batt. "I've been swindled!"

Kitten Brown knew more about women than did I. He said in a fairly steady voice:

"Madame, it *is* an outrage! The women of this mighty nation should make the Government answerable for its duplicity! Your lake should have been at least twenty miles long!"

Everybody turned and looked at Kitten. He was a handsome dog.

"This young man appears to have some trace of common-sense," said Mrs. Batt. "I shall see to it that the Government is held responsible for this odious act of insulting duplicity. I—I won't have my name given to this—this wallow!—" She advanced toward me, her small eyes blazing: I retreated to leeward of Arthur.

"Guide!" she said in a voice still trembling with passion. "Are you certain that you have made no mistake? You appear to be unusually ignorant."

"I am afraid there can be no room for doubt," I said, almost scared out of my senses.

"And on top of this outrage, am I to eat your cooking?" she demanded passionately. "Did I come here to look at this frog-pond and choke on your cooking? *Did* I?"

"*I* can cook," said a clear, pleasant voice at my elbow. And Miss White came forward, cool, clean, fresh as a posy in her uniform and cap. I immediately got behind her.

"I can cook very nicely," she said smilingly. "It is part of my profession, you know. So if you two guides will be kind enough to build the fire and help me—" She let her violet eyes linger on me for an instant, then on Brown. A moment later he and I were jostling each other in our eagerness to obey her slightest suggestion. It is that way with men.

So we built her a fire and unpacked our provisions, and we waited very politely on the ladies when dinner was ready.

It was a fine dinner—coffee, bacon, flap-jacks, soup, ash-bread, stewed chicken.

The heavy artillery, made ravenous by their journey, required vast quantities of ammunition. They banqueted largely. I gazed in amazement at Mrs. Doolittle Batt as she swallowed one flap-jack after another, while her eyes bulged larger and larger.

Nor was the capacity of Miss Dingleheimer and the Reverend Dr. Jones to be mocked at by pachyderms.

Brown and I left them eating while we erected the row of little tents. Every lady had demanded a separate tent.

So we cut saplings, set up the silk, drove pegs, and brought armfuls of balsam boughs.

I was afraid they'd demand their knitting and other utensils, but they had eaten to repletion, and were sleepy; and as each toilet case or reticule contained also a nightgown, they drew the flaps of their several tents without insisting that we unpack Arthur's panniers.

They all had disappeared within their tents except Miss White, who insisted on cooking something for us, although we protested that the scraps of the banquet were all right for mere guides.

She stood beside us for a few minutes, watching us busy with our delicious dinner.

"You poor fellows," she said gently. "You are nearly starved."

It is agreeable to be sympathized with by a tall, fair, fresh young girl. We looked up, simpering gratefully.

"This is really a most lovely little lake," she said, gazing out across the still, crystalline water which was all rose and gold in the sunset, save where the sombre shapes of the towering mountains were mirrored in glassy depths.

"It's odd," I said, "that no trout are jumping. There ought to be lots of them there, and this is their jumping hour."

We all looked at the quiet, oval bit of water. Not a circle, not the slightest ripple disturbed it.

"It must be deep," remarked Brown.

We gazed up at the three lofty peaks, the bases of which were the shores of this tiny gem among lakes. Deep, deep, plunging down into dusky profundity, the rocks fell away sheer into limpid depths.

"That little lake may be a thousand feet deep," I said. "In 1903 Professor Farrago, of Bronx Park, measured a lake in the Thunder Mountains, which was two thousand seven hundred and sixty-nine feet deep."

Miss White looked at me curiously.

Into a patch of late sunshine flitted a small butterfly—one of *Grapta* species. It settled on a chip of wood, uncoiled its delicate proboscis, and spread its fulvous and deeply indented wings.

"*Grapta california,*" remarked Brown to me.

"*Vanessa asteriska,*" I corrected him. "Note the anal angle of the secondaries and the argentiferous discal area bordering the subcostal nervule."

"The characteristic stripes on the primaries are wanting," he demurred.

"It is double brooded. The summer form lacks the three darker bands."

A few moments' silence was broken by the voice of Miss White.

"I had no idea," she remarked, "that Alaskan guides were so familiar with entomological terms and nomenclature."

We both turned very red.

Brown mumbled something about having picked up a smattering. I added that Brown had taught me.

Perhaps she believed us; her blue eyes rested on us curiously, musingly. Also, at moments, I fancied there was the faintest glint of amusement in them.

She said:

"Two scientific gentlemen from New York requested permission to join this expedition, but Mrs. Batt refused them." She gazed thoughtfully upon the waters of Lake Gladys Doolittle Batt. "I wonder," she murmured, "what became of those two gentlemen."

It was evident that we had betrayed ourselves to this young girl.

She glanced at us again, and perhaps she noted in our fascinated gaze an expression akin to terror, for suddenly she laughed—such a clear, sweet, silvery little laugh!

"For my part," she said, "I wish they had come with us. I like—men."

With that she bade us goodnight very politely and went off to her tent, leaving us with our hats pressed against our stomachs, attempting by the profundity of our bows to indicate the depth of our gratitude.

"*There's* a girl!" exclaimed Brown, as soon as she had disappeared behind her tent flaps. "She'll never let on to Medusa, Xantippe, Cassandra and Company. I like *that* girl, Smith."

"You're not the only one imbued by such sentiments," said I.

He smiled a fatuous and reminiscent smile. He certainly was good-looking. Presently he said:

"She has the most delightful way of gazing at a man—"

"I've noticed," I said pleasantly.

"Oh. Did she happen to glance at *you* that way?" he inquired. I wanted to beat him.

All I said was:

"She's certainly some kitten." Which bottled that young man for a while.

We lay on the bank of the tiny lake, our backs against a huge pine-tree, watching the last traces of colour fading from peak and tree-top.

"Isn't it queer," I said, "that not a trout has splashed? It can't be that there are no fish in the lake."

"There *are* such lakes."

"Yes, very deep ones. I wonder how deep this is."

"We'll be out at sunrise with our reel of piano wire and take soundings," he said. "The heavy artillery won't wake until they're ready to be loaded with flap-jacks."

I shuddered:

"They're fearsome creatures, Brown. Somehow, that resolute and bony one has inspired me with a terror unutterable."

"Mrs. Batt?"

"Yes."

He said seriously:

"She'll make a horrid outcry when she asks for her knitting. What are you going to tell her?"

"I shall say that Indians ambuscaded us while she was asleep, and carried off all those things."

"You lie very nicely, don't you?" he remarked admiringly.

"*In vitium ducit culpæ fuga,*" said I. "Besides, they don't really need those articles."

He laughed. He didn't seem to be very much afraid of Mrs. Batt.

It had grown deliciously dusky, and myriads of stars were coming out. Little by little the lake lost its shape in the darkness, until only an irregular, star-set area of quiet water indicated that there was any lake there at all.

I remember that Brown and I, reclining at the foot of the tree, were looking at the still and starry surface of the lake, over which numbers of bats were darting after insects; and I recollect that I was just about to speak, when, of a sudden, the silent and luminous surface of the water was shattered as with a subterranean explosion; a geyser of scintillating spray shot upward flashing, foaming, towering a hundred feet into the air. And through it I seemed to catch a glimpse of a vast, quivering, twisting mass of silver falling back with a crash into the lake, while the huge fountain rained spray on every side and the little lake rocked and heaved from shore to shore, sending great sheets of surf up over the rocks so high that the very tree-tops dripped.

Petrified, dumb, our senses almost paralyzed by the shock, our ears still deafened by the watery crash of that gigantic something that had fallen into the lake, and our eyes starting from their sockets, we stared at the darkness.

Slap—slash—slush went the waves, hitting the shore with a clashing sound almost metallic. Vision and hearing told us that the water in the lake as rocking like the contents of a bath-tub.

"G-g-good Lord!" whispered Brown. "Is there a v-volcano under that lake?"

"Did you see that huge, glittering shape that seemed to fall into the water?" I gasped.

"Yes. What was it? A meteor?"

"No. It was something that first came out of the lake and fell back—the way a trout leaps. Heavens! It couldn't have been alive, could it?"

"W-wh-what do you mean?" stammered Brown.

"It couldn't have been a f-f-fish, could it?" I asked with chattering teeth.

"No! *No!* It was as big as a Pullman car! It must have been a falling star. Did you ever hear of a fish as big as a sleeping car?"

I was too thoroughly unnerved to reply. The roaring of the surf had subsided somewhat, enough for another sound to reach our ears—a raucous, gallinaceous, squawking sound.

I sprang up and looked at the row of tents. White-robed figures loomed in front of them. The heavy artillery was evidently frightened.

We went over to them, and when we got nearer they chastely scuttled into their tents and thrust out a row of heads—heads hideous with curl-papers.

"What was that awful noise? An earthquake?" shrilled the Reverend Dr. Jones. "I think I'll go home."

"Was it an avalanche?" demanded Mrs. Batt, in a deep and shaky voice. "Are we in any immediate danger, young man?"

I said that it was probably a flying-star which had happened to strike the lake and explode.

"What an awful region!" wailed Miss Dingleheimer. "I've had my money's worth. I wish to go back to New York at once. I'll begin to dress immediately—"

"It might be a million years before another meteor falls in this latitude," I said, soothingly.

"Or it might be ten minutes," sobbed Miss Dingleheimer. "What do *you* know about it, anyway! I want to go home. I'm putting on my stockings now. I'm getting dressed as fast as I can—"

Her voice was blotted out in a mighty crash from the lake. Appalled, I whirled on my heel, just in time to see another huge jet of water rise high in the starlight, another, another, until the entire lake was but a cluster of gigantic geysers exploding a hundred feet in the air, while through them, falling back into the smother of furious foam, great silvery bulks dropped crashing, one after another.

I don't know how long the incredible vision lasted; the woods roared with the infernal pandemonium, echoed and re-echoed from mountain to mountain; the tree-tops fairly stormed spray, driving it in sheets through the leaves; and the shores of the lake spouted surf long after the last vast, silvery shape had fallen back again into the water.

As my senses gradually recovered, I found myself supporting Mrs. Batt on one arm and the Reverend Dr. Jones upon my bosom. Both had fainted. I released them with a shudder and turned to look for Brown.

Somebody had swooned in his arms, too.

He was not noticing me, and as I approached him I heard him say something resembling the word "kitten."

In spite of my demoralization, another fear seized me, and I drew nearer and peered closely at what he was holding so nobly in his arms. It was, as I supposed, Angelica White.

I don't know whether my arrival occultly revived her, for as I stumbled over a tent-peg she opened her blue eyes, and then disengaged herself from Brown's arms.

"Oh, I am so frightened," she murmured. She looked at me sideways when she said it.

"Come," said I coldly to Brown, "let Miss White retire and lie down. This meteoric shower is over and so is the danger."

He evinced a desire to further soothe and minister to Miss White, but she said, with considerable composure, that she was feeling better; and Brown came unwillingly with me to inspect the heavy artillery lines.

That formidable battery was wrecked, the pieces dismounted and lying tumbled about in their emplacements.

But a vigorous course of cold water in dippers revived them, and we herded them into one tent and quieted them with some soothing prevarication, the details of which I have forgotten; but it was something about a flock of meteors which hit the earth every twelve billion years, and that it was now all over for another such interim, and everybody could sleep soundly with the consciousness of having assisted at a spectacle never before beheld except by a primordial protoplasmic cell.

Which flattered them, I think, for, seated once more at the base of our tree, presently we heard weird noises from the reconcentrados, like the moaning of the harbour bar.

They slept, the heavy guns, like unawakened engines of destruction all a-row in battery. But Brown and I, fearfully excited, still dazed and bewildered, sat with our fascinated eyes fixed on the lake, asking each other what in the name of miracles it was that we had witnessed and heard.

On one thing we were agreed. A scientific discovery of the most enormous importance awaited our investigation.

This was no time for temporising, for deception, for any species of polite shilly-shallying. We must, on the morrow, tear off our masks and appear before these misguided and feminine victims of our duplicity in our own characters as scientists. We must boldly avow our identities and flatly refuse to stir from this spot until the mystery of this astounding lake had been thoroughly investigated.

And so, discussing our policy, our plans for the morrow, and mutually reassuring each other concerning our common ability to successfully defy the heavy artillery, we finally fell asleep.

III

Dawn awoke me, and I sat up in my blanket and aroused Brown.

No birds were singing. It seemed unusual, and I spoke of it to Brown. Never have I witnessed such a still, strange daybreak. Mountains, woods, and water were curiously silent. There was not a sound to be heard, nothing stirred except the thin veil of vapour over the water, shreds of which were now parting from the shore and steaming slowly upward.

There was, it seemed to me, something slightly uncanny about this lake, even in repose. The water seemed as translucent as a dark crystal, and as motionless as the surface of a mirror. Nothing stirred its placid surface, not a ripple, not an insect, not a leaf floating.

Brown had lugged the pneumatic raft down to the shore where he was now pumping it full: I followed with the paddles, pole, and hydroscope. When the raft had been pumped up and was afloat, we carried the reel of gossamer piano-wire aboard, followed it, pushed off, and paddled quietly through the level cobwebs of mist toward the centre of the lake. From the shore I heard a gruesome noise. It originated under one of the row of tents of the heavy artillery. Medusa, snoring, was an awesome sound in that wilderness and solitude of dawn.

I was unscrewing the centre-plug from the raft and screwing into the empty socket the lens of the hydroscope and attaching the battery, while Brown started his sounding; and I was still busy when an exclamation from my companion started me:

"We're breaking some records! Do you know it, Smith?"

"Where is the lead?"

"Three hundred fathoms and still running!"

"Nonsense!"

"Look at it yourself! It goes on unreeling: I've put the drag on. Hurry and adjust the hydroscope!"

I sighted the powerful instrument for two thousand feet, altering it from minute to minute as Brown excitedly announced the amazing depth of the lake. When he called out four thousand feet, I stared at him.

"There's something wrong—" I began.

"There's *nothing* wrong!" he interrupted. "Four thousand five hundred! Five thousand! Five thousand five hundred—"

"Are you squatting there and trying to tell me that this lake is over a mile deep!"

"Look for yourself!" he said in an unsteady voice. "Here is the tape! You can read, can't you? Six thousand feet—and running evenly. Six thousand five hundred! . . . Seven thousand! Seven thousand five—"

"It *can't* be!" I protested.

But it was true. Astounded, I continued to adjust the hydroscope to a range incredible, turning the screw to focus at a mile and a half, at two miles, at two and a quarter, a half, three-quarters, three miles, three miles and a quarter—click!

"Good Heavens!" he whispered. "This lake is three miles and a quarter deep!"

Mechanically I set the lachet, screwed the hood firm, drew out the black eye-mask, locked it, then, kneeling on the raft I rested my face in the mask, felt for the lever, and switched on the electric light.

Quicker that thought the solid lance of dazzling light plunged down through profundity, and the vast abyss of water was revealed along its pathway.

Nothing moved in those tremendous depths except, nearly two miles below, a few spots of tinsel glittered and drifted like flakes of mica.

At first I scarcely noticed them, supposing them to be vast beds of silvery bottom sand glittering under the electric pencil of the hydroscope. But presently it occurred to me that these brilliant specks in motion were not on the bottom—were a little less than two miles deep, and therefore suspended.

To be seen at all, at two miles' depth, whatever they were they must have considerable bulk.

"Do you see anything?" demanded Brown.

"Some silvery specks at a depth of two miles."

"What do they look like?"

"Specks."

"Are they in motion?"

"They seem to be."

"Do they come any nearer?"

After a while I answered:

"One of the specks seems to be growing larger. . . . I believe it is in motion and is floating slowly upward. . . . It's certainly getting bigger. . . . It's getting longer."

"Is it a fish?"

"It can't be."

"Why not?"

"It's impossible. Fish don't attain the size of whales in mountain ponds."

There was a silence. After an interval I said:

"Brown, I don't know what to make of that thing."

"Is it coming any nearer?"

"Yes."

"What does it look like now?"

"It *looks* like a fish. But it can't be. It looks like a tiny, silver minnow. But it can't be. Why, if it resembles a minnow in size at this distance—what can be its actual dimensions?"

"Let me look," he said.

Unwillingly I raised my head from the mask and yielded him my place.

A long silence followed. The western mountaintops reddened under the rising sun; the sky grew faintly bluer. Yet, there was not a bird-note in that still place, not a flash of wings, nothing stirring.

Here and there along the lake shore I noticed unusual-looking trees—very odd-looking trees indeed, for their trunks seemed bleached and dead, and as though no bark covered them, yet every stark limb was covered with foliage—a thick foliage so dark in colour that it seemed black to me.

I glanced at my motionless companion where he knelt with his face in the mask, then I unslung my field-glasses and focussed them on the nearest of the curious trees.

At first I could not make out what I was looking at; then, to my astonishment, I saw that these stark, gray trees were indeed lifeless, and that what I had mistaken for dark foliage were velvety clusters of bats hanging there asleep—thousands of them thickly infesting and clotting the dead branches with a sombre and horrid effect of foliage.

I don't mind bats in ordinary numbers. But in such soft, motionless masses they slightly sickened me. There must have been literally tons of them hanging to the dead trees.

"This is pleasant," I said. "Look at those bats, Brown."

When Brown spoke without lifting his head, his voice was so shaken, so altered, that the mere sound of it scared me:

"Smith," he said, "there is a fish in here, shaped exactly like a brook minnow. And I should judge, by the depth it is swimming in, that it is about as long as an ordinary Pullman car."

His voice shook, but his words were calm to the point of commonplace. Which made the effect of his statement all the more terrific.

"A—a *minnow*—as big as a Pullman car?" I repeated, dazed.

"Larger, I think. . . . It looks to me through the hydroscope, at this distance, exactly like a tiny, silvery minnow. It's half a mile down. . . . Swimming about. . . . I can see its eyes; they must be about ten feet in diameter. I can see its fins moving. And there are about a dozen others, much deeper, swimming around. . . . This is easily the most overwhelming contribution made to science since the discovery of the purple-spotted dingle-bock, *Bukkus dinglii.* . . . We've got to catch one of those gigantic fish!"

"How?" I gasped. "How are we going to catch a minnow as large as a sleeping car?"

"I don't know, but we've got to do it. We've got to manage it, somehow."

"It would require a steel cable to hold such a fish and a donkey engine to reel him in! And what about a hook? And if we had hook, line, steam-winch, and everything else, *what* about bait?"

He knelt for some time longer, watching the fish, before he resigned the hydroscope to me. Then I watched it; but it came no nearer, seeming contented to swim about at the depth of a little more than half a mile. Deep under this fish I could see others glittering as they sailed or darted to and fro.

Presently I raised my head and sat thinking. The sun now gilded the water; a little breeze ruffled it here and there where dainty cast's-paws played over the surface.

"What on earth do you suppose those gigantic fish feed on?" asked Brown under his breath.

I thought a moment longer, then it came to me in a flash of understanding, and I pointed at the dead trees.

"Bats!" I muttered. "They feed on bats as other fish feed on the little, gauzy-winged flies which dance over ponds! You saw those bats flying over the pond last night, didn't you? That explains the whole thing! Don't you understand? Why, what we saw were these gigantic fish leaping like trout after the bats. It was their feeding time!"

I do not imagine that two more excited scientists ever existed than Brown and I. The joy of discovery transfigured us. Here we had discovered a lake in the Thunder Mountains which was the deepest lake in the world; and it was inhabited by a few gigantic fish of the minnow species, the existence of which, hitherto, had never even been dreamed of by science.

"Kitten," I said, my voice broken by emotion, "which will you have named after you, the lake or the fish? Shall it be Lake Kitten Brown, or shall it be *Minnius kittenii?* Speak!"

"What about that old party whose name you said had already been given to the lake?" he asked piteously.

"Who? Mrs. Batt? Do you think I'd name such an important lake after *her?* Anyway, she has declined the honour."

"Very well," he said, "I'll accept it. And the fish shall be known as *Minnius Smithii!*"

Too deeply moved to speak, we bent over and shook hands with each other. In that solemn and holy moment, surcharged with ecstatic emotion, a deep, distant reverberation came across the water to our ears. It was the heavy artillery, snoring.

Never can I forget that scene; sunshine glittering on the pond, the silent forests and towering peaks, the blue sky overhead, the dead trees where thousands of bats hung in nauseating clusters, thicker than the leaves in Valembrosa—and Kitten Brown and I, cross-legged upon our pneumatic raft, hands clasped in pledge of deathless devotion to science and a fraternity unending.

"And how about that girl?" he asked. "What girl?"

"Angelica White?"

"Well," said I, "*what* about her?"

"Does she go with the lake or with the fish?"

"What do you mean?" I asked coldly, withdrawing my hand from his clasp.

"I mean, which of us gets the first chance to win her?" he said, blushing. "There's no use denying that we both have been bowled over by her; is there?"

I pondered for several moments.

"She is an extremely intelligent girl," I said, stalling.

"Yes, and then some."

After a few minutes' further thought, I said: "Possibly I am in error, but at moments it has seemed to me that my marked attentions to Miss White are not wholly displeasing to her. I may be mistaken—"

"I think you are, Smith."

"Why?"

"Because—well, because I seem to think so."

I said coldly:

"Because she happened to faint away in your arms last night is no symptom that she prefers you. Is it?"

"No."

"Then why do you seem to think that tactful, delicate, and assiduous attentions on my part may prove not entirely unwelcome to this unusually intelligent—"

"Smith!"

"What?"

"Miss White is not only a trained nurse, but she also is about to receive her diploma as a physician."

"How do you know?"

"She told me."

"When?"

"When you were building the fire last night. Also, she informed me that she had relentlessly dedicated herself to a eugenic marriage."

"When did she tell you *that?*"

"While you were bringing in a bucket of water from the lake last night. And furthermore, she told me that 1 was perfectly suited for a eugenic marriage."

"When did she tell you *that?"* I demanded.

"When she had—fainted—in my arms."

"How the devil did she come to say a thing like that?"

He became conspicuously red about the ears:

"Well, I had just told her that I had fallen in love with her—"

"Damn!" I said. And that's all I said; and seizing a paddle I made furiously for shore. Behind me I heard the whirr of the piano wire as Brown started the electric reel. Later I heard him clamping the hood on the hydroscope; but I was too disgusted for any further words, and I dug away at the water with my paddle.

In various and weird stages of morning deshabille the heavy artillery came down to the shore for morning ablutions, all a-row like a file of ducks. They glared at me as I leaped ashore:

"I want my breakfast!" snapped Mrs. Batt. "Do you hear what I say, guide? And I don't wish to be kept waiting for it either! I desire to get out of this place as soon as possible."

"I'm sorry," I said, "but I intend to stay here for some time."

"What!" bawled the heavy artillery in booming unison.

But my temper had been sorely tried, and I was in a mood to tell the truth and make short work of it, too.

"Ladies," I said, "I'll not mince matters. Mr. Brown and I are not guides; we are scientists from Bronx Park, and we don't know a bally thing about this wilderness we're in!"

"Swindler!" shouted Mrs. Batt, in an enraged voice. "I knew very well that the United States Government would never have named that puddle of water after me!"

"Don't worry, madam! I've named it after Mr. Brown. And the new species of gigantic fish which I discovered in this lake I have named after myself. As for leaving this spot until I have concluded my scientific study of these fish, I simply won't. I intend to observe their habits and to capture one of them if it requires the remainder of my natural life to do so. I shall be sorry to detain you here during such a period, but it can't be helped. And now you know what the situation is, and you are at liberty to think it over after you have washed your countenances in Lake Kitten Brown."

Rage possessed the heavy artillery, and a fury indescribable seized them when they discovered that Indians had raided their half ton of feminine perquisites. I went up a tree.

When the tumult had calmed sufficiently for them to distinguish what I said, I made a speech to them. From the higher branches of a neighboring tree Kitten Brown applauded and cried, "Hear! Hear!"

"Ladies," I said, "you know the worst, now. If you keep me up this tree and starve me to death it will be murder. Also, you don't know enough to get out of these forests, but I can guide you back the way you came. I'll do it if you cease your dangerous demonstrations and permit Mr. Brown and myself to remain here and study these giant fish for a week or two."

They now seemed disposed to consider the idea. There was nothing else for them to do. So after an hour or two, Brown and I ventured to descend from our trees, and we went among them to placate them and ingratiate ourselves as best we might.

"Think," I argued, "what a matchless opportunity for you to be among the first discoverers of a totally new and undescribed species of giant fish! Think what a legacy it will be to leave such a record to posterity! Think how proud and happy your descendants will be to know that their ancestors assisted at the discovery of *Minnius Smithii!*"

"Why can't they be named after *me?*" demanded Mrs. Batt.

"Because," I explained patiently, "they have already been named after *me!*"

"Couldn't *something* be named after me?" inquired the fearsome lady.

"The bats," suggested Brown politely, "we could name a bat after you with pleasure—"

I thought for a moment she meant to swing on him. He thought so, too, and ducked.

"A bat!" she shouted. "Name a *bat* after *me!*"

"Many a celebrated scientist has been honoured by having his name conferred upon humbler fauna," I explained.

But she remained dangerous, so I went and built the fire, and squatted there, frying bacon, while on the other side of the fire, sitting side by side, Kitten Brown and Angelica White gazed upon each other with enraptured eyes. It was slightly sickening—but let that pass. I was beginning to understand that science is a jealous mistress and that any contemplated infidelity of mine stood every chance of being squelched. No; evidently I had not been fashioned for the joys of legal domesticity. Science, the wanton jade, had not yet finished her dance with me. Apparently my maxixe with her was to be eternal. *Fides servanda est.*

That afternoon the heavy artillery held a council of war, and evidently came to a conclusion to make the best of the situation, for toward sundown they accosted me with a request for the raft, explaining that they desired to picnic aboard and afterward row about the lake and indulge in song.

So Brown and I put aboard the craft a substantial cold supper; and the heavy artillery embarked, taking aboard a guitar to be worked by Miss Dingleheimer, and knitting for the others.

It was a lovely evening. Brown and I had been discussing a plan to dynamite the lake and stun the fish, that method appealing to us as the only possible way to secure a specimen of the stupendous minnows which inhabited the depths. In fact, it was our only hope of possessing one of these creatures—fishing with a donkey engine, steel cable, and a hook baited with a bat being too uncertain and far more laborious and expensive.

I was still smoking my pipe, seated at the foot of the big pine-tree, watching the water turn from gold to pink: Brown sat higher up the slope, his arm around Angelica White. I carefully kept my back toward them.

On the lake the heavy artillery were revelling loudly, banqueting, singing, strumming the guitar, and trailing their hands overboard across the sunset-tinted water.

I was thinking of nothing in particular as I now remember, except that I noticed the bats beginning to flit over the lake; when Brown called to me from the slope above, asking whether it was perfectly safe for the heavy artillery to remain out so late.

"Why?" I demanded.

"Suppose," he shouted, "that those fish should begin to jump and feed on the bats again?"

I had never thought of that.

I rose and hurried nervously down to the shore, and, making a megaphone of my hands, I shouted:

"Come in! It isn't safe to remain out any longer!"

Scornful laughter from the artillery answered my appeal.

"You'd better come in!" I called. "You can't tell what might happen if any of those fish should jump."

"Mind your business!" retorted Mrs. Batt. "We've had enough of your prevarications—"

Then, suddenly, without the faintest shadow of warning, from the centre of the lake a vast geyser of water towered a hundred feet in the air.

For one dreadful second I saw the raft hurled skyward, balanced on the crest of the stupendous fountain, spilling ladies, supper, guitars, and knitting in every direction.

Then a horrible thing occurred; fish after fish shot up out of the water and foam, seizing, as they fell, ladies, luncheon, and knitting in mid-air, falling back with a crashing shock which seemed to rock the very mountains.

"Help!" I screamed. And fainted dead away.

Is it necessary to proceed? Literature nods; Science shakes her head. No, nothing but literature lies beyond the ripples which splashed musically upon the shore, terminating forever the last vibration from that immeasurable catastrophe.

Why should I go on? The newspapers of the nation have recorded the last scenes of the tragedy.

We know that tons of dynamite are being forwarded to that solitary lake. We know that it is the determination of the Government to rid the world of those gigantic minnows.

And yet, somehow, it seems to me as I sit writing here in my office, amid the verdure of Bronx Park, that the destruction of these enormous fish is a mistake.

What more splendid sarcophagus could the ladies of the lake desire than these huge, silvery, itinerant and living tombs?

What reward more sumptuous could anybody wish for than to rest at last within the interior dimness of an absolutely new species of anything?

For me, such a final repose as this would represent the highest pinnacle of sublimity, the uttermost zenith of mortal dignity.

So what more is there for me to say?

As for Angelica—but no matter. I hope she may be comparatively happy with Kitten Brown. Yet, as I have said before, handsome men never last. But she should have thought of that in time.

I absolve myself of all responsibility. She had her chance.

BIBLIOGRAPHY

I. Books by Chambers

The King in Yellow. New York: F. Tennyson Neely, 1895. London: Chatto & Windus, 1895. New York: Harper & Brothers, 1902. London: Constable, 1916. [*Contents:* The Repairer of Reputations; The Mask; In the Court of the Dragon; The Yellow Sign; The Demoiselle D'Ys; The Prophet's Paradise; The Street of the Four Winds; The Street of the First Shell; The Street of Our Lady of the Fields; Rue Barrée.]

The Maker of Moons. New York: G. P. Putnam's Sons, 1896. [*Contents:* The Maker of Moons; The Silent Land; The Black Water; In the Name of the Most High; The Boy's Sister; The Crime; A Pleasant Evening; The Man at the Next Table.]

The Mystery of Choice. New York: D. Appleton & Co., 1897. [*Contents:* The Purple Emperor; Pompe Funèbre; The Messenger; The White Shadow; Passeur; A Matter of Interest; Envoi.]

In Search of the Unknown. New York: Harper & Brothers, 1904.

The Tree of Heaven. New York: D. Appleton & Co., 1907. London: Constable, 1908. [*Contents:* The Carpet of Belshazzar; The Sign of Venus; The Case of Mr. Helmer; The Tree of Dreams; The Bridal Pair; Ex Curia; The Golden Pool; Out of the Depths; The Swastika; The Ghost of Chance.]

Police!!! New York: D. Appleton & Co., 1915. [*Contents:* The Third Eye; The Immortal; The Ladies of the Lake; One Over; Un Peu d'Amour; The Eggs of the Silver Moon.]

II. Publications of Individual Stories

"The Carpet of Belshazzar." *Harper's Weekly* (10 December 1904; as "The Tree of Heaven"). In *The Tree of Heaven* (q.v.).

"The Demoiselle d'Ys." In *The King in Yellow* (q.v.).

"The Harbor-Master." *Ainslee's* (August 1899). Incorporated into *In Search of the Unknown* (q.v.).

"The Ladies of the Lake." In *Police!!!* (q.v.).

"The Maker of Moons." In *The Maker of Moons* (q.v.).

"The Mask." In *The King in Yellow* (q.v.).

"The Messenger." In *The Mystery of Choice* (q.v.).

"A Pleasant Evening." In *The Maker of Moons* (q.v.).

"Pompe Funèbre." In *The Mystery of Choice* (q.v.).

"The Repairer of Reputations." In *The King in Yellow* (q.v.).

"The Sign of Venus." *Harper's Magazine* (December 1903). In *The Tree of Heaven* (q.v.).

"The Yellow Sign." In *The King in Yellow* (q.v.).

ABOUT S. T. JOSHI

S. T. JOSHI is the author of *The Weird Tale* (1990), *H. P. Lovecraft: The Decline of the West* (1990), and *Unutterable Horror: A History of Supernatural Fiction* (2012). He has prepared corrected editions of H. P. Lovecraft's work for Arkham House and annotated editions of Lovecraft's stories for Penguin Classics. He has also prepared editions of Lovecraft's collected essays and poetry. His exhaustive biography, *H. P. Lovecraft: A Life* (1996), was expanded as *I Am Providence: The Life and Times of H. P. Lovecraft* (2010). He is the editor of the anthologies *American Supernatural Tales* (Penguin, 2007), *Black Wings* I-VI (PS Publishing, 2010, 2012, 2013), *A Mountain Walked: Great Tales of the Cthulhu Mythos* (Centipede Press, 2014), *The Madness of Cthulhu* (Titan Books, 2014–15), and *Searchers After Horror: New Tales of the Weird and Fantastic* (Fedogan & Bremer, 2014). He is the editor of the *Lovecraft Annual, Spectral Realms,* and *Penumbra* (all published by Hippocampus Press). Among his works of fiction are *The Recurring Doom: Tales of Mystery and Horror* (Sarnath Press, 2019) and *Something from Below* (PS Publishing, 2019).

www.ingramcontent.com/pod-product-compliance
Lightning Source LLC
Chambersburg PA
CBHW050924030726
47503CB00007BB/2460